37653012893999
Williams JUV Fiction
JUV
FIC LOIZEAUX
Wings

CENTRAL ARKANSAS LIBRARY SYSTEM
SUE COWAN WILLIAMS BRANCH LIBRARY
LITTLE ROCK, ARKANSAS

WINGS

WINGS

WILLIAM LOIZEAUX

Pictures by LESLIE BOWMAN

Melanie Kroupa Books

Farrar, Straus and Giroux * New York

Text copyright © 2006 by William Loizeaux
Illustrations copyright © 2006 by Leslie Bowman
All rights reserved
Printed in the United States of America
Distributed in Canada by Douglas & McIntyre Ltd.
Designed by Barbara Grzeslo
First edition, 2006
1 3 5 7 9 10 8 6 4 2

www.fsgkidsbooks.com

Library of Congress Cataloging-in-Publication Data
Loizeaux, William.
Wings : a novel / by William Loizeaux.— 1st ed.
p. cm.
Summary: Ten-year-old Nick, who misses his father, finds companionship after rescuing an injured baby mockingbird.
ISBN-13: 978-0-374-34802-1
ISBN-10: 0-374-34802-2
[1. Mockingbirds—Fiction. 2. Wildlife rescue—Fiction. 3. Human-animal relationships—Fiction. 4. Loss (Psychology)—Fiction.]
I. Bowman, Leslie, ill. II. Title.

PZ7.L8295 Mar 2006
[Fic]—dc22

2005046351

For Beth and Emma

CENTRAL ARKANSAS LIBRARY SYSTEM
SUE COWAN WILLIAMS BRANCH
LITTLE ROCK, ARKANSAS

WINGS

SUMMERS AT OUR HOME in central New Jersey had always been pretty predictable for Mom and me. In the mornings, I had to do my chores. I took out the trash or swept the front porch, and every Friday I went with Mom and her envelope stuffed with coupons to buy our groceries at the A&P. In the afternoons, I often mowed yards, including our own. For fun I rode my bike or listened to Yankee games on the radio. Most days went by like freight cars on a trestle, slow and steady, evenly spaced, each day a lot like the day before, which was a lot like the day before that.

So when something new actually did come into my life that summer—something that would shake up my world and teach me some hard and surprising truths—it seemed like a big deal. It still seems like a big deal. Even if it was as small as a bird.

JUNE 1960

THE BIRD

ONE AFTERNOON IN LATE JUNE, I was pushing the mower home from the Finleys'. I had passed the woods, passed the field where they were building the new tract houses, when I saw something in the middle of the road. From a distance, it was just a small gray ball of fluff. Then I could see its beak and short tail. For a while I watched it. No cars came by, and no other birds came to help it. I walked closer, thinking I'd scare it off the road where it would be safer. But it didn't move, didn't even flinch, so I squatted down right in front of it.

And that's when it reached toward me, stretching its neck like a rubber tube and opening its beak like a hinge. It made a sound that I'll never forget. It went *TTCHAAAAAAACK!!!* Just once. Like a rusty gate. Such a big sound for such a small thing.

I picked up the bird in both hands, cupping it carefully to my chest. I could feel it breathing fast. But if it was scared, it didn't try to go anywhere. It wriggled down into my palms. Its feet felt dry and scratchy. I could see pink flesh through its furry wings. Around its head was a cloud of frizzy feathers, fine as dandelion seeds. It had a sad, scrunched-up old man's face, with a wrinkled neck, thin yellow lips, and a beak that was arrow-shaped. Its black eye blinked. It wasn't particularly beautiful or cuddly, but holding it made me shiver inside. It seemed like so much to carry, and at the same time so little and so light.

“Oh!” Mom said when I came into the kitchen and she looked into my hands. She was standing at the table, shelling peas into the colander, her green printed apron tied around her narrow waist. “It looks too young to fly. It must have fallen out of its nest.”

“Can I keep it?” I asked. We’d never had any pets, except for some goldfish, and it seemed that the bird needed me.

Mom bent even closer to see. She pushed her hair behind her ears.

“I’ll keep it in a box in the shed,” I told her. “I won’t bring it into the house, I promise.”

She looked at me. “But, Nick, if it fell from its nest, it might be hurt. It might not be able to live.”

“I know. I still want to keep it.”

“Sure?”

I nodded. I was still shivering inside.

Smiling to herself, she sighed, as if to say there was no stopping some things that boys do. She put her arm around my shoulder. “All right,” she said.

THE SHED

THE SHED WAS WHERE I ALWAYS PARKED the mower and my bike, and where Mom kept her gardening tools. Above the workbench was a small window with sticky cobwebs across its panes, and in the corner sat the wheelbarrow, heaped with peat moss, which made the air thick and heavy.

From the cellar, Mom brought out a cardboard box, about two feet square. She set it on the workbench and fit a few sheets of newspaper into the bottom. "There you go," she said.

I laid the bird in the corner of the box, where it sat just like it had on the road: still and quiet, its head, like my grandfather's, hunched down between its shoulders. I set a jar top filled with water right next to the bird, but it didn't seem interested. I fit a piece of chicken wire over the top of the box. Then, taking a shovel and an empty coffee can, I headed down to the corner of the backyard where we had the compost pile.

Ever since I could remember, that pile had been down there, growing taller and wider with leaves, bruised apples, and all those soft, rotted tomatoes and zucchinis that we'd find in the garden when we came back from our summer vacation. Now the pile was as tall as me, and near the bottom it was crawling with worms.

In about five minutes, I got a dozen in the can and brought them back to the shed. "I've got something to cheer you up!" I said to the bird, dangling a gooey worm above its head. But it didn't respond, didn't do anything.

I dangled the worm closer, until it touched the

bird's beak. "Just a bite," I said. "Come on, try." I even said, "Please . . ."

Nothing.

"It's had a big day," Mom said during supper. Then she tried to be a little funny. "Maybe your bird didn't like the menu today. By the way, you haven't touched your peas."

Afterward, though, when I checked on the bird again, there was nothing funny at all. It was trembling, its beak wedged into the corner of the box, where it made a sad, tiny tapping sound against the cardboard. It still wouldn't eat, and didn't move when I picked it up and touched the fuzz on its head. Its eyes didn't even blink.

"I'm sorry about your bird," Mom said after I'd gone upstairs and slid between my sheets. I was late to bed—it was already dark outside—but tonight she didn't mention that. She just said, "I wish your bird was feeling better."

"Do you know what's wrong with it?"

She shook her head. "I don't know."

I asked how a bird could live without eating, and again she said, "I don't know."

She switched off my lamp, and I felt her sit down on

the edge of my bed and put her hand on my arm. For a while, I couldn't see anything at all. Then, slowly, the shapes in my room came back: the desk, the bureau, my baseball mitt, my jeans hanging over the bedpost, and Mom's head, with her slender neck and wavy hair, very still in the light from the streetlamp. We were quiet, just listening to the sounds of bullfrogs drifting over the porch roof and through my window. Then she said, "You've done your best. Now go to sleep. Let's see what tomorrow brings."

MARCY

SOMETIME IN THE MIDDLE of that night or in the early-morning hours, I was suddenly wide awake. It seemed just seconds before that Mom had been there, saying "Go to sleep," but I knew it was much later because the air was cool, the windows were dark in the neighbors' houses, and the bullfrogs had quit groaning in the pond across the road.

I'd been dreaming of rowing a boat on flat, shiny water, but that wasn't why I was awake. It was because something had seemed to be happening just beyond the dream, something that I needed to see or touch. And now I thought that it had already happened.

I got up and went out of my room. I had to see if the bird was okay. In the hallway I listened at Mom's door. It was quiet in there—she slept like a log—so I turned and went down the stairs. At the bottom I walked across the braided rug and then the kitchen linoleum. The faucet dripped and the refrigerator hummed, much louder than they did during the daytime. I felt my way past the stove, the sink, and the drying rack until I reached the end of the counter. There, beneath it, was the drawer with the flashlights for when the electricity went out. When I pushed up on its bottom, I could slide it out quietly. I grabbed the first flashlight I touched. I tested it and the kitchen jumped alive. Then I switched it off. I wouldn't need it until I was outside.

I went past the pantry, through the mudroom, out the back door, and into the night. There weren't any stars out, no moon either. The air smelled like mown grass. The ground was cold and wet. I was wearing only my pajama bottoms, and I'd forgotten to put on shoes or slippers. I shined the flashlight around our backyard. There was Mom's garden, the compost pile in the corner, the sagging clothesline tied to the cherry tree, and the split-rail fence beyond the bushes, where the Carlsons' yard began. Everything was quiet, everything still—except for my feet in the grass.

I was coming around toward the back of the shed, when I stopped right in my tracks. I saw light flickering through the gap around the shed door, as if there was heat lightning inside. It glowed and dimmed. Then I heard the little metal bar scraping out of its notch. Something or someone was opening the latch. Something or someone was in there.

I couldn't move. I turned off my flashlight as the door swung open, and another beam of light swept out.

"Dad?" I said. The word sprang to my lips in a weird, high voice that didn't seem to be mine.

The beam of light in the doorway stopped still. I could hardly breathe.

"No," came another voice. There was something uncertain about it, but I could tell it was Mom's. "No," she said. "It's me."

I switched my flashlight back on and followed its beam to her slippers, her bathrobe, her long, thin fingers holding her own flashlight, and finally there was her face. Her eyes were tired, like she hadn't slept, but her lips were smiling at me.

"What's going on?" I asked.

She tilted her head and gave me her funny look, as if she could ask me the same question.

"How's the bird?" I said.

"About the same, I think. Come in and see."

I went into the shed, which seemed smaller at night. The air seemed thicker too. Our flashlights roamed over the shelves and tools, making swaying shadows.

"Where's your bathrobe?" she asked.

"I don't know."

"Well, shut the door. You must be chilly."

She sat on the stool and I sat on a crate that was standing on end, both of us side by side at the workbench. I shined my flashlight into the box, and there was the bird, that ball of fluff, crushed into the corner. It wasn't trembling. It didn't seem to be moving at all.

"Is it alive?" I asked.

She nodded. "I think so. I'm pretty sure. I think I can see it breathing."

Now I took the chicken wire off. The coffee can was still on the bench, and I fished out a worm. I dangled the worm over the bird, but the bird just stared ahead.

"Why can't it just . . . I don't get it," I said, and dropped the worm back into the can.

After a while, Mom said softly, "It's awfully late. Shall we go back in the house?"

"No," I said. "I'm going to stay here."

She said, "Mind if I stay too?"

We held our flashlights still as lamps, and for a time we just watched and waited, though nothing seemed to be happening.

"I think it's a mockingbird," Mom said at last, as though she'd been trying to figure this out. "See those white marks, like narrow stripes, across its wings? Mockingbirds. You must have heard them at night, singing all the songs of other birds, especially when the moon is bright."

"Why do they do that?" I asked.

"I'm not sure," she said. "But it seems like they're calling out in every language."

"I like those wings," I said after a while. "I'd like to see them open."

"That would be wonderful," she said. "You sure you're not cold? Goodness, Nick, you're shivering."

We didn't talk for a couple of minutes. Then she

turned to me with a strange look and said, "You know, a while ago, I heard you say 'Dad.' Were you thinking of him?"

"No, not really. I don't think I was thinking of anything, except maybe running. Your flashlight scared me." I looked at her, and it seemed like it'd be okay, so I asked, "Were *you* thinking of him?"

"Yes," she said after a moment. "I was thinking about how much he'd have wanted to be here right now, silly as it is, all of us out in the middle of the night in our pajamas."

I didn't know what to say to this. We were awkward when we spoke of my father. It didn't happen often, and when it did, it was usually in the wintertime. That's when his birthday—in January—came around, and that's when we always went to the cemetery outside of town, on one of those long, low hillsides that look like a wave held still. His grave is a flat stone, and beside it stood a small American flag that sometimes was covered in snow.

Now, as I thought of my father, I thought of the black-and-white photograph on Mom's nightstand. He was a handsome man with a kind smile, in a uniform with bright buttons. His dark hair was shiny and combed straight back. His arms seemed to dangle. "Except for his hair, he was a lot like you," Mom had told me. "A live wire. Lean as a bean." Before he went into the army, he worked at Yeager's Lumberyard. He cut boards to certain lengths and widths. So I thought that maybe if he were still alive, he might have come home from work smelling of wood, and with sawdust on his arms and in the folds of his shirt.

"How did he die—I mean, what really happened?" I said. I knew he'd died in the Korean War when I wasn't even a year old. But I'd never asked *this* before.

She drew in a breath and pulled something, a thread, from the hem of her nightgown. "Well, I suppose you're getting old enough to know. Your dad, he wasn't shot, or anything like that. He was in a battle way up in the mountains, near China, in a place called Yudam-ni. It was in the middle of a terrible winter. Below zero for weeks on end. His unit was trapped—they couldn't escape—and he froze in the cold weather."

"Well, what was that like—I mean, for him?" It was another question I'd never asked her.

"I don't know. But I like to think he died peacefully, like falling asleep. They say that's how it happens in the cold."

She looked off toward the shelves and tools. She let out a long breath. All at once, she straightened her shoulders, ready for business, just as I'd see her at the checkout desk in our school library, where she worked.

"Now," she said in her chipper voice, "what are we going to call this bird of yours? We can't just call it 'it'!"

I thought for a moment. Molly? Polly? Percy? Then in a flash it came to me. "Marcy!" I said. That's the name of a mountain near the lake where we always went on vacation. It was also a good name for a bird.

"Marcy. Why, it's perfect!" Mom said. "Our friend Marcy must be a girl. That's a girl's name, right?"

Suddenly she stopped. She'd noticed something. "Look," she said. "The dawn."

And she was right. We switched off our flashlights and turned to the window, where soft blue light was spreading across the yard.

That's when we heard a faint rustle in the box, like the sound of leaves blowing on the ground. For a second it was as though we were trying to figure it out, like we weren't sure that we'd really heard it, and to believe it we had to hear it again. But the next thing we heard was totally different, and it made Mom drop her flashlight and both of us jump to our feet. From inside the box came that sharp, loud *TTCHAAAAAAACK!!!* It seemed to fill up the shed.

"What a sound!" Mom said. "What do we do?"

Already I was in action: my flashlight on, a worm dangling from my fingers. In the box, Marcy's beak was stretched straight up and opened wide as the mouth of a trout. I dropped the worm down her bright yellow throat, and her beak snapped closed like a trap. Then, with a big pump of her head, she swallowed the whole thing down.

"Did you see that?" I shouted.

"I don't believe it!"

But now we could barely hear ourselves speak, because already Marcy had opened her mouth again, stretching and squawking for more.

"Hurry!" Mom said.

"I am! I am!" I found another worm, dropped it in, and—bang!—it went right down. I fed Marcy another, and another, and then a fat five-inch night crawler that took her three pumps to swallow. Finally she was quiet again, but this was a whole different kind of quiet.

"She's going to live!" I said. "See, she's looking all around!"

We watched Marcy turn her head in that way birds do, so fast that you can't see the turning. Then she lifted her body slightly and, balancing on her stick legs, wobbled out of the corner and planted herself right in the middle of the box.

"She *is* going to live!" Mom said, wiping her eyes with one hand. The other, I noticed, had been gripping my arm so tightly that it left red marks. Now she let it go. "I'm starved," she said.

"Me too."

"I'm going to make breakfast. Pancakes?" she said. "Come in soon. It's Sunday morning."

THE REST OF THE DAY

EXCEPT FOR MEALS and another trip down to the compost pile, I spent the rest of that day on the stool in the shed, just being with Marcy, watching her and waiting for the next time she tilted back her head and went *TTCHAAAAAAACK!!!* I could tell that she was feeling better. I think I saw her smile. After she'd bolted down a bunch of worms, she'd let out a little satisfied burp, and then she'd seem to settle into herself and be quiet again.

Most of the time she just sat in her box, resting. Sometimes she slept, her eyes closing like a glass that's filling from the bottom up. But watching her wasn't boring. I didn't feel lonely, and I didn't feel like going anywhere else, even though I could hear my friend Mate playing freeze tag in his yard with his brothers and I knew there was a doubleheader on the radio.

It's funny when you sit with something for a while. You see things you didn't notice right away. For instance, Marcy's breast feathers, which at first looked solid gray, had tiny brown and black streaks. And those narrow stripes on each of her wings were actually the white tips of eight or nine different feathers, all lined up in a perfect row.

With the lightest touch, I stroked those feathers and the frizzy ones on her head. She seemed to like it. I felt her lean against my fingers, and I took her out of the box and held her again in my hands. Except for her feet, she was soft and warm. She smelled like grass in the sun. She breathed slowly and evenly. She was getting comfortable—we were *both* getting comfortable—and I told her that she was safe, that nothing bad would happen here, that there were plenty of worms where these came from and she could stay as long as she wanted.

In the late afternoon, while I was holding her, I got drowsy myself and had to close my own eyes. I leaned against the wall, dozing off for a few minutes, everything slowing down, getting warm and numb until I couldn't feel anything.

When I opened my eyes again, Marcy was wide awake, watching me as carefully as I'd been watching her. She was still right there, resting in my hands, like this was where she most wanted to be.

After supper when Mom had called me in for bed,

Marcy did something new. She squawked right *after* I'd fed her a load of worms, so it had nothing to do with her being hungry. We'd been together for almost the whole day. She was back in her box and I was getting off the stool, saying good night, when she let out a softer, sort of baby *tchack* that made me turn my head.

"What was *that* all about?" I asked.

She didn't answer in a way that I could hear with my ears, though when she looked at me, with her face all disappointed, I swear I could hear her words in my head. It was like a whole different kind of talking and listening. And the words I thought she was saying were *Don't go.*

MATE

THE NEXT DAY, a Monday, Mate started helping me with the worm digging and feeding. He even helped clean up Marcy's box. His real name was David, but he'd been "Mate" to me ever since we'd built our raft the summer before, had taken it out on the pond, and

Mom, joking, had called to me across the road, "Hey, sailor, who's your mate?"

He was only nine, a year younger than me, and while he could have weighed about the same, he was a lot shorter. His nose was stubby, his head round as a kickball. He had freckles as big as ladybugs, and, like his two other brothers, he had a crew cut that made his ears stick out like a couple of car doors left wide open. He lived up the road, not far away, just beyond the Andersons' and the Hulberts', in an old clapboard house like ours. As if his brothers weren't enough already, he had two little sisters and a wild spaniel named Trixie, so he often came over to play at my house, where we could do some things in peace and without everything getting wrecked.

In the summers, we were together most mornings, except Sundays, when he had to go to Mass. He was Catholic. So he wasn't allowed to have hot dogs or hamburgers on Fridays, and he crossed himself before he ate anything, including soft swirl cones at Dairy Queen. His mother, he said, had been all excited recently about having another baby, and about a man named Senator Kennedy, who she said would be the next president. Mate said that when their new baby came, they were going to name him Fitzgerald.

"Why?" I asked. "That's a pretty weird name."

He said, "Because Fitzgerald is Mr. Kennedy's middle name, and John—that's his first name—is already used up." John was Mate's older brother.

"Well, what if the kid's a girl?" I asked.

Mate looked at me like I was nuts. "Can't be a girl," he said. He was absolutely sure. "I mean, how can you have a girl named Fitzgerald?"

Luckily, Mate didn't mind the idea of a bird that was a girl, or a bird with a name like Marcy. In fact, there was something about her being a girl—or a certain *kind* of girl—that made us like her more. The way she ate, for instance. She didn't pick at her food. And she sure didn't care about manners. She didn't look down her nose at you either. She didn't even have a nose! On top of this, she didn't call you names like "Shorty," meaning Mate, or "Scrawny," meaning me. And she wasn't mysterious and sulky, like certain girls I knew—like Debbie Sparks or Ingrid Castleman. Birds, I think, aren't as tricky as girls. Marcy, for example, always let you know what she was thinking. And she was usually thinking about worms.

“Wow!” Mate had said when I first took him into the shed to see her. “A wild bird!”

Hearing us come in, Marcy squawked for food.

“Can I feed her?” Mate said. “Can I hold her too?” These were questions I’d *never* heard him ask about either of his little sisters, or even about his dog, for that matter. So I showed him how to drop a worm into Marcy’s throat, and how to make his palms into a nest to hold her. You learn a lot about your friends when you have your own bird. When I slid Marcy from my hands into Mate’s, he held her closely, like a candle with a tiny flame in a breeze.

“Can you feel that sort of whirring thing?” I asked him. “Almost like a little motor?”

He was quiet for a few seconds, concentrating, as Marcy fit herself into his fingers.

“That’s her heart,” I said.

Then he whispered, “Yeah, I can!” his eyes all big and amazed.

RISE AND SHINE

ON THAT TUESDAY—and like so many days that followed—I was up at the crack of dawn. I threw on my clothes, went downstairs, brought in the milk, ran down the porch steps, grabbed the newspaper off the driveway, left the front section in the kitchen for Mom, and rushed around back to the shed. When I went inside, we were so happy to see each other, Marcy and I. It was like we'd been separated for months.

"Rise and shine!" I said.

She squawked, *I'm already awake! I'm already shining!* She reached toward me, as if her head might stretch right off her body, and I grabbed some worms and fed her. Afterwards, she gave me that soft *tchack* which meant "thanks," and I slid the sports section into her box, face up, so we could both look at the major league standings. My team was the Yankees. Being a bird, she chose the Orioles, and the Cardinals in the National League. We studied the box scores and batting averages. Then we talked and talked. She wanted to know all about me, about what I'd been doing all those years before she was born and we met.

So I told her I couldn't remember too far back. A lot of it was ancient history. I'd been going to school. I'd been playing with Mate. In the summers, I mowed yards. In the winters, I went sledding and skated on the pond.

She wanted to know my favorite subject at school.

I told her maybe science.

She wanted to know if I played any sports.

I told her I was in Little League, but I wasn't exactly the star of the team. When I wasn't sitting on the bench, I played way, way out in right field.

She wanted to know if I had many friends—there seemed to be other kids in the neighborhood.

I told her yes, some . . . Well, mainly just Mate.

Then, right out of the blue, she said, *I bet you miss your father.*

"How do you know about him?" I asked.

She shrugged her shoulders. *I haven't seen him around. So I figured you must miss him.*

"I guess so," I said. "But how do you miss someone you can't remember?"

She seemed to understand this, nodding her head. Then she asked another question that I didn't expect. She wanted to know if I was happy.

"Well . . . sure," I said. "Of course. Especially when I'm with you!"

FLUTTERING

SINCE THE DAY BEFORE, Mate and I had been digging like crazy at the compost pile, shoveling out the clods of earth, breaking them up with our bare hands, and pulling the slimy worms from their tunnels. And about as fast as we could dig them up and take them to the shed, Marcy gobbled them down. Then, about as fast as she gobbled them, she pooped them out on the sports page—mostly on the Yankees' box score! So by the time I'd had her just three or four days, Mate and I were wearing a path from the compost pile to the shed, and around the side of the house to the garbage can, where we threw out the soaking sheets of newspaper.

Already Marcy was getting bigger and fatter. It was amazing how fast she changed. New feathers unfurled, she was losing her fuzziness, and her tail seemed to have lengthened. More and more she was waddling around in her box, pecking at the newspaper and cardboard sides, dipping her bill into the water, then raising it to swallow. She was growing, getting stronger, doing more things. Which of course meant that she was eating more, which then meant that we had to make more trips to the pile, to the shed, to the garbage can.

"You're getting to know what it's like to be parents," Mom called out to us on that Tuesday afternoon, more amused than we were by her observation. From the kitchen window, she was watching us trudge up the backyard with our shovels and a fresh can of worms.

On that day, though, instead of feeding Marcy in the shed, we took her out of her box and into the yard for the first time. "Recess!" we told her, but she just sat for a while as Mate and I kneeled around her. Soon she started to wobble and walk, testing her feet in the grass. We called, "Mar-see!" She squawked, and I held a worm a few inches in front of her so she had to lunge and stretch to get it.

Then, as she was stretching for another worm, her wings opened like fans and fluttered twice. They pushed her not off the ground but a little bit higher, as if she was reaching on tiptoe.

"Whoa! See that?" I said to Mate. On the top and underside of each of her wings, I caught a glimpse of a big white patch that had been hidden while her wings were closed. It was like a secret that she'd kept to herself. And now, there it was.

"They're beautiful, those patches!" I said to Marcy. "Can you do that again?"

She rocked back on her feet and fluttered her wings, flashing the patches, only this time she wasn't stretching for a worm. Instead, she was showing off for us. *Hey, look what I can do!* She fluttered and walked, then fluttered and hopped, then fluttered and ran, stumbling this way and that like some crazy windup toy.

Then Mate and I, we couldn't help it. We jumped up on our feet and made our legs, like Marcy's, go funny and wobbly, flapping and flashing our arms and shirtsleeves, following her, going nowhere in particular. We were doing the "Marcy March," as Mate called it, though it was more like a kind of stagger. We just made believe that we were all wound up, then let our bodies go.

We were laughing and crazy-marching and cheering Marcy on, when it came to me with a twinge: that in that stumbling, fumbling, fluttering way, she was moving farther and faster than ever before, and in a while—maybe sooner than I thought—I might not be able to catch her.

"I think she's ready to go back in," I said to Mate, who must have been thinking the same thing. He helped me scoop her back into my hands, and though she was excited, she seemed grateful for this. She gave us a shy, tired smile as we took her into the shed. I said, "Time for a rest"—we were all suddenly tired—and in a moment she was sound asleep in her box.

BAPTISM

ABOUT NOON THE NEXT DAY, Mate came into the shed with a concerned look on his face. "Do you know what limbo is?"

"Sure," I said. "It's like a dance. You have to bend real low beneath a stick."

"No. I mean the *real* limbo. My mom just told me about it. It's a place. It's dark. Where you can't see God. It's where you go when you die if you haven't been baptized, and when you go, you go there forever." He looked at me hard. "Nick, has Marcy been baptized?"

"I don't know."

"Well, she should be."

"But she isn't even Catholic."

"Doesn't matter. When she dies, and if she hasn't been baptized, she goes to limbo. It's automatic. We can only see her again—in heaven, I hope—if she gets baptized."

That was always the thing about Mate. He *really* believed in certain things—and stuck with them—while I wasn't quite sure of anything.

"All right," I said. "How do we do it?"

"Can you get a bowl?"

From the kitchen, I brought out a cereal bowl which he'd asked me to fill with water. Back in the shed, I held the bowl for him as he leaned over the box. To Marcy he said, very slowly and seriously, "I baptize thee in the name of the Father . . . and of the Son . . ."

With the words "Father" and "Son," he poured water from his hand over Marcy's head, and she shook like a wet dog. *Hey, what's going on?*

"It's all right," I said, trying to calm her.

". . . and in the name of the Holy Ghost," Mate went on, dousing her again. Then, with his face relieved and beaming, he said, "We're done! Now she'll always be with us."

DEREK

SOMETIMES I THOUGHT OF HIM AS A FRIEND, and sometimes I didn't. He was twelve. He made fun of Mate, calling him a "pip-squeak" and a "shrimp," and asked me, "Why do you hang around with that altar boy?" But you didn't dare make fun of Derek.

He lived off Dogwood Lane, in one of the new development houses with a pool and a patio out back. He wore tight pants that made his legs look long, and white socks and shiny loafers instead of high-top sneakers. He combed his hair like Elvis Presley, in a rippling black wave. He had lots of cool friends, and a lot of them were girls. He didn't usually pay much attention to me, except that every once in a while when it was hot he'd walk over to our house, his thumbs hooked in his front pockets. "Hey, Slick," he'd say, "you want to come over? We can swim and listen to records."

Mom, as you might imagine, wasn't crazy about this. She said Derek was "growing up too fast for his own good." But sometimes, because she knew I loved to swim, she'd say okay.

So at Derek's house, while his mother lay on a towel getting a tan, we swam, dove, and splashed in his pool, which was shaped like a giant peanut. In his room, which was air-conditioned and cold as a refrigerator, he played his stack of Ricky Nelson records and showed me all his *Hep Cats* magazines, with those girls in their bathing suits and bright red lipstick.

When he came to our house, he didn't stay long. "There's nothing to do," he'd say.

"Oh, yeah?" I said a few hours after Mate had gone home on the day of Marcy's baptism. "I've got a bird. You should see her." I led Derek into the shed. "Take a look in that box."

He looked, then shrugged his shoulders.

"She's a mockingbird. See those white marks on her wings? And beneath them are huge bright patches!"

"Well, what does it do? Just sit there?"

I took off the chicken wire and picked Marcy up

with both hands. "One thing you can do with a bird," I said, "is hold her like this. Want to try?"

You'd have thought I'd offered him a lighted firecracker. He stepped back, saying "No!" He took another step out of the shed. "Look, I'm going swimming. You coming or what?" He spun away and strolled off toward his development, his shirttail flapping, his hair gleaming like chrome in the sun. Though he never turned around or said another word, it was like he was pulling me along.

Quickly I put Marcy back in her box, and inside the house I grabbed my towel and swimming trunks. I asked Mom if I could go. She said, "Well, it looks like you're already on your way." Then I hurried to catch up with Derek, though now and then—I couldn't help it—I kept glancing back toward our house and the shed.

PERCHING

THE NEXT DAY, after I'd done my chores, I tried to make Marcy's box more like a home. I wove some willow wisps and grass clippings together to make a nest. With crayons, I drew branches on the inside walls of the box and glued on leaves and chunks of bark. Then I stuck a long stick through the holes I'd poked in either end to make a perch, and Marcy knew just what to do. She hopped right on.

That gave me another idea. I cut a doorway into one side of the box that I could open and tape closed, and where I could slide in my hand. For a couple of minutes, I held my finger in there, still as a stick, and finally, after she'd pecked at it awhile, Marcy jumped aboard, balancing with a flick of her wings. Right away, I rewarded her with a worm, and then she hopped on again and stayed there when I pulled my finger out of the box.

"We're going for a ride," I said.

Wheee! she said, fluttering and balancing, holding on as I took her on a roller coaster, up and down, swerving through the air.

What a feeling that was! Marcy had three front toes and one in the rear, each sharp and bony, with a curved nail on the end like a claw. It was as if all her strength—it was like all of *her*!—was somehow inside those toes. Together they'd clench me tight as a fist, so hard that it hurt, that I thought I was bleeding . . .

And so hard that I didn't want her to ever let go.

FLYING

ON FRIDAY OF THAT WEEK, I introduced Marcy to my grandfather, who I always called Granddad. When we'd come back from the A&P and had finished lunch, Mom and I drove over to the Deaconry—"the Home" as she called it—to pick him up for the rest of the afternoon. He was my father's father, my only living grandparent. Mom's parents had died young, soon after they'd sold the farm on Meeker Road, and long before I could ever know them. So we tried to see Granddad a lot.

He was an old man. His head was sunk into his shoulders, and his white hair, though combed, always looked stiff and flattened on one side, as if he'd been lying down in one place for a while. His left eye was made of cloudy glass and looked like one of my marbles. Only his right eye blinked, but even that eye, when you looked closely at its center, was still as glass. Three years before, he'd had cancer in his left eye, and then he'd had a bad stroke. He didn't move much, and when he made sounds, they were usually a kind of soft lowing, like the noise calves made in the pasture out beyond the developments.

I know all this sounds a little strange, but really it was okay. I liked having Granddad around. You got used to his sounds and his stillness, and when he was with us, Mom was always especially cheerful and patient. She patted his shoulder and kissed his forehead. She wanted us all to enjoy ourselves—"in the time he has left," she once told me.

At the Deaconry, a nurse helped him out of his wheelchair and got him into our car. On the drive back to our house, Mom usually just talked about the weather, the book she was reading, the vegetables she was growing, or that handsome shirt that Granddad was wearing. At home, we'd get the wheelchair out of the trunk and carefully slide him back into it with his head propped between pillows. Mom arranged his hands in his lap and his feet on the metal rests. On nice days, like this one, I'd push him around to the backyard and he'd sit in the sun beside the garden, where Mom would weed and water.

"Can I go get Marcy?" I asked Mom after we'd gotten Granddad settled and I'd set the brakes on the wheelchair. "Can I show her to him now?"

"Time for a surprise," she said to Granddad from where she was kneeling among the lettuce and tomato plants, working with the trowel. She was in her usual gardening clothes: shorts, gloves, an old paint-speckled shirt with the sleeves rolled up above her elbows, and a red bandana on her head. I always thought she looked pretty that way. Some loose strands of hair danced in the breeze, and her arms were tan in the sun.

I got the cardboard box from the shed and set it in front of the wheelchair. I took Marcy out—she was perched on my finger—and showed her off to Granddad. "Her name is Marcy," I said. "I found her on the road last Saturday."

As usual, Granddad didn't say anything. He just sat there like a statue, so, as Mom always did, I kept on talking and doing things calmly, like this was just the way things were. "She's a mockingbird," I went on. "She doesn't sing yet, but I'm hoping she will. Sometime maybe she'll sing us to sleep. Maybe she'll sing for you too." I bent closer to him and, with my free hand, pried Marcy off my finger and got her onto his. His skin was loose, wrinkled, and dotted with dark brown spots, but Marcy wasn't afraid. She clamped right on. I could even see how she was pinching his finger, though he didn't seem to feel it or to know what was happening at all.

"He's back there somewhere," Mom had told me, "somewhere behind the stillness and silence."

"Want to see me feed her, Granddad?" I called Marcy's name. She squawked, loud, which made him twitch, like he'd hiccupped. Then he fell back into his stillness and I fed Marcy a few worms. I said, "Thanks, Granddad, for holding her. Now I'm going to take her off your hand, before those worms come out the other end." I went to unclasp Marcy's toes from his finger, but she held on to him as fiercely as she did to me, maybe even tighter.

Can't I stay? she seemed to be pleading. So I figured, Let her stay for a while. We can clean up the mess later.

But Marcy had something else in mind. As if mostly for him, she flashed her wings, showing her secret patches. Then, fluttering more wildly than I'd ever seen, she leaped from his finger and actually *flew* a few feet in the air, until she stumbled down into the grass.

I couldn't believe it. "Marcy, that's terrific!"

Something about this made Granddad twitch again and made Mom put down the trowel. "Nick?" she said in an excited voice that also seemed a little scared. "She can fly?"

Now Marcy swayed her shoulders, fluttered her wings again, leaped, and, flying in that frantic, zigzag way of a bat, hauled herself just above the ground, over the garden and under the clothesline, all the way to the bush at the far side of the yard. There she scrambled in the leaves, her wings still going, her feet clawing, until she grabbed a swaying branch and held on for dear life.

Mom and I watched her in amazement. So far away, Marcy looked so small and different, like any gray bird in the yard. Suddenly my mouth was dry. I couldn't swallow or speak. Then we heard a strange noise. It was Granddad, bellowing. He was staring at

Marcy too, pointing at her, his whole arm shaking.

"Mr. B?" Mom called to him. "Can you see her?"

He kept bellowing, shaking, and pointing.

Now something came free in my throat, and I was making my own sound: "Mar-see! Come back! . . . Marcy?"

In the bush, she rode the swaying branch until the breeze calmed down. She pecked at a leaf, rubbed her beak against the branch, then stood alert, jerking her head, lifting her tail and ruffling her feathers, as if she was feeling all the air around her—and paying no attention to me. She preened her wings, smoothing and smoothing her feathers, like certain guys I'd seen in the boys' room mirror combing those waves in their hair.

She flashed her patches and leaped again. Away she flew in that same desperate, darting way, farther and farther, as if to join the grackles and sparrows in the Carlsons' yard beyond the fence.

Once more Granddad bellowed. Standing, Mom said, very slowly and calmly—it seemed as much to herself as to me—"Well, maybe it's for the best. After all, she's getting older. She needs to be among her kind . . ." Then all at once she cried out, "Nick! For God's sake, call her again!"

I did. And above the Carlsons' yard now, still flapping frantically, Marcy tilted her body and turned in a wide, jerky circle, back over the fence, back over the bush, back under the clothesline and over the garden, nearly crashing into the wheelchair, until she landed with a flop at my feet. I was feeling so many things—good, bad, happy, and scared—that I couldn't really tell what I was feeling. Marcy looked confused herself.

Then I reached down and she scrambled into my hand, clenching my finger with all her might, like we'd never be apart again.

JULY 1960

WITH WINGS SO WIDE

THE FOLLOWING WEEK, which carried into July, was an amazing one. Marcy took to the air so quickly! Each day she flew longer and higher, even up to the peak of the roof. She learned to glide for short periods between her flutters, either by holding her wings straight out or by folding them close to her body so she flew like a shot from a cannon. She didn't go far—just around the yard, always in sight—and she liked to soar up to the tops of trees, where she'd perch like a little queen looking over her territory.

Meanwhile, I kept a bait tin of worms attached to my belt, just like you do when you're fishing. That way, I could feed Marcy anywhere in the yard without having to lug around the coffee can. When she was hungry, I'd open the lid and pull out a worm, or sometimes she'd perch on the bait tin itself and tap it with her beak.

I also carried a box of raisins in my pocket, the kind Mom put in my lunch box during the school year. One morning I'd dropped a raisin down Marcy's throat instead of her usual worm. She'd swallowed it, then paused, blinking, figuring out if she liked it. Then she'd squawked, *Hey, that's great!* and she opened wide again.

So now I alternated worms and raisins for Marcy's meals, and with the raisins we did some tricks. I began by dropping them into her mouth from a little higher each time, so she had to jerk her head to catch them. Then I started underhanding them to her from a few feet away, then from a few yards away, and she went after them like a shortstop. Soon I could actually throw them up high and way out in the yard, like long fly balls, and she'd streak after them and snatch them out of the air, smooth as Willie Mays.

Farther! Throw it farther! she'd say.

I'd heave the raisin, and she'd snag it over her shoulder as she flew above the split-rail fence.

"It's like you're playing catch!" Mate said when he first saw us doing this.

"You should try," I told him. "She fields like a pro."

Now Mate had his own box of raisins too.

But best of all—even better than feeding her or

playing raisin-catch—was that wherever Marcy went, whenever I called her, she always came right back. She knew her name. I'd yell "Mar-see!!" She'd squawk, *Coming!* and in a second she'd swoop down like a hawk, then hit the brakes, parachuting the last few yards, her legs and feet stretched toward me. Then I had to close my eyes, because I was never exactly sure where she'd land. Usually it was on my shoulder, but sometimes it was on my ear, on the top of my head, or even right on my nose, her toes biting into my skin.

It's hard to describe just how good this felt: to call something wild from out of the sky, and then to see her with her wings so wide, like open arms, racing home to me. Mate said it was a miracle. I said it was magic. And Mom, who I think got it most right, said that it was love.

IN THE EVENINGS

ONE OF MARCY'S FAVORITE PERCHING PLACES was the edge of our green awning, where she had a good view of the backyard. Like every early July, it was getting warmer, so Mom called the handyman—a new man that year named Glen—who came and got the rolled-up awning from the cellar. Standing on a stepladder, he hauled the awning up onto a frame made of metal poles that jutted out over our back door. Then he unrolled it and, moving his ladder from place to place, tied it on with rope. Spread out, it was about twelve feet square.

When he'd finished and taken away his ladder and toolbox, Mom and I brought out the card table and our rickety folding chairs, and set them under the awning. Sitting there, you felt like you were inside *and* outside, in a small breezy room with a rug of grass, a canvas roof, and three open sides. On hot days we ate lunch out there in the shade, and sometimes after supper Mom invited over a few of her "girlfriends," as she called them, to drink lemonade and play the card game hearts. Usually they were our school nurse, Miss Smeltzer, and my homeroom teacher, Miss Zamora, with her orange hand fan that she fluttered back and forth like a butterfly's wing. Though friends, they were different from Mom. Younger, louder. While she studied her cards and listened with that amused look on her face, they'd go on about the men teachers in our school. Mr. Hall, they'd say, was "on the measly side," and as for my gym teacher, Mr. Bullis, he was "a regular Rock Hudson," Miss Zamora said. "He can knock on my door anytime!"

In the backyard, I played with Marcy while they laughed and shuffled cards. She'd swoop to me from the trees or the edge of the awning, and we'd play raisin-catch until the fireflies came out and the darkness sifted down. Meanwhile, Mom lit citronella candles that flickered in glass globes on the card table. As I carried

Marcy back toward the shed, the smell of melting wax filled the air. Mom and her friends would be leaning back in their chairs, their voices weaving, the playing cards snapping, and the ice going *chink* in their glasses.

In the shed, with me on the stool and Marcy resting in my hands, we'd have our own evening get-together. We'd talk about whatever came to mind: how the Orioles and the Yankees were doing, or her newest flying technique, or how I felt I was being mean to Mate when I wanted to spend time with Derek. Eventually I'd put her back in her box, and we'd talk a little more. I'd check her water. I'd feed her again. The last light would fade from the window, and the shed would feel small and warm. We'd be tired in that calm, happy, emptied way that you feel when you've had a full summer day.

"See you in the morning," I'd say, and she'd settle down on her legs, then lower her head into her shoulders, pulling her wings around herself like a blanket. Next she'd close her eyes in that special way and I'd hear the softest *tchack*, which meant "Good night." Then I'd hear nothing, which meant she was falling asleep, and very soon, after I'd closed the shed and gone in to bed, I'd be drifting off too.

THE FOURTH

THE FOURTH OF JULY was especially magical that year, and it had a lot to do with Marcy, though she wasn't with us to celebrate it until the very end.

In the afternoon, I fed her a big meal, told her we'd be out for a while, and closed her up in her box in the shed. Then Mom and I drove to Aunt Deb and Uncle Jeffrey's house. Uncle Jeff had been a friend of my father and Mom when they went to high school together. And Aunt Deb was my mom's kid sister, though with four kids of her own—my crazy cousins—she wasn't exactly what you'd call a kid. We saw them every couple of months. We met up with them on our vacations up north too, and for as long as I can remember, we always went to their house on the Fourth.

On that Fourth, like most, we ate hot dogs and watermelon, and all of us kids ran hollering beneath the sprinkler and tried to walk with hula hoops swinging around our waists. Much later, Mom and I came home, and though it was dark, I phoned Mate to ask him over for a special treat. I met him outside, under our awning, where Mom lit the candles and gave us a handful of sparklers, which we stuck in the ground around the card table.

Then, as we were about to get them going, we heard Marcy squawking from the shed. She'd been cooped up all afternoon and evening, and now she'd heard us outside and was pleading to come join the fun.

Using a flashlight, I went to the shed, fed her, and brought her out on my finger. It was her first time out in the wide-open night since I'd found her. She looked all around as if to say *Wow!* as I took her over to the card table. Mate lit the sparklers one by one, so that, beneath the awning, we seemed to be in a room of shimmering brightness, all surrounded by the night. Unafraid, Marcy leaped from my finger and—this too was a first—shot out of sight, swallowed up in the dark.

"Where is she?" Mate asked, alarmed.

I could have called her, but I just said, "Shhh. Listen."

And we stood there, listening as we never had before, until, over the fizzle of the sparklers, we heard the flutter of her wings. She was soaring and diving around out there! It was exciting, but not as exciting as what

happened next, as if Marcy was giving us another show. The fluttering got louder, suddenly stopped, and she swooped straight *through* our little room of light, in one side and out the other, lit up for an instant as if caught in the flash of a camera, her wings stretched out and their patches glowing.

Then she was gone—poof!—just the breeze behind her and that fading fluttering, and our hearts thumping like drums. But a few moments later, she swooped through from the *other* side—another surprise—and again we saw her in that instant of light.

OUT AND ABOUT

WE DID ALMOST EVERYTHING TOGETHER those days, even when I was out and around the neighborhood. Like a dancing kite, Marcy flew behind me as I pedaled my bike up to Mate's house. When I sped up, she sped up. When I slowed down, she slowed down. And when I did figure eights, leaving my tire tracks in the tar, she did figure eights above me too.

One day, she came with Mate and me when we

pulled our old raft from the brush near the pond and launched ourselves out on the water. We pretended to be river rafters on the Mississippi. We dodged waterfalls, snags, barges, and pounding steamboats—then shot through rapids, everything rushing, roaring, swaying. And all the while, Marcy dove and darted ahead of us, our trusty scout showing us the way.

On another day, a Saturday right smack in the middle of the month, she followed our car all the way across town to my Little League game, near the new school that my classmates and I would attend in the fall. At the time, Mom and I didn't realize that Marcy was flying behind us. We were running late, and in our rush to leave, I'd forgotten to put Marcy in her box. So after Mom had dropped me off, and as I was standing near the bench with my teammates, it took me a while to understand what my eyes were seeing. It was Marcy way above us, circling the ball field, her wings beating slow and hard. She went around the field a couple of times. Then she glided down in a narrowing spiral. Down and down she came like a falcon, and all at once everyone saw her.

They stopped talking. We were all stunned. Down and down she came until she landed in my mitt, the best catch I'd made all summer.

"Hey!" someone called.

Someone else yelled, "There's a bird in your mitt!"

Everyone crowded around us. They wanted to know all about her. Where did she come from? Whose was she?

"This is Marcy," I said. I'd never felt prouder. "She's mine."

Because Marcy was getting older and loved to fly so much, I finally decided to take the chicken wire off the box. With a brick and a wooden wedge, I propped the shed door open just a few inches so cats couldn't get inside but Marcy could come and go as she pleased. This wasn't an easy decision for me, but Mom said, "She's earned it. She's ready for some more freedom. You don't want her to feel trapped."

Now Marcy could go off on her own, around the neighborhood, wherever and whenever she wanted. While I was in the house doing one thing or another, you might see her on the Bisbees' trellis, or whirring in the Andersons' birdbath, or balancing like a rodeo rider on Mr. Fuller's clothesline while he hung out his red socks.

But she always flew back whenever I called her. It was still a magical thing. And if we hadn't seen each other for a while, she'd return on her own, streaking toward me like a thought that had never left my mind. She came home ready for food, ready for fun, or ready to stand guard in her usual places: in our apple tree out front, on the peak of the roof, on the edge of the awning, or on the telephone wire outside my window. And even though she was free now to go wherever she pleased, she still slept most nights in her box—or sometimes on my windowsill, with her feathers pressed against the screen, so we could be as close as possible.

When Marcy wasn't with me, you'd often find her somewhere around Mom, especially if Mom was watering her garden. With her finger on the end of the hose, Mom made the water spray in a wide arc, which Marcy flew through again and again, wetting her face and wings. Then Marcy would land on one of the wooden stakes for the tomato plants and perch there for a long time. From the back door, I'd sometimes watch them: Marcy preening her wings, running her beak through her feathers, then relaxing—often on one foot, then on the other—as Mom made the water slowly sway, like a kind of moving rainbow. They didn't really "talk" in the way that Marcy and I "talked," something always going back and forth between us. Instead, they were like friends who sat quietly, so comfortable together, as if they'd known each other so long and so well that they didn't even have to speak.

Maybe because she had human friends, Marcy didn't seem very interested in other birds, though some, including a few mockingbirds, seemed to be interested in her. When they flew near her, or anywhere around our yard, she scolded them with harsh *TTCHAAAAAAACK!!!*s. If they walked toward her in the grass, sometimes with their chests pushed out and wings flashing, she turned her back, ignoring them. If they kept coming, she gave them a look that said *Get lost!* And if they still didn't quit, she flew over and perched on my shoulder until they got bored and left.

This made me feel both bad and good, though mostly it felt good. "Marcy," I'd say, "you could be more friendly. How would you like to be treated like that?" But then again, it felt pretty nice when she was on my shoulder, her toes digging in, telling those other birds to buzz off and saying to me, *I'd rather be with you. I'm glad you're not a creep like them!*

FROM THE TOP OF THE APPLE TREE

TOWARD THE END OF JULY, it turned terribly hot and humid, and Granddad was too weak and uncomfortable to come visit us at home. He couldn't even sit in his wheelchair. So for two Fridays in a row, we just stayed by his bed in the Deaconry, where we talked to him quietly as now and then he made his lowing sounds and Mom wiped his forehead with a handkerchief.

It was so hot that you didn't want to move. Everything felt like lead. The air wavered above the road, the yard turned brown, and the hills outside of town looked dull and hazy. At night, all you heard were the air conditioners buzzing in the development houses and the crickets shrilling in the grass, like sandpaper rubbed on metal. No breeze came through my window, and I tossed and turned on damp, sweaty sheets, with the electric fan pointed at me.

Somehow the weather didn't affect Marcy. *Heat? What heat?* she seemed to say. *Watch this!* While Mate and I lay in the shade of the cherry tree, she hopped like a rabbit across the yard on her tall, narrow legs. Like an acrobat, she flew through the tops of trees, coasting and flapping, turning and banking, shooting even through the thick willow beside the pond without touching a leaf. She somersaulted in midair. She'd dive-bomb, like a kamikaze, straight toward the ground, making you cover your eyes and hold your breath, until, at the last second, she'd pull out of the dive, skimming the grass like a swallow.

"She's already passed you," Mom said. "She's older—in bird years, that is. She's getting so sure of herself."

It was true. By now, Marcy was almost full-size.

Gone were those tiny brown and black streaks on her breast. Gone was all her round softness. Her tail, when she flew, flared with white, and her wing patches shone like decals. Perched on the roof, or high in our apple tree with her tail cocked up, she really did look like the queen of our yard. It was as though, from her height, she could see everything more clearly than I could from below. And one afternoon, at a moment when my own vision was blurred, she saw so clearly that she took some matters into her own hands. Or, I guess I should say, into her own claws.

Mate and I were sitting on the porch steps next to Mom's pot of geraniums, eating baloney sandwiches. Senator Kennedy had recently won the Democratic nomination for president, and Mate was telling me how his mom had been listening to the radio day and night, she was so excited. We were talking, our T-shirts off, our skin sticky with sweat, when we heard Derek's loafers clicking on the road. He strolled toward us and stopped at the end of the front walk, his hair gleaming and his thumbs, as always, hitched into his front pockets.

"Hey, Slick," he called to me, "I got some time to kill. You want to come over and swim?" He tilted his head slightly toward his development, and I could almost feel myself walking alongside him.

"So let's go," he said. He didn't say a word to Mate, who just looked down at his knees.

"Hold on," I said to Derek. I couldn't say no to him, even though I knew I should. "Just a second. I'm eating lunch."

"With that little saint?" he said, meaning Mate, which made me feel awful.

I saw a corner of Derek's mouth turn up, and with another pang, I saw Mate just close his eyes. Whose friend was I?

Then I saw another thing: a flash of wings at the top of the apple tree, where Marcy was perched and peering at us.

"You coming or what?" Derek said when I'd finished my sandwich. He was standing there, rocking on the heels of his polished shoes, arms crossed, waiting for the answer he wanted to hear, as if he already knew what I'd say.

In fact, at that moment, I didn't know what I'd say. I might have said anything, I was so confused. But I never had the chance to speak.

In an instant, Marcy shot down like lightning. Dead

on, she hit the top of Derek's head, exploding his hair, whipping it with her claws, jabbing with her beak. It sent him reeling forward and tumbling to the ground, one of his loafers flying clear off his foot, with Marcy squawking and still after him.

"Marcy, stop! That's enough!"

She flew back to the top of the tree.

Now Mate looked up at her, his mouth open, and crossed himself. I was as amazed as he was.

Meanwhile, Derek scrambled to his feet, his eyes looking scared like I'd never seen them, his hair a tangle of spaghetti. Without a word, he turned and ran like all get-out, arms churning, shirttail flying, hobbling in one shoe and one white sock, heading back to where he came from.

I felt bad for Derek, but not *that* bad. Mostly I felt relieved, and happy for myself and Mate. For the rest of that afternoon and the rest of that summer, I barely thought of Derek again. I heard from him once, a couple of weeks later. He called on the phone—he didn't dare come over—and asked if I wanted to "hang out" while his parents were away.

He'd hardly finished his question, when I told him, No, thanks. I was busy. With a friend.

GLEN

FOR TWO DAYS, we had heavy rain. Mom's garden really needed it, but the rain settled in our awning and stretched it out. Big round pockets of water, like bellies, sagged between the metal poles. So Mom called the handyman who had put up the awning, and on an afternoon when the sun had finally come out again, he returned in his pickup truck with his stepladder and his bright red toolbox.

As I said before, his name was Glen. He was a big, clumsy-looking man, though in fact he wasn't clumsy at all, and once you'd been around him a while, he didn't even seem big. He had sandy-colored hair. He was maybe thirty, maybe forty. It was hard to tell. He wore work boots, jeans, and a plaid shirt. He had wide hands, sloped shoulders, and a soft, shy voice. Like the other time he'd come here, he called Mom "ma'am."

"No, ma'am, I don't think it's ruined . . . Yes, ma'am, I think I can fix it." Then, as if he knew what was on Mom's mind, he added, "Of course, there's no extra charge."

"Well, can I get you some lemonade?" Mom asked him. She was standing in the back doorway, with her arms folded loosely across her blue-and-white checked shirt. "By the way, this is Nick, my son."

"I remember," he said. "I'm Glen." He held out his hand, and as we were shaking, he nodded over his shoulder, up toward the cherry tree where Marcy was staring down at us and flashing her wings. I could tell she was suspicious of him. "I see you've still got your little soldier watching over you," he said. "Tell her I'm okay. I'm a friend."

With a broom that he held upside down, he pushed against the underside of the awning and the water cascaded over the edge. Then he stood on his stepladder and, reaching up, began unlacing the crisscrossed rope on the poles the way you'd unlace a shoe.

Mom brought out his lemonade, placing it on the flat tray on his ladder, and I saw that it wasn't our usual lemonade from a can. Instead, she must have squeezed it fresh, left in a slice of lemon, and added some mint from her garden.

He took the drink, said it was great, and when she

went back inside he got on with his work. He unlaced the whole awning, then started relacing and knotting, pulling it tight as a drum. A couple of times he came down from the ladder, had another sip of lemonade, sat beside me on the back step, and, with a short length of rope, showed me the knots he'd been tying. A clove hitch. A square knot. A cool figure eight. "And here's one I won't use, because your bird won't like it. It's called a 'cat's-paw.' "

Meanwhile, Marcy was getting more used to Glen. She flew under the awning and perched on the open lid of his toolbox to have a peek inside.

"Looks like she might want to help us," he said. He was up on his ladder again. "Think she can bring over my tape measure?"

"No," I said, "but I can."

"Thanks, partner," he said in his easy voice, then asked, "How long have you had her, that bird?"

"Since the end of school."

"And you take care of her all by yourself?"

"Me and my friend Mate."

"Well, she sure looks happy and healthy. You must be doing a good job."

Stretching, he measured something along one of

the poles and put the tape measure in his rear pocket, where it had worn its shape in his jeans. "She's a mockingbird, right? Has she got a name?"

"Marcy."

He thought about this. "That's a fine name," he said.

Toward six o'clock, Mom, in her apron, started preparing supper, and she asked Glen if she could make a sandwich for him. He seemed to be working late.

"No, thanks," he said, but added that he was "much obliged." He said he'd be finished in a little while.

Soon Mom and I ate supper at the kitchen table while Glen continued working. That's when I noticed that she'd put on a white blouse I'd never seen before. It was pretty, with embroidered decorations around the neck, and it didn't have any sleeves, so you could see the tops of her arms.

"It'll be nice to be out under the awning again," she said to me, "after all that rain." In her face was a sort of odd, faraway look. She was looking at me, but not quite into my eyes. Now, resting her chin in one hand, she gazed out the screened back door. "It seems like the rain has washed the air clean. It feels soft tonight," she said.

UNDER THE AWNING

AFTER SUPPER, I helped Mom take the dishes to the sink, where she washed them and put them in the rack, singing along with the record player, her voice all low and sweet. I pedaled up to Mate's house, but he was out somewhere with his father. So Marcy and I went over to the pond to watch the carp feed on the surface, as the sun fell through the trees.

It was almost dark when I came back into our driveway and saw Glen's truck still parked near the house, with his ladder sticking over the tailgate. He must be packing up his stuff, I thought, getting ready to leave. But when I went around to the backyard, I saw them under the awning—Mom and Glen—and he didn't seem to be going anywhere. They were sitting at the card table, with the candles lit in the glass globes. They were talking quietly, bending toward each other, just their faces and arms in the flickering light, as if there was nothing else in the world around them.

"Oh! Nick!" Mom said. She seemed to have jumped

out of a dream. She leaned back from the table. "What time is it? Goodness! I must have lost track. Where've you been?"

"Just over at the pond."

"Well, better hurry upstairs. I'll be right up to say good night."

"And I'd better be heading home," Glen said to Mom. I noticed he didn't call her ma'am.

I got Marcy settled in her box in the shed. Then I headed for the back door, where Mom had hung her apron on the knob.

"Good night, partner," Glen said, standing now. He said "partner" in his warm, mild voice, just like he had that afternoon, but this time it felt different.

"Wash up," Mom said to me. "Brush your teeth."

I went upstairs to the bathroom, got into my pajamas, into bed, and turned off the light. A ball game was on my transistor radio, but I didn't feel like listening. Instead, I turned it off and listened to the crickets and frogs and anything else I might hear. But I heard nothing through the heat register in my floor and nothing drifting up the stairs. I waited for what seemed like a long time, though it was probably just four or five minutes. At last I heard the door of Glen's truck open and close. The engine started. The tires crunched over gravel. Kneeling, I looked out my window and saw his taillights turn away on the road.

Soon Mom came up and sat on my bed, her arms long and bare in the light from the streetlamp. She smelled like candle wax, citronella, and something sweet that I couldn't place.

For a while, we didn't say anything. The clock, as always, ticked on my bureau. Everything was the same, but strange. Then she asked, "What were you up to at the pond?"

"Not much. Just fooling around."

"See any frogs?"

"No."

"Any fish?"

"A couple."

We were quiet again. She looked out the window, then pushed her hand through her hair. "It's been a long day," she said. "Let's get some sleep." She touched my forehead and kissed me there, and I watched her move toward the door.

THROUGH THE TUNNEL

THE NEXT MORNING, I was hungry but didn't feel like eating. I couldn't sit still either. Lying in bed, I'd kept thinking about my father in that photo on Mom's nightstand, his dangling arms and kind smile, and how in a place on the other side of the world he had fallen asleep in the freezing cold.

When I'd gotten up, I told Mom I was going out, and I ran straight down to where the tiny stream from the pond flowed under the road through a big concrete pipe that Mate and I called "the tunnel." I pushed through weeds and blackberry bushes, down the bank to the water. I hadn't been there in a while—not since spring, when the stream was colder. I squatted at the dark, round mouth of the pipe. The opening was a yard wide. I could barely see to the other end, but the water inside made a gentle, inviting sound. Just an inch deep, it flowed smoothly, narrow and straight. With my hands and knees on either side of the water, I started crawling inside. This was a secret place that only Mate and I knew about, where nobody else could find us. Near the middle, we'd written our initials on the wall with nail polish that he'd borrowed from his mom. Now, when I got there, I could just read them, the only light coming from each end of the pipe. With my back against one side and my feet against the other, I made a kind of bridge with my legs, the stream flowing beneath them. Far off to my right, I saw the end where I'd started, small as a dime, like I was looking down the wrong end of a telescope.

Then, in that little circle of light, Marcy appeared. She was perched on a rock, peering into the tunnel, as though she was asking me, *What are you doing in there? Something bugging you? You okay?*

But I guess she didn't wait for an answer. Or maybe she already knew it. I heard her wings and felt the air beating. She was flying to me underground!

She landed beside me at the edge of the stream, standing on the curved concrete.

"This is our secret hideout," I explained to her. "For when Mate or I need to get away from things or we just want to be alone."

Do you want to be alone now? she asked.

I shook my head no.

So she hopped onto my knee and we sat there awhile, listening to the gurgling water. She looked up at me with her wide, round eyes, and though I barely knew it myself, she seemed to know just what I was feeling. I had the sense that if I was much smaller and she much bigger, she'd have taken me under her wings. *Try not to worry,* her eyes were saying. *It will all be okay.*

Together like that, we listened to the water, and little by little something drained out of me, and what was left was calm. Everything seemed cool, dark, and damp, but safe, like we were deep inside a shell. We could feel, but couldn't hear, a car pass above us. It seemed so far away.

After a while, Marcy said softly, *I think we can go out now. All right?*

As she fluttered in front of me, leading the way, we continued through the tunnel. Ahead, the circle of light got bigger and bigger. Behind us, the light dimmed. Now the water seemed to flow faster. And as we reached the end, there was the sense that we were coming out into a different kind of place, brighter, more wide-open, but almost blinding too. We had to squint so hard to see.

AUGUST 1960

THE CALENDAR

ONE SUNDAY AFTER WE'D EATEN DINNER, Mom turned the page of the calendar that hung on the cupboard door above the telephone. That's where I'd mark the Saturdays when my Little League team was scheduled to play. And that's where Mom wrote less-interesting notes like "Dentist—10:15," "Pay bills," "Trash pickup," or "Tutor—2:00–3:00," which meant that for that hour, on whatever day it was, I wasn't allowed into the kitchen, where Mom would be sitting with a second-grader, teaching the kid how to read. She did this tutoring for most of the summer, a few times a week, for "pin money," as she called it. She put some of this money in an envelope in the cupboard, beside her envelope stuffed with coupons.

Now she wrote her notes on the new page of the calendar, then stepped back and counted the neat rows of squares. "Guess what?" she said, her voice full of excitement. "In three weeks—no, a little less!—we'll be off to the lake!"

Of course she was talking about our vacation up north, and the thought of it made me excited too. Each year we drove way up to a lake in New York State, over three hundred miles away. That was where Mom's family had always gone since she was a kid. We met up there with Uncle Jeff, Aunt Deb, and my cousins. Mom and I had the cabin next to theirs. Together with the people in a couple of other cabins, we shared the boathouse, the little beach, and the swimming area, where we always made tidal waves doing cannonballs off the float.

Now when Mom said we'd be off to the lake, I was also thinking of another thing. This year, she'd promised, I could take the boat out all by myself as long as the weather was calm and I wore a life jacket. Before dawn, while everyone else was still asleep, I could dress, go quietly down to the boathouse, untie the boat, row way out on the water, and see what the morning would bring . . .

But what about Marcy? What about her? The question hit me like a hammer. Somehow I hadn't thought of it, or hadn't dared think of it. Where would she be while I was up on the lake all those miles away? Could she come with us? *Should* she come with us? Could I put her in a box and take her in the car for such a long ride? Would she make it? And even if she did, could I let her out in such a different place?

Or would I have to leave her at home?

That seemed impossible. But the look on Mom's face said she'd known we might come to this. Yes, it was possible. Very possible.

"But we can't go!" I said. "Not without Marcy! We can't just up and leave her!"

"Let's take one day at time," Mom said, trying to keep us calm. "Let's not get ahead of ourselves. Let's figure something out. Maybe, during the time we're gone, Mate can take care of her."

AT MATE'S

THOUGH MARCY SPENT THAT NIGHT on my windowsill, I couldn't sleep at all. A wind rattled the apple leaves and shook the phone line. Through the screen, I could see the willow beside the pond, its long branches thrashing.

Before breakfast the next morning, I sped on my bike to Mate's house, with Marcy flying hard to keep up. I knocked on the patched screen door to their kitchen. Mate was inside with his mom. He looked sleepy, slumped at the table in his pajamas, eating a piece of toast. His mom also looked tired. Her hair was in curlers, and she was pouring cereal into bowls. As she came toward the door, she tightened her bathrobe over her round stomach. I told Marcy to wait outside.

"Can I talk with Mate?" I asked as soon as his mom let me in the door.

"Sure. We're having breakfast. You okay? You want to sit down?"

"No, thanks. I just need to know something, Mrs. Connell." Then I looked right at Mate. "Can you do me a favor? Can you take care of Marcy while I'm away on vacation? You'll have to feed her, change her water and newspaper, and make sure the shed door's open just a few inches each night. She'll be lonely, so you'll need to be with her a lot. It'll be for a week. Think you can?"

Like a splash of water, this woke Mate up, and he

smiled big as the sun. "Why, sure!" he said. "Of course! We'll do everything together! I'll feed her. I'll take her to the pond. I'll take her to the stream. I'll take care of her as good as you do, Nick. I swear. Cross my heart!"

Now he was standing and we were hugging each other, then jumping around in their kitchen. We made the dishes clatter, and their dog, Trixie, started barking.

I said, "I can make a list of everything you'll have to do."

He gave me a look. "I already know." Then he said, "Know what? How about if *I* make a list? Each day I can write what me and Marcy do. I'll keep a notebook. Then you and me, we can read it together as soon as you get home. It'll be like you never went away!"

We were still jumping around when one of Mate's sisters and his older brother, John, came in.

"What's with them?" John asked, looking at us.

"They're happy!" Mate's mom said, putting silverware on the table. "Your brother's going to take care of Nick's bird. Isn't that great? Nick, where are you going on vacation?"

"Up north," I said. "To the mountains."

"Wonderful!" She poured juice. "When do you go?"

"On the twentieth."

Something about this stopped her cold. It made her face change. "You sure?"

I nodded.

Then she let out a little sound with her breath and said, "Uh-oh."

"What's wrong?" Mate asked.

She shook her head slowly. "That's the week when *we'll* be on vacation too. When we'll be away at the beach. Remember?"

I heard something boiling on their kitchen stove. For a moment, no one moved at all, until Mate dropped his face into his hands and his shoulders heaved. Just then his dad came in, buttoning his orange shirt that said "Eddie" in an oval patch. He was a short, thick man who looked like a wrestler. He drove a dump truck for the town road department. He saw Mate, stopped, and said, "Sonny?" Then he went right up to him, wrapped his big arms around him, and Mate, small as he was, burrowed in.

"There, there," his dad said softly, and he lifted Mate clear off the floor.

Suddenly I was feeling hungry and faint. The room swayed. I managed to say, "Mate, I'll see you later," as I pushed open the screen door. Outside, the sun was bright, and there was Marcy, waiting on the railing.

She looked at me. *Hey, cheer up! It's a beautiful morning!*

But I couldn't look her straight in the eye. How would I *ever* tell her?

DOWN AT THE POND

SO WHAT DO YOU THINK she's going to do?" Mate asked me.

That's how most of our conversations started after that morning in Mate's kitchen. Since then, Mom had been firm: Marcy couldn't come on our trip. At bedtime, I'd plead with her—"Mom, please!"—but again and again she'd told me, You can't just take a mockingbird away from its home and expect it to survive in the mountains. Those nights, when she'd left my room, I'd cry myself to sleep, and all the next day I'd feel groggy and mad, then defeated. Nothing seemed right in the world.

Now Mate and I were sitting cross-legged, Indian style, on the concrete dam of the pond, where the water spilled over a little chute. It was almost noon. Marcy was perched in the willow on the opposite bank, and in the brush we could see our raft where we'd left it after our adventure on the Mississippi. But we didn't even talk about hauling it out and putting it in the water. The air was hot and sticky. We didn't have the energy, and already the raft had vines growing over it, probably poison ivy. So we just sat there, lobbing pebbles out into the pond. *Plunk. Plunk. Plunk.*

"So what do you think?" Mate asked again.

"I've already told you—about a million times," I said. "Probably she'll fly away. There's nothing we can do to keep her here."

"But where will she go?"

"How am I supposed to know? Mom says she'll be interested in other birds pretty soon. So maybe she'll go someplace where teenage mockingbirds hang out. Maybe she'll go to Asbury Park."

He threw another pebble.

"Look," I said. "We have to get it into our heads. Once she knows we're gone, she'll have no reason to stay. She'll go wherever she can get food. And who knows where that'll be."

"But we won't be gone forever," he said, this too for the millionth time. "We'll be back."

"Well, how's she supposed to know that?"

He looked stumped for a while and gazed off toward the hazy hillside. "Well, maybe somehow she just *will.*"

"I don't think so," I said.

This seemed to put an end to that part of the conversation, and we just kept tossing pebbles. I told Mate about the lake in the mountains, trying to sound enthusiastic. Still trying to perk us up, he told me about the beach and the boardwalk and a place where you could play a game called Skee-Ball, and if you were good enough, you could win all kinds of cool things: yo-yos, cap guns, baseball cards, model airplanes, Silly Putty . . .

But none of those things—not even all of them put together—could come close to having a bird like Marcy.

THE BIRD FEEDER

SINCE THE END OF JULY, Glen had dropped by once after work to check on the awning after a rainstorm, and he had stopped in another time to see if his handiwork "was still holding up," as he said, though it had hardly rained at all. He was always nice to me, often asking what I was doing, but I didn't have much to say. When he was there, and even after he'd gone, Mom seemed to be in a different, private place, and there was nothing I could do about it. "Sometimes it's like she barely sees me," I complained more than once to Marcy.

Then one Sunday evening a week or so into the month, Glen came over again. He wore khaki pants, a short-sleeved shirt, and rubber-soled shoes that didn't make any noise when Mom let him in the front door. He looked shy and awkward, as though he didn't come calling like this often. Mom touched him lightly on one hand. In his other he held some white carnations.

All that afternoon I'd sensed that something was up, while Mom bustled around the house, vacuuming and dusting. It wasn't until supper that she told me Glen would be stopping by in half an hour to join us for dessert. Would I mind putting on a fresh shirt? She went upstairs for a while, and when she came down, she was wearing a tan skirt and that sleeveless blouse with the embroidery around the neck. Slender silver earrings in the shape of icicles dangled from clips on her earlobes. Her cheeks were redder. She smelled like lavender, and her eyes and hair seemed to shine.

Never before had I seen her so alive with something that had nothing to do with me. She hugged me and said, "Let's try to have a nice evening." I went out to find Marcy in the yard.

That's where I was sitting glumly, with Marcy perched on my knee, when I heard Glen's truck rattle into the driveway. Mom called me back inside to greet him.

The carnations, of course, were his gift to her. Taking them, she said, "Oh, they're magnificent!" though they looked like regular old flowers to me. She arranged them in a vase that she took out under the awning and put on the card table, along with the forks for dessert. She served her rhubarb pie with vanilla ice cream on top, which should have improved my mood but didn't. She seemed to enjoy watching Glen clean his plate, and she asked him if he wanted another slice, something that I was rarely allowed. He said no thanks, pushing back his chair, but it was "terrific." He'd "reached his limit."

I excused myself. I just wanted to be with Marcy in some other place, maybe over at the pond or deep in the tunnel, where everything here would seem far away.

I hadn't gone three steps when I heard Glen ask me, "Could you hold on a second?" He got up and, in his loose-legged way, walked around the house toward his truck. He came back with a package about twice as big as a shoe box and set it at my place at the table.

"I understand you're about to go on a trip," he said. "Maybe this will make the going easier."

I opened the box and inside was a kit—with all the nails, screws, glass sides, a cedar roof, and a metal tray—to make a good-sized bird feeder! Along with the kit were the building instructions and a plastic bag full of birdseed.

I didn't know what to say. How had *he* thought of this? Why hadn't I? A feeder could be just the thing to keep Marcy here while we were gone—provided she liked the seeds and the feeder didn't go empty.

"Let's see if she'll eat them," he said. "If she doesn't, we can try some other options."

I opened the bag, took out some seeds, and called Marcy over. She flew down, and I held the seeds out on my palm.

Eat them? she said.

"Go ahead. Try."

But you've got all those juicy worms in your bait tin and raisins in your pocket.

"I think you'll like these just as well."

Sure?

I said yes.

All right, just a taste. She jumped into my hand and picked at a seed, barely chewing it, ready to spit it out . . . but she didn't. She swallowed it. She grabbed another and another. One by one, the seeds disappeared!

"Now, I've got an idea," Glen said. "Maybe we can make a deal. If you build the feeder, set it up, and if, on your trip, you promise to enjoy yourself and not worry about your bird, then I'll stop by here every evening while you're away to make sure the feeder stays full. I'd like to do that."

I still didn't know what to say. Why was he doing this? Was it all because he liked Mom? Or was some of it because he also liked Marcy and me?

"You know, Audrey," he said to Mom. It was the first

time I'd heard him use her name. "You know, on second thought, I *will* have another slice of that pie."

"How about you?" he said to me.

SINGING

I TOLD MATE all about the feeder, and over the next few days, with Mom's help, we built it together. It was like a miniature glass-sided house, filled with seed, where birds could perch on the lip outside. As they ate, the seed would dribble through a gap beneath the glass, always replenishing the tray. It was ingenious. And it worked! We screwed the bird feeder to the top of a fence post, and in a second Marcy was at it, like a kid at a soda fountain.

Meanwhile, the date of our departure was approaching. More and more, Mom was talking with Aunt Deb on the phone and adding to her vacation list. On the Saturday a week before we were to leave, she drove me to my last Little League game, with Marcy flying behind as usual. On Monday she asked our postman to hold our mail the following week, and the next day Glen stopped by to see how the bird feeder was coming along. He was astounded. With gray paint and a tiny brush, I'd printed Marcy's name on the roof, along with pictures I'd drawn of her. He said Mate and I had done a bang-up job, and of course he'd keep his side of the deal. He'd check on the feeder, and while he was at it, he'd refill the water in Marcy's box every day.

Marcy's tastes now were suddenly expanding, as though her feasting at the feeder had sparked her appetite for different kinds of food. She started raiding the raspberry bushes near the pond and the blackberry bushes down by the stream, and she also managed to catch some butterflies. So on the sports page in her box, I'd find all sorts of colors, depending on what she was eating. Bright red meant raspberries. Dark purple meant blackberries. Gray meant cabbage butterflies or sunflower seeds. Orange meant she was sampling Mom's tomatoes. And all of it meant that she was providing more and more for herself, and that I, as far as she was concerned, could put away the shovel and bait tin, and eat all the raisins myself.

Then, on that Thursday evening, I mowed our yard for the last time before vacation, as Marcy perched at the feeder and darted after moths that I'd scared out of the grass. When I finished, we sat side by side on the fence, and I watched the shadows move across the yard, as if they were lengthening fingers.

It was time to say it, but it wasn't easy. It scared me, and I had to get up my nerve. "Marcy, there's something I have to tell you."

She turned her head toward me. *Go ahead.*

"I'm afraid it's bad news."

All right. I'm ready.

I tried to look right at her. I could barely get it out. "Marcy, I have to leave you soon. This Saturday morning. We're going away on vacation."

For a moment she was absolutely still. I couldn't tell if she understood or not.

"It's just a week," I went on. "I know it's going to feel like a long time, but there should be plenty of berries in the bushes, and Glen will keep the feeder full. Like always, I'll leave the shed door propped open, so you can sleep in your box."

She still hadn't said anything. Then she blinked her eyes and straightened her back, as if she'd made up her mind about something. *I'll follow. I'll follow the car. I'll fly to wherever you go!*

"No," I said, "it's hundreds and hundreds of miles away. You can't. It's impossible."

She thought about this. *Well, what about Mate? He'll be here, won't he?*

I told her that he'd be on vacation too, during the same week, "but we'll both be back. I promise." Then I tightened my grip on the fence rail. "You'll stick around? You won't go away, will you?"

She stared at me, wide-eyed, like she'd never thought of this before. A tiny shiver ran through her body, and though her eyes didn't make any tears, I thought she might be crying. *Where else would I go? Who else would be my friends? This is my home, right?*

"Of course," I said. "And when we're back, it'll be just like always. It'll be like we never left!"

This seemed to comfort us both a bit. *I guess I'll be okay.*

Now we were quiet again, just sitting, the sparrows chattering in the Carlsons' yard. She looked at me, and I could tell she wanted to say something else, though for once no words came to her, or maybe words couldn't express what was on her mind.

Instead, I heard something I'd never heard before, a soft, uncertain sound that seemed to come from far away, though it wasn't far away at all. It was a sound softer than a dove's, softer than when you blow across the mouth of a bottle, and so thin it could have been a thread in the air. But light as it was, it seemed to come from deep inside her, as deep, I think, as her heart: *Hew, hew . . . Hew, hew . . .*

It was a single note, repeated twice and drawn out at the end. *Hew, hew . . .*

I couldn't tell exactly what it meant, but this much I was sure of: "Marcy! Listen! You're singing!"

When I ran in and told Mom about this, she said, "You sure?" She dropped her pencil and pushed aside her vacation list, and we hurried out to the backyard.

But Marcy didn't sing right then. It wasn't until after supper, at dusk, when Mate had come back to play until dark, that we all heard her *hew*-ing at the top of the cherry tree. Mate and I froze. Mom looked up from her gardening, her face filled with wonder. "What a beautiful, fragile sound," she said. "It's like she's yearning."

Then as we listened, Mate's eyes went big, as if he was lit up from inside. "She's giving us something! A little song, something to remember while we're away. Until we see her again."

GOODBYE. FOR NOW.

ON THE NEXT DAY, Friday, Mom and I went shopping, visited with Granddad at the Deaconry, and then spent the afternoon filling our suitcases and packing the car so we could leave right away in the morning. After supper, I pedaled up to Mate's house to say a quick goodbye. A pile of beach chairs tilted on top of their rusty station wagon. A hooked-on trailer squashed the rear tires and pushed the bumper practically to the ground. Scattered on the driveway were boxes and bags that Mate's dad was loading into the trailer. Seeing me, he called into the house for Mate, while Marcy landed on one of the beach chairs.

When Mate came out, we greeted each other with our secret password, "Orroz," which is "Zorro" spelled backwards. We made a promise—cross our hearts—that whoever got home first from vacation would race straight to my backyard and let Marcy know we'd returned.

As I was about to go, he asked me if he could spend a moment alone with Marcy. I said sure, of course, and he walked over toward the garage, calling Marcy to follow. When she landed in the weeds near his feet, he squatted down right in front of her. I was watching from a ways off, looking over his shoulder, so I couldn't see that well. He seemed to be talking to her calmly and seriously, and she was nodding as if she understood, and then he sort of patted the air above her head.

"That Sonny," his father said to me. He seemed so proud and amazed. "Know what he's doing?"

I shook my head.

"I think he's giving your bird a blessing."

That evening I went to bed early, but I couldn't fall right asleep—not with the streaks of orange light lingering in the sky, and my suitcase on my desk, open like a book, all packed except for my clock and toothbrush. Again Marcy was snuggled up to my screen, and through the heat register I heard Mom cleaning up the dishes. Then I heard her take some last things to the car as the front door banged behind her.

Later, when the light was gone from the sky, the phone rang, and I knew it was Glen. Though I could only make out a few of Mom's words, she said them in a tone that she didn't use with Aunt Deb or any of her girlfriends. At one point she said, "There's no telling . . ." At another point she said, "I think he'll be okay . . ." And much later she said, "Take care."

Soon her light steps came up the stairs, and I saw her shape, thin as a reed, standing without a sound in my doorway. Beneath my sheets, I didn't move, and since it was too dark to see much of anything, she couldn't have known I was awake. Still, she stood there without moving for three or four minutes. It was like she was trying to hold on to that moment: the way the light of the streetlamp filtered through the leaves, the sound of the frogs, the smell of the grass still warm from the day—and Marcy asleep on the sill.

The dawn came through my window and lit up my suitcase. Mom was already awake—I heard her dressing in her room—so there wasn't much time left. I didn't say "Rise and shine!" to Marcy, and I didn't run out to get the newspaper so we could look at the baseball standings. Instead, I just said, "Marcy, I'll meet you out at the fence in a few minutes."

I got my clothes on and brushed my teeth. I put the clock and the toothbrush in the suitcase, then snapped it closed. I shut and locked my window. I went downstairs and through the kitchen, where Mom was making fried-egg sandwiches that we'd eat in the car.

When I got out in the backyard, Marcy was waiting on the top rail of the fence, huddled into her wings. She wasn't greeting the morning as she usually did. She wasn't standing tall, ruffling her feathers or twitching her tail. We both knew what morning this was.

On a whim, I grabbed the shovel from the shed, took it down to the compost pile, and dug out a worm.

I carried the worm over to the fence, climbed up, and, sitting beside her, fed Marcy out of my hand, just as I used to do. She tilted up her head, opened wide, and took the worm, but swallowed it slowly, like she wanted it to last.

When she was done, she gave me her shy and grateful look, and I said, "I guess we should say goodbye. For now."

She nodded, as if to say the same.

I said, "See you later," and climbed down off the fence, leaving the shovel against the post. The sun was rising, the shadows shrinking, the sparrows quarreling next door. The light went out in the kitchen window, and I heard Mom call gently, "It's time."

Then I walked toward the house, through the dewy grass. There was dew on the awning too. But before I got there, I felt the air beating. Next I felt that sharp, familiar pain in my shoulder—Marcy's claws digging in. I stopped and she made her *hew, hew* sound. She hopped down my arm to my wrist and looked up at me, waiting but not anxious, until I understood what she wanted. I brought my hands together close to my chest and made my palms into a bowl. Then, lifting her tail, she climbed in and settled herself inside.

She was so big now and so beautiful, her eyes bright yellow around their black pupils, her closed wings trimmed with white, her tail feathers so long and sleek. She was like an arrow or a boat, her whole body smooth and pointed straight ahead. She was so big that she didn't fit in my hands anymore. Her tail shot over one side.

For a moment we stayed like that, and I felt her heart beating. I think she felt mine as well. Then I raised my hands and she lifted off, wings flashing, slender legs trailing behind, and I watched her fly up toward the trees.

UP NORTH

FOR MOST OF THE TRIP, I thought about Marcy. I followed our progress on the map that was spread on my lap, every mile taking us farther from her. But as we got near the lake—as the air cooled and smelled like pines, as the road got steep, windy, and turned to dirt, and as I saw through the trees those sky-blue flashes of water—I was thinking of other things too. Like swimming.

Like fishing and hiking. And rowing way out on the water.

My cousins, who'd arrived an hour before, ran to our car the moment we parked, all of them shouting, filled with important news: There's spiders in the outhouse! Salamanders on the path! And this year there's a rope from the tree that hangs over the water! You can swing out real far, let yourself go, and fly into the lake!

They helped carry our suitcases to our cabin. Then we put on our bathing suits and charged down to the water, to the new rope swing. One by one, we took hold of it, sprinted toward the end of the rock ledge, and leaped out into the open air, letting go, arms flapping and legs still running, yelling *AHHHH-A-A-A-A-AHHHH!!!* like Tarzan.

We ate supper on the beach, ran three-legged races, played horseshoes and tag, and roasted marshmallows, all the time slapping at mosquitoes. Beneath the stars, we went swimming in the dark water. Shivering, we followed the beams of our flashlights up the split-log steps to the path to our cabins. Through the window, I called good night to my cousins, then slid into my sleeping bag on the cot. Soon Mom got into her bag and turned off the light. The air was cold, with that piney smell. I

was dead tired. All I heard was the soft *lap, lap* of water, and yet it didn't put me right to sleep.

In my mind, I was making a list of what I did that day and telling it all to Marcy. I imagined us sitting in the shed as always, me on the stool and she in her box or perched on my knee, everything feeling warm and wonderful. She was asking questions and listening intently, especially amused by how I'd leaped off the rock ledge, as if I thought I could fly. Then we talked all about *her* day. How she'd been to the pond and over to the stream. How she'd watched Mate's family leave after we had, their bumper scraping the driveway.

Was she feeling lonely?

Yes. But I'm doing okay.

Had she seen Glen in the evening when he refilled the feeder? Did that make her feel better?

It did.

Had she found enough food?

Yes, plenty.

And would she sleep tonight in her box?

No. I'd rather be on your windowsill—even when you aren't here.

ON THE LAKE

AS WITH ALL OUR VACATIONS, the time raced by. One day my cousins and I caught a few perch off the dock, cleaned them, and left the guts in the woods for raccoons. Another day we hiked to a waterfall, hopping up a stream from rock to rock without even getting our feet wet. On another day it rained, and we collected salamanders that we put in jars. Each night, on my cot, I imagined telling it all to Marcy, everything I did, every detail, and we talked until I fell asleep.

Now it was already Thursday night, and as we were going to bed, I asked Mom if I could take out the rowboat early the next morning. She said, "Fine. Wear the life jacket, be careful, and try to be quiet when you get up."

I set my alarm for five-thirty and put the clock under my pillow. In the dark, I told Marcy how much I was looking forward to going out all by myself on the lake, where everything I did would be up to me and everything I saw I'd see for myself, and she seemed to understand.

With the first hint of light, I was wide-awake. I turned off the alarm, dressed in my sweatshirt and jeans, tiptoed out the door and around the cabin, brushing through ferns, then went down the steps to the lake. Halfway there, I stepped into a cottony mist, so thick that I couldn't see far ahead of me, and I put my hand on the wobbly railing. At the bottom, I got to the beach and the back of the boathouse with its warped, paint-chipped door. Inside, I smelled wet wood, mildewed rope, and the muddy, animal scent of barn-swallow nests on the rafters. Along the wall, shapes slowly appeared, some leaning, some hanging: hourglass minnow traps, anchors, pulleys, bulblike buoys, and squat tackle boxes. Then came that sense of the lake itself, a little part of it inside the boathouse, and the rest spreading for miles. The lake was still and quiet, and I couldn't see it in the mist. But I knew it was out there—so much water, like something wide and waiting.

I put on my life jacket, untied the lines from the stern and bow, and, crouching, stepped into the boat. I used an oar to push off from the dock, gliding out of the boathouse and onto the lake with barely a ripple or a sound.

The air was even cooler out on the water. I slid the

pins into the oarlocks and, facing the stern, started rowing as steadily as I could, the way Mom had taught me the summer before. Bend your shoulders forward, hands out as far as you can, like you're reaching for something way behind the boat. Then, mostly with the strength in your legs and back, pull the blades evenly through the water—that's how you keep going straight. Nice and easy, that's the trick. You row forward by reaching back and back, and pulling the lake behind you.

Out and out I rowed, beyond the float, beyond the swimming area, and deeper into the mist. The cabins already had disappeared. Now the boathouse faded and was gone. It was like I was pulling through a cloud. Where was I going? I didn't know. I just felt the distance pulsing in my arms, my calves, and my head, and heard it in the creaking oarlocks and in the rush of water around the hull. I was moving, and it didn't matter where, as long as it was into an openness.

After fifteen or twenty minutes, I was warm and tired, so I paused, holding the oars straight out, like narrow wings. I let the boat coast. It left no wake. The water, what I saw of it, was like dark glass. It trickled faintly against the hull, and then it too was quiet.

I'm not sure how long I stayed like that, but it must have been a good while. I just drifted and watched as the light kept coming, gray, blue, and pink. Then a warm breeze, like a breath, kicked up, moving and softly shredding the mist, wispy rags of it floating up and away. I saw more and more water and more and more light, with orange now mixed in. Soon I heard faraway voices and an engine starting and the low *chunk . . . chunk* of someone chopping wood. A beat after each sound, I heard its echo, like an answer from even farther away. Next I saw the fuzzy green line of the shore. Then a boathouse. Another. Then a cabin with a speck of light in a window. Then the mist above was shot through with yellow, and as the yellow rose, I saw those big round-peaked mountains, like somebody's worn shoulders.

"How was it?" Mom asked as I glided back into the boathouse, stowing the oars inside the gunwales. It had become a clear, crisp morning. Mountain air. The sun slanted in and lit up the dock, where Mom was waiting in her sweater and jeans, a mug of steaming coffee in her hands.

"I saw the morning come!" I said. "I saw it happen!"

"Good for you!" she said, excited for me, though I noticed her take in a breath. She put down her mug. "You were gone so long. Here, I'll tie up the lines."

COMING HOME

MY COUSINS ALL WAVED TO US as Mom and I drove away from the cabin. Eight hours later, it was a warm, late Saturday afternoon as we pulled into town. The air was still. The gray sky felt heavy. Though we'd been away for only a week, it seemed that things were different. The summer, in full swing when we'd left, had petered out. The lawns looked browner. The trees seemed droopy, exhausted. On the dusty field where I'd played my Little League games, kids huddled in helmets and shoulder pads. In town, a banner announced the Labor Day fair, and in Woolworth's window a big sign said BACK-TO-SCHOOL SALE.

We stopped at the Deaconry to tell Granddad that we'd returned, but as he lay silently in bed, he seemed unaware that we had gone or that we were with him again. Still, I told him all about our trip and how I'd rowed the boat.

Fifteen minutes later we got back in the car, and now Mom drove very slowly and carefully, like someone who was unsure of her directions, though of course we knew those roads by heart. The half circle around the War Memorial on the green. The hill along the iron fence by the Catholic church. Then, on Maple Avenue, the old houses, lining either side. There was the tumbledown garage where Mr. Gould fixed mowers, and there was Dr. Foley's office, where he gave me shots that always made me dizzy. Now the pavement dipped, taking us under the railroad bridge. At the stone wall beside the Moffetts' yard, Mom braked and we turned onto our road.

For the past few minutes we hadn't said a word, but I knew we were wondering the same thing. Was Marcy home or not? We stared through the windshield as everything drifted by slower and slower, and I didn't know whether I wanted it to stop or keep going.

Mom gripped both hands on the wheel, and something about her neck and shoulders seemed tight and straight. We passed the fire hydrant. We passed Dogwood Lane, which led into Derek's development. Then we came to Mate's house. He and his family weren't back from their vacation yet. The windows were all closed, the driveway empty. And their mailbox—they must not have had their letters held at the post office—was crammed, with the little door half open.

We passed the Hulberts', the Andersons', and beyond the bushes on the left I saw the flat water of the pond . . . and, on the other side, the telephone pole with the streetlamp in front of our yard . . . and our mailbox . . . and our apple tree . . . and then the wire that stretched in a long arc from the telephone pole to the hook beside my window. A couple of sparrows were sitting on it.

Next I heard our tires crunching over gravel. The house looked the same. As we slowed, pulling up to the porch, I saw that Mom's geraniums on the step were still blooming. Glen must have thought to water them.

"Cross your fingers," Mom said as she brought the car to a stop and let her hands slide from the wheel. But I'd already crossed my fingers on both hands. I still had them crossed as I burst out of the car and raced around to the backyard.

When I got there, I saw the shovel where I'd left it the week before, still leaning against the fence post. But I didn't see Marcy. She wasn't perched on the top rail, or at the bird feeder, or in the cherry tree, or on the clothesline, or in the bushes, or on the peak of the roof, or on the edge of the awning, or on one of the stakes that held up the tomato plants that sagged with swollen fruit. I didn't find her in her box in the shed. The nest I'd made her was empty. A few quarter-size drops of poop were splattered on last week's baseball standings, but they were old and dry, almost white. They turned to powder when I touched them. She hadn't been here for days.

I went back out into the yard, and though I knew it was probably no use, I started calling her name. It came out like water rushing through the tunnel after a long, hard rain. "Mar-see!! Mar-see!!"

I called and called, then waited and waited, but nothing came back, not even a faint echo. My voice just went out, without any answers, soaked up by the soft, low hills.

Now I saw Mom under the awning. She'd come in from the car, through the house, and stepped out the back door. She'd heard me calling. She had her hands at her chest, like she was hurting there. Her heart was all in her eyes, which were sad and wet, but looking right at me.

Then she said something that I hope I'll never forget, that still feels like she's saying it to me. She said, "I know it hurts, it isn't fair, but you did the right thing—the only real thing. You loved what you'd lose with all your might. And the love, I think, is worth the sorrow. You can't have the one without the other. I don't know how else to live."

Just then it began to rain, a late-August rain that smelled like fall, that was less like rain than a cool drizzle which I couldn't tell from the tears on my face.

"Come on in," Mom said, reaching out her hand. "We're home. Come in under the awning."

THE SHELL

ABOUT HALF AN HOUR LATER, as Mom and I were taking the last bags out of the trunk, I heard Glen's truck rattle into our driveway, and then he was standing beside his open door in his rumpled work clothes, with his hands hanging down, empty. He looked at me and said, "I'm sorry. She was here through Tuesday. I saw her at the feeder and under the awning. I saw her at your windowsill, and I saw her fly into the shed. But on Wednesday, she had gone. I don't know where. I stayed until dark, but I didn't see her. I stayed until dark each night after that, but I never saw her again."

For a moment or two, I didn't hear anything. Then I heard Mate speed into our driveway on his bike. He skidded up behind the car. He was out of breath. He'd been squinting through the drizzle, but now his eyes were big, his face a wide-open question.

All I could do was shake my head. No, she wasn't here.

He stood there, stunned, with his bike between his

legs and his mouth a small O. His shoulders fell. He looked at Glen. He looked back at me in a pained way that made his freckles run together. Then he looked down at his sneakers. "I can't believe it," he said in a voice I could barely hear.

After Mom and Glen had gone into the house, we walked over to the pond. We searched the blackberry bushes and looked in the tunnel, but Marcy was nowhere to be found. I'd given Mate a model canoe—one I'd bought at the general store near the lake—and now he was holding it in his hands. It was made of tiny wood strips formed into a frame and covered with birch bark that was sewn together. He carried it like a precious thing. "Thanks," he kept saying.

We sat on the dam, where the water was barely trickling down the chute. The rain made tiny dimples on the pond, which otherwise looked green and gluey. We loaded the canoe with a couple of pebbles, then pushed it back and forth on the water. As we did this, I told Mate all about swinging on the rope and flying out into the lake, and he told me all about swimming with his dad in the ocean, way out where the waves lift you up and sometimes you can't touch the bottom.

We didn't say anything about Marcy. I don't know

what we could have said. Then Mate sat up straighter. "I brought you this," he said, and reached into his pocket. He had something in there about the size of his fist, and when he pulled it out, it was a shell.

He held it out to me. It was the sort of shell that's spiral-shaped, hollow, with a big long opening that leads inside, where something once must have lived. It was tan and pink, and looked as if it had been polished. He'd bought it at a shop on the boardwalk, he said, with some of his allowance.

I thanked him and told him it was really neat.

He looked at me like he had a secret. "If you hold it to your ear, you can hear the ocean inside. Go ahead. Listen."

So I held the shell close to my ear, and of course I knew it wasn't really the ocean in there. It must have been the sound of blood pulsing in my ear or some weird whooshing in my brain that echoed around in the shell. Still, when I listened to it for a while, especially when I closed my eyes and covered my other ear and concentrated and didn't think about anything else, it *did* seem that I could hear what wasn't there: the waves pounding, rushing up and whispering backward, then a split second of silence, and all of it starting over again.

APRIL 1961

ON THE ROOF

SOMETIMES YOU THINK you've come to the end of something, but it turns out not to be the end, or it turns out that there really isn't an end to the thing at all.

Since that summer with Marcy, there had been a lot of changes. Those tract houses they were building down the road were finished, and soon families were living in them. In October, the Yankees lost the World Series to the Pirates. Mate got a baby brother whose name—of course—was Fitzgerald. As his mother had predicted, Senator Kennedy became President Kennedy soon after the new year, and a lot of people seemed excited about that.

Then, on the Sunday after my birthday in February, a phone call came from the Deaconry. Mom and I sped right over, and there Granddad lay in his bed with his white hair combed, his glass eye open, his other eye shut tight, and his chest barely moving up and down. He was almost gone, the nurse whispered to Mom as we went in, but he seemed to be holding on, waiting. I think he wanted to say goodbye, for he kept on breathing until after Mom had told him we loved him, and after I had squeezed his hand, and after he, as if to give me something, had squeezed mine long and hard.

And there were other changes as well. On a bus, I now went to the new school with the rest of my grade, where Mom wasn't the librarian. Mate, who was a grade behind me, wasn't there either. On weekday afternoons, I got home later than he did, so we didn't have as much time to fool around before I had to do my homework and set the table for supper. Then, at about six o'clock, Glen would come over. He and Mom had been seeing a lot of each other. He had taken the awning down in the fall, and little by little he was dropping by more and more, until he became a sort of addition to our household. He'd knock lightly on the front door. Usually he brought ice cream or a fruit pie in a box that he'd picked up at the A&P. Soon Mom would serve our supper, and as we ate, Glen and I swapped riddles or talked about baseball—the Yankees, we said, would be even better this year. Then he and

Mom talked about their day at work. And later, before Glen headed home in his truck, they'd clean up the kitchen together.

That's what they were doing one particular evening in April as I got into my pajamas, set my alarm, and slid into bed. Through the heat register, I heard them talking in their easy voices as the dishes clinked and the refrigerator door banged, rattling the things on my bureau: my clock, the shell from Mate, and a framed photo of Granddad sitting in the sun in our backyard. Soon I turned off my light, and Mom came up to say good night. As always, she wanted to know how I was "doing." So I told her that at recess we were all dancing the twist, and in math I had gotten a B on my multiplication test. So I guess I was doing okay.

Though it was still cool outside, it was getting warmer. In a few weeks, Mom would be planting her lettuce and peas, and I'd be mowing the grass again. After she went back downstairs, I sat up and cracked open my window to let in some fresh air. Outside, the moon was full and high, glowing silvery white, so bright that I couldn't see any stars. It seemed to have painted the tops of everything. There was our mailbox, standing like a stork. There was the rounded hood of our car.

The branches and budding twigs of the apple tree made crisscross shadows on the yard. The road was quiet. The pond too. No groaning bullfrogs. No crickets yet in the grass.

Then I heard it. Like music, it poured through the crack beneath the window sash: *Chuley, chuley, chuley, shee . . . shee, shee, shee-da-lee-shee . . . chu-a-lee, chu-a-lee, chu-a-lee, shee . . . shee, shee-da-lee-shee . . .* Three times this came, then a whole different string of sounds, like someone hitting a snare drum: *CHICK! CHACK! CHECK! CHUCK! . . . CHUCK! CHACK! CHOOK!* Then a sweet, light, twittering song: *Swit-wit-wit, swit-wit-wit, ziti-ziti-ziti . . .* Then it seemed that someone was winding a clock: *Rrrrrrachhhhhh, rrrrrrachhhhhh, rrrrrrachhh-hhhh* . . . Then: *Chick-a-dee-dee-dee* . . . *chick-a-dee-dee-dee* . . . Then a wild and happy sound, like a kid on a swing: *See-mee? See-mee? WHEEEE-WHEEEEOOOOO-WHEEEE-WHEEEE!!!* And then I heard a gentle, liquid song, *Murm-ring, murm-ring, murm-ring*, like water sliding over smooth rocks.

My eyes followed the sounds to the apple tree, where a bird, just one, stood on the top branch, though it sounded like a dozen were up there. Against the shining sky, I saw it in silhouette, high on its legs, its tail straight out and its head stretched up, singing its heart out to the moon.

I pressed my face to the window so the bird might recognize me. I didn't know if it was Marcy or not. It didn't come closer, didn't come to the sill. It stayed where it was, singing. So I put on my robe, opened the window, unhitched the screen, and crawled headfirst out onto the porch roof. The shingles were warm from the day's sun. They made pebbly dents on my palms. The air was crisp and cool, the sky a bowl of light. It was the most beautiful night I'd ever seen.

I sat back against the house, with the rows of clapboard against my spine. Still the bird hadn't moved. For a second, I thought I'd cry out "Marcy!"—a word I hadn't said in months, except in all my dreams. But then I thought that if I spoke aloud, or if I waved or reached toward her—if I tried to make things the way they'd been—I'd break that moment like a spell. Even if it was Marcy, she'd fly away, and everything would be quiet again.

So I didn't say a word. I didn't move. I just sat there listening as the bird sang and sang, then sang even louder, until, it seemed, she was singing to me.

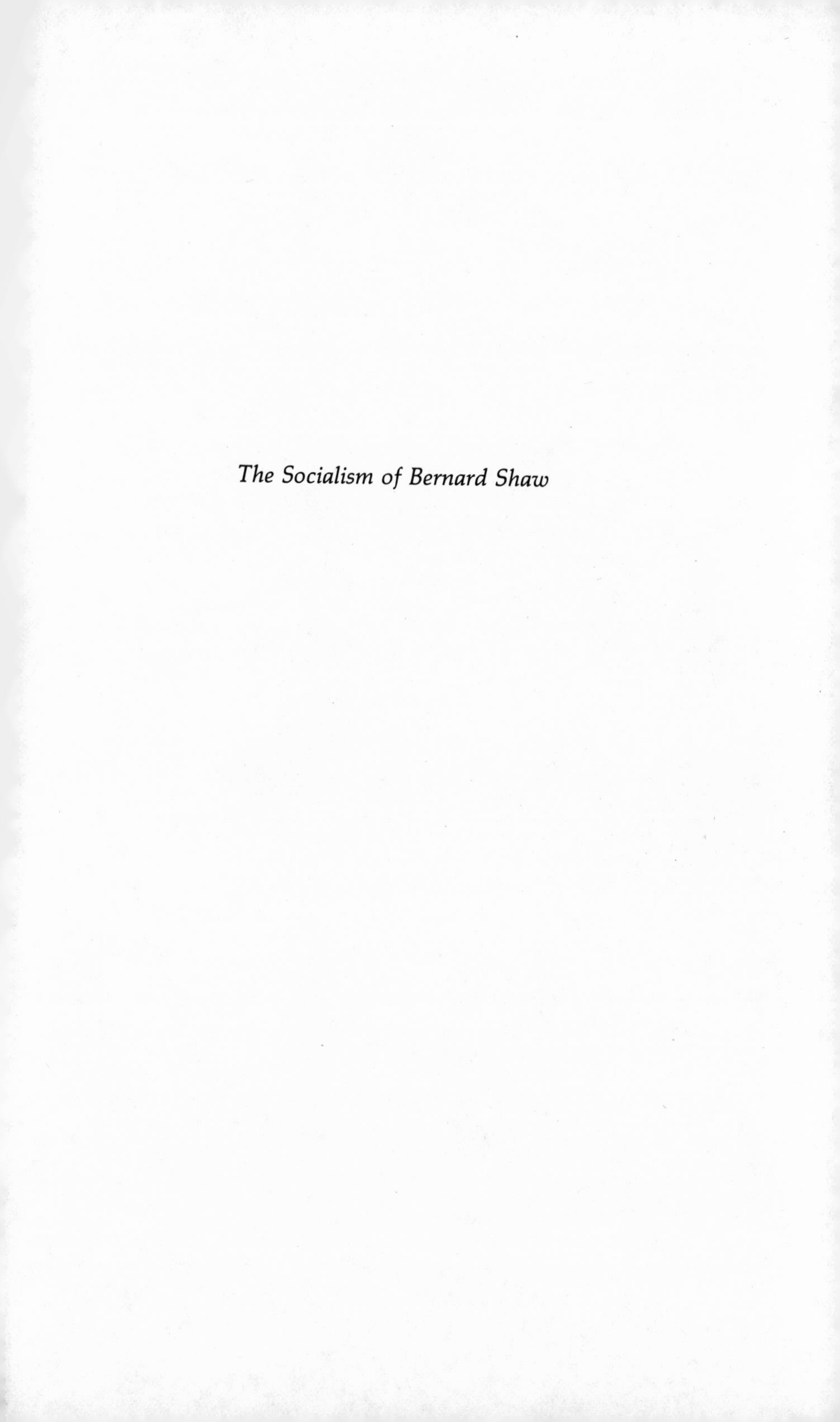

The Socialism of Bernard Shaw

THE SOCIALISM OF BERNARD SHAW

by
Harry Morrison

McFarland & Company, Inc., Publishers
Jefferson, North Carolina, and London

PR
5368
.S6
M67
1989
c.1

A Dedicatory Acknowledgment

For the World Socialist Movement, which I joined back in January of 1938, in Los Angeles; with special thanks to *The Socialist Standard* (SPGB), London, from which I learned and was inspired to learn, over a period covering more than a half century, the substance of Scientific Socialism; and to the memory of *The Western Socialist*, of Winnipeg and Boston, with which I was personally associated for many years.

Also, for my wife and comrade, Sally, who cooperated in her own way for some 47 years of commitment to the Movement, thereby helping to make this work possible. —Harry Morrison ("Harmo")

Extracts from *The Intelligent Woman's Guide to Socialism and Capitalism, Man and Superman, Androcles and the Lion, Back to Methuselah, Everybody's Political What's What, The Millionairess*, and two Shaw letters, 1943 and 1944, to *The Western Socialist*, are reprinted courtesy of the Society of Authors on behalf of the Bernard Shaw Estate. *Fabian Tract* numbers 2 and 3 reprinted courtesy of the Fabian Society. Material from *The Socialist Standard* reprinted courtesy of the Socialist Party of Great Britain; excerpts from *The Western Socialist* reprinted courtesy of World Socialist Party of the United States.

British Library Cataloguing-in-Publication Data are available

Library of Congress Cataloguing-in-Publication Data

Morrison, Harry, 1912–
The socialism of Bernard Shaw / by Harry Morrison.
p. cm.
[Includes index.]
Includes bibliographical references.
ISBN 0-89950-441-8 (lib. bdg.; 50# alk. paper) ♾
1. Shaw, Bernard, 1856–1950—Political and social views.
2. Socialism and literature—Great Britain. I. Title.
PR5368.S6M67 1989
822'.912—dc20 89-42738
CIP

©1989 Harry Morrison. All rights reserved.

Printed in the United States of America.

McFarland & Company, Inc., Publishers
Box 611, Jefferson, North Carolina 28640

Contents

Preface

Among the biographers of great persons there is a most persistent and popular belief that the subject's genetic, religious, and social background should be taken into consideration when estimating the importance – if not the validity itself – of the great one's utterances. Biographers of Bernard Shaw, for example, have made much of his toper father and pianist mother; the *ménage à trois*, as Shaw himself has referred to it, that included his parents and a friendly music teacher who had moved in with them during his youthful years in Dublin and again, later, in his mother's house in London where she had gone on her own; the reprobate uncle who delighted in recounting bawdy jokes to him when he was but a youngster; the Irish Protestant Church in which he was baptized and which he rejected at an early age; his formal schooling which he abandoned at age 15 . . . Shaw himself has made much of it in accounting for his talents.

So, if Bernard Shaw had helped to develop and to articulate a theory of municipal ownership known to the world as Fabian Socialism, a body of thought which has been an important force in British politics for most of the 20th century, especially during periods of Labour governments, it was largely due to all of those influences! Somehow, in order to understand the case for Fabian Socialism, one must at least recognize the more immediate generations of the personal family and the friends and acquaintances of Bernard Shaw; and, of course, the same reasoning should apply in assessing the scientific socialism of Karl Marx.

Silly as this may sound it isn't far from the way Shaw himself sometimes explained the *raison d'être* of the system of Marx and Engels which Shaw claimed to have accepted at a relatively early age. Marx's rabbinical forebears, as he seemed to indicate, were somehow responsible for the angry, Old Testament–style approach to the Marxian strictures and to the system of thought itself. No similar conjecture, of course, could be hung on Frederick Engels who, as far as heredity was concerned, could have passed as an example of the stereotypical Nordic German later made infamous by Hitler; and this should somehow have confused the issue for anyone as knowledgeable as Shaw was reputed to have been on Marx and his writings, for the experts on that subject, generally, have some difficulty in distinguishing which of the collaborator-friends wrote much of what is credited to each separately.

Nevertheless, this approach makes interesting reading if one does not become hypercritical and for that reason might seem to be appropriate here. But it has been done too frequently, and at length, in the cases of both Marx and Shaw and the validity of such an approach is at least questionable and unquestionably removed from the area of expertise of this writer.

In any event, the burden of this book will be to present in broad perspective, the basics of (1) Fabian Socialism as promulgated in the essays, books, plays and prefaces to the plays of Shaw; (2) a detailed treatment of him and others on some tangentially related areas as religion and Darwinian evolution; and (3) a running documentation indicating the basis and extent of the Shavian opposition to, rather than acceptance of, Scientific Socialism, despite his occasional bows of respect to Marx.

What will be presented is a well-documented description, largely from Shaw's own writings, of his brand of socialism. If it becomes necessary to show that his, and the widely understood socialism of Marx and Engels, is actually not that much different one from the other, that is a finding that Shaw himself came to conclude on the occasion of his visit to the Soviet Union in 1931. If there seems somehow to be a contradiction here it is only because there is, in truth, a vast difference between the theoretical system of Marx and Engels as detailed in their major theoretical works and what is declared to be Marxism in practice throughout the Communist and Socialist world.

Before plunging into our task, however, we will anticipate and respond to an objection that is certain to come from *some*

Marx aficionados: why bother presenting and analyzing *Fabian* Socialism? It is like kicking a dead horse since the designation, itself, is hardly known of in Britain today let alone anyplace else in the world. A good question.

The sole justification would seem to be that Shaw, through his extreme volubility to the point of literary diarrhea, has made it necessary. Sections of shelves and file-index drawers in public and college libraries throughout the world bulge with his books and with books about him; and his plays—even the more socialist oriented ones—still enjoy popularity in many lands. He has forced himself on the public as an authority on socialism in general and even if scant attention is paid to Fabianism as a brand name today, Shaw himself is considered widely to have been an archetype socialist. Almost any biography of the man tags him as having been an unrelenting socialist, converted through reading *Capital,* Vol. 1, and notwithstanding his later criticism of Marx he has been and continues to be recognized by editors of the mass media newspapers and periodicals as having been a top authority on Marx. Despite protest by more knowledgeable Marxists, Shaw, by his spate of writings and criticisms, has left a legacy of purported Marxism and criticisms of Marxism which should be dealt with by those who would do battle with the mass confusion on that subject.

Shaw is rightly famed as a playwright by anyone's standards; some of his writings have become required reading in schools in many countries, even if such reading be skimpy and hasty. True, the name and fame of Shaw is most widely connected with the musical *My Fair Lady,* a posthumous rewrite of his *Pygmalion* which he himself described as a "potboiler"—something to earn him the money to be able to concentrate upon his politically inspired plays and propaganda prefaces and treatises. He seemed to be, for many years, extremely dedicated to writing prefaces in order to help spread his political theories. As he put it himself in his penultimate paragraph of *The Intelligent Woman's Guide to Socialism and Capitalism:*

> One of the oddities of English Literary tradition is that plays should be printed with prefaces which have nothing to do with them, and are really essays, or manifestoes, or pamphlets, with

> the plays as a bait to catch readers. I have exploited this tradition very freely . . . (N.Y.: Brentano's, 1928.)

Plays such as *Man and Superman* and *Major Barbara* make clear his viewpoint as to what socialism and capitalism are all about and one does, occasionally, get such a response to a query as: "Socialism? Sure, I know about socialism. I saw *Man and Superman* and even read the Preface and *The Revolutionist's Handbook.*" And that is how many learn about socialism!

Actually, however Shaw's version of socialism may differ from that of most commentators and interpreters of Marx – even in the Shavian direct treatises and books on the subject – there is one thing they do have in common: socialism, according to all of them, equals nationalization, at least providing that the government terms itself socialist. Even that is not necessarily essential because the very tendency itself of converting private or corporate industry into government-owned industry is, supposedly, socialistic, if not downright socialism itself. Even the bailing out, with Federal money, of one-time near-bankrupt industries such as Lockheed and Chrysler, is termed socialistic. There is little to be found in public libraries, schools, or any place where such matters are read and discussed – other than the actual writings of Marx and Engels themselves – that dissociates Marxism from such an equation. And whatever attention is given Marxist works seems to be skimpy at best.

In the case of Shaw's views in regard to socialism there is no confusion on that particular aspect. He has spelled it out in a torrent of words in his prefaces and in his political, sociological, and religious essays and books. In the case of Marx, however, there really was no such equation and that should have been made clear enough from his writings but seems to have eluded most of those who profess to espouse his system. All but everybody – friend and foe, including Shaw at different stages, even at one and the same period – have interpreted Marx as advocating nationalization, even of capital; and this despite the reams of paper that Marx used up in his attack on the very existence of capital and of nations , and the patent fact that Marx called upon the workers of the world to unite in order to abolish the entire system of wage labor and capital relationships.

And it is not easy to fight this all but universal concept of socialism, especially when one considers that wherever one travels in the so-called Communist world one looks at the images of Marx and Engels flanked by various national Communist heroes and dignitaries of past and present. Ruling classes (or Communist bureaucracies), representing more than half of the world's population, have taken the founders of scientific socialism to their bosoms; acknowledged them as their inspiration. And they are somehow even able to justify their wars, their armed forces, and their frightful armaments on the basis of the writings of the founders of Scientific Socialism.

Now it is unlikely that anybody who has been exposed to the plays and – particularly – the prefaces of Bernard Shaw has missed grasping the fact that Shaw was, first and foremost, a propagandizer of socialism. In fact, one need not even crack the covers to make that discovery. On the back of some Penguin Book editions, for example, a thumbnail sketch of the man's credits informs us that:

> Meanwhile he had plunged into the Socialist revival of the eighteen-eighties and come out as one of the leaders who made the Fabian Society famous, figuring prominently not only as a pamphleteer and platform orator, but as a serious economist and philosopher . . .

Not being turned off by this admission by his publishers, one can go on to read Shaw's own assertions on the subject, as for instance, in the opening paragraph of his Epistle Dedicatory to his one-time journalist-colleague, Arthur Bingham Walkley, in *Man and Superman:*

> It is hardly fifteen years, since, as twin pioneers of the new Journalism of that time, we two, cradled in the same new sheets, began an epoch in the criticism of the theatre and the opera house by making it the pretext for a propaganda of our own views of life. So you cannot plead ignorance of the character of the force you set in action. You meant me to *épater le bourgeois:* and if he protests, I hereby refer him to you as the accountable party.

Readers of *Man and Superman,* inclusive of its introduction and its appendix, will not fail to get the significance of the Shavian message, that capitalism is the root cause of evils from mass poverty to mass hypocrisy and should be replaced by socialism. In fact, so much did authorities in New York City get the message that although the play was a smashing success on the stage of the Hudson Theatre the book was banned from the New York libraries on the ground that it would pervert the young.

As a further bit of documentation, take his *Major Barbara*, written in 1906 and revised in 1949. Herein, in his Preface, Shaw made it clear that:

> I am, and have always been, and shall now always be, a revolutionary writer, because our laws made law impossible; our liberties destroy all freedom, our property is organized robbery; our morality is impudent hypocrisy . . . I am an enemy of the existing order for good reasons. . . (*Six Plays by Bernard Shaw*. N.Y.: Dodd, Mead, 1945; p. 336.)

Now in the matter of the reaction by the library authorities of New York City, in 1915, to *Man and Superman*, it is understandable why there was some trepidation. The influence of the Socialist Party of America in the early years of the 20th century, especially in New York, was great enough to be at least worrisome despite the certainty that that party—notwithstanding the many examples of sound Socialist analysis in the texts and lectures of a number of its personalities—would approach its efforts at practical politics on a pragmatic, reform-of-capitalism basis. Eugene Debs, the party's best known spokesman and candidate for high political office at the time, had, in 1912, received some one million votes for president and Socialist Party politicians had cracked the New York state legislature. Attitudes such as those expressed by Shaw in *Man and Superman* against cherished institutions such as marriage, property and religion had to have been regarded as more scandalous in 1915, even in a city with a population as sophisticated as that of New York, than would be the case today. And despite our debunking of Shaw's socialism it must be admitted that such attitudes, if not the bulk of *The Revolutionist's Handbook*, were and are held by any socialist worth his or her salt.

Looking at the matter today, however, with hindsight's 20-20 vision, even the more scientific variety of Socialist would have to admit that man's ideological institutions do not necessarily have to be in harmony with the form of economic relationships. We have examples of state capitalist regimes – of the "Communist" variety – either throwing roadblocks against all religions or outlawing the entire kit and caboodle of them (as with North Korea and Albania); and at least interfering to greater degree than is done in avowedly capitalist lands with the rights to property ownership. As for marriage, skyrocketing divorce rates in both types of capitalism, and the proliferation and official/unofficial acceptance of unregistered and unsanctified conjugal unions, serve to minimize the importance of marriage and the nuclear family to the health and well-being of capitalism, itself. The bottom line seems to be, is there any widespread recognition of the slave-context of this social system, that a wage (or salary) envelope is but a "badge of slavery"? Obviously, there is no indication that any more than a relative handful of the population – even in the professedly Communist and Socialist world – holds such an attitude. Nor, for that matter, did Shaw, as we shall see.

Yet, despite all that is said above and subsequently, and reservations by some Socialists on his understanding, there is little doubt that Shaw avowed his socialism openly in most of his better known works throughout his long life. He never seemed to question, let alone abandon it, as did other one-time enthusiasts from the world of literature such as John Dos Passos and Edmund Wilson. What made Shaw unique, however, was his ability to ride two horses at the same time, each traveling in an opposite direction to the other. In fact, just as is said by a certain type of Christian that Satan can quote Scripture to serve his own ends, so could he – or any material body – quote Shaw on either side of almost any argument.

As an example of his double-exposure proclivity, Shaw wrote in his ninety-third year: "I never threw Marx over. In essentials I am as much a Marxist as ever..." (*Sixteen Self Sketches.* London, Constable, 1949; pp. 81–2); then went on to reiterate his diametrical differences with Marxian economic theory. He had rejected Marx's Labor Theory of Value (certainly an "essential" of Marxism) from his early Fabian years and, as he put it in that autobiographical digest:

> I found that neither Marx nor anyone else in the Socialist movement understood (capitalist political economy) and that as to abstract value theory Marx was wrong and Wickstead (a Jevonsian economist) right. Of the Law of Rent, which is fundamental in Socialism, Marx was simply ignorant, as his footnote on Ricardo shows.* His lack of administrative experience and of personal contacts with English society, both proletarian and capitalistic, disabled him dangerously as a practical politician in spite of his world-shaking exposure of the villainies of Capitalism, and his grasp of its destiny in the Communist Manifesto. (Ibid, pp. 49, 50.)

So he did reject an "essential" of Marxism—the Labor Theory of Value—preferring to go with Jevons' Theory of Marginal Utility which concerns itself with the area of circulation, mainly, rather than the more dangerous (to capitalist interests) area of production. Shaw seemed, in fact, to take turns at approving and denouncing Marx and Marxism in his outpourings of political writing. In the same book cited above, he tells us that "Marx's *Capital* is not a treatise on Socialism; it is a jeremiad against the bourgeoisie, supported by a mass of official evidence and a relentless Jewish genius for denunciation." And he argues that although *Capital* was "addressed to the working classes," that had to have been a mistake because "the working man respects the bougeoisie and wants to be a bourgeois." He reminds us that it was the "revolting sons of the bourgeoisie itself, Lassalle, Marx, Liebknecht, Morris, Hyndman, [add Lenin, Trotsky and Stalin] who painted the flag red . . ." (ibid, pp. 81–2.)

Shaw's most prominent contribution as a Socialist activist was his role—along with Sidney Webb—in building and disseminating the theories of the Fabian Socialist Society—theories that the former was largely instrumental in concocting. And there was little, if anything, about Fabian Socialism that could be mistaken by any serious student of the subject for the socialism of Marx and Engels. Shaw's old, 19th-century contem-

**Marx did not deal with rent in his Vol. I, assigning it in his intended sequence to Vol. III which was edited and published 11 years after his death in 1883 by Engels, a year before his own death in 1895. Shaw, a reputed authority on Marx, should have known that all of the drafts for his Vols. II and III were finished before the latter's own death.*

porary and friend, William Morris, who came much closer than did Shaw to being an exponent of Marxian Socialism, dismissed Fabianism as "gas and water socialism." But for Shaw, there was more than the attraction of municipal and government schemes – a more practical and immediate type of "socialism" (as it was designated then, and still is, almost universally). There was also the fact, as he made clear, that the advocates of Fabianism were of a different class than the mechanics and laborers who attended the meetings of organizations such as that of Henry Hyndman, a well-known economist and disciple of Marxism. The Fabians were a genteel, highly educated group that suited Shaw's tastes.

But as time went on, and new, revolutionary changes in Europe shook the first half of the 20th century, Shaw excelled more and more in squaring the circle. He embraced Stalin's Russia with its alleged Marxist background and philosophy (actually dubbing it the world's first Fabian Socialist state) in spite of the absence of that which he considered a *sine qua non* of socialism as he understood it (total equality in wage-income) in that allegedly socialist nation. Shaw even embraced Mussolini in Italy and Hitler in Germany and declared their respective dictatorships to be examples of socialism in action, thereby alienating himself from many of the old line Social Democrats who had previously regarded him as one of their stalwarts.

Not that an embrace of Fascism and Nazism by erstwhile Socialists of the Social Democratic or Labor variety was all that contradictory to their theories. Mussolini, of course, had been a well-known leader in the Italian Social Democratic movement prior to World War I. After organizing the Italian Fascist party he and this new, purportedly proletarian-based, organization were at least as active, if not more so, as any radical party of the left in Italy in fomenting and leading strikes by workers against Italian industry in the years immediately following the end of the war. Then, to boot, the new, Fascist nation dubbed itself a corporate state – supposedly a partnership between labor and the industrialists. It fooled a considerable number of militant, left-wing radicals in its early days.

Then there was that documentation by the Italian Social Democratic writer Ignazio Silone in his book *The School for Dic-*

tators, of the aid given the Nazis by the German Communists in the overthrow of the Weimar Republic (dominated by German Social Democrats). Communist party theory held, at that time, that Nazism was a historically progressive, last phase, of capitalism that would lead directly to the Socialist-Communist revolution.

Although the German Communist party was persecuted and crushed by Hitler—along with the Social Democratic party—immediately following his rise to political power, this did nothing to prevent the subsequent honeymoon period between August 1939 and June 1940, when Nazi Germany and Bolshevik Russia cooperated in a friendship pact. This confounded a minority of Communist party members and their sympathizers but won acceptance by a majority when the "line" was changed again—this time from "Popular Front Against Hitler" to "The Yanks Are Not Coming" (or whatever catchphrase the particular national situation might have called for). What should be noted here is the fact that although there certainly was a running hostility between Social Democrats and Communist party devotees, as far as Shaw himself was concerned he could embrace them both—along with the Fascists and Nazis.

Concerning his embrace of Nazi Germany: aside from the anti-Jewish program of the Hitlerites, which Shaw repudiated as an aberration (a "bee in Hitler's bonnet" was what he termed it) and urged him to abandon—largely, one would surmise, because of his sympathy for his friend Albert Einstein who had been forced into exile by Hitler (at least one could easily infer as much from his frequent references to that event)—there was not all that much difference between the stated goals of the Nazis, and those of the Fabian Society and of Shaw, in his political writings:

> He [Hitler] carried out a persecution of the Jews which went to the scandalous length of outlawing, plundering, and exiling Albert Einstein, a much greater man than any politician, but great in such a manner that he was quite above the heads of the masses and therefore so utterly powerless economically and militarily that he depended for his very existence on the culture and conscience of the rulers of the earth. Hitler's throwing Ein-

> stein to the Antisemite wolves was an appalling breach of cultural faith. It raised the question which is the root question of this preface: to wit, what safeguard have the weaponless great against the great who have myrmidons at their call? . . . (*Selected Plays of Bernard Shaw*—Preface to *The Millionairess,* Dodd, Mead, 1957; pp. 737–8.)

Plainly, to Shaw, the exiling of Einstein was even more to be deplored than the Nazis' pre-war treatment of the German Jewish population, as a whole (*The Millionairess* was written in 1936).

The declared program of the Nazis was "socialism"—but *National* socialism; and they even employed similar slogans to those of the German Social Democratic party that had influenced German politics for some 15 years prior to the Nazi rise to political power. But so was the program of the Fabians national in nature—one need only read Shaw's *Intelligent Woman's Guide to Socialism and Capitalism* to comprehend that here was no clarion call to the workers of the world to unite for Socialist revolution in the manner of Marx and Engels. The thrust seemed, rather, for the citizens of Great Britain (with particular emphasis on what he considered to be the middle class) to awaken and to convert the parliamentary democracy, which he decried as a useless, do-nothing institution, into something more practical and purposeful after the manner—as he saw it—of Mussolini in Italy under Fascism. As of 1928, when his *Intelligent Woman's Guide . . .* was written, he had not arrived at an approval of what was going on in the Soviet Union; was, in fact, quite critical of the Bolshevik regime's accomplishments and had turned down an offer by William Randolph Hearst to visit that "Land of Socialism" and do a series of articles on it. And, of course, the Nazi rise to power in Germany did not materialize until some five years later.

In fairness, however, it must be acknowledged that Shaw was far more knowledgeable in his criticisms of capitalism, as it existed, than were any of the propagandists of Hitler's National Socialism. Shaw's trenchant wit and withering sarcasm most effectively annihilated much of the propaganda of capitalism. He was tolerated by the political powers of wartime Britain in both world wars because, despite his criticisms of much of the government's propaganda and his well-known pro–Nazi and pro-Fascist stance), he performed valuable service for British capitalism when the chips were down. In fact, so startlingly opposite in sentiment was much of his writing and public utterances that one might indeed wonder if he was not a perfect example of a split personality. At least some of his plays and other writings will be cited in this work as evidence for that conjecture. In this effort, then, there will be the attempt to portray—from his overall writings—the contradictions that make it all but impossible to label him permanently, one way or another.

But in any case, despite his often seemingly odd departure from traditional Socialist thought, Shaw did belong with the mainstream of that movement, if one considers the Second (Socialist) and Third (Communist) internationals in their prime years (the first half of the 20th century) as constituting the mainstream of the movement for socialism. And this notwithstanding some major differences in approach between Fabian Socialists and Marxist scholars such as Karl Kautsky, Karl Liebknecht, and Rosa Luxemburg, in Germany; and even the Bolshevik chief, Nicolai Lenin, in Russia; but especially the Menshevik theoreticians Martov and Plekhanov in that country. Whereas the above mentioned revolutionists generally embraced the Marxian method in their writings, if not in their practical politics (which were opportunistic with effort spent mainly at the attempt to gain political power with aim at reforming capitalism "in the meantime"), Shaw and his fellow Fabians, in their main theoretical works, did not even identify themselves with Marxism but advocated a general revamping of British capitalism. In the final analysis, though, the differences between Fabian Socialism and what was and still is regarded widely as Marxism were not all that great when not only Shaw, but Sidney and Beatrice Webb, as well, could visit Soviet Russia as they did during some of that country's darkest years of hunger and political repression and yet extol it as the greatest democracy on earth and a veritable "worker's paradise" (!); and giants of social democracy throughout the world could find it not unreasonable to criticize the "Socialist Fatherland" only on the basis of its totalitarian regime and not at all for its basic relationships of wage labor and capital (a juxtaposition between classes within the population that is fundamental to capitalism). Neither Shaw nor the brains of social democracy seemed able to detect a contradiction there. Nor can most avowed Socialists and Communists spot that anomaly today.

The differences between Shaw and the Marxist scholars of the recognized Socialist movement were, at most, superficial. In fact, the literary critic and one-time Marx enthusiast Edmund Wilson almost made of Shaw, *vis-à-vis* Marx, that which Shaw attempted to make of himself as a playwright *vis-à-vis* Shakespeare: an "echo." In his *To the Finland Station,* Wilson had the following to say:

> These writings of Marx are electrical. Nowhere perhaps in the history of thought is the reader made to feel the excitement of a new intellectural discovery. Marx is here at his most vigorous—in the closeness and exactitude of political observations; in the energy of the faculty that combines, articulating at the same time it compresses; in the wit and the metaphorical phantasmagoria that transfigures the prosaic phenomena of politics, and in the pulse of the tragic invective—we have heard its echo in Bernard Shaw—(N.Y.: Farrar, Straus and Giroux, 1973 ed.; p. 237.)

Now Wilson, although a bit subdued in *To the Finland Station* from his zealous embrace of Marxism and Soviet Russia in his earler years, was by no means unfriendly to Shaw as a Socialist. But was Shaw really an "echo" of Marx even if only "in the pulse of the tragic invective" when inveighing against the obvious evils and hypocrisies of capitalism and of those who defend such hypocrisies? Certainly not if what is meant is an agreement with and employment of the Marxian method. The proof of the pudding is in the eating. A masticating and digesting of G.B. Shaw's profuse political writings, when compared to those of Marx and Engels, will show conclusively that Shaw—although *seeming* at times to grasp that Marxian analysis and even, on occasion, to make use of it—was certainly no echo. And that is unfortunate because not only were his general approach to the problems and his understanding of the solution radically different from Marx's; his audience—those willing to listen to and to directly read those of his plays that actually introduce and deal with *his* socialism—has been, possibly, greater than that of Marx.

He played to a wider aggregation than did Marx (at least so far as Marx's main works on economics are concerned); and because such plays as *Man and Superman* and *Major Barbara* will undoubtedly continue to live on pretty much throughout the world, Shaw's socialism will, almost certainly, continue to be confused with the socialism of Marx and Engels by a great many of Shaw's audience. It is unfortunately true that there are too many casual readers and listeners when it comes to political and economic writings and speeches. General knowledge of Marxism has been acquired, for the most part, not directly from Marx and Engels but from interpreters who have frequently been defenders of "practical" politics — advocacy of reform measures rather than of an outright abolition of the relationships of capitalism — "Abolition of the Wages System" — as Marx did in his pamphlet entitled *Value, Price and Profit.* When actual works of Marx are read — even carefully — they are most likely to be works such as *The Communist Manifesto,* which deals heavily with tactics that were applicable to the mid-19th century and which, notwithstanding its excellence as a historical statement, does not present a critique of the economics of capitalism, and is not intended as such.

Taking all of that into consideration and adding to it the fact that Bernard Shaw is so widely recognized as having been an authority on Marx and Marxism, clearing the confusion between the two systems (Fabian Socialism and Scientific Socialism) will not be easy, if at all possible, although it certainly does deserve a try. What will be attempted here will be a more or less chronological investigation of Shaw's socialist system and writings (novel, plays, prefaces, essays and treatises) dating from his early conversion to Marxism (as he, himself, maintained) and his immediately subsequent writing of *An Unsocial Socialist* (1883); to his joining — along with Sidney Webb — the then-tiny Fabian Society in 1884, or thereabouts; to certain of his plays and prefaces dating all the way through the final decade of the 19th century and on into the 20th century until the years immediately following the end of World War II. (Shaw died in 1950 at the age of 94.) One can only hope that a more-or-less thorough investigation of his socialism will at least help to clarify the present misreading that surrounds it.

1. Shaw Discovers Marx

Bernard Shaw left Ireland at the age of 20, in 1876, and settled down in London in his mother's house where he decided to become a writer of novels. During the next five years he ground out the manuscripts for five books for which he earned nothing but rejection slips. It was sometime during that period that he began to attend lectures and debates at the Democratic Federation (later, the Social Democratic Federation) of Henry M. Hyndman, a well-known economist of the Marxian persuasion. Karl Marx was still alive and living in London during those years; he died in 1883 and his *Das Kapital,* Vol. I, published in Hamburg, Germany, in 1867, had made an impression among English-speaking radicals even though it had not been published in English until 1887. Of course, many of his pamphlets and other writings, as was the case also with the works of Frederick Engels, Marx's close friend, collaborator, and benefactor, were available in English prior to the translation of *Capital.* Engels, who had inherited his father's woolen mill in Manchester, lived in that city until his later years when he also settled in London.

As Shaw tells it in his *Sixteen Self Sketches* and elsewhere, he was admonished by certain of the S.D.F. members: "If you haven't read Marx's *Capital* you are not qualified to discuss socialism," or words to that effect. So he began to frequent the reading room at the British Museum where he found that *Capital* was available in a French language translation. (Shaw was, in those times, fluent in French.) Curiously enough, he had the opportunity to meet the author himself since Marx still haunted that reading room in those last few years of his life when Shaw claims to have digested the book. For whatever reasons he did not make the effort, although, sometime after the death of Marx, he did become friendly with Marx's daughter, Eleanor, who was a member of the Socialist League of William Morris.

After absorbing the volume, he returned to the S.D.F. meetings only to learn that nobody else there had read the Marx tome (with the exception, surely, of Henry Hyndman).

But the question that interests us at this point is, To what extent did he comprehend what he had read? For *Capital* is not an easy book to read, not in its entirety, at any rate; it is, rather, a text to be studied, preferably, in class, many of which did spring up in the years and among the generations of interested working people since its publication. The answer can be ascertained by reading Shaw's fifth novel, which has long since now been published because of his subsequent fame.

We will, at this juncture, examine extracts from the novel which he entitled *An Unsocial Socialist.* Much has been made by Shaw's biographers and by Shaw himself when referring to this novel that he had mastered the labor process under capitalism as explained by Marx in his Part III of *Capital.* Whatever might be said one way or the other about it, it is evident that Shaw did not pay enough attention to the opening chapter of the book which deals with commodities and money, in which Marx went to great lengths to explain some basic terms in order that his readers would understand exactly what he was driving at. Take, for example, that word "value." In the Marxian context, "value" is nothing other than crystallized human labor or "socially necessary labor time" (that production time that is average in a given locale, intensity, and era); furthermore, "value" exists only as a *concept* because we live in a commodity society that makes such concepts necessary in order that products and services may be exchanged, by their owners, on a market with view to a realization of profit. Shaw evidently did not grasp this fact; nor did he exhibit a general comprehension of a Marxian Socialist viewpoint.

Shaw's Socialist protagonist, one Sidney Trefusis, was engaged in an attempt to convert to socialism a wealthy landowner and a poet who had dabbled mildly in radical verse. He has been showing them, and declaiming upon, a collection of pictures that he had of slum dwellings and general poverty and privation among the very people who had built his father's industrial empire. The younger Trefusis was seemingly scandalized by that fact, not being able to take the matter philosophically while bending all efforts to propagandize for socialism. He has talked the landowner (a baronet) into signing a militant petition and declaring himself openly as a Socialist. The poet reacts by laughing loudly at the baronet, calling him an "ass." "You, with a large landed estate, and bags of gold invested in railways, calling yourself a Social Democrat! Are you going to sell out and distribute—to sell all that thou hast and give to the poor?" (N.Y.: Brentano's, 1903; p. 304.)

There is more than a little bit of nonsense to that purported adjuration by Jesus of Nazareth that Shaw, as one who had supposedly mastered *Capital,* might have been expected to expose from a historical perspective, but did not. The era of the Gospels was the era of classical chattel slavery. Whatever production that was carried on was the work of chattel slaves, and the poor (free proletarians) could not be maintained—even in their poverty—without the labor of the chattels. And in fact, because of the lowly development of industrial know-how and machinery, slaves had to be numbered, in many cases, on a 10–1 ratio to free men in order to maintain the luxurious standards of the ruling class and the so-so life styles of the rest of the population. So giving one's money to the poor could do no good whatever to relieve the misery of the chattels.

Nor, for that matter, can the poor be kept alive in our own times without the continuous "free" labor of wage and salaried "slaves." As Oscar Wilde so eloquently put it in his *Soul of Man Under Socialism:* You cannot end poverty by keeping the poor alive. Labor today is "free" in the sense of an absence of chains and whips. There are only those *symbolic* chains and whiplashes of poverty—or the everhanging threat of poverty—for the producers of our times. Such might have been the approach of a knowledgeable Marxist.

But Shaw was content to have Trefusis handle the problem somewhat differently and not altogether soundly. He, in fact, had Trefusis imply that there is nothing wrong about such a (Christian) dictum but that it was impossible to carry it out in the England of capitalism. "All talk of practicing Christianity, or even bare justice, is at present mere waste of words." Does this not lead one to infer that in an ideal Britain—as Shaw would have had it—it would be *possible* for one to sell one's possessions and give the proceeds to the poor? That there is nothing intrinsically wrong about a system in which buying and selling, and riches and poverty, are still the vogue?

In capitalist Britain, Trefusis explains, selling one's possessions in order to feed the poor would solve nothing, for one's shares (or money) do not simply represent present wealth but, in actuality, constitute a mortgage on future production. Even were he to donate his land for a public park the value of the neighboring property would rise and the poor would be driven from their erstwhile slum to another one.

Not bad, to be sure, and in fact it calls to mind that ongoing process of "gentrification" that has been burgeoning in American cities for a number of years—forcing numbers of the existing slum dwellers from that turf entirely and into suburban slum areas. But the Trefusis tirade ends with the following popular example of faulty "Marxian" economics: ". . . how can you justly reward the laborer when you cannot ascertain the value of what he makes owing to the prevailing custom of stealing it!" (Ibid, p. 305.)

And with that, Shaw made it more than doubtful that he had understood what he had read in *Capital*—for a certainty he had not "mastered" the message. For, in the Marxian analysis, the worker has neither legal nor moral right to the *value* of what he makes, or to the product of his labor. It is obvious that there would be no profit for the capitalist class if such were the case since the function of the working class is to produce *all* of value while the function of the capitalist class is to own the means of wealth production and distribution and to appropriate the surplus value. There is nothing illegal or immoral about profits under the codes of capitalism.

In plain words, the worker is not, and cannot be, entitled to the value of what he produces; the wage or salary agreed upon compensates the worker—according to the rules of capitalism—for the value of the labor *power* which he has agreed to sell to the employer—the worker's mental and or physical abilities and energy. So the product of that labor belongs to the employer even before the labor has been performed. And one cannot sell what one does not own—excepting, of course, in the case of the legal procedure of "selling short" which is indulged in by Wall Street operatives.

Furthermore, "stealing" is a legal concept, the one really important taboo that exists throughout "civilized" societies—taboo even for the hungry when surrounded by mountains of food waiting for buyers or vacant dwellings seeking buyers or renters. But in the case of the appropriation of surplus value by the capitalist class, that is *not* stealing and in the opinion even of the working class, generally—as propagandizers of socialism keep learning—is the way it ought to be! Exploitation—to be sure—but not robbery (although even here there is no meeting of the minds for "exploitation," to the average individual, means being driven and underpaid beyond normal or average).

True, the legal concept and the system of legality extant under capitalism was originally introduced by the class that had usurped previous rights enjoyed by peasant proprietors and had driven them forcibly from their land in order to introduce sheep enclosure. But that was a long time ago and inasmuch as there is majority support, even if much of it is apathetic, for this system of ownership rights the system operates as it is supposed to operate and all attempts to reform it, in the interests of all mankind, throughout history, have had but marginal success. This has resulted only in a higher level of poverty for the poor—both working poor and unemployed.

Nor could there exist, in an "ideal" (socialist) society, such a practice as recompense of the value of what one produces. Leaving aside the obvious fact that it is not possible to determine the value of the labor of much of the population (teachers and other professionals, for example), there can be no such concept in a socialist society as value (at least not in that envisioned by Marx, although that concept is not at all in conflict or contradiction with the Fabian Socialism as later developed by Shaw, Webb, H.G. Wells, et al.). In the socialism of Marx, who could possibly care about the labor time, or the intensity of the labor, or the "cost" when there is no exchange on a market? In a society based upon free right of access, the concept of "cost" becomes irrelevant. In fact, William Morris described such a society in his utopian Socialist novel, *News from Nowhere* which was written, according to Morris, as a reaction to Edward Bellamy's *Looking Backward,* which Morris did not like because of its protrayal of regimentation, rather than freedom. Interestingly enough, young Shaw, who was a frequent visitor to the Morris home in those times, even having what he himself termed an "unspoken romance" with Morris's daughter, liked that Morris novel very much and recommended it to his own readers at various times. (It should be pointed out that although *News from Nowhere* is termed an "utopian" novel, Morris was no utopian; he understood that capitalism would have to go, before a free-access society would be possible, which is what had happened in the novel.)

But there is more confusion in Shaw's *An Unsocial Socialist* with little if anything of counterbalance, to follow. Trefusis is telling his two friends about an incident he had had with a painter friend, one Donovan Brown, over one of his canvases. Trefusis's mother had bought the picture from Brown when he was unknown and poor, for £30 (in those times, about $150.00). Years afterwards, when Trefusis's mother was dead and Brown famous, Trefusis was offered £800 for it (in his opinion, the picture was a poor one!). Trefusis believed, despite his solicitor's advice, that he could not conscientiously accept the profit "in reward for my mother's benevolence in buying a presumably worthless picture from an obscure painter." Trefusis continued:

> But he failed to convince me that I ought to be paid for my mother's virtues, though we agreed that neither I nor my mother had received any return in the shape of pleasure in contemplating the work, which had deteriorated considerably by the fading of the colors since its purchase... (ibid, pp. 306-07).

So Trefusis finally went to Donovan's studio and offered to sell the picture back to him for one-half of what his mother had paid so that Brown would be able to resell it at a magnificent profit. But Brown insisted on paying him the full, original £30 and Trefusis sent him to the man who had offered him £800. Then Brown refused to sell it, arguing that the painting was unworthy of his reputation, even though the man had bid up his price to £1500!

Next, Trefusis felt that rather than putting a profit of £770 into Brown's pocket he had actually taken £30 out of it and he wanted to return the £30 that Brown had given him for the painting. Brown, insulted, refused to accept it, the upshot being that he broke off communications with Trefusis. (But that was not the end of all of that foolishness.)

Trefusis insisted that the matter be submitted to arbitration, and demanded £1500 for full exchange value of the picture. The denouement of this farce is best told in Shaw's own words:

> All the arbitrators agreed that this was monstrous, whereupon I contended that if they denied my right to the value in exchange, they must admit my right to the value in use. They assented to this after putting off their decision for a fortnight in order to read Adam Smith and discover what on earth I meant by my values in use and exchange. I now showed that the picture had no value in use to me, as I disliked it, and therefore I was entitled to nothing and that Brown must take back the thirty pounds. They were glad to concede this also to me, as they were all artist friends of Brown and wished him not to lose money by the transaction, though they of course privately thought that the picture was, as I described it, a bad one. After that Brown and I became very good friends... (ibid, pp. 307–08).

And in that segment of his novel Shaw demonstrated that rather than digesting *Capital*, as he had claimed to have done, he must have gulped it in a manner as to give him indigestion. For if *value*, in the Marxian sense, is nothing other than crystallized labor, and even allowing for the painting, originally, to have been a true commodity, the price offered after Brown's rise to fame could have had nothing in common with the concept of socially necessary labor time and commodities, but only with status and potential investment quality. Shaw should have used a different illustration than a hand painting and he definitely should have delved into Marx's basic definitions.

To begin with, in the very opening paragraph of Marx's *Capital*, a book which Shaw claimed had made a Socialist of him, we read:

> The wealth of those societies in which the capitalist mode of production prevails, presents itself as 'an immense accumulation of commodities,' its unit being a single commodity. Our investigation must therefore begin with the analysis of a commodity.

And Shaw obviously did not bother to accompany Marx on that particular investigation for which the latter had seen fit to devote more than 50 pages in order to make clear, among other things, that "commodity" is not a synonym for "product"; that it is merely a particular relationship of a product at a certain stage of its existence—when it is carrying a price tag prior to its having been sold.

In the first place, a product must have been produced for sale on the market with view to profit in order to qualify as a commodity. And even if such can be said to be the intention of painters of art, an original hand painting, or any other *used* product that is re-sold at an outlandishly inflated price due to the eventual fame of its creator can hardly be classified as a commodity at that juncture.

In fact, the only way such an original product can be reproduced as an original at the time of its production—and commodities must be capable of reproduction—is through some form of fakery or quasi (legal) fakery.

Works of art such as paintings—like rare books, stamps, antique pieces; even letters, scraps of paper with squigglings and scrawlings by individuals who have achieved fame or notoriety—do take on the appearance of commodities because there certainly is a market for them and they are merchandised in much the same fashion as is everything else, but their values cannot be explained in the manner of commodities from a Marxian standpoint. In short, they are not commodities. The various prices that an original painting (or a faked "original" that fools the experts) will bring can hardly have been conceived of by the artist who originally created it. That usually hungry individual could only have thought in terms of toting up his costs, living expenses, and a margin of gain that would not be high enough to cause his potential patron to seek elsewhere.

In any event, and even allowing for Marx and Engels' famed

opening section of their *Communist Manifesto* in which they excoriated the bourgeoisie away back in 1848 for, among a number of abominations, turning all but everything into commodities, in the strict sense and when dealing with the economics of capitalism, as Shaw was certainly attempting to do in his *Unsocial Socialist*, Marxists advocate preciseness of terms. Better deal with wheat and iron, whiskey and bibles and the host of tangible, everyday commodities that exchange on the market than with original paintings by the occasional artist who had unexpectedly gained fame.

In the case of Shaw and his fictional characters, however, whatever merit might exist in the story (and it is certainly not without merit in that it does effectively expose much of the hypocrisy of capitalism), *An Unsocial Socialist* betrays his failure to master Marxian economics in that reading of the French translation of *Das Kapital* in the library of the British Museum. And the general agreement among his biographers that he was, indeed, an authority on Marxian economics can, in the final analysis, only indicate their own deficiencies in that area.

True, Shaw later on, did abandon Marx's Labor Theory of Value and, in consequence, did no longer recognize labor power as a commodity in his writings on economics (albeit with some seeming backsliding in the instance of his explanation, after his brief visit to Soviet Russia in 1932, of the reasons for the absence of equality of income in that "Socialist" nation). But when he wrote *An Unsocial Socialist* he was an avowed, dedicated devotee of Marx and since he was basing his novel on the labor process as explained by Marx in *Capital*, he most certainly should have taken the trouble to check on Marx's basic definitions. On the other hand, it does become easier to understand his reasons for abandoning a previously held theory when it becomes evident that his comprehension of the theory was faulty.

The excuse of extenuating circumstances might, of course, be given to explain his naivete in that book. He was a relatively young man when he wrote it and had not had enough time to develop his knowledge of economics. After all, as he tells it himself in his *Sixteen Self Sketches*, written in 1949, he had "mastered" that French translation of *Das Kapital* in the British

Museum at the same time that he was reading analyses of operas; and Marxian economics, fascinating as it is, is not that easily grasped—not even by a mind as brilliant as that possessed by Shaw.

Interestingly enough, and all unwittingly, a *coup de grace* was administered to his grasp of Marxism by a friend and biographer, one St. John Ervine, in his *Bernard Shaw, His Life, Work and Friends* (Wm. Morrow, N.Y., 1956). In this work, Ervine tells us that Shaw was "converted to Communism" (in the winter of 1882–83) by reading that French translation of *Capital* and that as a result of that reading he had accepted the view that all forms of capital should be nationalized!

To be sure, Shaw did advocate such a remedy for the ills of capitalism until the end of his days—in all of his writings on economics and politics—but he certainly did not get such an idea from Marx. And this is a serious blunder and one that is widespread even among people who have read *Capital.* The problem is, obviously, that they not only read the book but have read into it something that is not there. For, in fact, *Capital* is an analysis of capitalism and does not get involved with an attempt to describe Socialist society. Furthermore, Marx certainly did not offer advice on how capitalism might be reformed—through nationalization, for example. The entire thrust of *Capital* is a reasoned argument-for-the-prosecution in an effort to abolish, not to alter, the system.

To Marx, the number-one villain in the scheme of capitalism is *capital* and it is arrant nonsense to state, or even to suggest, that Marx conceived of the existence of capital, in any form, in Socialist society. Marx's Part II is generally headed, "The Transformation of Money Into Capital," and in the opening section, Chapter IV, Marx takes us through some 11 pages in which he traces the process by which money is transformed into capital. In a nutshell, money in itself is not capital. It must be transformed into plant, machinery, wage labor, etc. for the production of commodities through the extraction of surplus value from the hides of wage and salaried workers in order that profits and more capital may be realized. And as if to underscore his opinion of this transformed money Marx tells us, on page 257, in his chapter, "The Working Day," that "Capital is dead labour, that vampire-like, only lives by sucking living labour, and lives the more, the more labour it sucks."

To make the message even clearer, in Part VIII, "The So-Called Primitive Accumulation," Chapter XXVI, we are told:

> In themselves, money and commodities are no more capital than are the means of production and of subsistence. They want transforming into capital. But this transformation in itself can only take place under certain circumstances that center in this, viz., that two very different kinds of commodity-possessors must come face to face and into contact; on the one hand, the owners of money, means of production, means of subsistence, who are eager to increase the sum of values they possess, by buying other people's labour-power; on the other hand, free labourers, the sellers of their own labour-power, and therefore the sellers of labour. Free labourers, in the double sense that neither they themselves form part and parcel of the means of production, as in the case of slaves, bondsmen, &c., nor do the means of production belong to them, as in the case of peasant-proprietors; they are, therefore, free from, unencumbered by, any means of production of their own... (Kerr, ed., p.785).

It should help even further, at this point, to clarify the meaning of "commodity," "use value," and "capital," by relating an anecdotal situation that is used in the Socialist movement: A lady goes to a store that sells sewing machines. She sees one with a price tag, let us say, of $500. At that point, the sewing machine is a commodity. She purchases it and has it delivered to her home where she uses it to help keep her family in clothing repairs, or whatever. The sewing machine is no longer a commodity, it is a simple use value. But this lady is a dreamer. She founds a workshop by hiring another lady to sit at the machine for eight hours a day, at a wage, to make articles of clothing for sale with view to profit for the owner of the machine. The machine is no longer a commodity or a simple use value, it is now capital.

To be sure, this definition of capital is an over-simplification because, as Marx shows in his *Capital,* Vol. I, Chapter XXXIII, there is a considerable sum of money needed to meet the cost of employing a sufficient number of workers and of providing the necessary means of production if one is to really "join the capitalist class." (See Kerr, ed., pp. 336–338.) So one does not become a capitalist simply by owning a sewing machine and hiring a wage-worker to run it. The definition, as stated above, however, does serve to clear the air if its limitations are understood.

In any case, whatever its deficiencies, *An Unsocial Socialist* somehow caught the eye of William Morris and through his influence was published, serially, in an extant socialist journal. Once he attained fame, of course, Shaw found no real problem in finding a publisher and eventually all of his rejected novels—five—saw the light of day.

Now, although there are indications that Shaw did read some of Marx's copious writings, the tenor of his own works would indicate that he never acquired a similar viewpoint to that of Marx whether in the area of economics or the history of societies. Scientific Socialism, of course regards the state as an institution that evolved at a stage of history when individual economic interests overtly transcended in importance those of clan or family. Society developed, from then on, on a class basis and a life without poverty or insecurity only became possible in proportion to one's ownership of property. Marx ridiculed the idea that ownership of land, for example, or even the right of access to tillable areas, is the inherent right of each and every individual. That very concept, in fact, could not have possibly arisen before the era of capitalism—a comparatively recent development in history.

In previous societies, such as chattel slavery and feudalism, the population was mentally conditioned both by state and by church to accept the particular station in life to which it was born. If that is difficult to comprehend today it is only because it is not easy to understand the morals of a previous society or transcend the basic attitudes of the present one. It is a safe bet that mankind in a future, world socialist society, will look back in amazement at the indignities accepted by multitudes of their ancestors. For Scientific Socialism also sees society as continuing to evolve. The next meaningful change—world socialism—is possible only when a visible and vocal majority of the world's working class understands its role and organizes to end the wages, prices, profits and money system of society, world capitalism.

2. The Fabian Society

Whenever he described the Fabian Society and its membership, Shaw always made clear the fact that it was composed of highly educated and highly cultured individuals. The very name of the organization—Fabian—indicated a liberally educated body of people, acquainted with the history of ancient Rome and of the military strategist Quintus Fabius Maximus.

Rome, in the 2nd century B.C., had been invaded by Carthaginian armies and was seemingly unable, over a long period of time, to rid the country of the trespassers whose military strategists were better in normal battle tactics than were the Roman generals. But Fabius came up with a different-than-usual plan of action that did prove successful in driving out the enemy. After all, he reasoned, our desire is to rid our land of those hordes and that end can be had without our having to confront them in battle. Let us, instead, just wear them down to a point at which they will get tired, disgusted, and go back where they came from. (See *Plutarch's Lives*.)

So, other than an occasional swift sortie, Fabius had his army march in a parallel direction to the enemy, and at a safe distance, thereby wearying them to a point where they did throw in the towel and did leave the country entirely.

The Society of Fabian Socialists reasoned that their best bet was to emulate Fabius. They would remain a "Society" rather than to organize themselves into a political party; they would thereby avoid facing their political opponents in election battle, could defeat them in debate and indoctrinate them with their Socialist ideas to the end that full-blown socialism—as they understood it—would develop gradually in Britain.

Shaw first heard of this group — at the time numerically insignificant — just about the time that he had tendered an application-for-membership to the Social Democratic Federation. Although the S.D.F. did have some scholarly and urbane members — such as William Morris (noted poet, painter and furniture designer), Belfort Bax and Edward Aveling (well-known writers of Marxist persuasion), and Eleanor Marx (daughter of Karl Marx and common-law wife of Aveling) not to mention Hyndman himself, who was an aristocrat by temperament and the son of a wealthy banker — the main body of the group was composed of mechanics and unskilled laborers. On top of that, it was a professedly Marxist organization and it had apparently not taken Shaw very long to get over his initial infatuation with Marxism. He tells us in *Sixteen Self Sketches* that such a membership "could for me be only hindrances" and he withdrew his application in order to enroll with the Fabians.

Now in point of fact the S.D.F. was founded upon Marxist principles, nominally at least, albeit considerably diluted due to a program of immediate demands that ran the gamut from abolition of the Monarchy and the House of Lords to nationalization of trusts, railways, docks and canals; even to abolition of standing armies and establishment of citizen forces. There would not seem to have been much time, at meetings, for the discussion and absorption of Marxist theory, and as a matter of fact, Morris, Bax, Aveling, and Eleanor Marx — along with others of the more theoretically-oriented members — did secede and organized the Socialist League for that very reason.

But the emphasis of the League was on theory rather than on practical politics and such an organization was not for Shaw, either. He does admit that he was converted to socialism in the first place by his reading of *Capital,* but whatever influence Marx had on him did not last long. With the Fabians he adopted the value theory of marginal utility, known in England as the Jevonsian theory after the economist professor Stanley Jevons. This theory was a refinement of the Austrian School of Bohm Bawerk which was, itself, a reaction to the Marxian involvement with production, rather than with marketing, of the commodities. Referring to this in his Appendix to *The Intelligent Woman's Guide,* Shaw says:

> Marx's contribution to the abstract economic theory of value, by which he set much store, was a blunder which was presently corrected and superseded by the theory of Jevons; but as Marx's category of 'surplus value' (Mehrwerth)...represented solid facts, his blunder in no way invalidated his indictment of the capitalist system, nor his historical generalization as to the evolution of society on economic lines. (P. 467.)

And that was a curious endorsement of surplus value, indeed, from one whose entire approach, as will be shown, seems to negate it.

As for the labor theory of value, what bothered Shaw and the cultured professionals and business-minded Fabians was the fact that they were attuned more as buyers of consumer commodities and services than as sellers of commodity labor power. And they were in constant fear of impoverishment by the development of large scale capitalism. Furthermore, the working class, to them, was conservative. The middle class—or at least the highly cultured section of it who were squeezed out of actual ownership of industry—were the hope of the future, as Shaw and his fellow Fabians believed. These knowledgeable ones came, themselves, largely from Shaw's "capitalist class" (the financiers) but were not first-born sons and had gotten little of the family loot. What they had gotten, though, was a university education and degrees (Oxford and Cambridge) after prep schooling at Eton and Harrow, and had acquired cultured minds along with their talents. And it was, basically, people of that sort who made up the ranks of the Fabian Society.

Describing the Fabian membership, Shaw wrote:

> Now the significant thing about the particular Socialist society which I joined was that the members all belonged to the middle class. Indeed its leaders and directors belonged to what is sometimes called the upper-middle class: that is, they were either professional men like myself (I had escaped from clerkdom into literature) or members of the upper division of the civil service. Several of them have since had distinguished careers without changing their opinions or leaving the Society. To their Conservative and Liberal parents and aunts and uncles fifty years ago it seemed an amazing, shocking, unheard-of thing that they should become Socialists, and also a step bound to make an end

> of all their chances in life. Really it was quite natural and inevitable. Karl Marx was not a poor laborer: he was the highly educated son of a rich Jewish lawyer. His almost equally famous colleague, Friedrich Engels, was a well-to-do employer. It was practically because they were liberally educated, and brought up to think about how things are done instead of merely drudging at the manual labor of doing them, that these two men, like my colleagues in The Fabian Society (note, please, that we gave our society a name that could have occurred only to classically educated men), were the first to see that Capitalism was reducing their own class to the condition of a proletariat... (*Intelligent Woman's Guide*, p. 185).

It should now become clear why Fabian Socialists prefer a theory of value (Jevons and the Austrian School) that begins with the demand for consumer goods as the efficient cause of production, value, and price rather than the theory that makes of consumer goods a mere means to an end of further production. To Marx, the underlying motivation for earlier capitalism was:

> Accumulate, accumulate! That is Moses and the prophets! ... Therefore, save, save, i.e., reconvert the greatest possible portion of surplus-value, or surplus product into capital! Accumulation for accumulation's sake, production for production's sake... if to classical economy, the proletarian is but a machine for the production of surplus value; on the other hand, the capitalist is in its eyes only a machine for the conversion of this surplus value into additional capital... (Marx, *Capital*, p. 652).

The problem, according to this approach, is that the "robbery" takes place in the area of production—in the factories and workshops of capitalism—and is a matter of exploitation of the "great unwashed," of unpaid labor time. Any meaningful change calculated to benefit the majority of the population would have to be instituted and carried through by the working class.

And there also exists that question of psychology of the individual. To Marx, there certainly are individuals and he maintained, for example, that "Man makes his own history..." (*The 18th Brumaire of Louis Bonaparte*), but—to paraphrase—individuals are a part of a society and cannot be identified or in any way understood apart from that society. Such a theory does not go down well with middle class mentality and even those among Shaw's middle and upper middle class associates who recognized their own rapid descent to proletarian depths were still capable of middle class thinking.

The Fabian Society's Political Objectives

Now, what were the objectives of the Fabian Society? As quoted in *The* (London) *Times* of Saturday, Jan. 9, 1909,*

> The Fabian Society consists of Socialists. It therefore aims at the reorganization of society by the emancipation of land and industrial capital from individual and class ownership and the vesting of them in the community for the general benefit. In this way only can the natural and acquired advantages of the country be equitably shared by the whole people.
>
> The society accordingly works for the extinction of private property in land and of the consequent individual appropriation in the form of rent, of the price paid for permission to use the earth, as well as for the advantages of superior soils and sites.
>
> The society further works for the transfer to the community of the administration of such industrial capital as can conveniently be managed socially.

And *The Times'* journalist-commentator, after a page in which he exposes the "Involved and half-hearted pronouncement," which he claims is characteristic of the Fabians and which leaves the real position unclear, states:

> Its function has always been to educate, to instil Socialistic ideas gently, to inspire, to work indirectly through others, whom it has imbued with the principles of the faith. Hence its plasticity and absence of programme. It is an insidious rather than a powerful influence , and has hitherto taken visible effect chiefly in the sphere of municipal 'Socialism,' which is despised by the more robust brethren of the order, but is, at any rate, something

**Excerpted from* The Socialist Movement in Great Britain; *a series of articles reprinted from* The Times. *Printed and published by John Parkinson Bland at The Times Office. 2, Printing House Square, London, E.C. (no date).*

> practical. A conspicuous example is London, where Fabianism virtually ran the County Council for years, without appearing to do so, until the last election.

And *The Times* writer went on to tell us that at that time, 11 Fabians were members of Parliament (as Labour party representatives) but that "its real work lies outside of politics, and is carried on chiefly by the distribution of literature and by lectures. . . . The well-known volume of 'Fabian Essays' has for years had a large and increasing sale."

And just what was the gist of the message of the *Essays?* Shaw wrote:

> After Progress and Poverty (1883, by Henry George, father of the Single Tax movement for the complete nationalization of land) the next milestone is Fabian Essays, edited by myself, in which Sidney Webb first entered the field as a definitely Socialist writer with Graham Wallas, whose later treatises on constitutional problems are important, and Sydney Olivier (Lord Olivier) whose studies of the phenomenon of the 'poor white' in Africa and America, facing the competition of the black proletariats created by negro slavery should be read by Colonial Ministers. In Fabian Essays Socialism is presented for the first time as a completely constitutional political movement, which the most respectable and least revolutionary citizen can join as irreproachably as he might join the nearest Conservative club. Marx is not mentioned; and his peculiar theory of value is entirely ignored, the economic theories relied on being Jevons' theory of value and Ricardo's theory of rent of land, the latter being developed so as to apply to industrial capital and interests as well. In short, Socialism appears in Fabian Essays purged of all its unorthodox views and insurrectionary liberal associations. . . (*Intelligent Woman's Guide,* Brentano's, p. 468).

Now it should not be surprising that Marxist commentators were not generally complimentary in their references to either *Fabian Essays* or *The Intelligent Woman's Guide.* Commenting briefly in his *An American Looks at Marx* (1939), on minor British critics of Marx, William J. Blake wrote:

> In 1888 in the Fabian Essays, Bernard Shaw annihilated in a few pages both Karl Marx and Henry George and substituted for

> their unauthentic wisdom a few handpicked bouquets from the quasi-rent garden of Alfred Marshall. He declared Marx antiquated because he depended on the iron law of wages and a 'pure' labor theory of value. Having proved completely that he never read a line of Karl Marx, or if he did that he suffered from an infirmity of the senses, Shaw forty years later wrote a canonical system of socialism, based, if one pleases, on a 'better distribution of income.' He repudiates surplus-value and decides that the increment of the rich arises from mis-directed rents of ability, etc. This is interesting as proof that gall can be substituted for science. (N.Y.: The Cordon Company, 1939; p. 575.)

And we must here observe that, despite Shaw's repudiation of Marx, we are left with the question, did Blake actually read *The Fabian Essays?* Or was he just basing his dismissal of Shaw on the 1928 tome? For it is true that, other than two or three brief referencs in a footnote, the one quoted above—somewhat complimentary, at that—Marx is not mentioned in the *Essays.* So the "annihilation" of the Marxian system in that source is by implication. Shaw did not go after Marx in a frontal attack as he did in so many of his other books and essays.

Furthermore, there is plenty of indication in his works, beginning with his novel *An Unsocial Socialist,* that Shaw had read and absorbed, at least to some limited extent, Marx's *Capital* (or a section of it). But that does not necessarily indicate that he "suffered from an infirmity of the senses" when he wrote his so-called improvement on Marx's system. He just failed to comprehend the picture and pattern of what he had read—he must have if, for example, as Blake says, Shaw declared that Marx "depended on the iron law of wages," for that was a Lassallean tenet (Ferdinand Lassalle, German Socialist polemicist, contemporary and sometime friend of Marx), not a Marxian one. In fact, a paper was written by Marx and sent to the General International Congress of the International Working Men's Association to be read as his side of a debate with a delegate of the I.W.M.A., one Citizen Weston. Weston took the Lassallean position that wages are absolutely tied to the cost of living; that if wages go up the cost of living necessarily follows. Marx argued the negative explaining, among other facts of life under capitalism, that if the amount of national production is a fixed thing, and the magnitude of wages also fixed, as Weston argued, then the capitalists would be also silly to seek a reduction in wage levels, as they constantly do. The fact is, as Marx pointed out, that workers are constantly forced to resist attempts by employers to lower wage rates, which is one of the important reasons why labor unions exist.

The Marxian stand on wages is spelled out in that paper, published under the title *Value, Price and Profit,* one of the more widely read of Marx's pamphlets the existence of which Shaw, as a reputed authority on Marx, should have known.

Besides *The Fabian Essays,* among the more popular literature disseminated by the Society were the Fabian tracts. In 1884, the Fabian Tract No. 2, written by G.B. Shaw, was issued as a manifesto. Inasmuch as it is both an official publication of the Society and a statement by Shaw, himself, it merits reproduction here in full.

A Manifesto

THE FABIANS are associated for the purpose of spreading the following opinions held by them, and discussing their practical consequences.

That, under existing circumstances, wealth cannot be enjoyed without dishonour, or foregone without misery.

That it is the duty of each member of the State to provide for his or her wants by his or her own Labour.

That a life interest in the Land and Capital of the nation is the birth-right of every individual born within its confines: and that access to this birth-right should not depend upon the will of any private person other than the person seeking it.

That the most striking result of our present system of farming out the national Land and Capital to private individuals has been the division of Society into hostile classes, with large appetites and no dinners at one extreme, and large dinners and no appetites at the other.

That the practice of entrusting the Land of the nation to private persons in the hope that they will make the best of it has been discredited by the consistency with which they have made the worst of it; and that the Nationalization of the Land in some form is a public duty.

That the pretensions of Capitalism to encourage Invention,

and to distribute its benefits in the fairest way attainable, have been discredited by the experience of the nineteenth century.

That, under the existing system of leaving the National Industry to organize itself, Competition has the effect of rendering adulteration, dishonest dealing, and inhumanity compulsory.

That since Competition among producers admittedly secures to the public the most satisfactory products, the State should compete with all its might in every department of production.

That such restraints upon Free Competition as the penalties for infringing the Postal monopoly, and the withdrawal of workhouse and prison labour from the markets, should be abolished.

That no branch of Industry should be carried on at a profit by the central administration.

That the Public Revenue should be raised by a direct Tax; and that the central administration should have no legal power to hold back for the replenishment of the Public Treasury any portion of the proceeds of the Industries administered by them.

That the State should compete with private individuals—especially with parents in providing happy homes for children, so that every child may have a refuge from the tyranny or neglect of its natural custodians.

That Men no longer need special political privileges to protect them against Women: and that the sexes should henceforth enjoy equal political rights.

That no individual should enjoy any Privilege in consideration of services rendered to the State by his or her parents or other relations.

That the State should secure a liberal education and an equal share in the National Industry to each of its units.

That the established Government has no more right to call itself the State than the smoke of London has to call itself the weather.

That we had rather face a Civil War than such another century of suffering as the present one has been.

At the bottom of page 9 of a later tract, published in 1887, also written by Shaw, the names of the executive for 1887–88 are listed as follows: Annie Besant, Hubert Bland, Sydney Olivier, W.L. Phillips, Frank Podmore, G. Bernard Shaw, Sidney Webb.

The Manifesto's theme, of course, is that access to a meaningful share of the nation's wealth is, or should be, the birthright of every individual member of the nation. There is no breath of revolutionary agitation here, such as is found in the writings of the pioneers of Scientific Socialism. There is complete respectability, mute evidence of justification for the respect and affection given by Britain's rulers to homegrown Socialists of the Fabian variety. (The ashes of Sidney, and Beatrice Webb, in fact, are interred in Westminster Abbey largely through the efforts of their great friend and comrade, G.B. Shaw, during the post W.W. II Labour government tenure of Clement Attlee.)

The sole obstacle to socialism in Britain, according to the Fabians, was the absence of more-or-less total nationalization of land and basic industry. The system of "farming out" to corporations and to private individuals, prerogatives that by rights belong to the nation, was the reason for the existence of "hostile classes." In fact, not only did he differ fundamentally with the Marxists—at least with those who stubbornly adhered to the historical analysis of the founders of Scientific Socialism—on that question but his very definitions of the classes, themselves, differed antipodally. The capitalists, to Shaw, were the financiers and bankers from whom his "middle class" owners of industries had to borrow money for operating expenses. The employers of industrial labor were not capitalists, to him, but "middle class" with a legitimate function in society of hiring, organizing, and directing labor. The extra reward, over and above what they earned in their "legitimate" role, taken by the employers of labor was not profit but "rent of ability" and he fulminated against them, as he did in the case of the landowners, for making such a levy. It was, to Shaw, a sort of hold-up and he argued that those "middle class" employers should be satisfied with their earnings for their legitimate functions; in an ideal (Fabianized) Britain, as he saw it, that problem would not exist because income would be equalized for all, the only exceptions being those with special talents or other endowments pleasing to the eye and ear who would be permitted to be more equal than others by charging fees to all who would view or hear them perform. It is all explained in his *Intelligent Woman's Guide to Socialism and Capitalism.*

Although there seems not to have been an official spokesman for the Fabian Society, there was a generally recognized "old Guard" which were certainly the authors and chief promulgators of what came to be accepted as Fabian theory—the *Fabian Essays.* Chief among the Society's "watchdogs," were Sidney Webb and Bernard Shaw. Shaw edited the *Essays* (later bound as a book and published by the Society, selling like the proverbial hotcakes and becoming a chief source of the Society's income) and contributed the tract dealing with the economic basis of socialism as the Fabian Society understood it. His *Intelligent Woman's Guide to Socialism and Capitalism,* written some 40 years later, was couched in a somewhat more folksy—rather than literary—style but did not deviate noticeably from his original Fabian assumptions.

Marx, according to the Shavian viewpoint in 1888, was already passé chiefly because his theories were first drawn up in the 1840s and were, some four decades later, superseded by those of Professor Stanley Jevons (Marginal Utility) and Henry George (Economic Rent).

As for Webb, his main contribution to the *Essays* was the *Historical Basis of Socialism.* According to him, "The economic history of the [19th] century is an almost continuous record of the progress of socialism." (Quoted in *History of Socialism* by Harry W. Laidler, Thos. Y. Crowell, N.Y.) Webb maintained that the most important of the contributing factors behind Europe's steady march toward socialism in the century was the irresistible growth of democracy. In fact, socialism, he argued, was to a large extent already an established fact and needed only an expansion on the economic front and recognition in the area of politics. There is no documentation, he contended, for a sudden change or revolution from older societies to newer ones. Gradualism, or evolution, rather than revolution, has been the mechanism for social change. And it is easy to see that reasoning of that sort would be a great deal more likely to be acceptable to the middle-class membership of the Fabian Society than were the theories of Karl Marx with their emphasis on class struggle. As they understood Marxism, the struggle for socialism must involve agitation and organization of working people for violent confrontation with the police and even the military.

Interestingly enough, while Marx and Engels came to recognize and to accept democratic procedures as implements for revolution relatively early in their careers, both Shaw and Webb seemed to go all out in the opposite direction. Shaw denounced parliamentarianism most vehemently for many years, welcoming and defending all varieties of the European dictatorships and their "strong men" of the 20th century. They were all, to him, socialism and socialists in action; systems and "supermen" to be praised, not reviled.

As for Webb and his wife and collaborator, Beatrice (Potter) Webb, although originally put out by Shaw's rejection of democracy in favor of authoritarian regimes, they later succumbed to the enchantment of Bolshevik "communism." It seems that Beatrice, seeing the system that she and Sidney had portrayed as socialism in evolution—capitalism in the democratic West—all but collapsing around them during the years of the Great Depression, began to search out an existing alternative. She read up on the Soviet Union and, along with Sidney who was then a Cabinet minister (secretary of state for the Colonies), had become friendly with the Soviet ambassador, G.J. Sokolnikov. He, of course, assured them that they would be made most welcome were they to visit his country. So they did, in 1932, and they were, as Sidney put it, greeted like "a new type of royalty."

After their return they authored a distillation of what they had been shown and told on their three-month visit, entitled *Soviet Communism.* They went completely overboard in their adulation of the so-called Workers' Fatherland, declaring it to be the most democratic state on the face of the earth. And this must have come as somewhat of a shock to those who knew them best. For, up to shortly before their trip there, Beatrice had been openly condemning the Soviets for "brutality." But in the words of their biographers, Norman and Jeanne MacKenzie:

> The Soviet system touched deep-rooted elements in both their personalities—the streak of elitism and authoritarianism, intellectual dogmatism, the need for an all-embracing faith, the desire for a planned and efficient order, the belief in the rightness of the expert, the lack of sympathetic imagination for ordinary people and distrust of the people's capacity to govern themselves. In the depressing conditions of the early Thirties, when many intellectuals had begun to flirt with totalitarian solutions, Communism had come to seem to the Webbs the only

> hope for a genuinely new order of things. (*The Fabians*. N.Y.: Simon & Schuster, 1977; p. 408.)

And the MacKenzies conclude that segment:

> Sidney's intellectual and Beatrice's emotional needs were now satisfied. To the end of her life Beatrice did not waver, listening regularly to broadcasts from Moscow, taking in Communist publications and entertaining Soviet diplomats. Writing to the C.P. leader R. Palme Dutt in 1942, she described herself and Sidney as 'non-party Communists.' In the final years of their partnership their only political interest was in the survival of the Soviet state which they saw as the Fabian utopia.

The Webbs', G. B. Shaw, and the Fabian Society, generally, were interested in improving wages, salaries and political reforms under the existing social relationships. Marx and Engels, on the other hand, were uninterested in improving society; they felt that to devote one's time and effort to such a program would be tantamount to trampling a treadmill. Their efforts were aimed at changing the world from the roots up. Marx argued, in *Value, Price and Profit*, that whatever "fairness" or substance there was in the wage, wage labor itself is but a badge of slavery. His advice to the labor union movement was to rid itself of its conservative slogan "A Fair Day's Pay for a Fair Day's Work," and substitute for it the revolutionary watchword, emblazoned on their banners: "Abolition of the Wages System!"

But while Marxism and Fabianism were, originally, distinct and mutually hostile schools of socialism, events in the real world brought the two disciplines together—Fabianism melded into the neo-Marxism that developed out of the original theories. In the world of practical politics, the professedly Marxist political parties, whether of the Social Democratic or Bolshevik variety, for all practical purposes, changed the meaning of the words "Socialist" and "Communist." Whereas the terms had originally been used interchangeably by Marx and Engels, they came to mean something quite different, more acceptable to the mass of working people and even, to an important degree, to capitalists themselves.

One after another nation, since the end of World War I and

particularly after World War II, began to designate their economies as "Socialist" or "Communist" with the "Communist" countries embracing Marx and Engels along with such Bolshevik-style heroes as Lenin, Stalin, Tito, Mao, Castro, etc. How could British Fabians ignore this? Here was no uprooting of wage labor and capital relationships or even an advocacy of it unless relegated to the far distant future—some 500 years hence, as propounded by Mao. True, the overwhelming bulk of enterprise was generally taken over by the governments, but that had always been the program of the Fabians. So whatever animosities might arise because of clashing interests between political entities and blocs, the Fabians recognized their own ideals in the "Socialist" and "Communist" economies wherever they arose; while many professed Marxists—or neo "Marxists"—in the world today, would be likely to acknowledge the socialism of G.B. Shaw, as outlined in his plays and prefaces, to be at least akin to the genuine article, with whatever difference really being one without a distinction.

But what of Shaw and the Fabian Society on the question of "inherent" rights to ownership or access: in a five-page tract written by Shaw in 1887 for the Society, under a section heading *The True Radical Programme* to distinguish it from *The Official Liberal-Radical Programme*, we read:

Municipalization of Land and Local Government

> We want to RESTORE the land and industrial capital of the country to the workers of the country, and so to realize the dream of the Socialist on sound economic principles, by gradual, peaceful, and constitutional means.

True enough, before the era of capitalism in Britain there were tenured rights to land guaranteed the peasantry. True also, that such rights were ignored by the rising capitalist class who forcibly evicted the peasantry, sending them onto the highways and into the cities to seek employment in the burgeoning factory system. But industrial capital was never the property of the working class anywhere and, in any case, the Fabian program called for the right of municipally-owned enterprise to compete with private and corporate enterprise—a system termed today by Social Democrats as a "mixed" economy. But even total municipalization and nationalization of industry and land would have a market economy remain and one has but to look at the nations where such economies exist to note that the relationships of wage labor and capital remain—that is, if one actually *sees* what one looks at.

The Fabian Society reached its membership peak in March of 1943, just 3600 actual registrants; yet included in its body were 18 members of the House of Lords, 75 members of the House of Commons and numerous big names in business, labour and the professions. The "gas and water socialists," as termed by William Morris, certainly did influence British politics out of proportion to its membership to the greater glory of municipal ownership. Not that municipal ownership was the brainchild of Shaw and the Fabians—not by any means. E.R. Pease, long-time secretary of the Society from its foundation, pointed out in his *History of the Fabian Society:*

> Here, in passing, we may remark that there is a legend, current chiefly in the United States, that the wide extension of municipal ownership in Great Britain is due to the advocacy of the Fabian Society. This is very far from the truth. The great provincial municipalities took over the management of their water and gas because they found municipal control alike convenient, beneficial to the citizens, and financially profitable..." (Frank Cass Co., Ltd., 1963; pp. 81–2).

As a matter of fact, Sidney Webb—Shaw's alter ego in the building of the Fabian Society—in his Fabian essay entitled *The Historic Basis of Socialism,* asserted that socialism is but a further development of what had been evolving within capitalism, that the economic foundation was all but established, needing only extension. The evidence is all around us, he claimed, in the percentage of occupations that require no investment or participation by private enterprise. Small wonder that the ruling class of Britain, as well as the state capitalist bureaucrats of the Soviet Union, could embrace the Fabians and their program—after all, to paraphrase Robert Burns, capitalism by any other name smells as sweet, even when it is designated "socialism."

3. Shaw's Curious Socialism

Oddly enough, there was one important and seemingly irreconcilable difference between the approach of the Fabians and that of the presumptive Marxists of the Communist and Socialist nations. Whereas the alleged Marxists, in the main, did not adulterate Marxian economics (other than, in the Soviet Union, the identification of socialism as a transition stage between capitalism and communism) but somehow seemed to see no contradiction between it and their own systems, the Fabian Society rejected Marx out of hand. Shaw, of course, was seemingly the expert among the Fabians on economics and he certainly disseminated some viewpoints and theories that could only strike most Socialists as weird. Let us begin with his acceptance and description of the Jevons theory of Marginal Utility. In his *Economic Basis of Socialism* (his contribution to the *Fabian Essays)* he wrote:

> Fresh air and sunlight, which are so useful as to be quite indispensable, have no exchange value; whilst a meteoric stone, shot free of charge from the firmament into the back garden, has a considerable exchange value, although it is an eminently dispensable curiousity. We soon find that this somehow depends on the fact that fresh air is plenty and meteoric stones scarce. If by any means the supply of fresh air could be steadily diminished, and the supply of meteoric stones, by celestial cannonade or otherwise, steadily increased, the fresh air would presently acquire an exchange value which would gradually rise, while the exchange value of meteoric stones would be as un-saleable as ordinary pebbles. The exchange value, in fact, decreases with the supply. This is due to the fact that the supply decreases in utility

> as it goes on, because when people have had some of a commodity, they are partly satisfied, and do not value the rest so much. (*Selective Prose.* N.Y.: Dodd, Mead & Co., 1952 ed; pp. 705–6.)

Now the problem here begins with the fact that once again we have an example of confusion in definitions. We are supposed to be talking about the wealth of a social system and not about natural wealth. Marx saw no rhyme nor reason for injecting fresh air, sunlight, or meteor stones into a discussion of the system of commodity production and exchange—none are commodities. They are not produced for a market; they are, in fact, examples of natural wealth. Whatever value ("crystallized human labor") even meteor stones might possess, under special circumstances, would be exceptional. They are certainly not reproducible at will.

But he does go on from there to show that one can only use so much bread per week and that one will not give much for bread once one has had enough of it—its *utility,* as he calls it, drops. And then he takes us into the world of umbrellas and shows how umbrella utility drops the more umbrellas get produced. And he wants us to believe that this is not simply a case of supply and demand acting on price on a market. It is not as though Shaw did not know that millions of people, even in highly developed nations, can get no utility whatever from what they cannot afford to buy; need never be concerned with diminishing utility from oversatiation—not even from bread. Shaw did know this, a fact which makes of his conversion to Jevonsianism another contradiction.

However, let us not stray for the moment from the business of utility—demand for bread and umbrellas. One umbrella would have an exchange value of at least 15 loaves of bread. Would that be due to the umbrella having 15 times as much utility as one loaf of bread? Away back in David Ricardo's time (he died in 1823), he wrote:

> When I give 2000 times more cloth for a pound of gold than I give for a pound of iron does it prove that I attach 2000 times more utility to gold than I do to iron? Certainly not; it proves only that the cost of production of gold is 2000 times greater than the cost of production of iron. If the cost of production of the two

> metals were the same I should give the same price for them; but if utility were the measure of the value it is probable I should give much more for the iron. It is the competition of producers . . . which regulates the value of different commodities. If, then, I give one shilling for a loaf and 21 shillings for a guinea, it is no proof that this in my estimation is the comparative measure of their utility. (Quoted in his lecture entitled *The Final Futility of Final Utility* by H.M. Hyndman; book title *The Economics of Socialism.* The Twentieth Century Press, Ltd., London; 1909.)

Without dwelling here on Ricardo's own deficiencies—from a Marxian viewpoint—he hit the nail on the head with regard to utility.

So it seems that the main problem that bothered Shaw was his failure—despite his avowed socialism—to recognize the fact that society is organized for the purpose of producing commodities and surplus value and that, given such a fact and such a foundation, the system operates and functions normally. It takes but a glance at the economies of the Communist and Socialist nations, based also on production for sale on the market with view to profit, to discover that something other than nationalization and a change of vocabulary to describe the institutions is needed to end poverty, inequality, and exploitation.

Shaw Defines Capital

As noted above, Scientific Socialists define capital as wealth used to create more wealth with view to profit through exploitation of labor. Not so Shaw. In his *Intelligent Woman's Guide* he explains capital as follows:

> To begin with, the word Capitalism is misleading. The proper name of our system is Proletarianism. When practically every disinterested person who understands our system wants to put an end to it because it wastes capital so monstrously that most of us are as poor as church mice, it darkens counsel to call it Capitalism. It sets people thinking that Socialists want to destroy capital, and believe that they could do without it: in short, that they are worse fools than their neighbors.
>
> Unfortunately, that is exactly what the owners of the

> newspapers want you to think about Socialists . . . therefore they carefully avoid the obnoxious word Proletarianism and stick to the flattering title of Capitalism, which suggests that the capitalists are defending that necessary thing, Capital. (P. 100.)
>
> And, Land is not the only property that returns a rent to the owner. Spare money will do the same if it is properly used. Spare money is called Capital; its owner is called a Capitalist; and our system of leaving all the spare money in the country in private hands like the land is called Capitalism . . . (p. 127).

Capital, to Shaw, is simply "spare money" and this spare money "is the money you have left when you have bought everything you need to keep you becomingly in your station of life. . . . To be a capitalist, therefore, you must have more than enough to live on [p. 100]." But, he points out, even if it is "the root of all evil, [it] ought to be, and can be made, the means of all betterment."

So Shaw's newspaper owners are correct when they tell us—according to Shaw—that Socialists want to abolish capital in its entirety. And yet, when one takes into account the Communist bloc of nations, all of which embrace Marx and Engels as their inspirational leaders despite the flourishing of capital/wage-labor relationships in their domains, relationships which they obviously see as something other than what they are, how can one see Shaw as a lone aberrationist? Shaw, on the one hand, openly defended capital as being an all-time essential for society—even for a Fabian society; while on the other hand, the Communists simply ignore its existence, possibly on the premise that given the silent treatment, capital would—unlike the leopard—change its spots and become something different.

Rents and Commodity Costs

Two of Shaw's pet bugbears were ground rent (rent paid by industrial capitalists for the "ground" occupied by their plants and owned by aristocratic landowners) and—what he termed "Rent-of-Ability." They were, along with a number of other economic "facts," a prime cause of rising commodity costs. In the case of ground rent: at the time Shaw joined the Fabian Society, in 1884, England was the only country with a majority of urban, rather than rural population. So the heavy concentration of the Fabians on the parasitism of landowners was already somewhat anachronistic. Agriculture, of course, is essential to industrial capitalism because the working class must be able to purchase the food needed to keep them in shape for production duties. And, the lower such costs the lower the wage level in industry, generally, which is why the industrial capitalist class of Britain supported the repeal of the Corn Laws in 1846 (these had been a landowner maneuver designed to keep food imports low and agricultural prices high). The industrial capitalist class, however, had already won its long struggle against the landowning aristocrats with the aid, of course, of the working class, which had been hoodwinked into thinking that their food costs would drop while their wage levels would rise.

Actually, Shaw was wrong about rents being a factor in the raising of commodity prices. Such reasoning, to be sure, was not original with him but was stated by more renowned economists as far back as Adam Smith who advanced the proposition that

> In every society the price of every commodity finally resolves itself into some one or the other, of all three of these parts [viz., wages, profits, rent]. (See footnote on p. 981 of *Capital,* Vol. III, Kerr, ed.)

To which Marx responded:

> The entirely false dogma to the effect that the value of commodities resolves itself in the last analysis into wages plus profits plus rent expresses itself in the assertion that the consumer must ultimately pay for the total value of the total product, or that the money circulation between producers and consumers must ultimately be equal to the money circulation between the producers themselves (Tooke). All these assertions are as false as the axiom upon which they are founded. (*Capital,* Vol. III, p. 981.)

And he goes on to sum up the problem that since the worker receives only wages; the capitalist only profits; the landlord only rents; and the commodity's price represents a total of all three of these parts, how can any section of the society find the money to buy the commodity? ("How can they buy a value of four with a value of three?")

Let us now permit Marx to sum up on what actually takes place in the determination of price insofar as the role of the landowner was concerned:

> Just as the active capitalist pumps surplus labor, and with it surplus-value and surplus products in the form of profit out of the laborer, so the landlord in his turn pumps a portion of this surplus-value, or surplus product, out of the capitalist, in the shape of rent, according to the laws previously demonstrated by us. (*Capital,* Vol. III, p. 955.)

In other words, ground rent to Marx was a problem for capitalists and not one that should concern the working class.

Shaw was, in fact, altogether off base on the question of price determination, maintaining that additional involvement of entrepreneurs in distribution adds to the cost of a commodity. In *Intelligent Woman's Guide* he observed:

> Today the raising of the money to buy the materials is a separate business; the selection and purchasing is another separate business; the making is divided between several workers or else done by a machine tended by a young person; and the marketing is yet another separate business. Indeed it is much more complicated than that, because the separate businesses of buying materials and marketing products are themselves divided into several separate businesses; so that between the origin of the product in raw material from the hand of Nature and its final sale across the counter to you there may be dozens of middlemen, of whom you complain because they each, take a toll which raises the price to you, and it is impossible for you to find out how many of them are really necessary agents in the process and how many mere intercepters and parasites. (Pp. 333–4.)

One question in that approach must be, were all "non-essential" middlemen to be eliminated and prices proportionately lowered, would this not also affect wage/salary prices, since wage labor also has a price? Even in Shaw's times, wage levels had to be adjusted upwards and downwards to harmonize with general commodity prices. It would be nice, of course, were general prices to drop while wage/salary levels remain constant, or rise!

After some little thought, it would seem that Shaw's early abandonment of the economics of Marx may very well have been due to his failure to grasp the entire picture. He had never had the patience for Marx's historical approach and the economics of Scientific Socialism is bound up with that interpretation. For Marx was, above all, an historian with an evolutionary (dialectical) approach to all things. Such phenomena as value, exchange value, socially necessary labor time, capital, etc., are not intrinsic qualities but concepts relevant to a particular historical era, and there is much evidence of shakiness in Shaw's understanding of Marx's definitions. He wrote, for example:

> It is evident that the exchange value of anything depends on its utility, since no mortal exertion can make a useless thing exchangable." (*Selected Prose.* Dodd, Mead & Co., 1952; p. 705.)

This is obviously a thrust at the Marxian labor theory. He ignored Marx's own statement, if he did in fact notice it: "A commodity . . . by its properties satisfies human wants of some sort or another . . ." (*Capital,* I. Kerr, ed., p.41.). It is, of course, possible that the reason for Shaw's ignoring of that quote was that Marx went on to say, "The utility of a thing makes of it a *use* value." (Ibid., p. 42; ital. added.) And Shaw preferred to confuse use value and exchange value with value.

Valueless Land

The gist of Shaw's economics seems to have been his rejection of the Labor Theory of Value and his insistence upon the importance of ground rents (and "rents of ability") in determining values. A main point of departure between Shaw and Marx is that the Marxists insist that land, because it is not something that can be produced and reproduced for sale on the market and is not, in itself, the receptacle of crystallized human labor, has no value. Socially necessary labor must be performed before it does have value and it is that labor that gives the land its value. As a matter of fact, the fantastic prices paid for some land represents something other than the value. Such transactions are, in reality, like the purchase of annuity – not the exchange of values but a mere banking operation.

Actually, the best proof that land has no value is the fact that most land on the planet can be had free. In his *The Theoretical System of Karl Marx* (Chicago. Kerr Co., 1907), Louis B. Boudin pointed out:

> It is true that it is pretty inconvenient for us to get to a place where land is obtainable without price because of no value, and that as far as we are concerned the argument of the places where land is free seems, therefore, *far fetched*. But, first of all, it is certainly no fault of the Marxian theory that our capitalistic class has abducted from the people all the soil, so that there is none left either in its virginity or in the possession of lawful husbandmen. And, secondly, we might ask the great host of Marx-critics to point out one place on the face of the globe, where a single article produced by labor can habitually be obtained without giving an equivalent therefore. Not on the whole face of the globe, nor even in the clouds or among the stars where Bohm-Bawerk can get gold lumps free, can anybody find a place where chairs, coats or bicycles can be gotten free . . . (pp. 112–13).

So the Shavian position, partially based as it is on rent payments to landlords being a factor in the determination of cost and value, might very well have been expected to lead a Marxist such as Blake to protest that Shaw had either never read a line of Marx or had taken leave of his senses; for Shaw had established a reputation as a knowledgeable socialist and it would have been reasonable to have thought that he was aware of the Marxian approach to what he was attacking. On the other hand – and as remarked upon already – it might also be pointed out that many a Marxist authority who has read and claims to accept, the economics of Marx – those who equate the Communist nations, for example, with Marxism – can present an equally profound puzzle since all such nations display the essential hallmarks of capitalism: production for sale on a market with view to profit; wage labor and capital as the predominant relationships; even the spirit of nationalism and ethnic chauvinisms among the population.

Equality of Income

Throughout most of the years that Shaw propagandized for Fabian Socialism he argued that the *sine qua non* of a Socialist society was equality of income – with the exception cited above of those with special talents who would be permitted to pick up extra money through concerts, exhibitions, etc. He was cured of that theory upon his visit to the Soviet Union in 1931 – a land which he, from then on, enthusiastically regarded as a model Fabian state despite its typically capitalist system of income-differentiation. He was convinced, from then on, that the Bolshevik explanation was correct; that in time, equality of income would be possible in the U.S.S.R. after the existing "transition period" would make such a program feasible. But is socialism in the Marxian meaning, supposed to be a society based upon equality of income? Or is such a belief based upon nothing tangible?

It is a fact, to be sure, that the average person would respond to the question, How would (or how do) people live under socialism? by a shrug of the shoulders, a spreading of hands, maybe even a slight wrinkling of the brow, before saying: "You know! Everybody's equal. Everybody gets the same income. It's a government law in Socialist dictatorships," or something along those lines. Whether they get the idea from Socialists like Shaw – or vice versa – is a moot question. But Shaw went overboard for the important dictators in Europe – all varieties – and regarded them, and their systems, as socialist. The fact that he had embraced Mussolini even before his trip to Soviet Russia in 1931 would only further illustrate his being able to take conflicting positions on a question at one and the same time. For he could have seen no such phenomenon in Fascist Italy as equality of income.

But in any case, wherever and however Shaw arrived at that concept, he didn't get it from Marx. For traditional Marxists would not agree that such a goal as equality of income is possible, or even desirable, whatever the nature of the aspirations – the socialism of Shaw or the socialism of Marx. Inequality of income in a commodity society, of course, is an essential part of the economics of the system since labor power is a commodity and different types of labor power have different quantities of "crystallized human labor" incorporated in their production and reproduction and consequently must have different price tags. Not only that, but in the short run, market conditions for the various types of labor power will have an effect on the wage or price attached to each type. And it makes no difference to that law that the commodity society is labeled Socialism—as in the Soviet Union.

Shaw inveighed heavily against the successful businesspeople and the idle gentry with fancy unearned incomes. But given the class structure of society (and Shaw saw nothing wrong, intrinsically, with class structure; was proud to consider himself part of the "cultured" middle class) there is nothing immoral about property owners and exploiters of labor enjoying the fruits of their favored positions in proportion to their holdings of capital and commodities—not to knowledgable Marxists at any rate. A code of morality is part of the superstructure of a society's mode of production ("The ideology of the exploited class is the ideology of the ruling class"—Marx).

True, every society has produced its minorities who were able to rise above and fight against the morality of the times. But it was not the efforts of those champions of new morality that ended the chattel slave and serf societies of the past to whatever extent such efforts might have helped. It was the realization by slave owners, on the one hand, and the then-revolutionary bourgeoisie, on the other, that one need not own a slave outright in order to profit from him, and that feudal restrictions against the movement of the peasantry together with the modicum of security afforded them under feudal law, was not calculated to be of help to business interests. What was needed was mass insecurity and mass poverty in order to be able to recruit the new type of "free" slave to man the factories that were springing up everywhere. So a new code of morality was born.

This leads to the question of equalization of income and why Scientific Socialists disagree that such a condition of affairs will prevail in a Socialist world. To begin with, income itself implies an economy, with wages, money, and so forth. Wage labor cannot exist without its concomitance—capital. So right off the bat we are back to square one. It is all very well for Shaw and the Fabians, who seemed to believe that the leopard *can* change its spots, to think that way. Scientific Socialists, who make it their business to analyze and dissect capital and wage labor, disagree. So what must happen when capital and wage labor relationships are abolished? Only one alternative becomes possible: introduction of a system of free right of access to one's needs; the final realization of the revolutionary slogan, "From Each According to One's Ability; To Each According to One's Needs." Such a state of affairs does not require a population of kind-hearted people. What it does require is the removal of market restrictions on potential production capability with present supplies of raw materials and techniques. Just as the one-time revolutionary capitalist class required only the removal of feudal restrictions against trade and commerce in order to bring in a new and higher social order, so will a revolutionary proletariat eventually organize to abolish a market economy with all of its restraints against production.

Now Shaw was a notorious hedger of bets and can be quoted on both sides of many arguments. And the question of the potential for a free-access society was no exception. Fabianism, of course, envisioned a social order with the present arrangement of nations, trade, wage labor and capital relationships, but with general equalization of income and with nobody, not even the titled aristocracy, being permitted to live idly without returning something of value to the community in production. Shaw made that viewpoint clear in his political writings.

But he did know of and did comment upon the position of Marxists on the nature of the new social order—the traditional Marxists, that is. As noted above, he had been friendly with William Morris and had praised his *News from Nowhere.* First, let us cite an example of his negative attitude on the question, as he put it in one of his frequent religious speeches:

> The weak point of communism is that it does not give the consumer any control of production. If all things that are produced are thrown into the common stock, and everybody comes to take what they want, the result might be that everybody will not find what they want. The only way is to give everybody an equal

> income. The wonderfully beneficient invention of money makes this possible. (*Religious Speeches of Bernard* Shaw, Pennsylvania State University Press, p. 58.)

The implication here, of course, is that greed would take over; the grabbers would cart it all home. It is a common argument that flies in the face of all reason and dodges the real question – induced scarcity in the interests of the market. The emphasis in modern capitalism must be, How cán we keep from turning out more goods than the market can absorb? How to keep from piling up unsalable inventories – unsalable in the face of mass poverty and downright starvation.

On the other hand, we run into that proposition about one-half way through his 100-page Preface to *Androcles and the Lion* (1915), a commentary on Jesus, his disciples and apostles. In his section headed "Money: The Midwife of Scientific Communism" he discusses the pros and cons of classical communism as was, he contends, advocated by Jesus:

> It may be asked here by some simple-minded reader why we should not resort to crude Communism as the disciples were told to do. This would be quite practicable in a village where production was limited to the supply of the primitive wants which nature imposes on all human beings alike. We know that people need bread and boots without waiting for them to come and ask for these things and offer to pay for them. But when civilization advances to the point at which articles are produced that no man absolutely needs and that only some men fancy or can use, it is necessary that individuals should be able to have things made to their order and at their own cost. It is safe to provide bread for everybody because everybody wants and eats bread; but it would be absurd to provide microscopes and trombones, pet snakes and polo mallets, alembics and test tubes for everybody, as nine-tenths of them would be wasted; and the nine-tenths of the population who do not use such things would object to their being provided at all. We have in the invaluable instrument called money a means of enabling every individual to order and pay for the particular things he desires over and above the things he must consume in order to remain alive, plus the things the State insists on his having and using whether he wants to or not: for example, clothes, sanitary arrangements, armies and navies. . . (*Nine Plays: Bernard Shaw*, p. 890–91).

So it would seem, thus far, that Shaw deemed classical communism ("From each . . . to each . . .") to be unworkable outside a village economy. But wait: he makes another concession and all in the same paragraph:

> In large communities, where even the most eccentric demands for manufactured articles average themselves out until they can be foreseen within a negligible margin of error, direct communism (Take what you want without payment, as the people do in Morris's *News from Nowhere*) will, after a little experience, be found not only practicable but highly economical to an extent that now seems impossible. The sportsmen, the musicians, the physicists, the biologists will get their apparatus for the asking as easily as their bread, or, as at present, their paving, street lighting, and bridges; and the deaf man will not object to contribute to communal flutes when the musician has to contribute to communal ear trumpets. There are cases (for example, radium) in which the demand may be limited to the merest handful of laboratory workers, and in which nevertheless the whole community must pay because the price is beyond the means of any individual worker . . . (ibid, p. 891).

And even though he cannot shake the concept of cost and price and the continuation of the State with its coercive forces (armies and navies), these are concessions in this 1915 treatise that go beyond his economics of later years — or, for that matter, of the record from some of his writings previous to 1915.

But he stops short here of advocating outright abolition of money in its entirety. It will still, to some extent, be necessary, he insists. He is somehow able to isolate money from the economic relationships that make it essential:

> But even when the utmost allowance is made for extensions of communism that now seem fabulous, there will still remain for a long time to come regions of supply and demand in which men will need and use money or individual credit, and for which, therefore, they might have individual incomes. Foreign travel is an obvious instance. We are so far from even national communism still, that we shall probably have considerable developments of local communism before it becomes possible for a Manchester man to go up to London for a day without taking any money with him. The modern practical form of the

> communism of Jesus is therefore, for the present, equal distribution of the surplus of the national income that is not absorbed by simple communism. (Ibid, p. 891.)

And the foregoing excerpt from his Preface to *Androcles and the Lion* is apparently as close as he ever got to acknowledging the feasibility of the Marxist image of communism in action. This image is not nearly close enough and shot full of contradiction and confusion, carrying with it the trappings of class society, trappings which would not belong any more than would a buggy whip and a bale of hay belong as emergency items for an automobile or plane trip. In his major works on economics and politics, since then, he stayed close to his concept of a commodity society based upon buying and selling and the use of money—albeit apportioned equally by a benevolent State.

But how would such present evils as ostentatious luxury in the midst of poverty be eliminated through equalization of income? How would one guarantee that some people still would not prefer to buy necklaces, booze or fancy dogs before necessities? And, after all, don't the manufacturers and processors of luxury items provide employment? Shaw answers that argument forcefully:

> It is no excuse for such a state of things that the rich give employment. There is no merit in giving employment: a murderer gives employment to the hangman; and a motorist who runs over a child gives employment to an ambulance porter, a doctor, an undertaker, a clergyman, a mourning dress-maker, a hearse driver, a gravedigger: in short, to so many worthy people that when he ends by killing himself it seems ungrateful not to erect a statue to him as a public benefactor. The money with which the rich give the wrong sort of employment would give the right sort of employment if it were equally distributed; for then there would be no money offered for motor cars and diamonds until everyone was fed, clothed, and lodged, nor any wages offered to men and women to leave useful employments and become servants to idlers. There would be less ostentation, less idleness, less wastefulness, less uselessness; but there would be more food, more clothing, better houses, more security, more health, more virtue: in a word, more real prosperity. (*Intelligent Woman's Guide*, p. 52.)

And leaving aside the examples of his placing certain concepts, to a large extent, in proper if unfamiliar perspective to most people, Shaw herein hits one of his own misconceptions right on the button. Of the various dictionary definitions of *employ,* that best suited to the context of the above extract is, "to provide a job and a livelihood." Now this is no quibble for Shaw was nobody's fool when it came to the use and understanding of words. He was a wordsmith of the first order. He had to have known that to grant employment and a livelihood implies the authority to make such a gesture and, conversely, those in a position to need it.

In other words, Shaw's ideal nation would not represent the interests of all members of society any more than does the present state. It would be, one assumes from his copious writings, a sort of benevolent dictatorship (analogous to the *Tyrannies* of ancient Greece), ruled by the cultured middle and upper middle class. The manual, machine, and service workers of all types would be guaranteed employment—an equal share in the national income—and his own class would be stripped of its idlers, its members having all of the work they could handle turning out literary and artistic creations. At the head of government would be some modern Pisistratus—as far as England was concerned—bearing the title *Lord* (or, perhaps, *Lady*).

But of course that sort of concept, to Scientific Socialists, is not at all sublime and more than a little ridiculous. The Marxian revolutionary slogan "From Each . . . to Each" is good enough for most Socialists. An even more precise one, used by the descendants of those 1904 "Impossibilists" (the Socialist Party of Great Britain) who defected from the Hyndman S.D.F. and who, quite possibly, inspired Shaw to write his satirical piece on old Joe Budgett, the 100 percent non-compromiser (referred to later on), is: *Free right of access to what is in and on the earth by all mankind,* a subject we will also explore in due course.

For the moment, however, let us continue with Shaw. He saw the problem as one of widening public and municipal services, which he believed to be communism in action from away back in his career, and to make all men "supermen." In the first instance he shows what seems ignorance of, or utter disregard of, Marx's development of surplus value which he, nevertheless if only incidentally, praised in his footnote in *Fabian Essays* and, in passing, in *Intelligent Woman's Guide*, and briefly in *Everybody's Political What's What?* In the second instance, he seems to be putting the cart before his own horse, arguing that one must first change mankind in order to change society. Let us examine some evidence.

Some Shavian Economic Acrobatics

> There are many things that only a few people understand or use which nevertheless everybody pays for because without them we should have no learning, no books, no pictures, no high civilization. We have public galleries of the best pictures and statues, public libraries of the best books, public observatories in which astronomers watch the stars and mathematicians make abstruse calculations, public laboratories in which scientific men are supposed to add to our knowledge of the universe. These institutions cost a great deal of money to which we all have to contribute. Many of us never enter a gallery or a museum or a library even when we live within easy reach of them; and not one person in ten is interested in astronomy or mathematics or physical science; but we all have a general notion that these things are necessary; and so we do not object to pay for them.
>
> Besides, many of us do not know that we pay for them; we think we get them as kind presents from somebody. In this way a good deal of Communism has been established without our knowing anything about it... (*The Intelligent Woman's Guide*..., p. 16).

And so on.

Now one thing Shaw does make clear in the above extract: he may have praised Marx, on occasion, for his analysis of surplus value and there is even some evidence that he had a working grasp of it, but he was an expert at straddling two horses – each headed in an opposite direction – at the same time. Are museums and libraries examples of Communism in action? Let us retrace a bit of his acrobatics.

First, he made no bones about his rejection of Marx's Labor Theory of Value. So he did not see, or agree, that the worker produces a commodity, labor power, which he sells on the market at the market price, when he can command it, and at its value in the long haul. Not that he had no inkling of the predicament of the proletariat. He did even though he misunderstood the relationships. To him, the proletarian had no commodity whatever to sell in order to get his neccessities of life and so had to sell himself to the highest bidder. He puts it thus:

> The idea seems a desperate one; but it proves quite easy to carry out. The tenant cultivators of the land have not strength enough or time enough to exhaust the productive capacity of their holdings. If they could buy men in the market for less than these men's labor would add to the produce, then the purchase of such men would be a sheer gain. It would indeed be only a purchase in form: the men would literally cost nothing, since they would produce their own price, with a surplus for the buyer. Never in the history of buying and selling was there so splendid a bargain for buyers as this. Aladdin's uncle's offer of new lamps for old ones was in comparison a catchpenny. Accordingly, the proletarian no sooner offers himself for sale than he finds a rush of bidders for him, each striving to get the better of the other by offering to give him more and more of the produce of labor, and to content themselves with less and less surplus. But even the highest bidder must have some surplus, or he will not buy. The proletarian, in accepting the highest bid, sells himself openly into bondage... (from "The Economic Basis of Socialism," *Selected Prose*, p. 704).

So, palpably, there is some recognition here, even if a little upside-down, of the validity of surplus value and of the underlying fraud in capitalist bookkeeping which establishes fiction for fact—wages as a cost of production to the capitalist. Actually, the process works like this, throughout industry.

"Look what I have to do with most of my profit!" says the capitalist. "I have to plow it back into plant, equipment, and R & R." But that isn't profit he plows back. It is surplus value, though, and it is produced for him gratis by his workers. So he gets his wage labor free because he recovers the money-capital he has advanced when he sells his commodities; and he gets his plant, equipment, taxes and profits from the surplus value. You can't beat the price he pays for being a capitalist. He has an Aladdin's lamp for certain!

But we do not get much of a real perspective from Shaw on the historical process that made that supply of freed (from the means of a livelihood) labor possible. Unlike Shaw, for whom it was generally a case of he who got there first to claim the land bidding with his neighbors for the services of the propertyless, Marx – in language stark and savage – explains in his chapter "Legislation against the Expropriated" the process of creating a dispossessed class:

> Thus were the agricultural people, first forcibly expropriated from the soil, driven from their homes, turned into vagabonds, and then whipped, branded, tortured by laws grotesquely terrible, into the discipline necessary for the wages system. (*Capital,* I, Kerr, ed., p. 809.)

For, essential as ownership of land and industry is to a budding capitalist class, without a ready supply of free labor there can be no surplus value and no profit. Indeed, ownership in itself is not enough to make one a capitalist. One is still in the bud until one hires labor to produce surplus values. And, we should note well, that from its earliest beginnings the competitive nature of capitalism forced buyers of commodity labor power to buy it at its lowest possible price in order that commodities, generally, could be produced and sold more cheaply than those of the competition. The emphasis was on buying at the lowest price, not on bidding higher than the competition although that undoubtedly does play a role. The trick is to buy labor power at the cheapest price possible or, what amounts to the same thing, increase the output (productivity) of the worker, by hook or by crook, in order to realize more surplus value. *That* is the bottom line!

Needless to say, capitalism has learned that more flies are garnered with honey than with swatters. The entire system of exploitation – thanks to the "head-fixing industry" (education) – is now all but universally considered as natural and normal and those who oppose it kooky. Nor are any of the hallmarks of capitalism missing in the Socialist and Communist world, other than the vocabulary used to describe them.

But Shaw is also in grave contradiction when he throws out the Labor Theory of Value, yet seems to acknowledge the validity of surplus value. For the labor theory accounts for the bondage of the proletariat and, in fact, for surplus value. The fact is that, despite Shaw's denial, the worker does own one commodity which he sells in order to get his necessities of life—his labor power. (He does not sell himself as Shaw would have it. Such a relationship belonged to a previous historical epoch than capitalism, certain atypical exceptions such as the chattel slavery of plantation capitalism notwithstanding.) And commodity labor power, according to Marx, must sell on the average and in the long run according to the socially necessary labor time it takes to produce and reproduce it.

So, flowing from this, (1) the proletarians are getting all that is due them under the rules of capitalism (even in municipal and in state-owned industry), and (2) they do not pay for public libraries, art galleries, parks, or anything else that is paid for through tax revenues. Not in the long run, anyway. All of the cost of public and municipal service and industry comes from surplus value, which the proletarians do produce, for a certainty, but which they just as certainly do not own—under the rules of the system that they support. Surplus value is the property of the capitalist class. And if Shaw saw fit to at least acknowledge and compliment Marx on discovering and laying bare that "category," why could he not see the ramifications of it and follow it through?

So the entire approach of Shaw was to build upon nationalization and municipalization. He went to great lengths to show that when it came down to harbors, dockyards and the Post Office, capitalists are content to stay out of it because such industry operates much more cheaply and efficiently than it could were it privately owned. Like the libraries and the art galleries it is, according to Fabianism, an example of socialism (or communism) in action—and instituted by the capitalists themselves!

True as much of that statement appears to be, there are serious flaws in the reasoning. The fact is that such industries also operate under the rules of capitalism, and in the intended interests of the capitalist class or the state capitalist bureaucracy; and the emoluments received by the working people who operate them are determined in the same way as wage/salaried labor "reward" is determined in privately owned industry. As for the existence of libraries and museums, they are essential to the future—and the present—interests of capitalism or they would not be permitted to exist. True, they do provide valuable information that can also be used by awakening working people in the struggle for general emancipation from class society but that is a penalty capitalists must take.

Of course there is more than a germ of truth to the Fabian argument that socialism—the possibility of its materialization, at any rate—has been made possible by capitalism. Were it not for the discovery and the introduction of mass production techniques, and the necessary cultivation of a "One World" ideology through such institutions as the United Nations—without that sort of capitalist-instigated societal evolution—world socialism would be unimaginable. In fact, capitalism certainly has made it possible for world socialism, technically, to operate with smoothness and with minor birth pangs. The very process of operating the industries of production and distribution will not be all that different from what it will be at the time of world socialist revolution. The one important change will be that instead of being operated as commodity-instigated society, production and distribution will be based only on the needs of all mankind. The fetters on such production and distribution will be removed.

4. Shaw on Political Democracy

A pet gripe of some Socialists is the use of the qualifying adjective "democratic," by others, to differentiate themselves from the Bolshevik-style Communists. In actuality, the Socialist struggle throughout its history has been primarily one of struggle for democracy against the dictator-type regimes of late feudal-agrarianism – such as that of Bismarck in Germany and the tsarist governments of Imperial Russia – and late capitalism – Hitler, Mussolini, and others.

So the phrase "democratic socialism" to the more traditional Marxist is a tautology that lends credence to the fiction that there could be such a phenomenon as dictatorial socialism. Traditional Marxists usually counter with the emphatic assertion that there can be no real democracy without world socialism, nor can there be genuine socialism without democracy.

Bernard Shaw made no bones about his distaste for democracy; he was a champion of what is thought of as "dictatorial socialism." In order to get a proper understanding of his embrace of the European dictators – both left and right – it should be instructive to take a look at his attitude toward political democracy. Contradictory as he was in so many of his utterances he seemed to be firm in his jaundiced viewpoint of parliamentary democracy and universal suffrage. He did not consider such institutions as essential, or even valuable, in the struggle by Socialists to overthrow capitalism. He made his viewpoint in that area clear enough in his *Intelligent Woman's Guide:*

> The old parliamentary democrats were accomplished and endless talkers; but their unreal theory that nothing political

> must be done until it was understood and demanded by a majority of the people (which meant in effect that nothing political must ever be done at all) had disabled them as men of action; and when causal bodies of impatient and irresponsible proletarian men of action attempted to break up Capitalism without knowing how to do it, or appreciating the nature and necessity of government, a temper spread in which it was possible for Signor Mussolini to be made absolute managing director (Dictator or Duce) of the Italian nation as its savior from parliamentary impotence and democratic indiscipline. (P. 347.)

And, in the manner of one who was never at a loss for words, he went on:

> Socialism, however, cannot perish in these political storms and changes. Socialists have courted Democracy, and even called Socialism Social-Democracy to proclaim that the two are inseparable. Socialism is committed neither way. It faces Caesars and soviets, Presidents and Patriarchs, British cabinets and Italian Dictators or Popes, patrician oligarchs and plebeian demagogues, with its unshaken demonstration that they cannot have a stable and prosperous state without equality of income. They may plead that such equality is ridiculous. That will not save them from the consequences of inequality. They must equate or perish. The despot who values his head and the crowd that fears for its liberty are equally concerned. I should call Socialism not Democratic but simply Catholic if that name had not been taken in vain so often by so many Churches that nobody would understand me. (Pp. 347–8.)

So, despite his Fabian proclivities and the fact that its approach was intimately tied in with democracy—actually regarding the then-current democratic development as socialism in action on a lower plane, and despite his not (as of that time) gone all the way in intellectual alignment with the dictatorships, he was certainly more in tune with them than with democracy.

But he had much more to say on the subject, back in 1928, making his distaste for capitalism's democracy even more apparent: In Chapter 42 of his *Guide to Socialism* he unburdened himself of the following:

> It is a funny place, this world of Capitalism, with its astonishing spread of ignorance and helplessness, boasting all

> the time of its spread of education and enlightenment...Excuse my going on like this: but as I am a writer of books and plays myself, I know the folly and peril of it better than you do. And when I see that this moment of our utmost ignorance and helplessness, delusion and folly, has been stumbled upon by the blind forces of Capitalism as the moment for giving votes to everybody so that the few wise women are hopelessly overruled by the thousands whose political minds, as far as they can be said to have any political minds at all, have been formed in the cinema, I realize that I had better stop writing plays for a while to discuss political and social realities in this book with those who are intelligent enough to listen to me. (Pp. 163–4.)

Shaw's book, it should be noted, was addressed particulary to women of the "middle class"; club women who had asked him to explain his theories on socialism and capitalism. These were, essentially, property-owning women and there almost seems to have been a sort of petulant reasonableness—in that context—in what he was telling them. After all, he seemed to be implying, capitalists do not make a practice of having representatives from their hired hands sit in membership—or even cast votes—in the decision-making operations of their boards of directors. Perhaps Shaw, in the manner of a Marxian, rather than a Fabian, socialist, did regard the nation as a magnified business: The John Bull Manufacturing, Importing, Exporting, and General Merchandising Co., Ltd., with the government constituting its board of directors. If he did, however, the thought was more in line with what he thought it ought to be.

Now, one of the more fundamental quarrels that traditional Marxists have with the Bolshevik-style radicals is the insistence of the latter that the working class does not possess the mental capability of emancipating itself. Indeed, that essentially is also the attitude of Social Democrats and Fabians. As for Lenin, the number-one Bolshevik of his times, he maintained that the Revolution would have to be organized and led by a vanguard of professional revolutionists recruited from the ranks of the intelligentsia (an integral section of Shaw's middle class); and, as we have noted in our chapter on the Fabians, such was pretty much the attitude of the Shavian Socialists. In fact, it can be said that Shaw "wrote the book" on that theory even before Lenin.

The message runs through the *Fabian Essays* and some of his other early writings (*An Unsocial Socialist, Man and Superman,* and *Major Barbara*). It is explained in detail, however, in his *Intelligent Woman's Guide*... which was published a few years after Lenin's death.

So there you have it! Shaw's utter contempt for the minds of the working class—and the capitalist class as well, for that matter. Furthermore, the capitalist system, as he saw it, has gouged out or, at the very least, over-diluted their political brains to the extent that universal suffrage, rather than being a large step toward emancipation from class society—as traditional Marxian Socialists have always maintained—is actually but another stumbling block in the path of those few heroes and heroines who do understand what is needed to save us all from disaster! "The few wise women," said Shaw, "are hopelessly overruled by the thousands whose political minds as far as they can be said to have any political minds at all, have been formed in the cinema." Ah yes! But had Shaw, in his soapboxing days, been advocating the abolition of capitalism with all of its hallmarks—wages, money, buying and selling, national boundaries—he would have discovered how amazingly similar were the objections from his working class audiences to those of his cultured friends (and his own, for that matter). The "Headfixing Industry" operated democratically, even in those early years of this century, to mold attitudes in harmony with capitalism's interests, and did so without regard to class or "higher" education—as it still does.

Now it might, of course, be argued that Shaw's definitely political works such as *The Intelligent Woman's Guide*... and *The Fabian Essays* of a couple of generations earlier, even, have been out of print for many years and are not well known today. Fair enough, but the identical views are expressed in his prefaces to plays and have also been injected into the plays themselves, most of which are staged from time to time and or read in the various collections one finds on the shelves of public libraries. *On the Rocks* is a good example of a portrayal of the Shavian view of political democracy. It is centered on the Great Depression of the "Hungry Thirties" and its effects in Britain. His leading character is Sir Arthur Chavender, prime minister and a man who, after his conversion to Marx after having read the *entire* literature of Marxism on a two-week retreat to a specialized convalescent home dedicated to healing underexercised brains, obviously reflects the political opinions of Shaw. The Prime Minister speaks:

> Well, here is my ace of trumps. The people of this country, and of all the European countries, and of America, are at present sick of being told that, thanks to democracy, they are the real government of the country. They know very well that they dont govern and cant govern and know nothing about Government except that it always supports profiteering, and doesnt really respect anything else, no matter what party flag it waves. They are sick of twaddle about liberty when they have no liberty. They are sick of idling and loafing about on doles when they are not drudging for wages too beggarly to pay the rents of anything better than overcrowded one-room tenements. They are sick of me and sick of you and sick of the whole lot of us. They want to eat and drink the wheat and coffee that the profiteers are burning because they cant sell it at a profit. They want to hang people who burn good food when people are going hungry. They cant set matters right themselves; to they want rulers who will discipline them and make them do it instead of making them do the other thing. They are ready to go mad with enthusiams for any man strong enough to make them do anything, even if it is only Jew baiting, provided it's something tyrannical, something coercive, something that we all pretend no Englishman would submit to, though weve known ever since we gave them the vote that theyd submit to anything. (*The Bodley Head Bernard Shaw Collected Plays with Their Prefaces*, 6, p. 705.)

What's wrong with this message from a Scientific Socialist viewpoint? Perhaps as good an answer as we could give is contained in a brief review of that play in the journal of a Scientific Socialist party, *The Socialist Standard*, London (Socialist Party of Great Britain), September 1975:

> **ON THE ROCKS**
>
> The MERMAID THEATRE has revived Bernard Shaw's play *On the Rocks*, written in 1933 and given an up-to-date ring by the present depression. It is Britain that is on the rocks, with the

unemployed protesting and the Prime Minister at his wits' end. Enter an ancient left-winger, who tips off the Premier about Marx, and a lady homeopath, who prescribes a rest in which he reads all Marx's works.

Act two: Prime Minister, converted, is announcing the nationalization of practically everything thereby winning approval from financiers, landowners, police, etc. and the disapproval of the working class. Defeated by a Tory-Labour alliance, he retires from politics, accepting the left-wing sage's (Shaw speaking) view that a dictator is the solution.

It is excellently performed by a capable cast; much of *On the Rocks* is great fun. The types—trimming Prime Minister, choleric Tory, working-class representatives fiery and intellectual and stolid—are as recognizable as the situation, and Shaw's digs and quips are highly enjoyable. Who could resist the diagnosis that the Prime Minister ails not from over work but because his brain is unoccupied?

The trouble about it is, of course, the messge. For the sake of the play, overlook the idea of Marx's economics being absorbed in a fortnight; be charitable, and let pass also the allegation that nationalization is Marxism. What Shaw argues in this play is that democracy is no good. It has led nowhere and the working class has had enough of it. What they want is to be told what to do by a strong man who not only knows the answers but has the will to enforce them.

Shaw was speaking *post facto*, apparently without realizing it. Mussolini and Hitler had established themselves by 1933. Shaw expressed his admiration of them: *On the Rocks* contends with the voice of one who has seen everything else tried, for more of it. Their rise was for the reason given, that democracy had failed. Yet how had it failed? The European countries had had one or two generations of full or partial suffrage: during which Labour and social-democratic reformism, for which Shaw was a spokesman, had promised the earth and produced only misery. As a result, large numbers of working people thought democracy useless, and were ready to listen to the demagogues who said so.

It is Shaw's Fabianism that is shown on the rocks and waggishly saying it needs a strong man to rescue it, regardless of expense. An evening at the Mermaid can be recommended—good theatrical entertainment and food for thought. (R.B.)

And it is more than likely that Shaw's muddled grasp of Marxism was, like that of his fictional prime minister, largely founded on his "absorption" of the Marxian classics in too brief a time span. In fact, the text of the play has the P.M. reading not only the works of Marx in that brief fortnight at the lady homeopath's rest home. Here is the way Shaw did the dialogue ending Act One.:

> SIR ARTHUR. . . You will procure all the books you can find by a revolutionary German Jew named Harry Marks—
>
> HILDA (his sec'y.). Dont you mean Karl Marx?
>
> SIR ARTHUR. Thats the man. Karl Marx. Get me every blessed book by Karl Marx that you can find translated into English; and have them packed for the retreat.
>
> HILDA. There are much newer books by Marxists: Lenin and Trotsky and Stalin and people like that.
>
> SIR ARTHUR. Get them all. Pack the lot. By George, I'll teach Alderwoman Aloysia Brollikins to give herself airs. I'll teach her and her rabble of half-baked half-educated intellectual beggars-on-horseback that any Oxford man can beat them at their own silly game. I'll just turn Karl Marx inside-out for them. (*The household gong sounds*) Lunch! Come on: that woman's given me an appetite. . .

The Revolutionist's Handbook

G.B. Shaw wrote his *Man and Superman* and its Appendix, *The Revolutionist's Handbook,* back about the turn of the 20th century. In Section V of the *Handbook*—the work of his fictional protagonist John Tanner—he made plain his disapproval of universal suffrage and political democracy. He told us that what he called Proletarian Democracy, by which he meant universal suffrage, was forced upon the nation by the failure of previous systems that relied on individual "Supermen" acting as despots and oligarchs. This is how Tanner (Shaw) viewed the revolutionary new "Proletarian Democracy":

> Now we have yet to see the man, who, having any practical experience of Proletarian Democracy, has any belief in its capacity for solving great political problems, or even for doing ordinary parochial work intelligently and economically. Only under despotisms and oligarchs has the Radical faith in 'universal

> suffrage' as a political panacea arisen. It withers the moment it is exposed to practical trial, because Democracy cannot rise above the levels of the human material of which its voters are made. (*Nine Plays by Bernard Shaw.* N.Y.: Dodd, Mead, 1948; p. 704.)

In other words, if the vote is given to a population of mental incompetents (the proletariat), as Shaw—and traditional Bolsheviks, for that matter—deemed the working class to be, what should be expected other than what you have been getting? But there are strong indications, at least to many of those who pay close attention to history, that the bourgeoisie itself—Shaw's "middle class" employers of labor—prefer universal suffrage ("Proletarian Democracy") to dictatorships and only give noticeable support to political strong men of the Mussolini and Hitler type as a last resort, when popular support for such types is at a high level. Why?

To begin with, under political democracy and universal suffrage it is easier to gauge the temper of the population; what they are thinking on important subjects. Even in elections such as those in the United States, where voting is not compulsory, and where a relatively small percentage of eligible voters actually cast ballots, it is easier to detect tendencies than it is in one-party dictatorships.

It would seem to be apparent that, where universal suffrage is the norm, the vast numbers of working class voters will tend to regard themselves as an integral part of the nation, which is certainly preferable, to enlightened capitalists, to having them think of themselves as they really are—dispossessed wage slaves. Dictatorship nations of the left, and even the Nazi and Fascist regimes of bygone years, use a different ploy for hoodwinking their proletariat into the myth of joint ownership of the nation, a ploy which seems to have fooled Bernard Shaw and other prominent Fabians. They "abolish" capitalism!

But there is, also, a definite plus about universal suffrage for the working class and if relatively few realize it as yet, the day may well be coming when a significant majority will have organized politically to rid the world, finally and totally, of this last of the historic slave societies. The ballot, in itself, is not an educational tool; political awareness must come from the daily struggle in the workshops of capitalism and the continually mounting evidence that mere political reforms do nothing of consequence in alleviating working class misery and insecurity. But the ballot, when used intelligently, can serve two important purposes: (1) it can, as a thermometer, register the extent of working class awareness; and (2) it becomes an instrument for the final emancipation of all mankind from class society. Can it be easily taken away by a recalcitrant capitalist class? Not when there is a sufficient majority organized for meaningful change—revolution.

There was a time, long since past, when reforms within capitalism made some sense. Capitalism has not always had the capability of "overproducing" and flooding world markets with such ease as it has today. Nor has capitalism had the means, until relatively recent times, of wiping out all of mankind in war. It is now more vital than ever before in all of mankind's history to organize politically for world socialism and nothing short of it. Once a significant vote begins to materialize, the movement's growth should become geometrical rather than merely arithmetical, as it is today. Had John Tanner (GBS) emoted such a program from the stage in New York, or London, or wherever, back in 1915, the theatres might well have been raided by the police or the military—certainly in Britain where the government was embroiled in "the Great War," and he would have had scant sympathy from the Fabian Society whose membership, in the main, was supporting their government in that shambles as were the member parties of Social Democracy on the Continent. (Shaw, typically, can be quoted as criticizing *and* supporting his government's involvement, as we shall document in due course.)

In summing up his . . . *Handbook* segment on the "Political Need for the Superman," Shaw wrote:

> Finally, when social aggregation arrives at a point demanding international organization before the demagogues and electorates have learnt how to manage even a country parish properly much less internationalize Constantinople, the whole political business goes to smash; and presently we have Ruins of Empires, New Zealanders sitting on a broken arch of London Bridge, and so forth.

> To that recurrent catastrophe we shall certainly come again unless we can have a Democracy of Supermen; and the production of such a Democracy is the only change that is now hopeful enough to nerve us to the effort that Revolution demands.

And it is the production of a "Democracy of Supermen" that was paramount in his thinking for, as he made plain in *Handbook* in segment VII, Under the heading "Progress an Illusion," even the introduction of a Fabian social order without the population being made up of Supermen would be a long way from ideal. As he wrote:

> Of course, if the nation adopted the Fabian policy, it would be carried out by brute force exactly as our present property system is. It would become the law; and those who resisted it would be fined, sold up, knocked on the head by policemen, thrown into prison, and in the last resort "executed" just as they are when they break the present law . . . (ibid, p. 710).

So, to Shaw, while a social system based upon Fabian Socialism was possible with the population as it was, the main effort of the revolutionist should be the production of a society of Supermen.

He had already discussed this viewpoint in his section III, "The Perfectionist Experiment at Oneida Creek":

> The Perfectionists were mightily shepherded by their chief [John Humphrey] Noyes, one of those chance attempts at the superman which occur from time to time in spite of the interference of Man's blundering institutions. The existence of Noyes simplified the breeding problem for the Communists, the question as to what sort of man they should strive to breed being settled at once by the obvious desirability of breeding another Noyes. (Ibid, p. 699.)

Then Tanner begins to show why this experiment was bound to fail. He continues:

> But an experiment conducted by a handful of people, who, after thirty years of immunity from the unintentional child slaughter that goes on by ignorant parents in private homes,

> numbered only 300, could do very little except prove that Communists, under the guidance of a Superman 'devoted exclusively to the establishment of the Kingdom of God,' and caring no more for property and marriage than a Camberwell minister cares for Hindoo Caste or Suttee, might make a much better job of their lives than ordinary folk under the harrow of both these institutions. Yet this Superman himself admitted that this apparent success was only part of the abnormal phenomenon of his own occurrence; for when he came to the end of his powers through age, he himself guided and organized the voluntary relapse of the Communists into marriage, capitalism, and customary private life, thus admitting that the real social solution was not what a casual Superman could persuade a picked company to do for him, but what a whole community of Supermen would do spontaneously. If Noyes had had to organize, not a few dozen Perfectionists, but the whole United States, America would have beaten him as completely as England beat Oliver Cromwell, France Napoleon, or Rome Julius Caesar . . . (ibid, pp. 699–700).

So far so good? Not really! For the image one gets from this is one of a lone "Superman" trying to overthrow capitalism by organizing an entire population to operate a colony without first taking action to capture the political state. And of course that would be nothing short of lunacy. But what is Tanner really driving at? Is that really the problem or is there something more fundamental missing than conscious, political socialist, action? It all becomes clear some distance down the page:

> At certain moments there may even be a considerable material advance, as when the conquest of political power by the working class produces a better distribution of wealth through the simple action of the selfishness of the new masters; but all this is mere readjustment and reformation; until the heart and mind of the people is changed the very greatest man will no more dare to govern on the assumption that all are as great as he than a drover dare leave his flock to find its way through the streets as he himself would. Until there is an England in which every man is a Cromwell, a France in which every man is a Napoleon, a Rome in which every man is a Caesar, a Germany in which every man is a Luther plus a Goethe, the world will be no more improved by its heroes than a Brixton villa is improved by the pyramid of Cheops. The production of such nations is the only real change possible to us. (Ibid, pp. 700–01.)

And here, Shaw summed up as well as any place in his work, his own quarrel with (if not misunderstanding of) the Marxist approach. As we have already noted, Marxists maintain that man cannot be examined, meaningfully, apart from his society. Ordinary man's general attitudes—political, religious, and philosophical—are conditioned by the relationships, at least to a dominant degree, of the society in which he lives and earns his living. The "school" of wage slavery eventually must bring recognition to the toilers that they are, in fact, but slaves despite the songs of freedom, the pledges of allegiance to a "commonly-owned" nation, and other forms of ruling class propaganda lavished on them from childhood on. But this will be a class conscious realization, not one imparted by a "Superman" of any sort. As it is, in the final analysis, their leaders—"supermen" or not—are but followers themselves. They can lead only in the direction that their "followers" wish to go. Shaw should have learned that fact of life from his many years as a propagandist.

But that is the Scientific Socialist approach with which Shaw never in all of his productive life agreed. During all of his career he advocated political leadership (dictatorship) of the Lenin and Stalin, Mussolini, Hitler, and Franco varieties—during their regimes and before such regimes were given thought. Nor did the actual advent of such brutalitarianisms deter him; on the contrary, for he went overboard in his approval of all of the European dictatorships, not just the Bolsheviks, which fooled perhaps a majority of professed Marxian Socialists as well as it fooled Shaw.

He had an obsession for "supermen." In fact the theme of how to get a population of supermen was explored and developed further in some of his later, post-Bolshevik Revolution writing. For example:

> The notion that a civilized State can be made out of any sort of human material is one of our old Radical delusions. As to building Communism with such trash as the Capitalist system produces it is out of the question. For a Communist Utopia we need a population of Utopians; and Utopians do not grow wild on the bushes nor are they to be picked up in the slums; they have to be cultivated very carefully and expensively. Peasants will not do; yet without the peasants the Communists could never have

> captured the Russian Revolution. Nominally it was the Soviets of peasants and soldiers who backed Lenin and saved Communism when all Western Europe set on him like a pack of hounds on a fox. But as all the soldiers were peasants, and all the peasants hungry for property, the military only added to the peasants' cry of Give us land, the soldiers' cry of Give us peace. Lenin said, in effect, Take the land; and if feudally minded persons obstruct you, exterminate them; but do not burn their houses, as you will need them to live in. . . . (Preface to *On the Rocks,* Bodley Head, ed., p. 597.)

So that was the Shavian recipe for a socialist society: First, use "trash" to help get the "supermen" into political power. Then, without wasting time, weed out all degrees and types of "trash" left by capitalism, through the extermination process. With what is left, build a society of Supermen.

5. Shaw on the Soviet Union

As already noted, Shaw was not much more than lukewarm in his estimate of "socialism" in Bolshevik Russia when he wrote his *Intelligent Woman's Guide to Socialism and Capitalism* in 1928. Other than acknowledging, in the customary manner, the "overthrow of Capitalism" in Russia by the Communists of that nation, he had nothing glowing to say about it. In fact, some years later, when writing of his brief tour of Russia in 1931, he explained his earlier, negative, feelings:

> When Lenin came to power . . . I was . . . offered a very handsome commission by Mr. William Randolph Hearst to go to Russia and describe what there was to see there; but I refused because I knew only too well that what I should see was Capitalism in ruins and not Communism in excelsis . . . (*Autobiography, 1898–1950*).

That, of course, was in 1917 or thereabouts. He was apparently still somewhat negative about it in 1928 when he had written:

> In England, when Socialism is consummated it will plant the red flag on the summit of an already constructed pyramid; but the Russians have to build right up from the sand. We must build up Capitalism before we can turn it into Socialism. But meanwhile we must learn how to control it instead of letting it demoralize us, slaughter us, and half ruin us, as we have hitherto done in our ignorance. (*Intelligent Women's Guide* . . . , p. 376.)

And this statement might almost seem to indicate that he did have some significant grasp of Socialist essentials. At least it would seem that he saw the impossibility of socialism where mass production techniques were generally absent. So why, then, the nod to the Bolsheviks for their "overthrow" of something that hardly existed? After all, as Karl Marx expressed it, clearly, in his Preface to the first edition of *Capital:*

> One nation can and should learn from others. And even when a society has got upon the right track for the discovery of the natural laws of its movement. . . it can neither clear by bold leaps, nor remove by legal enactments, the obstacles offered by the successive phases of its normal development. But it can shorten and lessen the birth pangs. . . (Kerr, ed., pp. 14, 15).

Applying this reasoning to the Union of Soviet Socialist Republics, it would seem to be patent, then, that the best the Bolshevik regime could do was just what they have been doing since 1917—at least in essence—guiding the Soviet Union through its era of capitalist development however many years, decades, and generations are needed before it, and the world, generally, can achieve socialism.

Of course, the Bolsheviks never admitted that they have been doing just that. What they did was to "remove by legal enactment" (as Marx wrote could not be done) an obstacle of definition. The term *socialism* was re-defined to mean a "transition period" between capitalism and socialism during which one performs according to one's abilities and receives according to the quantity and quality of one's work (not according to one's needs, which had been the way that the revolutionary slogan was always worded), but which would not be possible of attainment until full-blown Communism has been achieved. In any case, whatever one calls it, the predominant social relationships of capitalism—wage labor and capital—are the order of the day in the Soviet Union so if it is different it is a difference without distinction.

But Shaw was even more critical of the early Bolsheviks in that 1928 work of his. On page 459 he asserted:

> Karl Marx would have recoiled if he had been foreshown what happened in Russia from 1917 to 1921 through the action of able and devoted men who made his writings their Bible.

Not that these "able and devoted men" were to be considered as bad, or evil. In order to help dispel such a notion he hastened to add:

> Good people are the very devil sometimes, because, when their good-will hits on a wrong way, they go much further along it and are much more ruthless than bad people; but there is always hope in the fact that they mean well, and that their bad deeds are the mistakes and not their successes; whereas the evils done by bad people are not mistakes but triumphs of wickedness.

A pertinent illustration of one of those "good people" who could turn into the very devil while carrying out deeds intended as good and humane, according to Shaw, was Felix Dzerzhinsky, director of the dreaded Secret Police of the Soviet Union, whom Shaw referred to as "gentle." In his Preface to *The Simpleton of the Unexpected Isles* he justifies and sympathizes with the perpetrator of the "evil deeds" with hardly a tear for the victims:

> Conceive, then, our horror when the Inquisition suddenly rose up again in Russia. It began as the Tcheka; then it became the Gay-pay-oo (Ogpu); now it has settled down as part of the ordinary police force. The worst of its work is over; the heretics are either liquidated, converted, or intimidated. But it was indispensable in its prime. The Bolsheviks, infected as they were with English Liberal and Agnostic notions, at first tried to do without it; but the result was that the unfortunate Commissars who had to make the Russian industries and transport services work, found themselves obliged to carry pistols and execute saboteurs and lazy drunkards with their own hands. Such a Commissar was Dzerzinsky, now, like Lenin, entombed in the Red Square. He was not a homicidally disposed person; but when it fell to his lot to make the Russian trains run at all costs, he had to force himself to shoot a station master who found it easier to drop telegrams into the waste paper basket than to attend to them. And it was this gentle Dzerzinsky who, unable to endure the duties of an executioner (even had he had time for them), organized the Tcheka. (*Bernard Shaw: Collected Plays with Their Prefaces,* Vol. VI, N.Y.: Dodd, Mead, 1975; pp. 753–54.)

And Shaw, like some talented and eloquent attorney for the defense, pleaded the case of the Tcheka:

> Now the Tcheka, being an Inquisition and not an ordinary police court dealing under written statutes and established precedents with defined offences, and sentencing the offenders to prescribed penalties, had to determine whether certain people were public spirited enough to live in a Communist society, and if not, to blow their brains out as public nuisances. If you would not work and pull your weight in the Russian boat, then the Tcheka had to make you do it by convincing you that you would be shot if you persisted in your determination to be a gentleman. For the national emergencies were then desperate; and the compulson to overcome them had to be fiercely in earnest.
>
> I, an old Irishman, am too used to Coercion Acts, suspensions of the Habeas Corpus Act, and the like, to have any virtuous indignation left to spare for the blunders and excesses into which the original Tcheka, as a body of well intentioned amateurs, no doubt fell before it had learnt the limits of its business by experience. (Ibid, pp. 754–55.)

And who were these people whom—in the Tcheka's and Shaw's opinion—were not fit to live in a Communist society? In this same Preface, Shaw explains:

> Now the heretic in Russia . . . is not content with a quiet abstract dissent from the State religion of Soviet Russia: he is an active, violent, venomous saboteur. He plans and carries out breakages of machinery, falsifies books and accounts to produce insolvencies, leaves the fields unsown or the harvests to rot unreaped, and slaughters farm stock in millions even at the cost of being half-starved (sometimes wholly starved) by the resultant "famine" in his fanatical hatred of a system which makes it impossible for him to become a gentleman. Toleration is impossible: the heretic-saboteur will not tolerate the State religion; consequently the State could not tolerate him even if it wanted to. (Ibid, pp. 752–53.)

But the resistance and sabotage by Kulaks (allegedly well-off peasants, mostly in the Ukraine) was triggered by the collectivization-of-farms policy of Stalin, the direct antithesis of the original Bolshevik policy of "land to the peasants." In truth, the support for the Bolsheviks by the peasantry was premised on the Bolshevik promise to turn them into land-owning farmers. Were they "public spirited enough to live in a 'Communist' society"? Obviously not—not even had they realized that the social system was state capitalism rather than communism—and had they dreamt of such an eventuality as forced collectivization of their newly-acquired property they certainly would not have supported the Bolsheviks in the revolutionary times of a decade earlier, with the likely result—in such an eventuality—that there would have been no successful Bolshevik Revolution in November of 1917.

And all of that calls to mind a particularly pithy and caustic comment on Shaw by Alexander Woolcott having to do with Shaw's defense of the liquidation of the Kulaks:

> It suddenly occurs to me that his angers and emphases are more understandable to any reader who realizes that there is one scent which offends the Shavian nostrils beyond all others, one smell which, quite literally, maddens him. That is the odor of burning flesh. He has, for instance, been able to contemplate the Soviet liquidation of the kulaks with singular equanimity so long as these recalcitrant farmers are merely exiled in droves or shot like grouse. But I seriously believe that if the Communists were to burn one of them at the stake, the Kremlin would lose Bernard Shaw overnight. (*While Rome Burns.* N.Y.: The Viking Press, 1935.)

A Woolcott gibe at Shaw's vegetarianism!

And Shaw's generally approving comments on the Soviet government's Great Kulak Liquidation, brings to the fore another of those more outlandish contradictions of himself, by himself, that makes quoting him risky unless one attempts to read *everything* that he wrote—a tough assignment! For, although in his *Shaw—"The Chucker-out,"* (Ams Press, 1971) Allan Chappelow makes the same charge re Shaw's defense of the liquidation, referring to ". . . Shaw's sympathy with Stalin's 'liquidation' of five million Ukranian Kulaks by starvation with collectivizing their farms" (p. 402); on the other hand, in the *Autobiography (1898–1950 The Playwright Years),* selected from his writings by Stanley Weintraub, Shaw tells us in his chapter entitled "Touring in Russia" (in July of 1931), when referring to some ruthless suppressions by the Bolsheviks:

> I know what Tolstoy's daughter felt about it: she told me herself; for she had seen a smiling countryside...where he had been born and brought up...where good farming had brought to everybody such prosperity as was possible for them in the days of Tsardom, blasted into ruin and desolation, squalor and misery, by the Soviet expropriation and persecution of the Kulaks...It was hard for her to forgive the Bolsheviks for that; *and she was quite right;* for the expulsion of the kulaks, like the confiscation of the shops, before the Government was ready to carry on, was a stupid, anti-Fabian blunder...(London, Sydney, Toronto: Max Reinhardt, 1970; p. 199).

So Shaw was one who believed in having it both ways and he did not need, by any means, a period of time to elapse between his contradictory and conflicting statements such as was the case with his sympathetic siding with Tolstoy's daughter, on the one hand, and his applause for Stalin's Kulak-liquidation program on the other. Some three years had elapsed between those conflicting opinions. But consider the following, the very next paragraph to the one quoted above:

> The persecution of the intelligentsia in Russia did not last very long. It was, I think, justified at the time when it was not yet perceived to be impracticable. I have often said myself that if I were a revolutionary dictator my first care would be to see that persons with a university education, or with the acquired mentality which universities inculcate and stereotype, would be ruthlessly excluded from all direction of affairs, all contact with education especially with their own children, and, if not violently exterminated, at least encouraged to die out as soon as possible. Lenin shared my views and attempted to carry them into action...(p. 200).

One cannot help but wonder how Shaw might have commented on—had he continued to live on like his Methuselah—the Cultural Revolution of Mao-tse Tung's People's Republic of China and the slaughter of intellectuals, etc., by the Pol Pot regime in Kampuchea. Had he been consistent with his past inconsistency, he most certainly would have had it both ways and would never have changed a line in future reprintings.

But generally, Shaw's all-out enthusiasm for the Soviet Union really jelled on the occasion of his brief visit there in July of 1931. He had made the trip with Lord and Lady Astor and Philip Kerr (later, in 1939–40, ambassador to Washington). As he pinpoints his feelings toward the "Workers' Fatherland" after experiencing what he firmly believed to be vast improvements in that economy of which he had been previously so critical:

> For ten days I lived and travelled in perfect comfort...and found no such horrors as I could have found in the distressed areas and slums of the Capitalist west, though the Soviet government was still finding out its mistakes... (*Autobiography*, p. 192).

At the border town of Nigoreloye, where he was met, he found:

> Not a band, not a flag, not a red scarf, not a street cheer from one end of the trip to the other* though I was certainly treated as if I were Karl Marx in person, and given a grand reception (a queer mixture of public meeting, snack bar banquet, and concert)...where they celebrated my seventy-fifth birthday...in the Hall of Nobles, which holds four thousand people and was crammed... (ibid, p. 195).
>
> And, "The climax of the tour," he tells us, "was an interview with Stalin...[who] played his part to perfection, receiving us as old friends and letting us talk ourselves dry before he modestly took the floor...." (Ibid, p. 195, 6.)

And to cap the highlights of his meeting the "Vozhd" he was granted an interview with the Great One that lasted some two hours and ten minutes, a fact that certainly attested to Shaw's reputation in 1931 as an influential voice in international politics. In any case, all it took to straighten out Shaw on the question of equality of income was that two hour and ten minute interview with the leader of the Third International brand of Marxism. Since that historic occasion—historic both for Shaw and for the Bolshevik regime—Shaw could explain with much more sympathetic feeling why the Soviet Union, although Socialist, had not yet introduced equality of wages, and explain it surprisingly enough in Marxian terms.

**We learn from the notes at the back that cheering thousands did meet him at the Moscow station, with brass band, and "Hail Shaw's!"*

> The cost of production of a worker as such varies with the sort of worker required. In Japan the cost of a cotton operative as such is a penny an hour. In Lancashire it is twenty pence. In Tsarist Russia the cost of production of a common Laborer as such was twenty-four shillings a month. Within the British Commonwealth we have black African workers who are expected by pink settlers to be grateful for a hut, a scrap of garden, the privilege of being British subjects, instruction in Christianity by missionaries, and eight shillings a month pocket money.
>
> Now legislators and administrators, managers and scholars, lawyers and doctors and clergymen, artists and philosophers, are not to be had on these terms: they cost education, culture, gentle nurture, privacy, decency, and some leisure. When the Soviet Government in Russia started with the intention of giving all workers an equal share of the national income their labor was producing, it found that they were not producing enough to give each of them more than the pittance earned by the cheapest labor under the Tsardom. It had either to increase the national income to such an amount as would enable it to pay every worker on the professional scale, which was not immediately possible, or else do without an educated public service, which meant pulling the linchpin out of the Communist cart and collapsing in hopeless bankruptcy. Equality of income had therefore to be dropped until the national dividend could be raised to the professional level. This level is attainable, and is within sight of being attained; but meanwhile Russia has a bureaucracy and a professional class with incomes ten times greater than the hewers of wood and drawers of water... (*Everybody's Political What's What.* London: Constable & Co., Copyright 1944 George Bernard Shaw, pp. 55–6).

What should have been the main thing wrong with that analysis, from the viewpoint of Shaw and the Fabian Society, is that it is based upon the Labor Theory of Value and not on Marginal Utility—setting aside, Shaw's references to the cost of the laborer (or professional) rather than the cost of producing their labor power, a distinction that is important but over which we will not quibble. Shaw had spent the bulk of his adult life in debunking the Marxian theory and insisting that what makes professional labor power more valuable is its utility to the consumer. Yet after 50 years, as of 1931, declaring the labor theory to be fallacious, it took but two hours and ten minutes for Stalin to convince him that he, and not Marx, was wrong on that score.

Not that there was no other error than our possible quibble. The explanation has incorporated in it the fantasy, if not the subterfuge, that an economy based upon the relationships of wage labor and capital, can, by bold leaps and legal enactments, ever overcome the commodity nature of labor power and introduce equality of income regardless of the level of the "national dividend." The only "remuneration" possible in a Socialist world—and socialism can only exist on a world basis—the Soviet Communist Party and the Fabian Socialist experts to the contrary notwithstanding—would be: "From Each According to Ability, To Each According to Need." And this could never mean equality of income; it can only mean absence of income.

Shaw and "The Western Socialist"

> On the occasion of the sixtieth anniversary of the death of Karl Marx (died on March 14th, 1883), a new edition of his selected works was reviewed by George Bernard Shaw in the *Daily Herald* (London). Strangely enough the review is headed 'What would Marx say about Beveridge?'* It appears to be an appreciation of the work and influence of Marx, but is in fact a mumble-jumble of ideas, mostly unconnected. In brief, the review is sufficient to show that if Shaw is great as a dramatist, as a guide to working class politics he is outside his sphere. The review proves that Shaw's knowledge of Marx's theories is painfully lacking.
>
> To begin with Shaw asserts that Marxism "has produced a new civilization in Russia and that the principles of Marxism have been carried into practice in that country. . ."

The foregoing is a tiny excerpt from a 2000-word article that appeared in *The Western Socialist* (Boston) in the issue of May 1943 of the defunct "Journal of Scientific Socialism in the Western Hemisphere." The author of the article, Clifford Allen, a member of the Socialist Party of Great Britain, was in frequent communication with his comrades of the World Socialist Party (U.S.), publishers of *The Western Socialist* (The Allen articles, complete, will be found in the Appendix.) A copy of the article

**Sir William Henry Beveridge, first Baron Tuggal, 1879–1963; British economist and sociologist; author of Britain's Welfare State plan ("From womb to tomb").*

was sent, as a courtesy, to Mr. Shaw – then in his 87th year and still actively engaged in writing. It elicited the following response:

> Sir,
>
> I am much indebted to Mr. Allan for having, by his article in your issue of May, called my attention to *The Western Socialist.* But I am sorry to have to add that if by some miracle a Socialist government were established in the United States tomorrow, its first painful necessity would be to shoot Mr. Allan. That is the worst of being a thorough-going out-and-out revolutionist. If the revolution is successful they have all to be shot by their old comrades because, as the victorious socialists must take on the government of the country instantly, and the change from capitalist to socialist institutions cannot be instantaneous and its new rulers take some time to learn their new business, they are denounced by the thorough-going out-and-outers as betrayers of The Cause, no better than the bold bourgeois rulers. The Possiblist and the Impossiblist may be old friends and comrades; but the Possiblist must shoot the Impossiblist because half a loaf is better than no bread. Stalin had to exile Trotsky, and to liquidate several of his old friends to save Socialism in a Single Country, without which beginning for an example Socialism can never be established in any country. If I could be made President of the United Socialist States of America, as somebody will some day, Mr. Allan would shoot me unless I shot him first for not having learnt that nature does not make a Socialist world at once with a wave of a Marxian wand. She makes it as she makes skeletons, by making spots of bone here and there which gradually coalesce.
>
> Let me, however, make the more friendly and probable supposition that Mr. Allan and not I am elected President. He will be surprised to find that at least nine-tenths of his work will be precisely the same old bourgeois routine now practised by Franklyn Roosevelt, Winston Churchill, and Stalin. Currency, wages, banking, police and prisons, unemployment, allotment of capital between industry and agriculture, length of the working day, and dozens of pressing questions which Capitalist governments abandon to selfish private enterprise, will press on President Allan harder than they do on President Roosevelt and his Secretaries of State, who will all find themselves not in a new world in which everything is changed, and the old problems no longer exist in short, in an earthly paradise – but in a very tough

job with a peck of troubles now undreamt-of by our political careerists. And Marx will not help him in the least; for Marx had no administrative experience, and dealt with epochs and classes, not with the daily drudgery of government.

John Burns, once The Man with the Red Flag, said to "Shaw: the first hour I spent on Committee that had half crown of public money to spend, knocked all the anarchism out of me." The same experience will certainly knock all day-dreaming out of Mr. Allen; and until he gets it he will waste his time and other people's in trying to discredit the better informed Socialists as he is trying to discredit me. However, his sympathies are all right. He may have the makings of a good Fabian in him yet.

Faithfully,

G. Bernard Shaw

The Editor,
The Western Socialist,
12 Hayward Place,
Boston, Mass.,
U.S.A.

Now, the editorial committee of *The Western Socialist,* as would have been the case with any other publication under similar circumstances, was quick enough to follow through by speeding a copy of the Shaw communication back across "the Pond" to their comrade Cliff Allen, and he responded again with some 3500 words, dealing point by point with Shaw's barbs. Allen's second article appeared in *The Western Socialist* for December 1943. An interesting sidelight on this affair was the length of time that it sometimes took, during World War II, to have airmail letters cross the Atlantic and be delivered, a situation noted by Shaw in his second, and final, communication with *The Western Socialist.*

Your letter dated the 26th Dec last was delivered today, the 15th February. The U.S. Air Mail takes more than twice as long as the ordinary mail to cross the Atlantic.

The packet of your issues since May with which you threaten

me has not yet arrived. I hope it never may. You forget the old precept "No use giving tracts to a missionary."

My time—of which there is so little left—is too precious to be wasted on W. Allen, whose utter ignorance of the real world created a vacuum into which Marx (what he could understand and misunderstand of him) rushed with irresistible force. Experience alone can drive it out.

G. Bernard Shaw

Without going into the specifics of the Allen reply, detailed and lengthy as is the article, let us just point out that the major difference between Shaw's concept of socialism and that of the "Impossiblists" (a term used by H.M. Hyndman against a group of secessionists from his Social Democratic Federation in 1904 who founded the Socialist Party of Great Britain) was Shaw's—and the more widely held belief among professed Socialists—that Socialism finally materializes out of a series of social reforms (of welfare state variety) under capitalism. That, and the concomitant belief that socialism is possible of attainment in a single country.

The "Impossiblist" rejoinder would be, in substance, that no reform that evades the central problem—the organization of society according to the predominant social relationships of wage labor and capital, can further the interests of a movement for socialism. Furthermore, that the capitalist class (or a state capitalist bureaucracy) will consider and even, more often than not, approve any reform so long as it does not disturb the basic social relationships as now exist.

But there is another point of departure between Shaw, as depicted in his correspondence with *The Western Socialist*, and traditional Socialists of the "Impossiblist" type. (At the time he pinned that label on the Socialist Party of Great Britain, Hyndman is said to have commented, "They want it to be 12-noon at 9 a.m.," or words to that effect.) For Shaw demonstrated in his initial reply to Allen that he was paying scant, if any, attention to the major point being made by Allen, to wit, that socialism will be impossible of achievement without a population the majority of which is ripe and ready for socialism.

It follows, then, that there can be no such phenomenon as

a "Socialist Government" attempting to operate affairs in the manner of current governments. What possible difference can be achieved by simply adopting a different nomenclature for the political realities of the time? It is the intrinsic nature of capitalism, not the abilities, such as they may be, of those who run it, that creates the multitude of insolvable problems.

The reason there can be no such phenomenon should be apparent, at least to a person with the degree of Socialist information of Bernard Shaw. "Government" implies governors over people, and people being governed. A Socialist world could only produce an administration over *things.* How long or short a time span would need to elapse until operations would run smoothly is a question for the future since there seems to be no indication of even a sizable minority wanting socialism today. With the "Impossiblists," then, it has to be all or nothing and if it takes another 500 years—as Lenin and Mao-tse Tung are both reputed to have opined—to produce a majority of Socialists in the population, that is how long it will have to take for the "impossible" to become possible.

Now although Shaw had to have known, early in his career as a Socialist soapboxer around London, that there were Socialists in that city who took such a position, he generally avoided referring to them in his own copious Socialist writings. He was an inveterate orator—both outdoor and indoor—as were a number of the members of The Socialist Party of Great Britain—Hyndman's "Impossiblists,"—and it is highly unlikely that he never encountered them around Hyde Park and other popular London spots for working class declamation.

As a matter of fact, though, Shaw did refer to them, by inference, at least once in a short story, published by a journal called *The Clarion,* in its March 1915 edition. The story, entitled *Death of an Old Revolutionary Hero,* dealt with a character by the name of Joe Budgett—an uncompromising revolutionist. Budgett opposed the Reform Bill of 1832, Shaw said, on the grounds that it was a conspiracy to enfranchise the middle class at the expense of the workers. He opposed every Parliamentary attempt at reform down to the enfranchisement of women (the property restrictions to that "victory" remained, however, signifying the fact that the vast bulk of women of the working class remained disenfranchised). He even called Karl Marx, Shaw wrote, a compromise between a Jew and a German, "Neither one nor the other." He criticized workers for "crawling" in labor demonstrations led by the likes of John Burns in order to beg publicly for sixpence instead of demanding the whole business. Shaw's narrator in the story (Shaw, himself) called Budgett a nihilist. "As it is quite certain that you won't get ALL, you are practically the propagandist of Nothing," he told Budgett.

Had the author been one with "Impossiblist" leanings, rather than Fabian, Budgett's response might well have been the reiteration of his philosophy: "If all you are demanding is a handout of crumbs from the master's table you'd stand a better chance of gettin' a bigger fistful by demandin' the whole bloody loaf -- that is, if there'd be enough of you to rattle him."

The fictional Budgett could very well have been one of the Hyndman-designated "Impossiblists." Even the reference to Karl Marx as being "a compromise between a Jew and a German, 'neither one nor the other'" was really not unthinkable language for a Socialist. Marx was not a German in the sense that, as a revolutionary Socialist he would not have tended to identify with a nation. On the other hand, referring to Marx as a Jew is fallacious for two good reasons. To begin with, chronologically speaking, he was but six years old when his parents converted to the Prussian State Church, at that time thought of as a haven for those with liberal leanings. Whatever religious training, if any, that Marx received after that was the equivalent of what was given Shaw; they both were connected, as youngsters, with the counterpart (in Ireland and in Germany) of the Anglican Church.

But in any case, again as a revolutionary Socialist, Marx would have naturally rejected the tag of Jew in the sense that it can only refer to a religion or a sect, neither of which designations could possibly have fit Karl Marx. He was *descended* from Jews but hardly, himself, should have been designated as a Jew!

It is interesting to contemplate, however, were there anything to the theory of reincarnation, just how Marx would be received were he to return as himself and elect to live in the land where his works -- according to Shaw -- had created a "new civilization." Would he be issued an internal passport stamped

"Jew"; or would he, perhaps, be awarded a designation of "honorary Slav" or "Great Russian"?

Finally, in the matter of Shaw's championing of Joseph Stalin, he was at least spared the embarrassment—felt by so many of Stalin's erstwhile admirers—of witnessing the posthumous stripping of the Great One's Demi-God stature during the regime of Nikita Khrushchev, by the Politburo; and the ousting of his remains from inside the Kremlin walls. For Shaw died in 1950, Stalin in 1952. Not that GBS could ever suffer from mortification when those whom he had extolled as examples of his Supermen were overturned and widely denounced, even in death, by most who had hailed them in life. He had lived to see it happen to Benito Mussolini and Adolf Hitler and had never amended a line of what he had written in praise of them—although he did back away somewhat during and after the end of WWII without, however, referring to his own erstwhile championing of them.

6. Shaw on Italian Fascism

Benito Mussolini, born in the year of Karl Marx's death (1883) was, in the years immediately preceding the outbreak of World War I, and until shortly before Italy's entry into that slaughter on the side of the Allied powers (France, Great Britain, and Czarist Russia) a prominent member of the Socialist party of Italy. He, in fact, was co-editor of the party's newspaper *Avanti*, along with Angelica Balabanoff, a self-exiled Russian Social Democrat who had settled in Italy and had become an active propagandist of the Socialist party there. The executive offices of the party paper had been moved from Rome to Milan, where Mussolini and Balabanoff both lived. (Balabanoff, shortly after the Bolshevik Revolution of November 1917, returned to Soviet Russia and became the first general secretary of the Third International, organized in 1919, until she had a belly-full of aggravation from the top Bolshevik politicans and got out of the country once again—while the getting was good!)

In harmony with the official party position on the war, which was supportive of the Italian government stance of neutrality, Mussolini was actively engaged in condemning the conflict and in agitating for its cessation with neither victors nor vanquished. According to Balabanoff, however, in her *My Life as a Rebel*, (Harper and Brothers, 1938), he had been bought off by agents from France and began to editorialize in *Avanti* for Italy's entry on the side of the Allied powers. Immediately following his first such editorial he was haled before a party meeting, denounced, and kicked out, although he continued, at that meeting, to profess his loyalty to Socialism. In *Mussolini as Revealed in His Political Speeches—Nov. 1914–Aug. 1923* (selected, translated and edited by Barone Bernardo Quaranti di San Severino), he is recorded as having emoted: "Do not think that by taking away my membership card you will take away my faith in the cause." But, according to Balabanoff, even as he spoke he had in his pocket a contract and the down payment on the money needed to found and operate a paper of his own, delivered by a propagandist from France. This was no doubt the case because living as he had to, in those years, a hand-to-mouth existence, always needing financial help from his comrades, he suddenly did come out with his own paper, *Il Popolo d'Italia* which, after his rise to political power, became the official newspaper of the government. As far as the Allies were concerned, he had at least two assets: he was a fair propagandist and he had a proneness for selling out his comrades. They had picked the right one for the job and he immediately went all-out, in his new paper, at denouncing the socialists and agitating for Italy's entry into the war on the Allied side.

But the situation seems not to have been as cut-and-dried as revealed by Balabanoff in her memoirs – she was, after all, relying much on her memory. The actual position of the so-called Socialist party of Italy was not that inflexible as indicated by her. In the *New York Times Current History of the European War*, Volume 1, No. 1 (The New York Times Company, 1914) the Manifesto of the Socialist Party of Italy on the war, issued on September 3, 1914, was reproduced. True enough, it did call for immediate cessation with neither "conquerors or conquered" but it did not quit while it was ahead. It went on to state:

> But if now this hope is vain, we express our desire that this infamous war may be concluded by the defeat of those who have provoked it; the Austrian and German Empires, since the empires of Austria and Germany form the rampart of European reaction, even more than Russia, which is shaken by democratic and Socialist forces, which have shown that they know how to attempt a heroic effort of liberation; since if the German and Austrian Empires emerge victorious from the war it will mean the triumph of military absolutism in its most brutal oppression, of a barbarous horde massacring, devastating, destroying and conquering in violation of every treaty and every right and law...

> Since, finally, the victory of the French republic now imbued with genuine socialism, and that of England, where the truest democracy flourishes, signifies the victory of a European political regime open to all social conquests and desiring peace, it signifies the agreement between States at last free and naturally reinforced by the limitation of armaments and the substitution of a system of national defense in the place of hordes professionally organized for aggression, which would imply the liberation as well of the German people.
>
> Therefore, under actual conditions, while nearly the whole of Europe is at war, we may well raise our cry of horror, and of protest; but our protest strikes only those who desired the war, not those who submit to it to defend themselves against oppression.
>
> In this war is outlined on one side the defense of European reaction, on the other the defense of all revolutions, past and future, brought about by historical necessity stronger than the intention of continued governments. And because of this we must confirm that there remains for us only one way of being internationalist—namely, to declare ourselves loyally in favor of whoever fights the empires of reaction, just as the Italian Socialists residing in Paris have understood that one way only remains to be anti-militarist—to arm and fight against the empires of militarism.
>
> This is our answer as Italian Socialists to the German Socialists. (Pp. 408–09.)

Now this statement, without doubt, showed the Socialist party of Italy as being no more socialist, in the original meaning of the term, than any of its sister parties of the Second (Socialist) International. But what makes it particularly interesting is when it is compared to the 60-page "manifesto" of Bernard Shaw on that war, originally published and copyrighted by the New York Times Co. in its *Current History of the European War* (Vol. 1, No. 1). Shaw drew down on his shoulders a storm of protest and criticism from a number of his fellow "men of letters" such as H.G. Wells and Arnold Bennett, who were more inclined to be one-sided in their patriotic fervor rather than to emulate Shaw in his penchant for embracing both sides of an argument.

Whereas the Socialist party of Italy was demonstrably equivocal in its opposition to the war, actually urging workers of other nations—including their own comrades—to do the job of conquering those whom they deemed to be the instigators of the carnage, Shaw, also equivocal, was nevertheless quick to point out that there was little, if anything, to choose between the ruling classes of the various belligerents; that Britain, in fact, was as thoroughly dominated by "Junkerism" as was Germany. Furthermore, he charged Britain as being just as guilty of wartime atrocities as were the Germans and, in fact, justified wartime acts of "savagery" as being an essential part of warfare.

He made haste, however, to demonstrate that he was really as patriotic as the next one and that he was primarily interested in having the conditions of those in the military, along with their families, improved. A situation had developed, for example, wherein hordes of Belgian refugees were flooding the labor market in England thus adding to the turmoil in that quarter. Shaw, perhaps with tongue-in-cheek, suggested that Belgians, before leaving their homeland, should appropriate uniforms of slain soldiers since members of the military—even from the enemy—were accorded better treatment in England than civilian unemployed.

In fact, Shaw went all-out in his pitch for improved conditions within the military—trade union representation; pay rates consistent with those earned by civilian workers in dangerous occupations; guarantees that the military personnel would not be dumped on the labor market immediately upon the end of hostilities; abolition of the phrase "by Almighty God" in the Oath of Allegiance in deference to atheist-enlistees, along with "the King" since he saw no need to drag in that dignitary; and, of course, elimination of the program of compulsory inoculation (four shots) against various diseases!

The fact was, that Shaw was no more in opposition to that war than was the Socialist party of Italy. And he was every bit as patriotic to British capitalism as were his fellow "men of Letters" and others who denounced him for his *Commonsense About the War* which, incidentally, has become as scarce as the proverbial hen's teeth in its later, pamphlet form but which is still available in libraries in its the New York Times' *Current History* compendiums of that era.

Nevertheless, Shaw had different visions of how the affairs of Great Britain should be conducted—of how the government should be constructed. For despite his alleged socialism he apparently envisioned a socialist world as one with continuing separate nations and governments; continuing trade and commerce; military organizations, analogous to what existed; and all of the other trappings of what thrived in his times. Not long after the end of the Great War there developed in Italy, with Mussolini's rise to political power and the Fascist party, a perfect role model for him given his comprehension of Socialism.

Shortly after the end of the war, Mussolini organized a "party of action," the Fascist party, the name deriving from the Roman rods, or *fasces,* which were carried by the lictors (minor functionaries), before the chief magistrate of the State, as emblems of authority. It was to be a party of discipline: strict, Spartan, virile, and it was intended to be a party to rule the nation, with an iron fist, and with no legal opposition. Mussolini, of course, had had his basic training among the proletariat with the Socialist party and when it comes right down to it, the tactics needed to organize supernationalistic, nominally anticapitalist parties, unaccompanied as they are by socialist education rather than mere slogans and catch phrases, are not all that different from the training one gets in the Social Democratic and Communist party movements. In fact, in the years immediately following the end of the war—years of turmoil and misery for the bulk of the Italian working class despite that nation's membership in the Alliance of the conquerors—Mussolini and his Fascists fomented more strikes than did the official, left wing radical parties of Italy and thus he gained much support from the militant Italian workers of that postwar era. And after his seizure of political power, Bernard Shaw—in his many writings and speeches on the subject—became one of his admirers and champions, to the dismay of the leaders of Social Democracy.

How could this be? Here was a terrible example—from a socialist perspective—of a political party seizing control of a nation—ostensibly by swift coup,* wholesale murder, and in

**There was, however, much widespread support for Mussolini among the masses of unruly, striking, Italian workers as well as substantial assistance during the Civil War of 1921–22 by finance from the banks, the big industrialists, and the landowners; by guns, bombs and transport for his Blackshirt (unofficial) army, from the military authorities, etc. (See Shaw, "The Chucker-out," by Allan Chappelow, Ams, N.Y.)*

this case organization of castor oil squads to administer toxic and frequently lethal doses of the laxative to its captive opponents; and there was Shaw, that internationally famed champion of the oppressed and outstanding socialist enemy of capitalism, writing and voicing his approbation of Il Duce and his openly brutal regime. The answer, of course, was simply that he regarded Mussolini and his party as another form of socialism and socialist – in essence, another harbinger of the end of capitalism, as he understood capitalism to be. By November 1933, when Mussolini's Corporate State was declared, his theory was that socialism had been superseded by the syndicate type of rule – a partnership, so to speak, among labor, industry, experts, and, of course, the National Fascist Party. Capitalism, according to Mussolini, was all but finished everywhere. (*The Corporate State*. N.Y.: Howard Fertig, 1975.) Shaw's feelings on that subject were, to a great extent, molded by his contempt for parliamentary-type democracy. Long afterwards, in 1946, he had the following to say about both Mussolini and Adolph Hitler:

> Adolf Hitler and Benito Mussolini found, as Cromwell found before them, that with a New Model army, well paid, and a network of local prefects chosen by themselves and backed by this army (major-generals in effect), they could get anything they wanted done, and sweep all parliamentary recalcitrants into the dust-bin, alive or dead. To the people it seemed that the dictators could fulfill their promises if they would, and that the parliamentary parties could not even if they would. No wonder the plebiscites always gave the dictators majorities of ninety-five percent and upwards. (*Everybody's Political What's What*, p. 263.)

Shaw, it seems, had a penchant for mixing his centuries in his comparisons of historical events and personalities. The social forces that created the dictatorship of Oliver Cromwell in 1653–58 were not analogous to those that gave rise to Benito Mussolini and Hitler.

Nor were Hitler and Mussolini able to consolidate their power merely by organizing a "New Model Army" (of Brown-shirts and Black-shirts), by organizing riots and administering castor oil to captive opponents. Not until they had the mass support needed to capture the government and consequent control of the regular armed forces were they in a position to "get anything they wanted done."

As for the plebiscites always showing 95 percent or so in favor the modern dictators, what could one expect when voting was compulsory and no alternatives were offered? Even if general support did exist—and it no doubt did—there had to have been a significant percentage of dissatisfied, who were not permitted to legally raise their voices.

Now, one of the more comprehensive sources for Shaw's views on the subject of Italian fascism was his correspondence with the leader of the Austrian Labour party and secretary of the Labour and Socialist International, Dr. Friedrich Adler. This correspondence was made public in the *Daily News* (London) on October 13, 1927, and also in the *Manchester Guardian* of the same date. An abbreviated version was published in the *New York Times* of October 14, 1927, some of which follows:

> "The only question for us is whether Mussolini is doing his job well enough to induce the Italian nation to accept him faute de mieux. It is irrelevant and silly to refuse to acknowledge the dictatorship of Il Duce, because it was not achieved without all the usual villainies.
>
> "Some of the things Mussolini has done and some he is threatening to do are further in the direction of socialism than the English Labor Party could yet venture if they were in power. They will bring him presently into serious conflict with capitalism, and it is certainly not my business nor that of anyt other Socialist to weaken him in view of such a conflict."

The sad fact is that, in the perspective of a traditional Marxist* Shaw made less nonsense in this exchange than did Adler. The one major difference between the Shavian and the

**Here we must confess that our use of the term "traditional" is not altogether sound since there have been a number of "traditional" Marxian theoreticians who have contributed mightily to socialist knowledge through their texts and their lectures but who, as practical politicians, concerned themselves with the advocacy of capitalist reform measures. Within the Second (Socialist) International there were a significant number of such "traditional" theoreticians—Kautsky, Martov, Boudin and a host of others. At least part of our problem is "poverty of language."*

Adlerian concept of Socialism in operation was in the *style* of government. Whereas Adler and Social Democrats, generally, favor parliamentary democracy, Shaw favored the dictatorships of both left and right that opt for iron-fisted totalitarianisms. None of these regimes, however, is remotely akin to the socialist concept of administration of things rather than government over people and, indeed, could hardly be expected to be since they are all concerned with operating the wages, prices, profits system—capitalism.

So, indeed, why should Shaw or anybody else be expected to have lectured Mussolini on the brutalities connected with his regime? At best, the degree of suffering experienced by so many in all varieties of capitalism is only a matter of degree; and that, even as regards the United States of America, the administrations of which successively lecture various other governments on their lack of humanitarianism—that is a subject in itself for a book-length response.

An interesting sidelight on the Shaw-Adler debate via subsequently published correspondence was Shaw's charge that Socialists had been shown to be incompetent; in so many words, they were a bunch of armchair philosophers who do not know how to deal with *real politik*. Shaw, of course, was referring to the type of socialists that run the capitalisms of their respective countries via parliamentary democracy. Adler was particularly upset by the charge and replied:

> I believe that on this point you are no longer serious... According to my experience, Socialists are perfectly capable of conducting the business of government with just as much understanding, and indeed success, as any aristocrat or bourgeois, provided only they possess the foundation for all true government—*i.e.*, the assured support of the majority of the people. Whenever that stipulation is not fulfilled those in power either break down or else are driven into the employment of violence. This latter feature may be observed not only in countries of Fascism, but likewise in Russia...if you would see how Socialists can administer public money and direct the work of tens of thousands of municipal employees, then I can only advise you to STUDY SOME DAY THE MUNICIPAL ADMINISTRATION OF Vienna. (Oct. 7, 1927: Shaw, "The Chucker-out," p. 193.)

But Adler should have realized that politicians—not even those who profess Socialism—cannot run the system in the interests of the working class as a whole. And the support of the majority of the population for any type of capitalist administration is a tenuous business. For whatever benefits accrue for one section must be at the expense of another or others since wealth—not even the portion that constitutes national wages and working class conditions—is not self-expanding but depends, in final analysis, on market "temperature." Indeed, it was but a half dozen years after that correspondence that Austrian Fascism, headed by Engelbert Dolfuss, seized power in that country and murdered and exiled hordes of Vienna's socialists. Balabanoff ends her brief account of that tragedy:

> In Red Vienna, gallows were erected for the survivors, including the wounded. The monuments which had symbolized human progress and freedom were removed. The houses built for the workers, as forerunners of a new society, were destroyed or mutilated—at the order of a man who was later to fall a victim to the Nazi bullets of his collaborators. . . (*My Life as a Rebel,* p. 306).

Now, notwithstanding the outrage of most nominal Socialists and Communists, and indeed of all varieties of Fascists and Nazis, at being lumped together in their vision of an ideal type of government—there is more than a little truth in such an assertion. Even if they do not all use the term "Socialist" or "Communist" and if the "right wing" varieties denounce Marx and Engels rather than flaunt their portraits along with those of their national strong-men, they all, at one time or another, have declared the abolition of capitalism in their respective countries. And the average individual would tend to agree with such a viewpoint since the general tendency, even in official education mills, is to confuse political systems with societal systems. A political system is but the mechanism used to administer (govern) the business of the economic structure of society. Government is, in other words, part of what Marx called the superstructure and although governments do have differences in how they are constructed, they are not all *that* different; in one way or another, they all must appeal to their nation—and frequently—for mass support despite the dissimilarity in superficial structure. Insofar as configuration is concerned, however, there is strong similarity among the totalitarian regimes.

So Shaw, at least in that regard, was the soul of consistency. He had no reason to denounce any of the dictators although, actually, he was somewhat inconsistent in not attacking Mussolini for his use of the castor oil squads. One of Shaw's pet abominations was the practice by governments of compulsory inoculation of whole populations against smallpox and other contagions. So far as he was concerned, Jenner was no better than a charlatan and the entire approach of inoculation was false. Germs do not cause disease, he contended. Disease causes germs: and if people would all become vegetarians, they would not contract diseases. So it would seem that a zealot such as he was, on that subject, would at least be anxious to reprove—if only with mildness—the Fascists for their forced feedings of castor oil to their opponents. As Allan Chappelow footnotes it on page 187 of his *Shaw "The Chucker-out"*:

> The castor oil torture could be as cruel as almost any ever invented (although this naturally depended on the dosage and over what length of time, and how frequently it was repeated). Some subjected to it died from weakness and exhaustion. Those who survived were often invalids for their rest of their lives, the mucous membranes lining their intestines having been partially or wholly destroyed.

The only extenuating circumstance in the reluctance of Shaw to lecture Mussolini and his cabinet on their "castor oil squads" was the fact, as he put it in his letter to Dr. Adler, that he considered the Mussolini cabinet to be a socialist one! The fact of its embrace of what to him was socialism gave the Fascist cabinet, in Shaw's opinion, a blank check to commit any sort of atrocity. And anyway, even if it should be considered as a blot, the blemish should be charged against human nature rather than against Mussolini and Fascism!

In that regard, nowhere does he make his position clearer, with less mincing of words, than in his Preface, written in August of 1935, to his political comedy *The Millionairess.* After noting that the institution of Parliament in Europe had fallen into "contempt"; that "ballot papers were less esteemed than toilet paper"; and that "the men from the trenches had no patience with the liberties that had not saved them from being driven like sheep to the shambles"; (p. 861), Shaw continued:

> Here was clearly a big opportunity for a man psychologist enough to grasp the situation and bold enough to act on it. Such a man was Mussolini. He had become known as a journalist by championing the demobilized soldiers, who, after suffering all the horrors of the war, had returned to find that the men who had been kept at home in the factories comfortably earning good wages, had seized those factories according to the Syndicalist doctrine of 'workers control,' and were wrecking them in their helpless ignorance of business. As one indignant master-Fascist said to me "They were listening to speeches round red flags and leaving the cows unmilked."
>
> The demobilized fell on the Syndicalists with sticks and stones. Some, more merciful, only dosed them with castor oil. They carried Mussolini to Rome with a rush. They gave him the chance of making an irreparable mistake and spending the next fifteen years in prison. It seemed just the occasion for a grand appeal for liberty, for democracy, for a parliament in which the people were supreme: in short, for nineteenth century resurrection pie. Mussolini did not make that mistake. With inspired precision he denounced Liberty as a putrefying corpse. He declared that what people needed was not liberty but discipline, the sterner the better. He said that he would not tolerate Opposition: he called for action and silence. The people, instead of being shocked like good Liberals, rose to him. He was able to organize a special constabulary who wore black shirts and applied the necessary coercion. (Max Reinhardt, *The Bodley Head Bernard Shaw—Collected Plays with Their Prefaces:* London, Sydney, Toronto, p. 862.)

And Shaw went on to describe, and to approve, the action of Mussolini in assuming the full responsibility for the excesses of his Black Shirts, even the "ruffians and Sadists" (to use Shaw's own terms) among them; in repressing and transporting the Liberal opponents to the Lipari Islands, ending his panegyric on Il Duce in his successful elimination of civil and political rights with the following assertion:

> Parliaments are supposed to have their fingers always on the people's pulse and to respond to its lightest throb. Mussolini proved that parliaments have not the slightest notion of how the people are feeling, and that he, being a good psychologist and a man of the people himself to boot, was a true organ of democracy.
>
> I, being a bit of a psychologist myself, also understood the situation, and was immediately denounced by the refugees and their champions as an anti-democrat, a hero worshipper of tyrants, and all the rest of it. (Ibid, p. 864.)

By 1935, when Shaw wrote the above, he had had plenty of practice writing statements in his Prefaces that stretch one's credulity. To be sure, it is at least doubtful that many of those who read his plays bother about the prefaces. In any case, many of those who actually do read his political "tracts" (as he, himself, has called his prefaces) must wonder, if they give serious thought to what he was saying, how one so seemingly bright could make so many silly errors of judgment and of fact.

To begin with: it is difficult to imagine a government that would deliberately keep significant numbers of able-bodied, draftable, men at home, during wartime, to work in factories—and at good wages plus comfort. One needs special political pull for such treatment and those selected would more likely be from what Shaw called the middle and upper middle class, the sons of industrialists, for example, who are hardly the type to join Syndicalist unions and seize factories. In any case, having gone through the experience in the United States of World War II, this writer recollects that although many workers did earn more money than they had ever earned in their lives before, it was by dint of working 60 to 70 hours and more per week (the compulsory work week was 48 hours with time-and-a-half after 40). He also recalls the large numbers of elderly men and women, and even youngsters with special work passes, who had joined the labor force, not necessarily because of patriotic fervor but largely because of wartime inflation. It should also be kept in mind that the Italy of the immediate post–World War I years was in as much chaos—if not more—as were the vanquished nations of the erstwhile Central Powers.

Secondly, to state, as he did, that the forceful administering of toxic dosages of castor oil is more "merciful" treatment to captive enemies than is peppering them with sticks and stones, borders on inanity, especially for Shaw with his attitude toward governmental inoculation of any kind. One has but to read his Preface to *The Doctor's Dilemma* to appreciate the contradiction here. There was nothing "merciful"—to him—about the medically-controlled dosages of vaccines administered to patients by medical doctors, let alone—one would imagine—the toxic quantities of castor oil forced upon the enemies of Fascism by Mussolini's Black Shirts!

Thirdly, Mussolini, by that time, was in no danger of being jailed for his activities. He was popular enough to have received an invitation from the King—representing much of Italy's capitalist class—by that time worried enough to be looking for a "strong man" to form a cabinet. His personal March on Rome was performed as a passenger in a first class carriage on the railway. His "Indomitable Black Shirt Army" (as Mussolini referred to his goon battalion) was met at the gates by the Regular Army and ushered in peacefully.

Shaw, however, if unwittingly, did recognize here that leaders are, indeed, but followers. Mussolini, he noted, was psychologist enough to recognize where the population wanted to go; so he "led" them. And when the overwhelming bulk of the population had had a bellyful of him, they dumped that leader!

Mussolini ended his speech of November 14, 1933 (*On the Corporate State*) with the following dictum:

> In conclusion, let us ask ourselves: can Corporativism be applied to other countries? We are bound to ask ourselves this because the same question is being asked in all countries where efforts are made to study and to understand this problem.
>
> There is no doubt that, in view of the general crisis of capitalism, the Corporate solution will force itself to the fore everywhere, but if the system is to be carried out fully, completely, integrally, revolutionarily, three conditions are required.
>
> A single political party, in order that political discipline may exist alongside the economic discipline and the bond of a common fate may unite everyone above contrasting interests. Nor is

> this enough. Besides the single political party there must be a totalitarian State, a State which by absorbing the energy, interests and aspirations of the people, may transform and uplift them.
>
> But even this is not enough. The third and last and most important condition is to live in an atmosphere of strong ideal tension.
>
> We, in Italy, are living in this atmosphere today.
>
> That is why, step by step, we shall give force and consistency to all our achievements, why we shall translate all our doctrine into action.
>
> Who can deny that the Fascist Era is an era of great ideal tension? No one can deny it. This is an age in which arms are crowned by victory, institutions renewed, land redeemed, and new cities founded. (*On the Corporate State,* Howard Fertig, Inc., ed., 1975.)

Now of course Mussolini, in 1933, had a role model in the Soviet Union; indeed it had served as such since his so-called March on Rome in 1922. Italy, to be sure, was not as backward a nation in those times as was Russia; it did have a relatively powerful bourgeoisie that could not be excluded from the political arena; powerful enough—in fact—to be at least to a degree a power behind the Throne. Other than that, though, what Mussolini detailed as the three vital needs of corporativism certainly did fit the Russian version of state capitalism. But there is something to consider about that speech of even greater importance.

It would seem to be apparent from the blustering and swashbuckling ending to a speech outlining the revolutionary benefits to all by this "brand new" social system that the designers of the corporate state program were not all that confident that it would solve the perpetual turmoil of Italy's capitalism. This actor with the out-thrust jaw was telling his countrymen, in so many words, that the success of this "revolutionary" society would be underwritten by a program of military conquest—along with its own repressive state; that universal contentment would be assured by a life of tension; that the opportunity for relaxation in secure comfort would be minimal, at best. In fact, it was not long after that speech, in 1934, that Mussolini's war against Ethiopia was launched.

Now, Mussolini had been in power, as Il Duce, for some 11 years. Clearly, he and his backers must have been convinced, by then, that they were on shaky ground and that something new had to be added. The fact that the plan was couched, at least partly, in terms used by the anarcho-syndicalist-minded workers, of whom there were a significant number in Italy, indicates that it was thrown as bait and from all reports of its effect it did fool many Syndicalist working people. So it wouldn't be 100 percent, those duped by it would reason. The working class would have to share the wealth with syndicalist professionals, owners, and politicians from the National Fascist party. But it had to be better, they thought, than the old capitalism. And the fact that it would be the same old wage labor and capital relationships, did not seem to enter the consciousness of many, if any.

Yet how could it have? In all of those years prior to Mussolini's rise to power as a Fascist, when did the Socialist party of Italy ever explain to their members and their supporters that the most that could be done, should they win an election and assume political power, would be a continued operation of capitalism and that no reforms that might be instituted would be of benefit to the working class, as a whole, because they would remain as wage slaves—until the desire to end capitalism and establish socialism swept the working class, internationally? To be sure, in the event of a significant strengthening of the international movement for socialism, reforms would come thick and fast as the capitalist class would attempt to hold back the flood. But even that was never the message of social democracy.

Yet, have the Social Democrats learned from past history that naming the country and its institutions "Socialist" when that party wins national elections is a bad joke? Apparently not, for the tune goes on and on like a cracked phonograph record long after Mussolini was killed and hung from his feet in a public square, alongside of his latest mistress. And we have the spectacle of "Socialist" parties in Britain, France, Greece, Austria and Scandinavia, carrying on capitalism in the name of socialism—not to mention Soviet Russia and the rest of the Communist bloc.

But what of Bernard Shaw? Was there, by any chance, an indication of a change of opinion in regard to the dictatorships — at least the right-wing dictatorships — in his writings during World War II and in his remaining years after the end of that war? Well, to our amazement, it seems that there was, albeit without so much as a reference to his previous and long-held identification of Mussolini and Hitler with Socialism. In his *Everybody's Political What's What* we read:

> A movement grew up to steal the thunder of the Socialists and substitute State Capitalism for private Capitalism whilst maintaining private property with all its privileges intact and buying off the proletariat with doles and higher wages. This movement was called Fascism in Italy, and National Socialism (or, for short, Nazi-ism) in Germany, in both of which countries it captured and financed proletarian leaders and put them in command of the government — namely Benito Mussolini and Adolf Hitler. In England and America, where it was much less lucid, it was called the New Deal and the New Order, thus securing a footing in both the democratic and plutocratic camps, but at the cost of a war with Italy and Germany for European hegemony; for when the new Fascist dictators invited the western States to join them in a grand attack on proletarian Russia they were rebuffed as dangerous and subversive revolutionaries whereupon the two dictators desperately undertook jointly the subjection not only of Russia but of recalcitrant Britain and America as well. The only comfortable ally they gained was Japan, leaving them in the position of having to fight both the Communists and the plutocracies in a paradoxical but terribly formidable combination to destroy them. (Constable & Company, Ltd., London, 1944, p. 12.)

But what of the other side of the coin? What of the line-up of bourgeois democracy (Western capitalism) with Russia's professed Communists? Not a word about that "paradox." And Shaw did live long enough after the war to have learned of the cynical carving up of the spoils by the victor nations; of the fact that the Soviet bureaucracy was no less interested in reaping the harvest of victory than were their avowedly capitalist allies. Insofar as recognizing Russia's state capitalism, Shaw died in blissful ignorance.

7. Shaw and Nazism

In the years that the German Social Democratic party had come to dominate the government of the Weimar Republic (after the overthrow of the Kaiser in the German Revolution of 1918), Marxist catchwords and slogans became popular among large sections of the working class of that country; in fact, even under the monarchy and as far back as the latter years of the 19th century, the German Social Democratic party was not only permitted to exist and to contest elections but was relatively strong. So much were the superficial trappings of socialist propaganda familiar and acceptable to the mass of German workers that when Hitler went after substantial support from the proletariat he knew better than to identify with the traditional parties of German capitalism. Instead, he railed against the "plutocracy" with the one significant variation of fingering the Jews as the arch plutocrats—a tactic certainly not a part of the socialist movement in any of its previously known varieties. The political climate in Germany was right for such an approach: deep and pervasive depression; a large and highly noticeable Jewish minority; a longstanding tradition of anti-Semitism.

So, the political scene in Germany at the time of Hitler's ascendancy to power was one in which the dominant parties were his National Socialist German Workers party, the Social Democrats and the Communists; and in truth—insofar as a basic approach was concerned—there was not a great deal to choose between them. True, neither of the professed Marxist parties had an anti-Jewish program; true also that the Social Democrats were basically parliamentary-democratic in approach; but the message of all three was: support us because we will correct the present problems simply by reforms and or drastic alteration of the type of government. There was no visible understanding on the part of the masses that short of worldwide socialist revolution—abolition of the wages, prices, profit, money, system of society, no change in government could accomplish much that was worthwhile. Nor—aside from some theoretical texts by members of the Social Democratic party—was any noticeable attempt made by that party to spread such an understanding among the working class.

In fact, so much were the approach and tactics of Nazis and Communists alike that in the few years preceding the rise to power of Hitlerism, when the Weimar Republic was showing signs of tottering, there was an actual merging of effort between Nazis and Communists in confrontation with the government's forces of "law and order." In his *School for Dictators*, the Italian Social Democrat and author Ignacio Silone informed us that:

> In Germany, between 1930 and 1933, whole groups went over bag and baggage from the militant Communist organization to the Brown-shirts. To understand that phenomenon a rapid sketch of its political causes is necessary. When one looks back now on the policy of the Communist International in Germany before 1933, it is impossible to avoid the conclusion that it was a precious and indispensable aid to Hitler's victory. From 1926 to 1929, when the world economy was on the up-grade, the Communist International decided that capitalist society had entered "the Third Period" of its fatal decline, a period of new revolutions and proletarian insurrections, during which the activities of the Communist parties should be concentrated on the fomenting of general strikes and the struggle for the dictatorship of the proletariat. . . The fantastic theory of "the Third Period" and the imminence of a new revolutionary cycle led to feverish activity among the German Communists, who set themselves to the systematic provocation of obvious and resounding revolutionary acts. . . (Harper & Bros. Publishers; New York and London, 1938; translated from the Italian by Gwenda David and Eric Mosbacher; p. 227).

In short, the main goal of both parties was the overthrow of the Weimar Republic, dominated by Social Democrats. Communist hoodlums joined Nazi storm troopers in confrontations and riots during the chaotic times of German and worldwide depression. Put in simplest terms, the Communist line had become: "First we take care of Weimar, then we'll take care of Hitler!"

But it had to be embarrassing times for Communists and communist sympathizers of Jewish persuasion and, indeed, a large percentage of them, if not the majority, in the years to come deserted the Moscow ranks. To be associated with an approval – to any degree – of Hitlerism was all but impossible for adherents to the religion or the cult of Judaism. Interestingly enough, Mussolini had not needed the anti-Semitic approach during most of the years of his rule and it was not until well into World War II, when the tide was beginning to turn sharply against the Axis powers, that an anti-Jewish policy was introduced into Italy. Until that time, Jewish bourgeois organizations had nothing of a derogatory nature to say against Fascist persecution of radical workers. There were even some Jewish members on Mussolini's Fascist Grand Council. Nor was there any use for anti-Semitism in Franco's Spain, there being no important or noticeable Jewish population in that land since the times of the Inquisition. So it can be safely extrapolated that, had it not been for Hitler's anti-Jewish campaign and his attempt to exterminate Jews *as* Jews, there would very well have been widespread Jewish support for National Socialism in Germany and also of the German war effort – as was the case in World War I.

(In this regard, it should also be noted that until the last years of Stalin, when his regime opened a drive against "cosmopolites," – a code word for Jews – a program of discrimination that has continued, on different levels of virulence, down to these late 1980s – there had been widespread support for Soviet Russia among world Jewry – and quite understandably. As had been the case in the 18th and 19th centuries' overthrow of feudal regimes in Europe, the Bolshevik Revolution of 1917 freed Jewry from a host of feudal restrictions against them, not to mention putting an end to the periodic pograms under the Tsars. So the Jews had much to be grateful for in earlier Bolshevik rule and, in fact, a number of the more prominent members of the Politburo were of ethnic Jewish background.)

Shaw on the Extermination of "Undesirables."

Although there is evidence in his writings that Shaw did favor extermination of "un-desirables" by revolutionary regimes, even that such eliminations be effectuated in lethal gas chambers (and *that*, incidentally, before the advent of Hitler on the scene), we can document his opposition to Hitler's anti-Jewish program as a "bee in Hitler's bonnet" that he ought to abandon. He did come on strong, however, in support of the practice, by victorious revolutionary governments, of liquidating opponents. In his Preface to his play *On the Rocks* he contended that it was a fact of life. He wrote:

> Let us then assume that private property, already maimed by factory legislation, surtax, and a good deal of petty persecution in England, and in Russia tolerated only provisionally as a disgraceful necessity pending its complete extirpation, is finally discarded by civilized communities, and the duty of maintaining it at all costs replaced by the duty of giving effect to the dogma that every ablebodied and ableminded and ablesouled person has an absolute right to an equal share in the national dividend. Would the practice of extermination disappear? I suggest that, on the contrary, it might continue much more openly and intelligently and scientifically than at present, because the humanitarian revolt against it would probably become a humanitarian support of it; and there would be an end of the hypocrisy, the venal special pleading, and the concealment or ignoring of facts which are imposed on us at present because extermination for the benefit of a handful of private persons against the interests of the race is permitted and practiced. . . (London: Constable & Co., pp. 150, 51, reprinted 1949).

Sentiments such as these would appear to be enough to convict Shaw as an inveterate tyrant, or at least a friend of tyranny; especially since his play *On the Rocks* was written as a sort of defense of the ideas of Hitler's National Socialism. The humanitarian revolt *against* extermination, he claimed, can very well become the humanitarian support for it, and consequently be carried out with more openness; and intelligently and scientifically—the hypocrisy usually connected with it would be missing.

But looking at the statement closely, a question comes to mind: So what's new about that? For who would be delegated to determine the victims? Why, of course, it would be folk with sufficient humanity in their souls and, in fact, that would be not all that different from the way that it is done today, even in the "humanitarian-minded" West—at least in wartime, both declared and undeclared varieties. It is certainly a fact that the military personnel who are selected to plan and to carry out bombing missions over "enemy" cities are not, as a rule, known hoodlums. They are, generally, really nice young men with—in many instances—advanced college degrees and even Sunday School background. They are certainly not the type that carry gats and machine guns hidden in trombone cases. And yet they seem to feel no compunction nor remorse at wiping out whole blocks of cities without knowing of or caring about the numbers of men, women and children of all ages—even unborn fetuses that the "right to life" zealots, during peacetime, defend with such vehemence. The same men, if ordered to toss armloads of infants into furnaces would, no doubt, demur and even accept prison terms for disobedience. Yet they do believe they are performing a humanitarian task by following orders of the more usual type from their commanding officers; and they wear their medals proudly.

And on the matter of Shaw's advocating the use of lethal gas chambers for "undesirables" he is even on record as remarking that Hitler should have assigned the credit for that form of extermination system to himself. (See Shaw, *"The Chucker-out"* by Allan Chappelow, p. 403.) He had been arguing against the practice of imprisonment as punishment for crime, taking the position that the world would not come to an end if we simply did not imprison offenders. How about those who just keep on breaking the law? How should we handle the habitual criminal? He put his answer with succinctness in his Preface to *Major Barbara:*

> We do not imprison dogs. We even take our chance of their first bite. But if a dog delights to bark and bite, it goes to the lethal chamber. That seems to me sensible. To allow the dog to expiate his bite by a period of torment—and then let him loose in a much more savage condition (for the chain makes a dog

> savage) to bite again and expiate again, having meanwhile spent a great deal of human life and happiness in the task of chaining and feeding and tormenting him, seems to me idiotic and superstitious. Yet that is what we do to men who bark and bite and steal. It would be far more sensible to put up with their vices, as we put up with their illnesses, until they give more trouble than they are worth, at which point we should, with many apologies and expressions of sympathy, and some generosity in complying with their last wishes, place them in a lethal chamber and get rid of them... (N.Y.: Dodd, Mead, 1945; p. 337).

But wait! As we know, Shaw's philosophy was much like Mark Twain's comment on New England weather. If you abhor what he has been quoted as stating, wait a minute! In a Preface to a book written by his friends and fellow Fabians, Sidney and Beatrice Webb, entitled *English Prisons Under Local Government,* he has much to say on the subject of how to correct the cruelty-impulses that seem to infect some people as, for example, those who derive pleasure from wife and child beating and who "lust after the spectacle of suffering, mental and physical, as normal men lust after love:"

> Now in the present state of our knowledge it is folly to talk of reforming these people. By this I do not mean that even now they are all incurable. The cases of no conscience are sometimes, like Parsigal's when he shot the swan, cases of unawakened conscience. Violent and quarrelsome people are often only energetic people who are underworked; I have known a man cured of wife-beating by setting him to beat the drum in a village band; and the quarrels that make country life so very unarcadian are picked mostly because the quarrelers have not enough friction in their lives to keep them goodhumored. (P. xxvi, Longmans, Green & Co., N.Y., London, Bombay, Calcutta & Madras, 1942.)

So why, then, in a society that has gotten rid of private property—even in a society such as Shaw envisioned, with equality of income for all—would a humanitarian-minded population wish to practice extermination of their fellows rather than simply setting up drum bands in every block? But Shaw is not trying simply to make a joke of it. He continues, in a vein that was just unusual for him, given his antipathy to members and practices of the medical profession:

> Psycho-analysis, too, which is not all quackery and pornography, might conceivably cure a case of Sadism as it might cure any of the phobias. And psycho-analysis is a mere fancy compared to the knowledge we now pretend to concerning the function of our glands and their effect on our character and conduct. In the nineteenth century this knowledge was pursued barbarously by crude vivisectors whose notion of finding out what a gland was for was to cut it violently out and see what would happen to the victim, meanwhile trying to bribe the public to tolerate such horrors by promising to make old debauchees young again. This was rightly felt to be a villainous business; besides, who could suppose that the men who did these things would hesitate to lie about the results when there was plenty of money to be made by representing them as cures for dreaded diseases? But today we are not asked to infer that because something has happened to a violently mutilated dog it must happen also to an unmutilated human being. We can now make authentic pictures of internal organs by means of rays to which flesh is transparent: This makes it possible to take a criminal and say authoritatively that he is a case, not of original sin, but of an inefficient, or excessively efficient, thyroid gland or pituitary gland, or adrenal gland, as the case may be. This of course does not help the police in dealing with a criminal; they must apprehend and bring him to trial all the same. But if the prison doctor were able to say "Put some iodine in this man's skilly, and his character will change," then the notion of punishing instead of curing him would become ridiculous. Of course the matter is not so simple as that; and all this endocrinism, as it is called, may turn out to be only the latest addition to our already very extensive collection of pseudoscientific mares' nests; still, we cannot ignore the fact that a considerable case is being made out by eminent physicians for at least a conjecture that many cases which are now incurable may be disposed of in the not very remote future by inducing the patient to produce more thyroxin or pituitrin or adrenalin or what not, or even administering them to him as thyroxin is at present administered in cases of myxedema. Yet the reports of the work of our prison medical officers suggest that hardly any of them has ever heard of these discoveries, or regards a convict as anything more interesting scientifically than a malingering rascal. (Ibid, 27, 28.)

What Shaw overlooked in doing that piece, however, — and something that he himself had touched upon in his *Intelligent Women's Guide to Socialism and Capitalism* (p. 52) and quoted here in our Chapter 3, is the tremendous boost that crime gives to the economy. Imagine the depths of the depression that would follow an outburst of honesty throughout an entire community! It is probable that even a majority of occupations that keep people employed are constantly, and to a considerable extent if not mainly, dependent upon the existence of dishonesty and outright crime. Karl Marx had something to say about that business and it is pertinent enough to reproduce it here:

Karl Marx on Crime

The criminal produces not alone crimes, but also criminal law and thence the professor who gives lectures thereon, together with the inevitable text-books in which this very same professor throws his discourses in the quality of "goods," on the world market. Thus is an increase of the national wealth produced, without counting the individual job which, according to a competent witness, Prof. Roscher, the manuscript of the text-book affords to the author himself.

Moreover, the criminal produces all correctional and criminal justice, the police, judges, hangmen, juries, etc., as well as the various branches of industry, which form just as many categories of the division of social labor, develop different faculties of the human mind, create new wants, and new means of satisfying them. Torture more than anything else has given place to the most ingenious mechanical inventions, and employs in the production of its machines quite an army of honest artisans.

The criminal produces an impression, good or bad, as the case may be, and thus renders a "service" to the movement of the moral and esthetic sentiments of the public. He produces not only text-books on criminal law, not only the penal law and thereby the legislators of the penal law, but also art, literature, novels and even tragedies, as is proved by the "Faute" of Mullner, the "Brigands" of Schiller, and even by "Oedipe" and "Richard III." The criminal breaks the monotony and daily security of bourgeois life, and thus guarantees it against stagnation and arouses that excitement and restlessness without which even the spur of competition would be blunted. In this manner he furnishes a stimulant to the productive forces. While crime

> withdraws from the labor market a part of the superfluous population, thus diminishing competition among the workers, and preventing to a certain degree the fall of wages below the minimum, the war against crime absorbs another part of this same population. Thus it is that the criminal intervenes as a natural leveller, which restores a just equilibrium and opens up a new perspective of branches of "useful" occupations.
>
> The influence of the criminal on the development of productive forces can be shown even in detail. Would the locksmiths have arrived at their present perfection were there no burglars? Would the making of bank-notes have reached its present perfection if there were no forgers? Would the microscope have found its way in certain commercial spheres (see Bannage) without the existence of fraud in trade? Does not practical chemistry owe as much to the adulteration of goods, and to the efforts made for its detection, as to the noble zeal for production? Crime, by every new means of attack against property, calls into being equally new means to defend it, and thus exercises an influence quite as productive as strikes on the invention of machines.
>
> And, if we leave aside consideration of individual crime, would the world market have existed without national crime, would even the national market have existed? Is it not the tree of sin which is, at the same time, since Adam, the tree of science? . . . ("Theories of Surplus Value," the posthumous manuscript on the "Critique of Political Economy" by Karl Marx, edited by Karl Kautsky (in German) Vol. 1.)

Shaw on Anti-Semitism

Now, in fairness to Shaw, it must be stated that there is no hard evidence in the record to indicate that he favored the Nazi theory of a super Aryan race and the need to exterminate "lesser races," such as the Jews. In fact, he is on record as approving of exogamy and miscegenation as a means of improving the stock—as we shall take note of shortly. In regard to his reaction to the Nazi persecution of Jews, in particular, Shaw had the following to say:

> Now no doubt Jews are most obnoxious creatures. Any competent historian or psycho-analyst can bring a mass of incontrovertible evidence to prove that it would have been better for

the world if the Jews had never existed. But I, as an Irishman, can, with patriotic relish, demonstrate the same of the English. Also of the Irish. If Herr Hitler would only consult the French and British newspapers and magazines of the latter half of 1914, he would learn that the Germans are a race of savage idolaters, murderers, liars, and fiends whose assumption of the human form is thinner than that of the wolf in Little Red Riding Hood.

We all live in glass houses. Is it wise to throw stones at the Jews? Is it wise to throw stones at all?

Herr Hitler is not only an Antisemite, but a believer in the possibility and desirability of a pure bred German race. I should like to ask him why. All Germans are not Mozarts, not even Mendelsohns and Meyerbeers, both of whom, by the way, though exceptional, desirable Germans, were Jews. Surely the average German can be improved. I am told that children bred from Irish colleens and Chinese laundrymen are far superior to inbred Irish or Chinese. Herr Hitler is not a typical German. I should not be at all surprised if it were discovered that his very mixed blood (all our bloods today are hopelessly mixed) got fortified somewhere in the past by that of King David. He cannot get over the fact that the lost tribes of Israel expose us all to the suspicion (sometimes, as in Abyssinia, to the boast) that we are those lost tribes, or at least that we must have absorbed them . . . (Preface to *The Millionairess*, pp. 867, 68).

But he soon goes on, in the same essay, to show his unwavering support for Nazism, generally, and tries to talk Hitler out of the anti-Semitic aspect of it:

Now Herr Hitler is not a stupid German. I therefore urge upon him that his Antisemitism and national exclusiveness must be pathological: a craze, a complex, a bee in his bonnet, a hole in his armor, a hitch in his statesmanship, one of those lesions which sometimes proves fatal. As it has no logical connection with Fascism or National Socialism, and has no effect on them except to bring them into disrepute, I doubt whether it can survive its momentary usefulness as an excuse for plundering raids and *coups d'etat* against inconvenient Liberals or Marxists. A persecution is always a man hunt; and man hunting is not only a very horrible sport but socially a dangerous one, as it revives a primitive instinct incompatible with civilization: indeed civilization rests fundamentally on the compact that it shall be dropped. (Ibid, pp. 869, 70.)

And there can be small doubt that a majority of Hitler's ethnic victims would have eagerly supported him if not for that "bee in his bonnet."

But, as we have pointed out, Shaw was generally the soul of inconsistency and can be quoted—like the Scriptures—on either side of almost any important argument. In the instance of his condemnation of atrocities by the Nazis, for example, as brought out by the post-World War II tribunals, he felt compelled to find justification for the defendants. Writing in his Preface to *Geneva,* he opined:

> As I write, dockfulls of German prisoners of war, male and female, are being tried on charges of hideous cruelties perpetrated by them at concentration camps. The witnesses describe the horrors of life and death in them; and the newspapers class the accused as fiends and monsters. But they also publish photographs of them in which they appear as ordinary human beings who could be paralleled from any crowd or army.
>
> These Germans had to live in the camps with their prisoners. It must have been very uncomfortable and dangerous for them. But they had been placed in authority and management, and had to organize the feeding, lodging, and sanitation of more and more thousands of prisoners and refugees thrust upon them by the central government. And as they were responsible for the custody of their prisoners they had to be armed to the teeth and their prisoners completely disarmed. Only eminent leadership, experience, and organizing talent could deal with such a situation.
>
> Well, they simply lacked these qualities. They were not fiends in human form; but they did not know what to do with the thousands thrown in their care. There was some food; but they could not distribute it except as rations among themselves. They could do nothing with their prisoners but overcrowd them within any four walls that were left standing, lock them in, and leave them almost starving to die of typhus. When further overcrowding became physically impossible they could do nothing with their unwalled prisoners but kill them and burn the corpses they could not bury. And even this they could not organize frankly and competently; they had to make their victims die of illusage instead of by military law. Under such circumstances any miscellaneous collection of irresistably armed men among them would wallow in cruelty and in the exercise of irresponsible

> authority for its own sake. Man beating is better sport than bear baiting or cock fighting or even child beating, of which some sensational English cases were in the papers at home at the time. Had there been efficient handling of the situation by the authorities (assuming this to have been possible) none of these atrocities would have occurred. They occur in every war when the troops get out of hand. (N.Y.: Dodd, Mead, 1963; pp. 637, 38.)

Now inasmuch as the vast majority of the victims of the Nazi concentration camp massacres were ethnic Jews, a case could possibly be made in the matter of Shaw as an anti-Semite. Here is a defense of the people who had been carrying out the orders of their superiors, who were conducting an orchestrated effort to wipe out an entire ethnic cult, rather than themselves—for the most part—being the victims of uncontrollable conditions. How could those who carried out such orders, as a daily routine, not be infected with the same virus of bigotry carried to extreme? Yet, however the degree of truth in such an observation, Shaw himself is firmly on record as favoring ethnic and even "racial" mixture, through marriage or otherwise, to "improve the stock." Whatever was the extent of his admiration for the British upper classes, he could well have scandalized them with his views on that subject because he went beyond the advocacy of miscegenation between the English, for example, and their colonials of any and all colors and ethnic origins; he even advocated the legitimizing of such unions. The British aristocracy never objected to the physical unions so long as it was kept on casual level. In a paragraph that addresses itself, particularly, to his rejection of the Nazi racial and breeding line of "thought," he tells us:

> The statesman must therefore abjure all forms of endogamy, whether of caste, nation, or color, whilst giving the fullest scope to natural selection between the sexes. This is not easy in our far flung commonwealth. We whites have signally failed to populate New Zealand, where we number only a million and a half instead of tens of millions in each of the two islands. When I was in Durham in 1935 the transport minister made an appeal for more British immigration to keep up the British population in South Africa. We have given up Australia as uninhabitable except in

> a few corners. Meanwhile the aboriginal blacks, the inventors of the miraculous boomerang, are not sterile, nor are the black tribes in Africa, or the Maoris in New Zealand now that they have stopped eating one another. *The remedy appears to be miscegenation.* In Jamaica this has been so freely practiced that when I was there in 1911 some of the whitest and most civilized men I met had brown fathers; and in Hawaii, where I wanted to hear some genuine native music instead of the British and American popular tunes with which our tourists are humbugged, I found that pure bred descendants of the old Sandwich Islanders are now human curiosities: Only the Japanese are endogamous. They also are trying the Hitlerian genetic experiment in the east; *but* I should bet *on the mongrels for the long run if I were a sportsman.* (*Everbody's Political What's What?* pp. 249–50. Emphasis added.)

And in the same book, written during World War II after he had apparently gotten rid of some of the enchantment with Hitler, he commented as follows:

> Adolf Hitler might leave George Washington nowhere in an examination (his book Mein Kampf contains a good deal of sound doctrine), but as his conclusions include German hegemony, subjugation of 'non-Aryans' as such, extirpation of Jews, with hostage slaughter and military terrorism as his method, the wisdom of entrusting him with political power is so questionable that the objection to it has produced a world war. He has neither done justice nor loved mercy nor walked humbly with his god. Neither have we nor any of our Allies; but that is not a reason for tolerating Herr Hitler; it is a reason for reforming ourselves as well as dethroning him. (P. 324, ibid.)

In his Preface to *Geneva,* written some two years after the defeat and demise of Hitler, Shaw went to work on the "great man" image of the quondam Fuehrer which, in fact, he himself had been suckered into portraying during the pre-war years of the National Socialist regime. The most interesting aspect of this expose, however, is the absence of reference to his own, previous, words of approval of Hitler's "socialist" dictatorship in, for example, his Depression-years play *On the Rocks.* In fact, even in his Preface to *Geneva* he had not abandoned, in its entirety, his previously-held admiration for the man. Consider the following:

> Power and worship turned Hitler's head: and the national benefactor who began by abolishing unemployment, tearing up the Treaty of Versailles, and restoring the selfrespect of sixty million of his fellow countrymen became the mad Messiah who, as lord of a Chosen Race, was destined to establish the Kingdom of God on earth—a German kingdom of a German God—by military conquest of the rest of mankind... (Vol. V, *Complete Plays with Prefaces*, Dodd, Mead & Co., Inc., 1963).

In so many words: To Shaw, Hitler was just another case of an otherwise decent sort of national hero who allowed success to "go to his head" and thereby change the course of history from progressiveness to retrogression!

Turning Marx on His Head

There is a saying about Karl Marx *vis-à-vis* Georg Hegel in regard to the Hegelian Dialectic: Marx, it is said, turned Hegel "on his head." Whereas Hegel began with the idea and had the materiality flow from it, Marx had the idea flow from the materiality. What Shaw did to Marx was to stand *him* on his head in regard to the primacy of the economic structure of society over the superstructure (in particular, the variety of government). To Shaw, the rejection of parliamentary-style democracy by the Bolshevik, Fascist, and Nazi dictatorships was what determined the fact that they had all overturned capitalism and were operating, each, a variety of socialism.

In reality, the only one of the three dictatorships that had actually undergone a revolution, in the classical sense of that much maligned word, was the Soviet Union. But it was not a revolution overthrowing capitalism; it is not possible to abolish something that does not exist. Whatever capitalism that was extant in the Russia of 1917 was exceptional in an economy predominantly of feudal-agrarian nature. The Soviet Communist party, to be sure, maintained that the first (February) Revolution was the overthrow of feudalism while the second (October)—just eight months later!—transformed Russia from capitalist to socialist. So Shaw and the Fabian Society were not the only ones to turn Marx on his head. In fact, Marx and Engels had had something to say about that sort of phantasmagoria away back in 1848 in their *Communist Manifesto:*

> The Socialist and Communist literature of France, a literature that originated under the pressure of a bourgeoisie in power, and that was the expression of the struggle against this power, was introduced into Germany at a time when the bourgeoisie, in that country, had just begun its contest with feudal absolutism.
>
> German philosophers, would be philosophers, and *beaux esprits,* eagerly seized on this literature, only forgetting, that when these writings immigrated from France into Germany, French social conditions had not immigrated along with them. In contact with German social conditions, this French literature lost all its immediate practical significance, and assumed a purely literary aspect. Thus, to the philosophers of the Eighteenth Century, the demands of the first French Revolution were nothing more than the demands of 'Practical Reason' in general, and the utterance of the will of the revolutionary French bourgeoisie signified in their eyes the laws of pure Will, of Will as it was bound to be, of true human Will generally.

And in those paragraphs, the founders of Scientific Socialism made clear an important fact, which most of their professed adherents – including that on-again-off-again professed adherent, Bernard Shaw – seem to have lost sight of. The desire for a new social order must arise from the generally existing material conditions within the particular country and not from literature that had emanated from industrially-advanced nations. Although written in 1848, those words of Marx and Engels certainly applied to the situation in the Russia of some 69 years later. And yet the Bolsheviks – allegedly Marxian – along with most of the professed friends of Marxism – believe firmly that a relatively tiny group of Russian socialists could foment and carry out a socialist revolution in a feudal-agrarian society such as the Russia of 1917 simply because a number of Bolshevik leaders had lived in exile for a number of years and had come in contact with the most advanced literature of the day on the subject.

8. SHAW ON RELIGION

Without a doubt, the overwhelming majority of those professing to be socialist, or even communist in sympathy – outside of the officially communist nations – believe in one form or other of religion. In fact, it is even doubtful that any of the parties of social democracy has ever asked a prospective member about his religious opinions. And the purportedly Scientific Socialist DeLeonist parties are officially of the conviction that religion is a private matter and of no concern to socialists.

Such an attitude seems paradoxical to traditional Marxists who regard religion as a social matter, rather than private, and who therefore prefer to examine the origins of religion and its role in society. They reason that although, for primitive people, religion did offer enlightenment on scientifically unexplainable natural phenomena, despite the significant remnant of unexplainable processes in the modern world, we do know that answers – when they come – will be material in nature and not spooky. So the sole important role of religion in the advanced world of these times is as a pillar of class society – world capitalism.

But what of Shaw and *his* religious opinions. As with most other topics of importance he had a great deal to say and to write. He was one professed socialist who certainly did *not* regard it as a private affair and one to be shunned in political discussion. His approach, however, was not based upon any known scientific opinion, as we shall see. He was on record, to be sure, as a debunker of much of Christianity but he was also on record as an upholder of much of its purported history against the researched findings of other debunkers. In any case, he certainly did believe, and argue, that religion is a necessity for mankind, only he favored a different than usual variety—one along the lines of the one that he, himself, is credited with having developed. He called it his Life Force. In a nutshell, as Allan Chappelow put it in his *Shaw the Villager* (N.Y.: The Macmillan Co., 1962):

> Out of concepts drawn fromn Lamarck, Shopenhauer, Nietsche, Bergson, and Butler, he evolved a weird mystic power which he named the Life Force after the *elan vital* of creative evolution. This immanent force is slowly evolving through the aeons—amoeba, orangutang, man, superman, angel, archangel—toward ultimate Godhead. Not long before his death Shaw asserted that his was the only credible religion; but he seems to have been his only convert... (p. 332).

Now another one-time Fabian and a sometime crony of Shaw's, H.G. Wells (along with Julian Huxley and G.P. Wells) disposed of this matter with a minimum of space in their *The Science of Life:*

> The most celebrated creative force is Bergson's *elan vital* or vital urge, which reappears, expounded in exaggerated form a pantomime of giant as the Life Force of Mr. Bernard Shaw. The Shavian Life Force need not detain us long. It is Lamarckian in caricature, Life evolves, says Mr. Shaw, by trying, by more or less conscious effort. Evolution takes place because all life is purposeful in its degree. In ourselves the Life Force may be at cross purposes with our conscious, but more superficial selves; racial purpose may conflict with individual purpose. But however disguised, however deep below the level of ordinary consciousness, the essence of the Life Force is purpose. Quite apart from the difficulty of ascribing even rudimentary purpose and foreknowledge to a tapeworm or a potato or collective aspiration to the tapeworm race or the potatoes of the world, there remains the impossibility of transmitting the results of this purposeful striving to posterity. If, as we have given ample reason for believing, acquired characters cannot be inherited, Mr. Shaw's Life Force does not exist. (P. 638, The Literary Guild, ed., N.Y., 1934.)

But Shaw was not one to be convinced by scientific evidence, produced by Darwinian biologists, invalidating his

Lamarckian-based theory. His credo on that score seemed to have been, if the facts refute the theory, get some new facts. For example, there was his reaction to those careful experiments by the biologist August Weissman on mice. Weissman was determined to find out if acquired traits were passed on to offspring in successive generations so he cut off the tails of his rodents, for several generations. In no case were his mice born without tails. In the Preface to his *Back to Methuseleh* Shaw answered Weissman as follows:

> A vital conception of Evolution would have taught Weissman that biological problems are not to be solved by assaults on mice. The scientific form of his experiment would have been something like this. First, he should have procured a colony of mice highly susceptible to hypnotic suggestion. He should then have hypnotized them into an urgent conviction that the fate of the musque world depended on the disappearance of its tail, just as some ancient and forgotten experimenter seems to have convinced the cats of the Isle of Man. Having thus made the mice desire to lose their tails with a life-or-death intensity, he would very soon have seen a few mice born with little or no tail. These would be recognized by the other mice as superior beings, and privileged in the division of food and in sexual selection. Ultimately the tailed mice would be put to death as monsters by their fellows, and the miracle of the tailless mouse completely achieved.
>
> The objections to this experiment is not that it seems too funny to be taken seriously, and is not cruel enough to overawe the mob, but simply that it is impossible, because the human experimenter cannot get at the mouse's mind. And that is what is wrong with all the barren cruelties of the laboratories. Darwin's followers did not think of this . . . (pp. vii, lviii; Brentano's, N.Y. 1921).

And he continues with a lengthy tirade against such cruelties and the scientists who perpetrate them against the defenseless animals.

Unfortunately for Shaw's theory of general foreknowledge and purpose in the animal and vegetable kingdoms, it cannot be proved objectively and is based, as is all religion, on the faith of a little child. Darwin, years before Mendel's times, postulated that there is a hereditary factor in every part of the body that contributes to reproduction. If this conjecture were inaccurate then an injury to hereditary particles should produce corresponding injury to the next generation. No corresponding injury appeared in the succeeding generations of Weissman's mice; nor has the circumcision of Jewish male infants, over a period of some 5000 years, as yet produced a penis without a foreskin. The 20th century discovery of the genetic factor, of course, sounded the absolute death knell of Lamarckism, Bergsonism, and Shaw's Life Force.

Now Shaw, of course, was a bundle of contradictions and despite his recorded rejection of Christianity was, for many years, a paid-up "pew member" of the Parish Church at Ayot St. Lawrence where he lived for his last 44 years. The Reverend R.J. Davies, Rector, had the following to say, *inter alia,* in his eulogy of Shaw on November 5, 1950:

> Most of us will remember the occasion on Palm Sunday two years ago when Mr. Shaw made his last public speech.
>
> Who would forget [its] conclusion...? "The gate," he said, "was placed not as a barrier, but as an invitation." It was most fitting, he added, that we should dedicate a gate on Palm Sunday, for that week we would all be singing "Lift up your heads O ye gates, and be ye lift up ye everlasting doors." And, then, pointing to the partly demolished church, he concluded: "This is His House. This is His Gate, and this is His Way." (Pp. 312–13, *Shaw the Villager*; The Macmillan Co., N.Y. 1962.)

So, even though he had written reams of pages to demonstrate his rejection of organized religion, particularly in the instance of what he liked to call *Crosstianity* – the religion with a "gibbet" for an emblem or symbol – and despite his having been widely known as an atheist, he was far from total rejection of all forms of even organized Christianity. According to Allan Chappelow, Shaw's own credo was:

> I am a resolute Protestant; I believe in the Holy Catholic Church, in the Holy Trinity of Father, Son (or Mother, Daughter) and Spirit; in the Community of Saints, the Life to Come, the Immaculate Conception and the everyday reality of Godhead and the Kingdom of Heaven. (*Shaw the Villager,* p. 333.)

And even though those words were uttered, no doubt, with tongue in cheek; with a shade of meaning other from the traditional, it should be remembered that Shaw was an expert equivocator, a hedger of his bets. He could have been playing it safe—just in case...

Now, as already indicated, nothing about Shaw serves more to underline his negative attitude toward Socialism as a philosophy and an interpretation of history—in the manner of Marxism—than his attitude on religion. To Marx, the problem with organized religion is its communion with private (capitalist) interests. It is one of those forces that scientific enquiry must do battle with. As he put it in his Preface to *Capital*, Vol. 1, first edition (italics added):

> In the domain of Political Economy, free scientific enquiry meets not merely the same enemies as in all other domains. The peculiar nature of the material it deals with, summons as foes into the battle the most violent, mean and malignant passions of the human breast, the Furies of private interest. The *English Established Church*, e.g., will more readily pardon an attack on 38 of its 39 Articles than on 1/39th of its income. Now-a-days atheism itself is *culpa levis* [lightly blamed] as compared with criticism of existing property relations.... (P. 15, Kerr, ed.)

So much for Marx; but Shaw was cut from a different mold; he was no echo on that subject of either Marx or of any of the established religions. In fact, he had become convinced that organized religions and logical destructionists of belief in God, between them, had all but destroyed religion and it was high time that a new credo became established; a credo based upon what he regarded as a scientific approach to creation and evolution—Lamarckism—as opposed to Darwinism which he regarded as, perhaps, the greatest calamity ever visited upon mankind. What Darwin had done with his natural selection (which Shaw preferred to label "Circumstantial Selection") was to remove will and purpose from the world.

For it is demonstrable, said Darwin, that design plays no role whatever, nor is conscious effort involved. It is all simply a random, hit-and-miss or trial-and-error proposition. Short-necked giraffes, for example, had simply died off as giraffes multiplied in numbers and as the food they could reach diminished to the vanishing point. The long necks had not resulted from conscious effort to reach the high branches. Acquired characteristics are not passed on in inheritance. With the same reasoning people with dark pigmentation are descended from those who survived under certain solar ultraviolet ray conditions in the tropics. So it is not just a case of healthy, permanent tanning, and this is easy to comprehend because it is patent that blacks could live in Alaska, for example, and never lose their color, providing that they are not the progeny of intermarriage with whites.

And because natural selection is easy to understand and, despite some extended argument to the contrary within and among groups with rival class interests, does not really violate class interest or political ideology, in general, not too many decades had to pass before it overcame resistance and became all but universally accepted—or, at very least, winked at by the large established churches whose priestly professors assure us that there is no basic conflict and allow the matter to rest in peace. Anyway, as Shaw saw it, the ancient mythology of organized religion had had it! It was time for a change to a mythology based upon his concept of scientific evolution—Lamarckism. As he put it in the *St. Martin-in-the-Fields Review*, "Catechism," on his creed:

> *What effect do you think it would have on the country if every Church were shut and every parson unfrocked?...*
>
> A very salutory effect indeed. It would soon provoke an irresistable demand for the Re-establishment of the Church, which could then start again without the superstitions that make it so impossible today. At present, the Church has to make itself cheap in all sorts of ways to induce people to attend its services; and the cheaper it makes itself the less the people attend. Its articles are out of date; its services are out of date; and its ministers are men to whom such things do not matter because they are out of date themselves... (*Shaw on Religion*, Dodd, Mead & Co., pp. 130–31).

The fact that Lamarckism and its exponents, once considered scientific by the scientific community, were now also out-of-date (exploded insofar as the scientific community was concerned), was of small matter. Shaw knew better.

In the course of his criticisms of the mythology of organized religion, Shaw had the following to say:

> In 1562 the Church, in convocation in London, 'for the avoiding of diversities of opinions and for the establishment of consent touching on true religion,' proclaimed in their first utterance, and as an Article of Religion, that God is 'without bodyparts, or passions,' or, as we say, an *Elan Vital* or Life Force. Unfortunately neither parents, parsons, nor pedagogues could be induced to adopt that article. St. John might say that 'God is spirit' as pointedly as he pleased; our Sovereign Lady Elizabeth might ratify the Article again and again; serious divines might feel so deeply as they could that a God with body, parts, and passions could be nothing but an anthropormophic idol: no matter: people at large could not conceive a God who was not anthropomorphic: they stood by the Old Testament and finally set up as against the Church a God who, far from being without body, parts, or passions, was composed of nothing else and of very evil passions too. They imposed this idol in practice on the church itself, in spite of the First Article, and thereby homeopathically produced the atheist, whose denial of God was simply a most unchristian idolatry. . . (p. xiii, Preface to *Back to Methuseleh).*

So, in effect, Shaw found the Church of England not guilty of complicity in the anthropomorphization of God by "higher authorities than its own or even of the State"—people-at-large (including the lesser clergy). As for Shaw's own belief: even though he seemed to reject the anthropomorphic view, and despite his frequent gibes at orthodoxy, he was no more willing to place himself completely outside of it than were the higher authorities of the Church of England in 1562 after losing out on their effort at de-anthropomorphization. In fact, as we shall demonstrate from his own writings, he still put up a remarkable defense of the tales as recounted in the Gospels: a defense that true believers can point to when discussing Shaw's rock bottom religious views. At worst, they might contend, he was not certain and was open to conversion—just in case!

It is said that as far back as the 1890s Shaw had suggested

that he would eventually write a "gospel of Shawianity" which is what *Back to Methuseleh* is: a "Metabiological Pentateuch" complete with a Preface. The kernel of his creative evolution was, as already noted, the philosophy of Henri Bergson, French philosopher (1859–1941) who argued that all living forms arise from a persisting natural force. It is, said Shaw, a life force which drives us ever upwards toward that ultimate goal of superman and maybe even beyond!

Finally, on the subject of Shaw's religious philosophy, a further example of his consistent inconsistency is in order. "Will," "Purpose," "Conscious striving" of all living matter ever upward to perfection? Yes, but it seems that random, trial-and-error, hit-and-miss experimentation on the part of that creator force out there, which he invariably referred to as God, was also part of his argument. The theme of his "Metabiological Pentateuch" is his belief that a lifespan of three-score years-and-ten is not nearly enough to make of man (the Englishman, at any rate) an intelligent being politically. He needs at least 300! And this can materialize, and will, by consciously willing and striving toward that goal. In the second section, entitled "The Gospel of the Barnabas Brothers," his characters are contemplating that assertion by Conrad Barnabas, a biologist, and his brother Franklyn, a writer, that man's lifespan could easily be three hundred years:

> BURGE (a liberal party politician)...we must keep the actual secret to ourselves.
>
> CONRAD. (staring at them) The actual secret! What on earth is the man talking about?
>
> BURGE. The stuff. The powder. The Bottle. Whatever it is...
>
> CONRAD. My good sir: I have no powder, no bottle, no tabloid. I am not a quack: I am a biologist. This is a thing that's going to happen.
>
> FRANKLYN. We can put it into men's heads that there is nothing to prevent its happening but their own will to die before their work is done, and their own ignorance of the splendid work there is for them to do.
>
> CONRAD. Spread that knowledge and that conviction; and as surely as the sun will rise tomorrow, the thing will happen...

But Shaw had created a loophole, a way out, as we read a couple of pages earlier; and this seeming variation in his theory also appears in his Preface and in his published religious speeches (Pennsylvania State University Press):

> LUBIN . . . (to Conrad). May I ask are there any alternative theories? Is there a scientific Opposition?
>
> CONRAD. Well, some authorities hold that the human race is a failure, and that a new form of life, better adapted to high civilization, will supersede us as we have superseded the ape and the elephant.
>
> BURGE (another Liberal party pol). The superman: eh?
>
> CONRAD. No. Some being quite different from us.
>
> LUBIN. Is that altogether desirable?
>
> FRANKLYN. I fear so. However that may be, we may be quite sure of one thing. We shall not be let alone. The force behind evolution, call it what you will, is determined to solve the problem of civilization; and if it cannot do it through us, it will produce some more capable agents. Man is not God's last word: God can still create. If you cannot do His work He will produce some being who can.
>
> BURGE (with zealous reverence). What do we know about Him, Barnabas? What does anyone know about Him?
>
> CONRAD. We know this about Him with absolute certainty. The power my brother calls God proceeds by the method of Trial and Error; and if we turn out to be one of the errors, we shall go the way of the mastodon and megatherium and all the other scrapped experiments.

In effect, Shaw seems to be hedging here just a little in his theory of grand design and evolution through will and conscious effort. As he worded it in his Preface:

> This does not mean that if Man cannot find the remedy no remedy will be found. The power that produced Man when the monkey was not up to the mark, can produce a higher creature than Man if Man does not come up to the mark. What it means is that if Man is to be saved, Man must save himself. There seems no compelling reason why he should be saved. He is by no means an ideal creature. At his present best many of his ways are so unpleasant that they are unmentionable in polite society, and so painful that he is compelled to pretend that pain is often a good. Nature holds no brief for the human experiment: it must stand or fall by its results. If Man will not serve, Nature will try another experiment.

> What hope is there then of human improvement? According to the Neo-Darwinists, to the Mechanists, no hope whatever because improvement can come only through some senseless accident which must, on the statistical average of accidents, presently be wiped out by some other senseless accident. (Pp. xv–xvi.)

So again he is having it both ways. It is not necessarily a grand design; will and purpose in evolution may not succeed; the grand design might just be one of trial-and-error, hit-and-miss experimentation. But heavens no! Is that not what the Neo-Darwinists are saying? So he proceeds in his very next section to reassure us:

> But this dismal creed does not discourage those who believe that the impulse that produces evolution is creative. They have observed the simple fact that the will to do anything can and does, at a certain pitch of intensity set up by conviction of its necessity create and organize new tissue to do it with. To them therefore mankind is by no means played out yet. If the weight lifter, under the trivial stimulus of an athletic competition, can "put up muscle," it seems reasonable to believe that an equally earnest and convinced philosopher could "put up a brain." Both are directions of vitality to a certain end. Evolution shews us that direction of vitality doing all sorts of things: providing the centipede with a hundred legs, and ridding the fish of any legs at all; building lungs and arms for the land and gills and fins for the sea; enabling the mammal to gestate its young inside its body, and the fowl to incubate hers outside it; offering us, we may say, our choice of any sort of bodily contrivance to maintain our activity and increase our resources. (P. xvi.)

Free will, powerful enough to create the body's raw material and eventually turn it into parts! Obviously, if we all will *will* intensely enough to fly on our own—without machines—man will sprout wings. Birds have done it!

Traditional Socialism and Religion

But in order to make a beginning to a discussion on the conflict between Shaw and the traditional socialists on religion it might be appropriate, inasmuch as Shaw did maintain in his *Self Sketches*, that he never threw Marx over on essentials, to present the Marxian attitude at this time; even though it is a fact that small emphasis, if any, has been placed on it by the majority of avowed Socialists in the West, or even in the East; and despite the hundreds of millions in the so-called socialist and communist nations who seem able to co-exist with it within their own societies. We have many examples of practicing Christians (of one sort or another);* practicing Moslems; and nominally practicing Jews also espousing what they and most of the world insists is socialism. Even the vast Hindu nation of India was led by the avowed Marxist Nehru and his socialist cronies of the Congress party (and still is); and we see the philosophy of Marxism supposedly making inroads among Buddhists—as in Sri Lanka. Truly, Marx and the collective saints must all be turning in their graves!

But traditional Scientific Socialists cannot help but regard all of this with jaundiced eye. Religion did not pop full-blown from the skies into the minds of men. It had a materialist foundation and can be explained with that socialist tool known as the materialist conception of history, a tool that neither G.B. Shaw nor the overwhelming majority of contemporary socialists/communists have made use of.

Marx on Religion

Now, were one to ask: what did Marx have to say about religion? the answer might very likely be that Marx called religion "the opium of the people" and that is true enough but the statement loses much of its punch when given out of context. These words were used in the course of his *Introduction to a Contribution to the Critique of Hegel's Philosophy of Right*, and the paragraphs surrounding it read as follows:

**This writer remembers an occasion when, in a discussion with some Jesuit priests who happened to be friendly to Marxism, generally, that they reasoned that Marx's views on religion were an aberration and not really essential to his philosophy.*

> The basis of irreligious criticism is this: *man makes religion;* religion does not make man. Religion is indeed man's self-consciousness and self-awareness so long as he has not found himself or has lost himself again. But *man* is not an abstract being, squatting outside the world. Man is *the human world,* the state, society. This state, this society, produce religion which is an *inverted world consciousness,* because they are an *inverted world.* Religion is the general theory of this world, its encyclopedic compendium, its logic in popular form, its spiritual *point d'honneur,* its enthusiasm, its moral sanction, its solemn complement, its general basis of consolation and justification. It is *the fantastic realization* of the *human being* inasmuch as the *human being* possesses no true reality. The struggle against religion, is, therefore, indirectly a struggle against that world whose spiritual *aroma* is religion.
>
> *Religious* suffering is at the same time an *expression* of real suffering and a *protest* against real suffering. Religion is the sigh of the oppressed creature, the sentiment of a heartless world, and the soul of soulless conditions. It is the *opium* of the people.
>
> The abolition of religion as the *illusory* happiness of man, is a demand for their *real* happiness. The call to abandon their illusions about their condition is a *call to abandon a condition which* requires *illusions.* The criticism of religion is, therefore, *the embryonic criticism of this vale of tears* of which religion is the *halo.* (Italics in text.)

Now, whereas religion has been a fetter, historically, on scientific research, it has learned how to cooperate—indeed it *must* now cooperate since, with a few exceptions, it no longer dominates the mundane affairs of society, and it has been encouraged by ruling classes that realize the dangers to their societies of uncurbed scientific attitudes on the nature of the universe.

So the populations—even the scientific section of the population—have been conditioned into developing a type of water and airtight, two-compartmented, mind that is able to hold at one and the same time ideas and attitudes that blatantly contradict one another. Scientists, generally, will pay lip service to religion, if only in an abstract manner; and it must be noted that a large percentage of the institutions of higher learning—science departments and labs and all—are owned by organized religions with no apparent embarrassment to them.

There is, then, a twofold reason why traditional socialists reject religions and insist that any variety of religious belief is inconsistent with an espousal of socialism: (1) Religion is founded upon a dualistic concept of the universe—physical and metaphysical; spiritual and material—whereas socialism embraces a monistic philosophy in line with the physical sciences. Scientific Socialism, then, is in harmony with science generally, not in spite of its different convictions but because of its understanding; (2) Religion—whatever its form—serves the interests of the ruling class rather than those of the subject class or classes. Religious institutions, as they develop, in fact become a part of the exploiting class through their acquisition of property. The state may intervene, as it frequently does, to hamper or to outlaw individual cults—new or old—but it is always eager to maintain, or cooperate with, to one extent or another, organized religion which functions as a pillar of class society.

Shaw on the Gospels' Historicity

Bernard Shaw was, essentially, a creative writer. He had begun his career with that concerted but abortive attempt at novel-writing; had switched to literary and music criticism as a journalist; went on from there to a different form of creative fiction, playwriting. During all of the half century as a dramatist he turned out reams of observations on politics, economics, and history but, apparently, allowed his analyses to be influenced by his creative aptitudes. To the creative writer, the fictional invention is the way it should have happened; the character as true as a true life individual. He creates a "white" lie and allows himself to believe it as gospel. He is not interested in—or not enough interested in—the social relationships in which his hero lives and which frame his attitudes. It is the hero and his ideology and philosophy which must be studied and emulated. Hang the forces! Who's interested in them?

This manner of thinking is no better exemplified than in Shaw's Preface to *Androcles and the Lion,* in Shaw's attitude toward the question of the historicity and importance of the person of Jesus. He sums up his approach to the question of credibility most lucidly, after having discussed the four Gospels—their similarities and their contradictions:

> It will be noted by the older among my readers, who are sure to be obsessed more or less by elderly wrangles as to whether the gospels are credible as matter-of-fact narratives, that I have hardly raised this question, and have accepted the credible and incredible with equal complacency. I have done this because credibility is a subjective condition, as the evolution of religious belief clearly shews. Belief is not dependent on evidence and reason. There is as much evidence that the miracles occurred as that the Battle of Waterloo occurred, or that a large body of Russian troops passed through England in 1914 to take part in the war on the western front.
>
> The reasons for believing in the murder of Pompey are the same as the reasons for believing in the raising of Lazarus. Both have been believed and doubted by men of equal intelligence. Miracles, in the sense of phenomena we cannot explain, surround us on every hand; life itself is the miracle of miracles. Miracles in the sense of events that violate the normal course of our experience are vouched for every day: the flourishing Church of Christ Scientist is founded on a multitude of such miracles. Nobody believes all the miracles: everybody believes some of them. I cannot tell why men who will not believe that Jesus ever existed yet believe firmly that Shakespear was Bacon. I cannot tell why people who believe that angels appeared and fought on our side at the battle of Mons, and who believe that miracles occur quite frequently at Lourdes, nevertheless boggle at the miracle of the liquefaction of the blood of St. Januarius, and reject it as a trick of priestcraft. I cannot tell why people who will not believe Matthew's story of three kings bringing costly gifts to the cradle of Jesus, believe Luke's story of the shepherds and the stable. I cannot tell why people, brought up to believe the Bible in the old literal way as an infallible record and revelation, and rejecting that view later on, begin by rejecting the Old Testament, and give up the belief in a brimstone hell before they give up (if they ever do) the belief in a heaven of harps, crowns, and thrones. I cannot tell why people who will not believe in baptism on any terms believe in vaccination with the cruel fanaticism of inquisitors. I am convinced that if a dozen sceptics were to draw up in parallel columns a list of the events narrated in the gospels which they consider credible and incredible respectively, their lists would be different in several particulars. Belief

is literally a matter of taste. (Penguin Books, Baltimore, 1969 ed., pp. 50, 51.)

The attitude expressed in this unreasonable piece of reasoning may be especially fitting for a creative fictionist or a dramatist but it hardly is suitable for a commentator on historical events. With Shaw, fact had become so intermixed with fiction in the creation of his prefaces, plays, and his political and religious speeches that he found it a plain nuisance to separate truth from the mélange in his brain. "What is the difference?" he must have asked himself. "In any case, as my 16th century counterpart put it: 'The play's the thing!'" So he was willing to accept Christianity in its earliest form as the creation of a single man, Jesus, and was unwilling to discuss the question of the actual historicity of Jesus. He contends, however, as we shall see, that Jesus was superseded by Paul (Saul of Tarsus) as the chief shaper of the Church, depicting Paul as the heavy in his story. The emphasis of Shaw, the dramatist, was on the heroes and the villains and on the flavor of the stories told by the evangelists; this despite some cursory acknowledgment of the class angle with little if anything to say regarding the material conditions and the class struggle that raged among the Jews of Judea.

For Shaw the creative artist was interested chiefly in the stories and characters. Why should he concern himself with historicity and credibility even when dealing with purportedly historic matters? As examples of this attitude, he delighted in mixing his epochs as though the material forces operating behind the scenes were essentially alike: he wrote "John the Baptist may have been a Keir Hardie [a modern Scottish miner; founder of the British Independent Labour Party]; but the Jesus of Matthew is of the Ruskin-Morris class [wealthy aristocrats and avowed Socialists, also, contemporaries of Shaw].

Apparently paying scant heed to the evidence indicating that the gospels had all been written as late as the second century A.D. he observed that they had to have all been written during the lifetime of Jesus since they all indicate, to one extent or another, that the writer expected to be around when Jesus returned. (In the case of St. John, of course, since the claim was that Jesus had conferred upon him eternal life he could still be around awaiting that Second Coming.) And, as noted, Shaw had no respect for documentation, was unwilling to accept any of it. On the subject of more expert testimony from scholarly researchers, he wrote:

> But I repeat, I take no note here of the disputes of experts as to the date of the gospels, not because I am not acquainted with them, but because, as the earliest codices are Greek manuscripts of the fourth century A.D., and the Syrian ones are translations from the Greek, the paleographic expert has no difficulty in arriving at whatever conclusion happens to suit his beliefs or disbeliefs; and he never succeeds in convincing the other experts except when they believe or disbelieve exactly as he does. Hence I conclude that the dates of the original narratives cannot be ascertained, and that we must make the best of the evangelists' own accounts of themselves . . . (p. 46, ibid).

So on the question of the historicity of the gospels, Shaw was definitely a sceptic to the extent that he rejected all of the expertly researched evidence of forgeries and interpolations. He maintained that no subsequent forger—and he did recognize that there were many of them—would perpetrate such an interpolation knowing that the event had not come to pass. As far as he was concerned:

> The paleographers and daters of first quotations may say what they please: John's claim to give evidence as an eyewitness whilst the others are only compiling history is supported by a certain versimilitude which appeals to me as one who has preached a new doctrine and argued about it, as well as written stories. This versimilitude may be dramatic art backed by knowledge of public life; but even at that we must not forget that the best dramatic art is the operation of a divinatory instinct for truth . . . (p. 47, ibid).

And how does one argue with an expert at divination? Nevertheless, it will be of interest here to cite an 1887 published account of research into the historicity of the gospels. The author, Lewis G. James, was a lecturer in an advanced Sunday school of the Second Unitarian Church, Brooklyn, N.Y. According to him, "We have absolutely no contemporary record of the life and teaching of Jesus, either in or out of the writings of the New Testament." And, he avers:

> The four canonical Gospels are preserved to us in extant manuscripts of the fourth, fifth, and later Christian centuries. All of them were originally written, probably, during the second century of our era. Their authorship is unknown, and, with the possible exception of the Third Gospel, it cannot even be conjectured with reasonable probability. Renan supposes that Mark and Luke were written in Rome and Matthew in Palestine; but for these hypotheses we are obliged to rely mainly upon uncertain traditions, sustained or corrected by the known character of the documents themselves. Tradition also asserts that the Fourth Gospel was composed at Ephesus, but it presents strong internal evidence of Alexandrian origin or influence. Prof. Robertson Smith terms them all "unapostolic digests of the second century". . . (*A Study of Primitive Christianity*, pp. 72–3, Chas. H. Kerr & Co., Chicago).

In reference to the "superseding" of Jesus by Paul and Paul's remaking of Christianity, Shaw had the following to say, also in his Preface to *Androcles and the Lion:*

> Years ago I said that the conversion of a savage to Christianity is the conversion of Christianity to savagery. The conversion of Paul was no conversion at all: It was Paul who converted the religion that had raised one man above sin and death into a religion that delivered millions of men so completely into their dominion that their own common nature became a horror to them, and the religious life became a denial of life. Paul had no intention of surrendering either his Judaism or his Roman citizenship to the new moral world (as Robert Owen called it) of Communism and Jesuism. Just as in the XIX century Karl Marx, not content to take political economy as he found it, insisted on rebuilding it from the bottom upwards in his own way, and thereby gave a new lease of life to the errors it was just outgrowing, so Paul reconstructed the old Salvationism from which Jesus had vainly tried to redeem him, and produced a fantastic theology which is still the most amazing thing of its kind known to us. . . (p. 83, ibid).

But how can one argue with an expert who sees no difference in belief that there actually was a Battle of Waterloo from belief in the chronicle of Biblical miracles and the lives of people with no documented historicity from their contemporaries? Certainly, accounts of actual historical events are frequently distorted, depending upon the perspective of the chronicler or journalist. The textbooks on the United States' Civil War, for example, must have a different orientation—even regardless of the author's perspective—for Southern schools than for those in the North in order to be acceptable. And sale at a profit is the bottom line for book publishers as it also is for the publishers of newspapers and journals. Yet we do know that Napoleon and Wellington and Grant and Lee did actually exist; and that Waterloo and Gettysburg did really occur; that Julius Caesar, Pompey, and John F. Kennedy were the victims of assassination, as were a host of other prominent leaders, not to mention the uncounted millions of ordinary folk who die in wars and famines. Future researchers can also determine, easily enough, that Bernard Shaw was not really a figment of the imaginations of a number of creative and polemical writers whose lives spanned the latter half of the 19th and the first half of the 20th centuries; that, despite the innumerable contradictions in his utterances he was, indeed, one person. Researchers can really separate truth from fiction—unless it is Biblical research (much of it, at any rate) or unless the researcher is, first of all, a creative writer!

But let us assume, for the sake of the argument, that Paul and Jesus were historical personalities; that Paul should have presented Christianity as delineated by Jesus—as should Karl Marx, some 1800 years later, Shaw argues, have allowed economics to proceed as newly presented by vulgar economists, without challenge. Paul's successors would learn that his creed would be unacceptable to the rulers of Rome and witness the installation of a different theology, such as Mithraism, as the official religion of their state.

As for Karl Marx, he was not interested in falling in line with the needs of a developing capitalist system. But there can be no comparison made between his efforts and those of Jesus for, despite the lack of relevance in Jesus' version of Christianity to the material interests of the Roman ruling class, there is no indication in the early gospels that he propagandized against chattel slavery, itself, as a system of society. But had Marx been willing to simply build upon economics according to the needs of capitalism, it is certain that somebody else would have exposed it for what it is—a higher form of slavery; and that somebody else would have gotten no further, by now, than did Marx and his successors have gotten in spreading the word in the manner intended.

9. Darwinism and Socialism

The viewpoint that discerns and identifies an historic linkage between Charles Darwin and Karl Marx in regard to their respective, earth-shaking theories seems not to be shared by scientists, generally, in our times. Most scientific people, to the extent that they do attempt an analysis of our social system, are no more cognizant of the traditional Marxist critique than is the bulk of the population. When it comes to political science, their thinking is dominated by the ruling class approach to an extent, in fact, of permitting their particular political views to influence, or to color, their research efforts. In any case, a century and a quarter after the publication of Darwin's *Origin of the Species*, it would not be easy to find scientists, other than an occasional Marxist, who do see a connection between scientific evolution and scientific socialism.

This was not always the case and in the decades immediately following the publication of Darwin's monumental work in 1859, there was frequent and heated debate among scientists over the question. For example, in 1877, Ernest Haeckel, the famed German embryologist, delivered an eloquent address at the Congress of Naturalists meetings, being held in Munich, in which he defended and propagated Darwinism, at the time under violent attack by other scientists.

A few days afterwards, one Rudolf Virchow, a noted pathologist, assailed the Darwinian theory of organic evolution, raising a terrible cry of alarm: "Darwinism," he warned, "leads directly to socialism."

The German Darwinians, headed by Haeckel and Oscar Schmidt, immediately protested—not, however, in defense of

Socialism but in disagreement with Virchow's premise – arguing that the theory of descent, in fact, invalidates the socialist case because it demonstrates the fact that variation and consequent inequality among humanity is inherent and that, consequently, the socialist dream of a society based upon absolute equality of all is impossible of attainment. In fact, they argued, Darwinian evolution would seem to justify and to lead to a society based upon aristocratic control rather than socialism or democracy in any form.

The theory of descent, they claimed, demonstrates the fact of variation and consequent inequality, upholding even inequality of reward and recompense for services rendered. (The position of these pro-Darwinian, anti-Socialist scientists was quoted at length in a work by Enrico Ferri, *Socialism and Modern Science,* International Library Publishing Co., 1900, N.Y. Translated by Robert Rives LaMonte.)

Now, it did not seem to dawn upon those naturalists that it was their understanding of the goal of Scientific Socialism that was faulty, and not socialism itself. For the revolutionary slogan "From Each According to Ability; To Each According to Need" was not a demand for absolute equality among all, but simply an insistence upon an equal *right of access* to the products, services, and territory of the planet. And when it comes right down to the nitty gritty, how could an individual of exceptional ability and talent resent those of lesser genius or expertise receiving according to their needs as long as the master, or specialist, is having his or her requirements satisfied?

There is, to be sure, the argument, Why would one bother to become a brain surgeon or a nuclear physicist when one's material rewards would be no greater than those with lesser talents and skills? But that type of reasoning can only be a product of a commodity society where everything – including brain power and talents – is for sale on the market! The fact that there are individuals, even if a distinct minority, who do not reason that way even in capitalist society demonstrates that such thinking is a product of the system of society and not of one's organic system.

It must be admitted, of course, that the mass production techniques of the late 19th century were not nearly as developed as they are today. In our times, however, it is not easy to understand why scientists, brilliant in their own areas as they are, cannot seem to comprehend that the problem of industry today is not one of how to produce an abundance but, rather, how to keep from producing more than the market can dispose of—at a profit! It is simply a case of understanding that the fetters on productive capacity can only be removed by universal abolition of the system of production for sale with view to profit and introduction of a universal system of production for use.

But, as has been noted, the debate over whether Darwinian evolution leads to socialism or, conversely, to aristocratic rule, was argued out a century ago and little, if anything, seems now to be said about a relationship between it and human societies other than an assertion one hears from time to time that Darwinism provides a logical explanation for individual prowess in the field of financial manipulation. It is the "fittest" who survive in the no-holds barred struggle in the markets.

In point of fact, Darwinism has nothing to do with democracy, aristocracy, socialism, or any other sort of civil social system. The theory of natural selection, no doubt, was somewhat applicable to primitive man but once he got organized into civilized societies (chattel slavery, serfdom, capitalism) his survival depended more upon man-made factors than natural ones.

True, there is a ferocious competition among members of the same class for profits and for jobs, as well as a relentless contention between the classes (workers vs. capitalists) in capitalist society. But that is a by-product of a man-made social order and would become nonexistent in a society based upon common ownership and free right of access to all wealth.

But aside from this factor, scientists for the most part have gone overboard on natural selection. As Darwin also pointed out, man has always been a social animal with the propensity to give mutual aid. At the end of Chapter 11 of his *The Descent of Man* he wrote:

> The small strength and speed of man, his want of natural weapons, &c are more than counterbalanced, firstly, by his in-

> tellectual powers, through which he has formed for himself weapons, tools &c, though still remaining in a barbarous state, and, secondly, by his social qualities which lead him to give and receive aid from his fellow-men. No country in the world abounds in a greater degree with dangerous beasts than Southern Africa; no country presents more fearful physical hardships than the Arctic regions; yet one of the puniest races, that of the Bushmen, maintains itself in Southern Africa, as do the dwarfed Esquimaux in the Arctic regions... (p. 333, Mod. Libr. ed.).

So much for what Haeckel had to say—especially on that "pitiless" struggle for existence that supposedly has always taken place among mankind. Even among the most primitive it was not that pitiless—according to Darwin and to "mutual aid" naturalists such as Peter Kropotkin. And populations among the more primitive have always been small—whereas in civilized societies, despite the most horrible hardships, and death-dealing implements and instruments and pollutants unimagined by primitives, populations have continued to multiply, creating a different problem at least in some areas. Mutual aid does play an important role, even under advanced capitalism.

Socialists' Reaction to Darwinian Evolution

But what of the socialists and their reaction to Darwinism? Beginning with Marx, there was tremendous enthusiasm. Coincidentally, Darwin's book had been published in the same year as Marx's *A Contribution to the Critique of Political Economy.* In the words of John Spargo of the old Socialist Party of America:

> Marx regarded it as a fortunate coincidence that his own book appeared in the same year as that of Darwin. He recognized at once the importance and merit of Darwin's work, and at once brought it to the attention of his fellow radicals at their meetings. Liebknecht has told us how for months the Marx circle spoke of nothing except the value of Darwin's work. With great frankness Marx likened his own work in the sociological field to that of Darwin in the biological field, and he was always manifestly pleased when others made the comparison. Once, in the late

> sixties, when it had become commonplace in Marxian circles, W. Harrison Riley, editor of the *International Herald*, made the now familiar comparison and Marx replied: "Nothing ever gives me greater pleasure than to have my name thus linked with Darwin's. His wonderful work makes my own absolutely impregnable. Darwin may not know it, but he belongs to the Social Revolution." (*Karl Marx: His Life and Work*, by Spargo; B.W. Huebsche, N.Y., 1910; p. 200.)

It did not take long, in fact, for Darwin to indicate that he was not anxious to be thought of as belonging to "the Social Revolution." Isaiah Berlin writes, in *Karl Marx, His Life and Environment:*

> [Marx] offered to dedicate his *Capital* to Darwin, for whom he had a greater intellectual admiration than for any other of his contemporaries, regarding him as having, by his theory of evolution and natural selection, done for the morphology of the natural sciences what he himself was striving to do for human history.

But alas! Darwin was apparently not interested in being identified with a revolutionary socialist. He must have realized that his own book would give him more than enough troubles as it was, so:

> [He] hastily declined the honour in a polite, cautiously phrased letter, saying that he was unhappily ignorant of economic science, but offered the author his good wishes in what he assumed to be their common end—the advancement of human knowledge. (A *Galaxy Book*, N.Y., Oxford University Press, 1959, p. 232.)

We should also have a brief look at what Engels had to say on the subject. Engels, we must remember, was Marx's literary partner. In his *Anti-Duhring*, Engels devotes some 11 pages to a defense of Darwin against the attack by Eugen Duhring, a German "reformer" of socialism who seemed to have had an antipathy toward Darwin that equalled that of G.B. Shaw's. Engels wrote:

> The main reproach levelled against Darwin is that he transferred the Malthusian population theory from political economy to natural science, that he was held captive by the ideas of an animal breeder, that in his theory of the struggle for existence he pursued unscientific semi-poetry, and that the whole of Darwinism, after deducting what had been borrowed from Lamarck, is a piece of brutality against humanity. (Foreign Languages Publishing House, Moscow, 1954, p. 97.)

Then, after outlining Darwin's discoveries, Engels tells us:

> Against this Darwinian theory Herr Duhring now says that the origin of the idea of the struggle for existence, as he claims Darwin himself admitted, has to be sought in a generalization of the views of the economist and theoretician of population, Malthus, and that the idea therefore suffers from all the defects inherent in the priestly Malthusian ideas of over-population. (P. 93.)

To which Engels responds:

> Now Darwin would not dream of saying that the origin of the idea of the struggle for existence is to be found in Malthus. He only says that the theory of the struggle for existence is the theory of Malthus applied to the animal and plant world as a whole. However great the blunder made by Darwin in accepting the Malthusian theory so naively and uncritically, nevertheless anyone can see at the first glance that no Malthusian spectacles are required to perceive the struggle for existence in nature—the contradiction between the countless host of germs which nature so lavishly produces and the small number of those which ever reach maturity, a contradiction which in fact for the most part finds its solution in a struggle for existence—often of extreme cruelty. . . the struggle for existence can take place in nature, even without any Malthusian interpretation. For that matter, the organisms of nature also have their laws of population, which have been left practically uninvestigated, although their establishment would be of decisive importance for the theory of the evolution of species. But who was it that lent decisive impetus to work in this direction too? No other than Darwin.

Now, in retrospect, one can understand the excitement of revolutionaries like Marx and Engels, in the latter half of the 19th century, over a book such as *Origin of the Species.* The basic message of Darwinian evolution, they were certain, would sweep the world and with the spread of scientific information superstition would be forced into swift retreat. The superstition of religion had been historically a major pillar of capitalism. *Origin of the Species* seemed to have knocked the very props from under it. And the general acceptance of biological evolution must, they thought, lead inexorably to an acceptance of social evolution and the principles of socialism.

But to put it mildly, the pioneers of Scientific Socialism were over-optimistic. On the one hand, in these last two decades of the 20th century, we have a battle still being waged between so-called scientific creationists and evolutionists in this most highly-developed nation of capitalism in the world—the United States; while religions such as Roman Catholicism and various Protestant denominations are able to teach Darwinian evolution in their church-owned schools of higher learning with no apparent damage to the future stability of their adjoining temples of superstition. The explanation can only be found in what has been termed the double-compartmented, watertight mind.

On the other hand, some nations of state capitalism of the left variety such as the Soviet Union, the People's Republic of China, Albania, and North Korea, have demonstrated that they are able to carry on the basics of a capitalist economy with little more than a limited toleration of religion—or no apparent organized religion whatever.

So the general acceptance of Darwinism in modern biology, even in the communist and socialist worlds, added not an iota to the basic political understanding of the workers. As in highly developed America, even laboratory workers in biology, from technicians to Ph.D.s, go about their appointed experiments, uninfluenced one whit in their social thinking; hardly, if at all, aware that they are, so to speak, standing on the shoulders of Darwin—let alone recognizing a connection between their science and Marxian Socialism.

Shaw on Darwinian Evolution

But what of Bernard Shaw on the subject of Darwinian evolution? To him, the central crime in Darwin's theory of natural selection was the abandonment of will and individual striving as an explanation for the evolution of species. It was a matter of simple accident of nature that the fittest were enabled to survive and this argument, after a great deal of debate among and testing by scientists, relegated Lamarckism to the dust heap of history.

Shaw was appalled—with good reasons—when the Darwinian approach and explanations really began to take hold for they also knocked the props from under his own philosophy—"wisdom" based heavily on Lamarckism. So, while Shaw was in agreement with most socialists that there is a connection between Darwinism and socialism, he was on an entirely different wavelength insofar as general agreement with Darwin's approach to evolution was concerned. Not only that, in his penchant for blowing hot and cold on Marx and Scientific Socialism, to blast Darwin was also, as he saw it, to blast Marx. He was unhappy about the connection between the two systems, as understood by socialists generally. For example, his *Back to Methuseleh* Preface became, in part, a tirade against Marx. For instance:

> [He] had proclaimed in his Communist Manifesto of 1848 (now enjoying Scriptural authority in Russia) that civilization is an organism evolving irresistably by circumstantial selection. . . (pp. lxviii).

and

> The revolt against anthropomorphic idolatry, which was, as we have seen, the secret of Darwin's success, had been accompanied by a revolt against the conventional respectability which covered not only the brigandage and piracy of the feudal barons, but the hypocrisy, in-humanity, snobbery, and greed of the bourgeoisie, who were utterly corrupted by an essentially diabolical identification of success in life with big profits. The moment Marx shewed the relation of the bourgeoisie to society was grossly immoral and disastrous, and that the whited wall of starched shirt fronts concealed and defended the most infamous of all tyrannies and the basest of all robberies he became an inspired prophet in the mind of every generous soul whom his book reached. He had said and proved what they wanted to

> have proved; and they would hear nothing against him . . . (p. lxviii).

Then G.B.S. took off his gloves and went to work on Marx, exposing him for the lightweight he, Shaw, considered him to be:

> Now Marx was by no means infallible: his economics, half-borrowed and half home-made by a literary amateur, were not, when strictly followed up, even favorable to Socialism. His theory of civilization had been promulgated already in Buckle's *History of Civilization*, a book as epoch-making in the minds of its readers as *Das Kapital*. There was nothing about Socialism in the widely read first volume of *Das Kapital*; every reference it made to workers and capitalists shewed that Marx had never breathed industrial air, and had dug his case out of bluebooks in the British Museum. Compared to Darwin he had no power of observation . . . (pp. lxviii, lxvix).

And so on!

What should be borne in mind, to be sure, when considering the animus in the above Shavianisms, is the fact that Shaw wrote his *Back to Methuseleh* in 1920, a long time after he had recovered from his early admiration of Marx and some eleven years before his brief visit to Soviet Russia put him back on what he believed to be the Marxian track. Throughout the years of his writing career he was able to switch mental gears on the subject of Marxism—as he understood it—rather facilely, leaving behind a rich lode of his pro- and anti-sentiment in regard to Scientific Socialism.

Not so, however, with Darwin and with the Shavian hostility towards the theory of natural selection. He never seemed to lose that nor did it even appear to wane in bitterness and intensity. He went so far, indeed, as to apply it to the at-that-time current political scene, blaming Darwinism for the mess that the world was in at the time of civil and interventionary wars. The world, as he saw it, was in the grip of the evil influence of Darwin's *Origin of the Species* some 60 years after its original publication. As he put it:

> If the Western Powers had selected their allies in the Lamarckian manner intelligently, purposely, and vitally, *ad*

> *majores Dei gloriam,* as what Nietzsche called good Europeans, there would have been a League of Nations and no war. But because the selection relied on was purely circumstantial opportunistic selection, so that the alliances were mere marriages of convenience, they have turned out, not merely as badly as might have been expected but far worse than the blackest pessimist had even imagined possible. (P. xvii.)

Now Shaw, in that observation, might well have been merely charged with second guessing but anyone making such an accusation would surely be guilty of naivete. What else can military alliances be but "marriages of convenience" in a world run on the principles of business? The Triple Alliance (England, France, Czarist Russia) was no Darwinian accident but a union made necessary by the arrival of Germany on the scene as a competitor for empire and trade. A world in which military alliances could be negotiated on the principle of "The Greater Glory of God" should be a world—according to believers—in which military alliances would be unnecessary. And anyway, Shaw should have known, when he wrote *Back to Methuseleh* only two or three years after the end of World War I, that "God" had been with both sides—according to the vying propaganda mills, blasting "Himself" in the trenches for four long years.

Should one grant Shaw extenuating circumstances in his bemoaning the missing League of Nations (founded in 1920, dissolved in 1946; succeeded by the United Nations) not being able, when he wrote *Back to Methuseleh,* to forsee the utter helplessness of that peacetime alliance in averting war? One thinks not because of his supposed socialist understanding.

But *Back to Methuseleh* was first published in 1921 and revised at least twice more during Shaw's lifetime with no further comment. Had he thought of the matter in 1936, and especially in 1949, he might have reasoned: why fight success? He was a good businessman. His writings were all doing well on the market and that, to him, might well have been the bottom line. In any event, had Shaw been an echo of Marx, as Edmund Wilson had observed in his *To the Finland Station;* if, indeed, he had been influenced by Marx to any degree, let alone to the extent to which he, himself, at times avowed, he would have known that the very existence of nation states had long since become an anachronism; that the answer to the problems that seem to be tearing the world apart lies not in a League of Nations nor a United Nations, but in an understanding that Darwinian evolution might very well suggest—whether or not this possibility is generally recognized among scientists in our times—that social systems have also evolved, from primitive communism through the various slave systems to modern capitalism, and will eventually evolve into world communism/socialism once a majority of the working class awaken to the con-game nature of world capitalism and organize politically for the appropriate action.

But even if he would have rejected Marx's theory of societal evolution—a theory that not all traditional socialists necessarily accept—he certainly would have understood that the essential economic structure of capitalism (wages, prices, profits, money, buying and selling) would have to go if mankind itself is to survive or, at very best, not to be thrust back into a state of primitive savagery.

10. Patriotism and Shaw

On a stretch of Boston's Commonwealth Avenue that is devoted to a series of monuments to some of its—and the nation's—noted personalities, there is a statue of William Lloyd Garrison, the outstanding 19th century enemy of chattel slavery in America. Etched in the concrete is his famous statement: "My country is the world; my countrymen are mankind." Superficially, this is, indeed, a noble statement, and were it not for one unfortunate fact that is still true more than a century after the sentiment was expressed by Garrison, it might have become a motto for socialists.

The problem is that the world is divided on another and even a more malignant basis than nationalistically or ethnically, a division predicated on economic class. So that, while socialists regard wage-workers everywhere as their fellows, they can hardly feel that spirit of camaraderie for the capitalist class, generally; and that, incidentally, pretty much sums up the attitude of capitalists on the subject. They have to feel more comfortable with "their own kind," regardless of color, nationality, or ethnic background—than with working people from their own country. As for the other part of the Garrison maxim, the capitalists can feel that the world is their country since, as a rule, their investments know no boundaries and it is even common for them to possess and even to occupy, at times, residences in different nations. As for the working class, living in countries other than their own is generally always predicated on the fact that jobs are not available for them at home.

Now all of this cogitation is intended as a basis for an examination of Bernard Shaw on the question of ideological identification with a particular country. While it is all but impossible for anybody to avoid national identification, on a practical level, it would seem to be a subjective tendency of socialists to reject such identification, at least ideologically.

Shaw, of course, almost always referred to himself as an Irishman but like so many of the native Irish he preferred to live out the bulk of his life elsewhere – in his case, since the age of 20, in England. He did, in fact, regard himself as British as he made clear in the final paragraph of his last will and testament drawn on June 12, 1950, in which he stated that, although registered as a citizen of Eire he considered himself to be British since Ireland, at the time of his birth, was a part of the United Kingdom. He requested that his will "be construed and take effect according to English Law."

And in case it is argued that that was a mere legal technicality and proves nothing about his personal feelings on the subject of national sentiment, there are those instances of his support of Britain in her various wars such as the Boer War (1899–1902); World War I (1914–1918); and World War II (1939–1945). In the case of Britain's war against the South African Boers, his approval was uncritical as well as unequivocal (to the dismay of many of his comrades) on grounds that Britain, as a colonizer, could be a more civilizing agency in South Africa than the Dutch Boers. As an avowed socialist he should have known that neither side was interested in anything other than the opportunity to pump surplus value, so to speak, from the skins of black and white workers of the area or they would not have been there to begin with. Civilizing, to colonizers, has always meant the conditioning of natives of industrially backward areas to the "glories" of class society and to the production of profits for the masters.

In the instance of World War I, despite his criticisms of British atrocities, placing them on a level with the atrocities of the German war machine (see Chapter 6 and the chapter headed "War Madness" in his *Autobiography* [1898–1950]) he demonstrated his patriotism to British capitalism by accepting the government's request that he tour the battlefields as a morale builder. And in the chapter of his autobiography immediately following his denunciation of "War Madness," headed *Joy Riding at the Front,* one can read the somewhat 5500–6000 words of Shavian chortlings anent his adventures on the Western front; his pleasurable communions there with important British Army officers, while young men of the warring powers were mowing each other down in job-lot numbers during the horrendous Battle of the Somme.

And he relates how his play *Augustus Does His Bit* (a spoof of those who guarded the home front) "opened the heart of every official to me. I have always been treated with distinguished consideration in my contacts with bureaucracy during the war; but on this occasion I found myself *persona grata* in the highest degree. . . ."

Shaw, the Fabian Socialist, then, was actually on the same wavelength with social democracy in World War I—in the final analysis, on the side of his government; excepting for the fact that he was more efficient at talking out of both sides of his mouth at one and the same time than were the renegades of social democracy on the Continent.

Had he wished to take a genuine socialist position, one which, however, would have put at least a temporary halt to his career, he would have had to emulate the stand of the numerically tiny Socialist Party of Great Britain which, in their Manifesto published in their monthly journal *The Socialist Standard* in its September 1914 issue, minced no words, stating boldly—*inter alia*—that they would

> Keep the issue clear by expounding the CLASS STRUGGLE, and while placing on record its abhorrence of this latest manifestation of the callous, sordid and mercenary nature of the international capitalist class, and declaring that no interests are at stake justifying the shedding of a single drop of working-class blood, enters its emphatic protest against the brutal and bloody butchery of our brothers of this and other lands, who are being used as food for cannon abroad while suffering and starvation are the lot of their fellows at home. . . .

But, then, with such a position Bernard Shaw would have made himself *persona non grata* to the nth degree and might well have wound up on the run in an attempt to dodge the British military, as a number of genuine British socialists were compelled to do in wartime, in their desire to avoid slaughtering (or being slaughtered by) their fellow workers from others lands for the sole reason that they were citizens of different lands.

As for World War II, notwithstanding his analogy of British and German capitalisms as fleets of pirate ships preying on one another, he declared that since he and his family were, so to speak, aboard a ship flying the "Jolly Roger," his support had to go to his own government (see *Everybody's Political What's What)*, a sentiment, incidentally, that he had also expressed in his "War Madness" chapter of his autobiography. With all of his criticisms of the atrocities committed by both sides, there is an underlying note of pride—almost of jingoism—in his Preface to *Geneva* (1945), wherein he boasts of the superiority of British prowess in war over her various enemies throughout history. In his section headed "England Frightened and Great," he lists a number of occasions when England was frightened (and great):

> England will do nothing outside her routine until she is thoroughly frightened; but when England is frightened England is capable of anything. Philip II of Spain frightened her, Louis XIV of France frightened her. Napoleon frightened her. Wilhelm II of the German Reich frightened her. But instead of frightening the wits out of her they frightened the wits into her. She woke up and smashed them all. In vain did the kaiser sing *Deutschland uber Alles*, and Hitler claim that his poeple were the Herrenvolk created by God to rule the earth. The English were equally convinced that when Britain first at Heaven's command arose from out the azure main she was destined to rule the waves, and make the earth her footstool. This is so natural to Englishmen that they are unconscious of it, just as they cannot taste water because it is always in their mouths. Long before England first sang Rule Britannia at Cliveden she had annilhilated Philip's Invincible Armada to the music of the winds and waves, and after being defeated again and again by General Luxemburg, made hay of the French armies at Blenheim, Ramilies, and Malplaquet to the senseless gibberish of Lillibullero-bullenalah. She not only took Hitler singlehanded without a word to the League of Nations nor to anyone else, but outfought him, outbragged him; outbullied him, outwitted him in every trick of warfare, and finally extinguished him and hanged his accomplices. (Pp. 625–6, *Bernard*

Shaw, Complete Plays with Prefaces, Vol. V; Dodd, Mead & Co., N.Y. 1963.)

Now a statement such as that, glorifying the military excellence of England, is not a sentiment one would expect from a confirmed socialist such as Shaw was considered to have been. Let us, for an example, take just one—the most recent of his illustrations of England, in her time of "greatness"—World War II.

To begin with, just whom was he including in that England that his mind had fashioned? Was a part of it composed of that not inconsiderable percentage of the population that caused him such irritation by living "on the dole," during the Depression years prior to World War II, and living quite comfortably "like ladies and gentlemen" in cases where they could pool their doles within a family unit? Generally, complaints about the dole, from those who had to live on it and from social-minded folk who resented the fact of its existence because of the indignity associated with it—who would much prefer employment, over it, in spite of the indignities usually associated with employment, were the gripes that concerned socialists. Not so with Shaw who was irritated for the opposite reason. On page 147 of his *The Intelligent Woman's Guide to Socialism and Capitalism* he unburdened himself of the following complaint:

> A man who has had his dinner is never a revolutionist; his politics are all talk. But hungry men, rather than die of starvation, will, when there are enough of them to over power the police, begin by rioting, and end by plundering and burning rich men's houses, upsetting the government, and destroying civilization. And the women, sooner than see their children starve, will make the men do it, small blame to them.
>
> Consequently the capitalists, when they have sent their capital abroad instead of giving continuous employment with it at home, and are confronted at home with masses of desperate men for whom they can find no suitable jobs, must either feed them for nothing or face a revolution. And so you get what we call the dole.

And, completely oblivious to the fact that the *purpose* of capital may be to provide jobs, but only in order that profits may be maximized, and if there are more such opportunities for that, abroad, then so be it, he continued to denounce the recipients of the dole:

> Now, small as the dole may be it must be sufficient to live on; and if two or three in one household put their doles together, they grow less keen on finding employment, and develop a taste for living like ladies and gentlemen; that is, amusing themselves at the expense of others instead of earning anything. We used to moralize over this sort of thing as part of the decline and fall of ancient Rome; but we have been heading straight for it ourselves for a long while past. . . .

Now in light of such Shavianisms expressed by him away back in 1928, some questions concerning his outburst of British chauvinism in 1945 come to mind. For example, did the fact that, during the war years, unemployment in Britain had all but ended; that the entire working class was then either in the armed services or the workshops; that even with strict food rationing, workers and their families were having their dinners with fair regularity; and that despite the significant improvement in their living standards—their hunger a thing of the past—they were now being licensed by their government to join in the general effort at destroying (European) civilization; did all of that, perhaps contribute—along with fear of Hitler—to England's greatness"? To be sure, Shaw must have felt that it was a shame that this newly great England was extinguishing those heroic anti-Parliamentarian dictators, Benito Mussolini and Adolf Hitler. It all had to be confusing for him—even "great" Great Britain's alliance with Stalin's "Proletarian Democracy"!

The Business of International Warfare

Now Shaw was by no means naive when it came to a comprehension of business, its whys and its wherefores. Although his wife was a wealthy woman when he hardly had two bobs to rub together, he became a millionaire in his own right through his writings and some of his works. They show indications of his understanding of the business of capitalism. He had to have been aware that the worst scoundrel to use patriotism as a last (and first) refuge is the scoundrelly system of capitalism. It is a safe bet, too, that he was aware of the fact that wars cost the economies of the nations involved a heap of money and that capitalism—an international system—must have avenues by which nations (whether at war or peace) can transact essential business with one another.

The chances are strong that he knew of the existence, for example, of the Bank for International Settlements that had been established in 1930, one of the functions of which is to move money capital from markets of low interest rates to markets of high interest rates. The bank obviously does not shut its doors during wartime, but continues to go on with its business, and without interruption from the belligerents who might very well be plundering one another in other ways but who would not dream of interrupting the normal functioning of the B.I.S. Nor does the bank, apparently, try to cloak its activities even in wartime as witness this story in *The New York Times* of May 19, 1943, in the midst of the guns and bombs of World War II:

> In the seclusion of a Swiss city American, German, French and Italian bankers, not to mention Belgian, Swedish, Swiss and Netherland representatives, are still at work side by side and attend to a common business.
>
> In a Europe where closed economy is the rule, where exchange and trade controls reign supreme they carry out transactions across national frontiers and, so far, they have regularly paid a six percent dividend.
>
> Most of the funds deposited at the Bank for International Settlements by the various central banks or governments associated with it . . . have been loaned to German economy.
>
> But, far from dealing roughly with it, the Nazi government has hitherto transferred in dollars, at the appointed dates, the interest accruing on its debt. Indeed, the German payments have enabled the bank to this day to remunerate its shareholders.
>
> The bank, therefore, is left to the discretion of its executive officers: Thomas H. McKittrick (American), president; Roger Auboin (French), general manager; Paul Hechler (German), assistant general manager; Dr. Raffaele Pilotti (Italian), secretary general; and Marcel Van Zeeland (Belgian), manager.
>
> Nevertheless special facilities continued to be extended to Mr. McKittrick. Four months ago he was in the United States. For his

> return journey he received an Italian diplomatic visa, he was allowed to fly to Rome and he reached the Swiss frontier in a private railroad compartment.

The Bank for International Settlements is also outlined by James Stewart Martin in his *All Honorable Men* (Little Brown & Co., Boston, 1950). Martin, a minor official in Franklin D. Roosevelt's government was one of a group sent to Western Europe in the final days of World War II to collar all of the documents they could get hold of in the vanquished Nazi territories that would help identify the role played by German industry in the German war effort. What was discovered, of course, was the fact of international industry and its cooperation with both sides. Grim stuff! Specifically, in the case of the B.I.S., Martin had the following to say:

> The American president of the bank, Mr. McKittrick, apparently shared none of the views of the International Monetary Conference about the Bank for International Settlements, nor the official determination of the United States to change the pattern of German economic domination in Europe. In May 1944, just before D Day, Mr. McKittrick was quoted as saying: 'We keep the machine ticking because when the armistice comes, the formerly hostile powers will need an efficient instrument such as the B.I.S.'
>
> Mr. McKittrick remained as president for two more years after the Bretton Woods resolution, and his 'efficient instrument' never stopped ticking. In the autumn of 1948 the 'efficient instrument' quietly moved in to become an agency for clearing foreign-exchange transactions among the countries participating in the European Recovery Program. Mr. McKittrick himself, by then a vice president of the Chase National Bank, became for a time financial adviser to W. Averell Harriman, roving ambassador in Europe of the Economic Co-operation Administration.

Now it seems, according to James Stewart Martin, that as of 1950 there were still many unanswered questions about the Bank and its role in the general war efforts of its member nations. For example, the Nazis had apparently deposited much of the gold that they had looted from some of the countries they occupied and, as of 1950, there had been no accounting of it. Martin went on to say:

> Dr. Emil Puhl, the vice president of the Reichbank, when picked up for questioning after we entered Germany, revealed that the last time he went to Switzerland in April 1945, a few days before the final collapse of Germany, he had succeeded in getting his friends to defer the publication of the bank's financial statement because he wanted to conceal the extent of the Nazi gold transactions.

What was known definitely, however, by 1950 was that

> Over four hundred million dollars in German assets, spirited out of Germany before the end of the war, never have been traced. These funds are now being used somewhere in the world by ex-Nazi Germans and their friends. They can finance propaganda and German nationalist "recovery" programs at will. We know that in Spain, Portugal, and Argentina there are large colonies of ex-Nazis showing no signs of money worries. The same is true in Sweden and Switzerland. No one knows when whether any of the "spontaneous" sympathy in the United States for a resurgent Germany is the product of a well-paid public relations program... (pp. 281–82).

Neither philosophically, nor historically, does patriotism make sense. Ask the average person with patriotic feelings, Would you grant that the citizens of an "enemy" country have a right and a duty to be patriotic to *that* country? The answer will all but invariably be in the affirmative. So why, then, do we want to murder one another when we are only acting the way we are supposed to act and which neither of us are taught to believe is wrong? America's worst betrayer in her early history was Benedict Arnold, whose very name, in this country, is synonymous with one who commits treason; yet Benedict Arnold, as a consequence of his treason to the Americans, became a hero to the British and is buried in Westminster Abbey. And what of some more recent defectors from Communist bloc, state capitalist, countries who have been rewarded by American capitalism for their treachery to their own countries, with honors and riches? Evidently, treason, in itself, is not necessarily evil!

And dozens of examples can be given, right off the top of one's head, of corporations with names familiar to all that have operated, by virtue of international investments, on both sides of enemy lines during wartime (one can read of such patriotism in books such as Martin's *All Honorable Men,* already cited and quoted from above). And this is not to mention the palpable fact that the first obligation of any corporation is, supposedly, to its shareholders, not to the nation. In the final analysis, Karl Marx's dictum "The working class has no country" applies equally, but for a different reason, to the capitalist class. The world is not only their oyster but their country, at least in the area of investment—the "bottom line."

11. Echo or Caricature of Marx?

As we have noted in our Preface, the literary critic Edmund Wilson in his *To the Finland Station,* suggested that Bernard Shaw was an "echo" of Karl Marx in the wit of his political observations and the pulse of the tragic invective. There can be no question, of course, that he did have the skill needed to nail penny-pinching and hypocritical employers of labor and government officials to the wall in his early soapboxing efforts and in at least some of his plays. Take, for example, his *Mrs. Warren's Profession.*

He wrote that play in 1894, when he was 38 years of age and a socialist activist of some ten years' standing. But the government examiner (censor) forbade its being performed on stage, other than in private clubs, and the ban remained in effect for eight years. Shaw, understandably, was furious and in 1902 he wrote what he titled *The Author's Apology* as a new Preface to the play, in which he was able to vent his spleen in the manner at which he excelled.

As he made clear, the banning could not have been the examiner's reaction to lustful or bawdy content because there was none of that in the play. Shaw, it must be said, was not given to that type of plot, preferring to concentrate on messages of political reform. But, as he pointed out, he had witnessed performances of plays – two of which he named – in London that had unmistakably lecherous scenes that apparently had not ruffled the censor's sense of moral propriety one whit. He not only named them but outlined the pertinent scenes. Plainly, his play was offensive only because of its theme: that girls who prefer a life of prostitution to that of toil in factories under the conditions forced upon them could hardly be blamed; that it is not innate licentiousness on the part of the girls, but the brutality of the working conditions and the stinginess of the employers that was responsible for the creation of bawdy houses. The censor must certainly have been shocked at the enormity of such a message.

But, unfortunately, he created a false impression by the banning. When the ban was lifted, the reviewers, expecting much titillation, were disappointed at what they saw, and panned it—and the author. Hence, his tongue-in-cheek *Apology*, an excerpt of which will illustrate:

> Play Mrs. Warren's Profession to an audience of clerical members of the Christian Social Union and of women well experienced in Rescue, Temperance, and Girls' Club work, and no moral panic will arise: every man and woman present will know that as long as poverty makes virtue hideous and the spare pocket-money of rich bachelordom makes vice dazzling, their daily hand-to-hand fight against prostitution with prayer and persuasion, shelters and scanty alms, will be a losing one. There was a time when they were able to urge that though "the white-lead factory where Anne Jane was poisoned" may be a far more terrible place than Mrs. Warren's house, yet hell is still more dreadful. Nowadays they no longer believe in hell; and the girls among whom they are working know that they do not believe in it, and would laugh at them if they did. So well have the rescuers learnt that Mrs. Warren's defense of herself and indictment of society is the thing that most needs saying, that those who know me personally reproach me, not for writing this play, but for wasting my energies on "pleasant plays" for the amusement of frivolous people, when I can build up such excellent stage sermons on their own work. Mrs. Warren's Profession is the one play of mine which I would submit to a censorship without doubt of the result; only, it must not be the censorship of the minor theatre critic, nor of an innocent court official like the Lord Chamberlain's Examiner, much less of people who consciously profit by Mrs. Warren's profession, or who personally make use of it, or who hold the widely whispered view that it is an indispensable safety-valve for the protection of domestic virtue, or, above all, who are smitten with a sentimental affection for our fallen sister, and would 'take her up tenderly, lift her with care, fashioned so slenderly, young, and *so* fair.' Nor am I prepared to accept the verdict of the medical gentlemen who

> would compulsorily examine and register Mrs. Warren, whilst leaving Mrs. Warren's patrons, especially her military patrons, free to destroy her health and anybody else's without fear of reprisals. But I should be quite content to have my play judged by, say, a joint committee of the Central Vigilance Society and the Salvation Army. And the sterner moralists the members of the committee were, the better. (*Nine Plays by Bernard Shaw;* N.Y.: Dodd, Mead, 1948; p. 5.)

And he went on and on, for some 30 pages, in his counter-attack on the government censor, the press review people and the theatre owners.

Now, of course, Marx had done much the same thing—more extensively—in researching the material for *Capital* at the library of the British Museum. He dug out many examples from government blue books of the horrors suffered by men, women and children, in British industry. Indeed, Frederick Engels had done the same earlier in the Manchester area in his *Condition of the English Working Class in 1844.* So, in that sense, Shaw might very well have been considered as an "echo" of Karl Marx excepting for one important difference: whereas Marx was calling loudly for Revolution, Shaw and his fellow Fabians were agitating on a much more respectable level—that of extending the "socialism" that they maintained had already evolved under English capitalism—municipalization and government ownership.

In a sense, of course, the bourgeoisie in England had more to fear from Shaw's type of propaganda than from that of the Marxists just because it could be perceived, by a great many in the population, that what he was agitating for was something that could very well be achieved in the immediate future but that would, unfortunately, from the bourgeois's view, cost a pretty penny. And, in fact, the ban on *Mrs. Warren's Profession* was lifted in a mere eight years just because it was apparently agreed and acknowledged by the censors that propaganda of that sort was not all that dangerous to the basic health of the system. And so, notwithstanding preliminary fears by some employers of labor, it has been proven again and again that the bourgeoisie, with a certain amount of haggling, to be sure, will agree with almost any sort of proposal by reformers providing that the basic relationships of wage labor and capital remain undisturbed. Not that the reformers ever intended to disturb those relationships!

True, long and bitter battles had to be waged between labor and capital over such reforms as the eight-hour day and, much later, the 40-hour week before they became the law in advanced capitalist nations. But a large, if not the largest, contributing factor to such victories was the realization by enough of the bourgeoisie that such legislation would by no means augur the death, or even serious illness, of capitalism and might very well lead to even greater margins of profit through technological improvements that would make possible greater productivity which is capitalism's bottom line.

"Dividing Up" Is No Echoing of Marxism

According to Shaw—and this viewpoint is far more prevalent than that of the Marxian explanation—poverty in the midst of abundance is largely caused by improper "dividing up." Ask almost anybody who professes to have a smattering of knowledge in economics—especially of the left-wing variety—to put his or her finger on the problem of economic and financial insecurity and downright indigence and the answer almost surely will be: we've solved the problem of production; we just have to straighten out the method of distribution.

In Shaw's understanding, for example, modern industry is owned according to the principles of Communism, i.e., that no one shareholder can point to any part of a factory or whatever it is in which he owns stock, that belongs to him. He brings that out in his Preface to *Androcles and the Lion.* As he points out in the final sentence of that section:

> There is no longer any practical question open as to Communism in production: the struggle today is over the distribution of the product: that is, over the daily dividing-up which is the first necessity of organized society.

Now the problem with that sort of estimate, from a Marxian viewpoint, is that it assumes something that just is not so. It assumes that there is some sort of inherent right of the population, as a whole, to share in the distribution of the products of industry. The truth of the matter is something altogether different. The vast bulk of the population gets no share at all in the distribution of the product that they are paid to turn out. True, their wages must be spent on goods and services which they produce but the employing class is interested in that part of production only to the extent that without it there could be no working class. That part of production is what is called "necessary value." The part that is of most interest to the capitalist class is the surplus value, which is the property of the capitalist class and from which comes the wherewithal to continue the operation of capitalism, itself, and the individual capitalist's profit. And that is rarely, if ever, divided up with the population at large.

Inasmuch as Shaw did claim to have mastered Marx's Chapter VII, Part III of *Capital,* Vol. 1, on the labor process, which is, to all intents and purposes, a response to that dividing-up business, it should be instructive to allow Marx to speak for himself. It is all simple enough:

> The labour-process, turned into the process by which the capitalist consumes labour-power, exhibits two characteristic phenomena. First, the labourer works under the control of the capitalist to whom his labour belongs; the capitalist taking good care that the work is done in a proper manner, and that the means of production are used with intelligence, so that there is no unnecessary waste of raw material, and no wear and tear of the implements beyond what is necessarily caused by the work.
>
> Secondly, *the product is the property of the capitalist* and not that of the labourer, its immediate producer. Suppose that a capitalist pays for a day's labour-power at its value; then the right to use that power for a day belongs to him, just as much as the right to use any other commodity, such as a horse that he has hired for the day. To the purchaser of a commodity belongs its use, and the seller of labour-power, by giving his labour, does no more, in reality, than part with the use-value of his labour-power, and therefore also its use, which is labour, belongs to the capitalist. By the purchase of labour-power, the capitalist incorporates labour, as a living ferment, with the lifeless constituents of the product. From his point of view, the labour-process is

> nothing more than the consumption of the commodity purchased, *i.e.* of labour-power; but this consumption cannot be effected except by supplying the labour-power with the means of production. The labour-process is a process between things that the capitalist has purchased, things that have become his property. The product of this process also belongs, therefore, to him, just as much as does the wine which is the product of fermentation completed in his cellar. (P. 206, Kerr ed.)*

And in a footnote, Marx quotes James Mill who has said the same thing in quite similar language. So it would seem that Shaw was surely not echoing Marx on that score.

In fact, Shaw, in that section of his Preface to *Androcles and the Lion,* called for a change in the system of distribution, examining different alternatives, including that of Scientific Socialism ("From each . . . to Each . . . . . ."), but winding up with his favorite: "Equality of Income for all," which he only began to soften up on at the time of his tour of the Soviet Union in July of 1931.

We know that by the time that Shaw joined the tiny Fabian Society at the age of 28, in 1884, he had abandoned the Marxian system as *he* understood it, for the system of Marginal Utility of Professor Stanley Jevons; and he helped mightily in building the Fabian Society's brand of "English Socialism" on that foundation. He would certainly have rejected anybody's suggestion during those years of his Fabian activity that he was an echo of Marx; and while there certainly were occasions between 1928 and 1948, for example, that he did have glowing words for Marx the following two excerpts from his writing would indicate otherwise. First, in his *Intelligent Woman's Guide to Socialism and Capitalism,* writing of those whom he termed "the preachers" of the Third (Communist) International, he stated:

**There are seeming problems in this analysis when one considers the gigantic retail distribution industry and the capitalists who wax rich on the purchasing power of the proletariat. This is an illusion. The source of the distributor/capitalists' profits has to be found in production where production/capitalists must leave enough profit to take care of the distribution end—or distribute the commodities themselves. The sum total of the proletariat's purchases can only equal the sum total of the wages/salaries paid.*

> Their metaphysical literature begins with the German philosophers Hegel and Feuerbach, and culminates in Das Kapital, the literary masterpiece of Marx, described as 'The Bible of the working classes,' inspired, infallible, omniscient. Two of the tenets contradict one another as flatly as the first two paragraphs of Article 27 of the Church of England. One is that the evolution of Capitalism into Socialism is predestined, implying that we have nothing to do but sit down and wait for it to occur. This is their version of Salvation by Faith. The other is that it must be effected by a revolution establishing a dictatorship of the proletariat. This is their version of Salvation by Works.
>
> The success of the Russian revolution was due to its leadership by Marxist fanatics; but its subsequent mistakes had the same cause. Marxism is not only useless but disastrous as a guide to the practice of government (a fair enough statement although not in the sense meant by Shaw—H/M). It gets no nearer a definition of Socialism than a Hegelian category in which the contradictions of Capitalism shall be reconciled and in which political power shall have passed to the proletariat... (p. 441).

And that second quote, two decades on:

> *You ask when I began to be interested in political questions and in what way they affected my work?*
>
> Well, you know how at the beginning of the eighties I heard an address by Henry George and how he opened my eyes to the importance of economics. I read Marx. Now the real secret of Marx's fascination was his appeal to an un-named, unrecognized passion; the hatred in the more generous souls among the respectable and educated sections from the middle-class institutions that starved, thwarted, misled, and corrupted them spiritually from their cradles. Marx's *Capital* is not a treatise on Socialism: it is a jeremiad against the bourgeoisie, supported by a mass of official evidence and a rentless Jewish genius for denunciation. It was addressed to the working classes; but the working man respects the bourgeoisie, and wants to be a bourgeois. It was the revolting sons of the bourgeoisie itself; Lasalle, Marx, Liebknecht, Morris, Hyndman, all, like myself, bourgeois, who painted the flag red. Bakunin and Kropotkin, of the military and noble caste, were our extreme Anarchist left. The professional and penniless younger son classes are the revolutionary element in society; the proletariat is the Conservative element, as

> Disraeli, the Tory Democrat, well knew. Marx made me a Socialist and saved me from becoming a literary man. (*Sixteen Self Sketches*, pp. 83–4.)

Now much could be written in response to the confused jumble of Shavian wit and invective in these two quotes. To begin with, what Shaw seemed not to have grasped in the charge of "predestination" ("Salvation by Faith") is the predicted development of awareness, by the working class, of its position as an oppressed class and the consequent need to organize, as a class, on the political field if it is to emancipate itself from this last of the slave societies. However, one may agree or disagree with that theory, it certainly cannot be interpreted as did Shaw—not reasonably, at any rate.

Insofar as the "Dictatorship of the Proletariat" constituting a tenet of Marxism is concerned, one will search in vain through the main works of Marx and Engels such as *The Communist Manifesto*, *Capital* (all three volumes), *The 18th Brumaire of Louis Bonaparte*, *Anti Duhring*, *Critique of Political Economy*, etc., for a reference, let alone any details of that tenet of Marxism. True, Marx used it in a famous "Letter to Bracke," later and after Marx's death, published as a pamphlet under the title *Critique of the Gotha Program:* and it can be found in Engels' preface to Marx's *Civil War in France*. But the nearest either came to delivering an opinion of what such a regime should look like was Engel's contention, in that preface, that the Commune of Paris was the Dictatorship of the Proletariat. But the Paris Commune was composed of representatives from the Blanquists (named after Louis Blanqui, an advocate of conspiratorial, *coup-d'etat*–type revolution), and the Proudhonian anarchists (after Pierre Joseph Proudhon, known both as an anarchist and an Utopian Socialist); plus a small minority of Marxists. So neither Shaw nor anyone else is echoing Marx on the business of a one-party dictatorship and whatever one may think of his seeming approval of that short-lived attempt by working people in Paris at the close of the Franco-Prussian War of 1870–71 to set up their own government it was anything *but* a one-party dictatorship. (The word "commune," to the French, has nothing to do with communism but is used only to depict city governments.)

The quotation from *Sixteen Self Sketches* is a reiteration by Shaw, in his final years, of his long-held belief in the revolutionary potential of the middle class. His image of that section of society was that of a sort of chosen people which, by virtue of its education and standing in society, together with its grasp of reality, can be trusted to carry out its historical mission. Whatever one might think of such an approach it is hardly an echoing of Marx, whose theory of history (Materialist Conception of History) was one of class struggle between enslaved classes and their oppressors. It is not likely that even Shaw ever regarded those "penniless" sons of the industrialists and merchants of Britain as having been enslaved.

But there was another trait of Shaw, having to do with his skill at invective, that was by no means an echoing of Marx, not as regards content, at any rate. Whenever he was in one of his anti-Marx snits he would delight in referring to Marx's rabbinical forebears; his "relentless *Jewish* genius for denunciation," and so forth. It never seemed to strike him as incongruous on his part to employ such a tactic inasmuch as he, too, excelled at denunciation. Was his competence in that area traceable to his (Protestant) Irish forebears? He might very well have thought as much but there is no evidence that Marx ever entertained such notions. Marx, in fact, created an impression that he was anti-Semitic. But his not infrequent cracks at Jews and Judaism, generally, in one way or another, had to do with the association of Jewry with the quest for money. To him, living as he did and writing his works some scant 50 years after the French Revolution and its dissemination of capitalism's verities throughout feudalistic Europe, the Jews—as money lenders of long standing—were an integral part of his main target. That, together with his science-based animosity towards *all* religions, motivated his criticism of Jews and Jewry. But he would certainly not have included himself as a Jew or agreed to the notion of his inheriting "Jewish" characteristics.

Did Shaw imagine that Marx's own snide criticisms of Jews and Judaism were products of a "relentless Jewish genius for denunciation?" That this "genius" compelled Jews and descendants of Jews to denounce even themselves? It would seem to have been so since Shaw's thrusts were all based upon his apparent belief that there is something programmed into Jewish genes that has to do with skill at denunciation and revolution. As a Lamarckian evolutionist, he might very well have believed that nonsense; in fact to him, as it is with so many others in our own times, the characteristics that make one Jewish are passed on from generation to generation through inheritance, rather than being acquired through learning; that one cannot "resign" from the Jewish cult and or religion as Karl Marx's parents both did when he was but a child of six. And so, to Shaw, it made some sort of sense to refer to Marx, as he did a number of times in his writings, as "Harry Marks, the German Jew."

12. The Fusion of Fabianism and "Marxism"

In its very early years and, in fact, up to 1931, almost five decades after its founding, the Fabian Society, in its approach to socialism, was definitely hostile to Marxism. In its economics, it was influenced by Henry George ("Single Taxer"), and Professor Stanley Jevons ("Marginal Utility"); in its membership composition it preferred to recruit from what it called the middle class (industrialists—the younger and "penniless" members rather than the heirs apparent), considering that element to be the revolutionary wave of the future; in its philosophy of action it espoused the conception of gradualism in reform, extension of municipal and government ownership of industry and land. In short, it courted respectability in its approach and shunned the very aroma of revolution of the Marxist type.

As late as 1928, Bernard Shaw, its most vocal spokesperson, was downplaying the significance of the Bolsheviks' system in Soviet Russia in his *Intelligent Woman's Guide to Socialism and Capitalism,* arguing that England was closer to full-blown Fabian Socialism by a long shot; and insisting that absolute equality in income (with the exception of special privileges for performing artists, e.g.) is a *sine qua non* of fully materialized socialism. That, together with the absolute necessity of every able-bodied person contributing his work equivalent to the community in return for that guaranteed income.

But that was by no means the sum and substance of its message. The Fabian Society also maintained that socialism was rapidly becoming an accomplished fact in their own England;

that it was evolving out of capitalism; that all that was left for it was to keep on evolving until the full measure of the Fabian program would come to pass. It will be instructive to have a look at one of Shaw's early works for the Society and his comments on its long term agenda.

In 1885, he authored Fabian Tract No. 3, worded as follows:

TO PROVIDENT LANDLORDS AND CAPITALISTS.

A Suggestion and a Warning.

The Fabian Society, having in view the advance of Socialism in England, and the threatened subversion of the powers hitherto exercised by private proprietors of the national land and capital ventures plainly to warn all such proprietors that the establishment of Socialism in England means nothing less than the compulsion of all members of the upper class, without regard to sex or condition, to work for their own living. In such a state of things, not even noble or royal birth would enable a delicately nurtured lady to obtain the most menial service from a vulgar person without suffering the humiliation of rendering an equivalent service in exchange. The Fabian Society, assuming that the proprietary classes are willing to leave nothing undone that may tend to avert conditions so frightful and unnatural to them, beg to recommend to their earnest support all undertakings having for their object the parcelling out of waste or inferior lands among the labouring class, and the attachment to the soil of a numerous body of peasant proprietors. A bare statement of the probable results of such a reform will sufficiently recommend it to proprietors.

I. It will provide purchasers for land hitherto unsaleable: and the purchase-money will be guaranteed by opulent joint stock companies.

II. If its effect be to enlarge the total area already under cultivation by the addition of inferior land, it will, according to a well known economic law, increase the amount of paid labour that ultimately determines the value of farm produce. The consequent rise in the price of wheat will enable the farmers of all land now under cultivation to pay higher rents, whereby the landlords will be enriched.

III. The enrichment of the landlords will enable them to employ more of our starving poor as domestic servants, as well as to purchase more of the products of artists and traders, and so greatly ameliorate the condition of the destitute, and stimulate Commerce and the Fine Arts.

IV. Those habits of idleness which are the bane of our national prosperity will be effectually checked in the peasant proprietors by the competition of capitalist farmers at home and abroad using improved machinery to cultivate large tracts of superior land with an economy unattainable by the small farmer, whose time will be so completely occupied by the excessive labour imposed on him by this competition, and whose mind will be so full of anxiety, that he will have neither time to attend Socialist meetings, nor leisure to consider the justice of schemes of Land Nationalization that menace the very existence of the Landlord class.

V. THE PEASANT PROPRIETOR, HAVING A STAKE IN THE COUNTRY, WILL, UNLIKE THE LANDLESS LABORER OF TO-DAY, HAVE A COMMON INTEREST WITH THE LANDLORD IN RESISTING REVOLUTIONARY PROPOSALS.

VI. Rent, which cannot be abolished, will continue to support the class that is, in its own opinion, most deserving of it. For, to quote one of the most celebrated prose writers of the present century (Thomas De Quincey): "*Rents are themselves inevitable consequences, bound up with the necessities of the case. As inevitable results, these increments on land import no blame to landlords, seeing that under any system of civil interests, and any administration of those interests, such increments eternally arising must be enjoyed by somebody. Having thus reduced the question to a simple case of comparison between country gentlemen (as the most ordinary class of rent-receivers) and any other assignable receivers, Ricardo was too conscientious to pretend that this class was not, amongst us, one of our noblest. If we have led Europe in political counsels since 1624: if we first founded a representative government—by whom else than our country gentlemen, in Parliament assembled, were we ourselves guided!*"

Now there are two items of importance about this document that merit attention: (1) Under full-blown Fabian Socialism, it seems that the titled aristocracy and royalty will continue to exist, albeit with present economic prerogatives sharply curtailed, if not abrogated entirely—unless the vision was to make the national equal-dividend equivalent to the standards of aristocracy and royalty! But in any case, the fact that they would continue to exist as a separate social class would seem to indicate that, to the Fabians, there is something about them other than their wealth that entitles them to the special respect they now get from the *hoi polloi.*

And (2), the Fabian Socialists were particularly concerned with the parasitism of the landlord class even though the freeloading of that caste has to be at the expense of the middle class (the Fabian term for employers of labor in the urban industries – the capitalist class, to everybody else). The majority of the population – the working class – already had all of the surplus value pumped out of it by that "middle" class so the landlords had to chisel their pound of flesh from the original expropriators, for their rents.

And so, aside from one or two off-beat tenets – equality of income (more-or-less soft-pedalled after the visits by Shaw and the Webbs to the "Workers' Fatherland" in 1931 and 1932) and equality of work-input by all, Fabianism was a middle-class (capitalist-oriented) movement, and indeed, over the years, the Fabian Society aided and abetted the efforts of the British Labour and Coalition-governments most mightily in their operation of British capitalism in peace and through two world wars.

Equality of Income

Shaw had an interesting argument in support of his pitch for equality in income. According to him, there already existed a degree of uniformity in pay, at least within various trades and occupations. So there remains only the transcendence of class and skill categories to achieve his goal. He discusses this in his Preface to *Androcles and the Lion:*

> EQUAL DISTRIBUTION
>
> When that problem is at last faced, the question of the proportion in which the national income shall be distributed can have only one answer. All our shares must be equal. It has always been so: it always will be so. It is true that the incomes of robbers vary considerably from individual to individual; and the variation is reflected in the incomes of their parasites. The commercialization of certain exceptional talents has also produced exceptional incomes, direct and derivative. Persons who live on

> rent of land and capital are economically, though not legally, in the category of robbers, and have grotesquely different incomes. But in the huge mass of mankind variation of income from individual to individual is unknown, because it is ridiculously impracticable. As a device for persuading a carpenter that a judge is a creature of superior nature to himself, to be deferred and submitted to even to the death, we may give a carpenter a hundred pounds a year and a judge five thousand; but the wage for one carpenter is the wage for all the carpenters: the salary for one judge is the salary for all the judges.

Which may be true, to a degree, with the unionized carpenters, but hardly with judges who are relatively few in number and whose salaries are set by legislatures. But it is hardly true with commodity labor power, generally, which like all other commodities will sell for as high a price as the market will allow while, at the same time, its owner—the worker—must always strive to underbid his competition—his fellow workers. Shaw continues, dragging Jesus into the question:

> *The Captain and the Cabin Boy*
>
> Nothing, therefore, is really in question, or ever has been, but the differences between class incomes. Already there is economic equality between captains, and economic equality between cabin boys. What is at issue still is whether there shall be economic equality between captains and cabin boys. What would Jesus have said? Presumably he would have said that if your only object is to produce a captain and a cabin boy for the purpose of transferring you from Liverpool to New York, or to manoeuvre a fleet and carry powder from the magazine to the gun, then you need give no more than a shilling to the cabin boy for every pound you give the more expensively trained captain. But if in addition to this you desire to allow the two human souls which are inseparable from the captain and the cabin boy, and which alone differentiates them from the donkey-engine, to develop all their possibilities, then you may find the cabin boy costing rather more than the captain, because cabin boy's work does not do so much for the soul as captain's work. Consequently you will have to give him at least as much as the captain unless you definitely wish him to be a lower creature, in which case the sooner you are hanged as an abortionist the better. That is the fundamental argument.

And one cannot help but notice that he was aware, in 1915 – some 16 years before his conversations with the Bolshevik leaders in the Soviet Union on the subject of income equality – of the importance of the cost factor, in the production of labor power, in determining wages/salaries. But he got around that obstacle, back in 1915, by bringing the soul into the argument. The problem with that approach is that in a system that has cost for a factor, the soul has no more material existence than it has in an autopsy laboratory. It may exist as a conjecture but it has no place in bookkeeping.

His Fabian Socialism was, in fact, a sort of extension, to national proportions, of the "socialism" of a commune or an Israeli kibbutz. Unfortunately, nothing basic is really changed because communes, even were it possible to enlarge them to national proportions, will still have to operate in a commodity world with buying and selling, wage labor and capital, and all the rest.

Socialism in One Country

Since the consolidation of power in Russia by the Bolsheviks under Lenin and Stalin, the traditional socialist viewpoint that socialism has to be a worldwide system without nations and without boundaries came to an end for all but a small minority of traditional "Impossibilists." In this latter part of the 20th century, more than half of the world lives under allegedly socialist/communist systems and yet there are many more nations and national borders than there ever were before.

It is a mistake, however, to think that the idea of Socialism operating in national units originated with Lenin and Stalin. As far back as the mid-1880s, Bernard Shaw, Sidney Webb, and a host of other prominent English Fabians were spreading their brand of socialism among the middle class, stumping for a socialist England. There was, to be sure, a difference in approach between Fabians and Bolsheviks. Many years before the party of Lenin was even called Bolsheviks (the name simply means "majority"in the Russian language) they were members of Russia's Social Democratic party and of the Second (Socialist)

International; advocates of parliamentary action in the traditional Marxist *modus operandi;* whereas the Fabians never did organize as a political party but sought to "bore from within" parties such as the British Labour and Liberal parties.

In short, the pre-Revolution Bolsheviks operated on the theory, along with social democracy in general, that when socialist majorities capture parliaments and governments, through the electoral process, in a large enough area of the world, the socialist revolution would come to pass and the changeover from capitalist to socialist methods will be instituted, with speed as deliberate as possible. The Fabians, on the other hand, maintained (as Sidney Webb explained in his Fabian Tract: *Historical Basis of Socialism* that there is no documentation anywhere of social changes occurring through revolution, all at once; that it is always a gradual, evolutionary, process that takes place within the old society and that socialism, indeed, had been evolving in England for some years through municipalization and government ownership of various industries; and that it only required more evolution—not revolution—to attain full blown socialism.

That the parliamentary procedure was the approach of the pioneers of Scientific Socialism is evident from the interest and support given by Marx to the Chartist movement for universal suffrage and the attitude of Engels in regard to the rapid growth of the German and other European parties of social democracy. As he put it in the Preface to the 1895 (the year of his death) edition of Marx's *Class Struggles in France:*

> The time is past for revolutions carried through by small minorities at the head of unconscious masses. When it gets to be a matter of the complete transformation of the social organization, the masses themselves must participate, must understand what is at stake and why they are to act. That much the history of the last fifty years has taught us. But so that the masses may understand what is to be done, long and persistent work is required, and it is this work that we are now performing with results that drive our enemies to despair....

And he went on to gloat over the numbers of socialists elected to political office throughout Europe, even to predicting socialist representation in the Duma of the Russian Czar! Of Germany, he wrote:

> This mass (the 2,000,000 voters that German Social Democracy sends to the hustings...") already furnishes more than 25 per cent of the total vote cast; and, as shown by the special election for the Reichstag, the Diet elections in the several States, the Municipal Council and the Industrial Court elections, it is growing apace, un-interruptedly...if this goes on, we shall at the close of the century win over the greater part of the middle social layers, petty bourgeoisie as well as small peasants and we shall come to be the decisive power in the land, before which all other powers must bow whether they like it or not...(ibid).

The fact that history has proved both Marx and Engels to have been over-optimistic in their predictions for election success for socialism in their own foreseeable futures or, in any case, to be definitely on the road to realization, is beside the point. What is important is that Marx and Engels did recognize bourgeois democracy as an important tool that would enable the working class to fulfill its historic mission. It was not something to be "smashed" and replaced by a one-party dictatorship. What they apparently failed to see was the dangers involved in socialist parties actually attempting, through occupancy of government offices, to conduct the business of capitalism in the interests of the working class. In order to improve working class conditions, under capitalism, taxes must be raised to a point where sections of the population, that get hit severely in the wallets and bank balances, resist in force and crush the revolutionary tide as they did in Germany and in Austria's capital city of Vienna in 1934, where thousands of socialists were murdered in the streets and other thousands forced to flee the country.

It would seem, in retrospect, that notwithstanding the active and enthusiastic support given by the founders of Scientific Socialism, themselves, to the German Social Democratic party, and the Second (Socialist) International, in general, that there was something about that approval inconsistent with the theme of their system. From the thorough and painstaking analysis of capitalism, detailed in the major works of Marx and Engels, it would seem to be patent that capitalism simply cannot be made to operate in the interests of the bulk of the population—regardless of who controls the government. Yet there was social democracy, campaigning for political offices on programs of reforms of capitalism, rather than outright revolution, and building a following running into the millions, that was obviously interested in the betterment of their conditions—"in the meantime"—by having professed socialist politicians run the governments.

Despite the enthusiasm of Engels, the millions of supporters of social democracy were no more socialists than the millions of supporters of New Deal Democrats, for example, at the time of the "revolution" of Franklin D. Roosevelt in November of 1932. And old Engels, in 1895, was apparently postulating the same nonsense that Bernard Shaw had pontificated some 33 years later in his *Intelligent Woman's Guide to Socialism and Capitalism*, to the effect that the socialists can, in the meantime, learn to control capitalism "instead of letting it demoralize us, slaughter us, and half ruin us, as we have hitherto done in our ignorance."

For all but a century since Engels wrote those words of commendation and applause for the efforts of the German Social Democrats, there have been example after example of aborted attempts and successful-and-enduring seizures of political power—and even legitimate electoral victories through democratic procedures—by purported socialists/communists. Yet nowhere in the world is there any indication of an increase in the numbers of those who understand and desire a society such as world socialism—a non-market system of production solely for use rather than for sale with view to profit. Who can predict when such a movement will begin to show signs of vibrancy? Until such signs are detectable, genuine socialists can but continue their efforts in that direction and persist in their refusal to be lulled—or hoodwinked—into a belief that socialism is possible in a single country, or even in a group of countries; that socialism can control capitalism in a manner beneficial to the working class as a whole. Socialists simply cannot believe that the leaky ship of capitalism can be effectively patched and made secure for all on board. Socialists argue that it is long past the time when a brand new ship is needed.

APPENDIX

The Western Socialist May 1943 page 31

Shaw vs. Marx

Before the conditions of the working class can be fundamentally changed, it is essential that the workers begin to think for themselves about their social problems, about Capitalism and Socialism. It is fatal to allow a few "high-ups" to have a monopoly of thought on these matters. The worker must cease being awed by great names, for as the Socialist has so often maintained, a person may be outstanding in one branch of knowledge and completely incapable in another. Thus we have scientists, literary giants and other experts worthy of close attention when they deal with their own particular subjects, hopelessly incapable when they come to write on working class problems and politics with a view to bringing enlightenment to the masses.

To illustrate our point, we shall see how well equipped Mr. George Bernard Shaw—without doubt an outstanding dramatist—is to add to the clear thinking of the workers.

On the occasion of the sixtieth anniversary of the death of Karl Marx, a new edition of his selected works was reviewed by Shaw in the "Daily Herald" (London). Strangely enough the review is headed "What Would Marx Say About Beveridge?" It appears to be an appreciation of the work and intelligence of Marx, but is in fact a mumble-jumble of ideas, mostly unconnected. In brief, the review is sufficient to show that if Shaw is great as a dramatist, as a guide to working class politics he is outside his sphere. The review proves that Shaw's knowledge of Marx's theories is painfully lacking.

To begin with Shaw asserts that Marxism "has produced a new civilization in Russia" and that the principles of Marxism have been carried into practice in that country. Shaw asserts this in spite of the fact that the lessons Marx had to teach were not allowed at any time by the Bolsheviks, and although the "new civilization" in Russia is Capitalism with which we are all only too familiar.

Unlike many of the literary experts who have entered left wing groups and parties, Marx and Engels were never vague when writing on the fundamentals of Socialism. Their examination of Capitalism and their experiences with working class movements led them to draw certain conclusions and to lay down certain principles clearly and definitely. Let us look at some of these conclusions. They will help us form opinions about the Bolsheviks, Shaw and Russia.

Marx held that Society evolved and changed its form. He showed how one form grows out of another. In his preface to "Capital" Marx stated that in the process of evolution the intermediary stages or forms cannot be jumped. By this he meant that a society could not, for instance, jump from Feudalism to Socialism; it must first pass through the stage of Capitalism. As this teaching of Marx is particularly important for an understanding of present day Russia, we will quote his words. He says: —

"One nation can and should learn from others. And even when a society has got upon the right track for the discovery of the natural laws of its movement. . . , it can neither clear by bold leaps or remove by legal enactments the obstacles offered by the successive phases of its normal development. But it can shorten and lessen the birth pangs."

Secondly, Marx maintained that before Socialism can be established there must be a majority of wage-workers and this majority (or the bulk of them) must understand what Socialism is and must strive to achieve it. This is made clear in "The Communist Manifesto" where Marx and Engels wrote: —

"All previous historical movements were movements of minorities or in the interest of minorities. The proletarian movement is the CONSCIOUS movement of the IMMENSE MAJORITY in the interest of the immense majority."

Now, in Russia, where, according to Shaw, Marxian tactics were used, the bulk of the population consisted of peasants in 1917. There was not a majority of wage workers, and the social system was predominantly feudal.

In addition, the peasantry was backward, economically and ideologically, individualistic in outlook, thinking mainly of preserving or extending private property. To gain power, then, the Bolsheviks could not put forward a Socialist programme. Such would have won them little support. They chose, therefore, to play up to a war-weary, starving, individualistic population and came out, not with the Marxian demand, "The Abolition of the Wage System" (See "Value, Price and Profit"), but with the vote catching slogan "Peace, Bread and Land."

Shaw's ignorance of Marx and Bolshevik history thus becomes evident, for the Bolsheviks won power supported, not by a majority of class-conscious workers, but by a population desiring peace and an end of starvation.

Furthermore, Shaw claims that Russia is socialist. And yet Socialism implies the end of Capital and Wage Labour. It must be remembered that Capital, whether wielded by the State or by the individual, is still Capital. Capital and Wage Labour are the roots of Capitalism and these must be eradicated before Capitalism has been abolished and Socialism established. As Marx points out in "The Communist Manifesto", "the essential condition of capital is wage-labour." In the "Communist Manifesto" he writes: — "There can be no more wage-labour so soon as there is no more capital." Similarly, we could quote from Marx's "Wage-Labour and Capital" to show that, in his views, these two phenomena of Capitalism were inseparable and that the one cannot exist without the other. Instead of the slavery of the wages system, in Socialist society, its members will have free access to the means of life. Trade, currency, banking, wages, capital, foreign loans, etc., are all evidence that a society is capitalist. With the advent of Socialism, these features will disappear.

It is strange, is it not, that Marx whose works, according to George Bernard Shaw, contain so much 'dead wood' could understand and give lucid expression to these things and yet the great Shaw himself, still does not perceive what goes to make up a Capitalist society, in spite of his dabbling in political thought for so many years? And the tragedy lies in this fact: Shaw, in passing on his misconceptions and half digested ideas, brings not enlightenment to the workers, but adds to the confusion that already exists in their heads.

Shaw's review contains many more inaccuracies which convince one he knows little about what he undertook to explain. He tells his readers, for example, that Marx's historical materialism is an out of date theory. Yet he warmly recommends the famous "Eighteenth Brumaire" of Marx, which is itself an application of historical materialism to a particular epoch. As Engels once wrote in a letter "One can say that Marx has written nothing in which some part of the theory is not found. An excellent example of its application in a specific way is the "Eighteenth Brumaire of Louis Bonaparte"."

This should be enough to prove to our readers how little Shaw understands Marx's "Materialist Conception of History."

With equal confidence – and ignorance – Shaw attacks Marx's greatest achievement in the realm of economic thought. Shaw writes: – "Marx's attempt to measure value by abstract labour-power. . . can lead only to nonsense and bankruptcy." (Indeed, after reading Shaw's appreciation (!) one is puzzled to know Marx was right on any point).

Here we must point out that Marx's Theory of Value is the only economic theory which enables one to understand, among other things, how in capitalist production profit is realized and how the worker is exploited. As Marx's analysis showed all commodities contain only one thing in common, i.e. worked up labour power, or the expended energy of the worker. Profit is realized in the process of production because, on the average, goods are sold at their value and the workers labour power is itself a commodity to be bought and sold. But, in production, the labour-power of the worker is capable of producing greater values than it, itself, possesses. When the worker eats, takes rest, or relaxation to maintain his labour power, that is when he spends his wage on necessities, he uses up fewer values than he produces when he applies his labour-power to raw materials in order to work them up into commodities. Far from being nonsense and leading to bankruptcy of thought, Marx's theory of value, besides explaining the workings of Capitalism, shows the workers why they must end commodity production and the wages-system. So long as Capitalism (the wages-system) lasts, their labour power will be bought and sold like any other commodity. It will be employed to make profits for the owning class and the exploitation of the workers will result.

We could take up other points with Shaw and show his lack of understanding of working class problems and their solution. We will, however, not go into his scanty comments on Beveridge, Fenner Brockway, etc. But we must deal with one of the main ideas that runs through Shaw's review. It is this: that Socialism can exist in a single country.

Let us point out at once that Shaw and the others who advocate "Socialism in a single country" believe that under Socialism, wages, currency, buying and selling will still be with us. As we have shown, when the workers abolish Capitalism, these things which are but features of Capitalism, will be ended too. In other words, the exponent of the "Socialism in One Country" theory are not striving for Socialism at all, but merely another form of Capitalism.

But, apart from this very important point, it can be shown by other arguments that Shaw's theory is unsound.

Advancing Capitalism has brought specialization. Different regions of the world specialize in particular products. The result is that countries have become dependent on others for a great variety of things – raw materials, tools, machines, markets, and often technical experts. Thus Great Britain, in spite of war-time efforts is still dependent on imports for many items of food. Imagine a single Socialist country, dependent on a Capitalist world for a multitude of goods and services! It would not survive a day – the capitalist states would not cooperate. There are many obvious reasons for this, but we will content ourselves by stating just one. As Mr. Churchill said in his broadcast (March 21, 1943) "Foreign trade to be of value must be fertile. There is no use of doing business at a loss." And yet trading with a Socialist country would be a dead loss, as the Socialist country would have no currency with which to pay for goods. (But as we have shown, in actual fact there will be no trading at all under Socialism. Goods will flow about the world freely, from the places of their production to the places where they are required).

The social problems of today are too big to be solved nationally. They are caused by Capitalism which is international and the application of the solution – Socialism – must be international. The workers, whether British, American, German, Japanese or Russian are all suffering from the same evil – from poverty. Furthermore, this poverty is suffered by the workers of each and every country for the same reason. He is exploited by an owning class, is compelled to work for their profit and in return receives a wage which, on the average, just enables him to live and recreate his kind, i.e. future wage-workers. This is the problem with which the worker is faced; it is an international problem and its solution must be international.

The call of Marx is, therefore, as valid today as it was when he made it nearly a hundred years ago: – "Workers of the World, Unite!", for not till the workers are internationally class-conscious, not till they, in close communication and with socialist knowledge and conviction, set about the task of establishing Socialism, will they be able to rid themselves of their poverty.

Before concluding our article, let us remind our readers of our original idea. Shaw is just one example of those experts who won a reputation in one sphere of thought and, on that account, consider themselves competent to offer themselves as guides and advisors to the working class on matters they do not understand. We have seen how this happens with Shaw. The reader can, no doubt, call to mind many other instances.

The hope of a better world, of Socialism, lies not in a famous few but in the majority of the working class. Let, then, the workers set about their task seriously. Let them read and think for themselves and develop their critical faculties. Until they do so, they will be misled by the Shaws. Remember—**"The proletarian movement is the conscious movement of the immense majority in the interest of the immense majority."**

C. ALLEN (The Socialist Party of Gt. Britain)

The Western Socialist Vol. X–No.86
Boston, Mass. December 1943

ALLEN'S REPLY TO SHAW

On the occasion of the sixtieth anniversary of the death of Karl Marx, a new edition of his selected works was reviewed by Mr. George Bernard Shaw in the (London) "Daily Herald." In this review Mr. Shaw revealed his lack of understanding of Marx. Indeed, he seemed to know very little about his subject, or about Socialism. Using Mr. Shaw's review as a basis, I wrote an article "Shaw vs. Marx." This I submitted to the Editors of "The Western Socialist," who published it in their May 1943 issue.

It is in answer to that article that Mr. Shaw sent the above reply [see pp. 70–71], which the Editors of "The Western Socialist" have passed on to me for my comments.

Instead of trying methodically to prove my arguments unsound, he prefers to write in general terms and to avoid any direct reference to my criticisms of his interpretations of Marx. Conveniently omitting any reference to his original review, he now brings forward additional points and arguments. These I shall deal with later and again prove that Mr. Shaw's knowledge of Socialism and Marx is "painfully lacking," but before doing so, I must recapitulate for the benefit of those readers who have not a May issue handy, the points I made in the "Shaw vs. Marx" article.

The aim of that article was twofold. First, to show that many people who are considered "great men" can be outstanding in one or more branches of knowledge and yet have no knowledge of Socialism. I showed that "Though Shaw be great as a dramatist, as a guide to working-class politics he is out of his sphere." Secondly, the conclusion drawn was sound, viz., if the workers wish to know about Marx and Socialism, the best thing for them to do is to read Marx and study Socialism for themselves and not rely on reviews, etc., written by professors of economics, dramatists, and others who have become famous in some other sphere and who know very little about the subject of Socialism.

In his "Daily Herald" review, Shaw asserted that "Marxism has produced a new civilization in Russia." I proved by reference to the writings of Marx and by reference to the Russian Revolution that the teachings of Marx were ignored by the Bolsheviks. Marx showed that before Socialism can be established two things are essential:

1. The economic conditions must be ripe, i.e., Capitalism must have reached a high stage of development and have giant means of production

capable of turning out huge quantities of goods with relatively little human effort.

2. The majority of the population, the majority of the workers, must have an understanding of Socialism and desire it.

The Bolshevik Party, grown up within a semi-feudal Russia, dependent largely on an illiterate superstitious peasantry, had NO CHANCE OF GAINING POWER FOR SOCIALISM. They had to use the slogan "Peace, Bread and Land" to gain power, and having got it in such a way, they had no alternative but to carry on the development of Capitalism.

Another point. Mr. Shaw, in his review, claimed that Marx's historical materialism is out of date. Yet he warmly recommended Marx's "Eighteenth Brumaire of Louis Bonaparte," which Engels quite correctly described as "an excellent example of its application in a specific way." What would Mr. Shaw think of me as a dramatic critic were I to write "George Bernard Shaw is a very poor dramatist, but you must read his "Man and Superman"—it is brilliant."

Shaw ignores that paragraph in which I show that Marx's theory of value stands—sound and unshaken—in spite of Shaw's affirmation that it leads to "nonsense and bankruptcy." I showed how only the labor theory of value could explain to the workers why, "so long as Capitalism (the Wages-System) lasts, their labor power will be bought and sold like any other commodity. It will be employed to make profits for the owning class and the exploitation of the workers will result." One looks in vain in Mr. Shaw's reply for any answer to my arguments for any attempt on his part to substantiate the wild statement he made in his review that Marx's theory of value leads to "nonsense and bankruptcy."

WHEN REVOLUTION COMES

Let us now turn to the letter Mr. Shaw sent to "The Western Socialist."

Judging from this letter, he sees the Socialist Revolution heralded by shootings on all sides. Mr. Shaw's difficulty lies in the fact that he believes the Socialist movement has its wings, its left wing, its right wing, and its center. When the Socialist Revolution comes, he thinks squabbles will arise between these wings and that then "old comrades" will set about shooting each other.

Mr. Shaw's view is totally incorrect. It is incorrect because the Socialist movement does not, and cannot, consist of "wings." The Socialist movement is composed only of Socialists; yes, Mr. Shaw, of none other but "thorough-going out-and-outers." Socialism involves a complete break with Capitalism; it is a completely different form of society because its economic base will be totally different from that of Capitalism. The overthrow of Capitalism is essential before Socialism is possible.

There is no question of degree about the matter at all; one is either a Socialist or a supporter of Capitalism. The Socialist movement, therefore, is united in its one aim; there are no side issues to sap the energies of its members and no reform program to divide them.

Furthermore, Mr. Shaw has not yet learned that Socialism can be established only by a majority of workers who understand Socialism and organize politically to obtain it. Socialism, by its very nature, "the ownership of the means of production by all society" cannot possibly be imposed by a few on an apathetic majority. Until the working class learns these things, Socialism is out of the question, but once they do, they will stand united for Socialism.

Marx, of course, explains these points as Mr. Shaw, a reviewer of his works, ought to know. But no, Mr. Shaw believes that even after the day of the Revolution the working-class will still remain as clay to be molded by "new rulers." (See his first paragraph.)

When the working class is ready for Socialism, it will not need rulers. It will be politically mature, determined on one single object—Socialism. Those elected will be delegates in the real sense of the word. The workers will give the orders and the delegates will take orders. Nor could Socialism function in any other way.

Engels, Marx's collaborator, whom Mr. Shaw claimed to know something about in a recent newspaper article, dealt with these matters in his Preface to Marx's "Class Struggles in France." Readers of "The Western Socialist" will see from the quotation I give that the position of the Socialist Party of Great Britain and the Workers' Socialist Party of the U.S.A. is identical with the views Engels puts forward, when he says.

> "As conditions have changed for warfare so not less for the class struggle. The period of sudden onslaughts, of revolutions carried out by small conscious minorities at the head of unconscious masses, is past. Where the question involves the complete transformation of the social organization, there the masses themselves must be consulted, must themselves have already grasped what the struggle is about and what they stand for. . . But in order that the masses may understand what is to be done, long and persistent work is needed." ("Preface to 'Class Struggles in France'.")

Therefore, (to turn to Mr. Shaw's reply) should he be elected as the first president of the Socialist U.S.A. and wish to shoot anyone, he would first have to get permission for that action from the majority. However, it is obvious that the first act of a Socialist elected as President, if such an election was considered necessary would be to resign in favor of a fully democratic Socialist administration.

Mr. Shaw says I should shoot him if he were elected the first Socialist president of the U.S.A. No doubt, Mr. Shaw is striving after humor. The humor, however, lies not where he thinks it does. The joke lies in this fact: that Mr. Shaw could possibly imagine that a working class, ripe for Socialism, understanding it and determined to get it, would think of electing Mr. Shaw, or any other anti-Socialist with similar views, as a delegate.

We will pass over the joke and give our attention to the general idea. It is this: that terrorist methods will be used by socialists to make their delegates toe the line.

As we have already pointed out, the working class, ready for and determined on Socialism, will be united in object. They will give instructions to their delegates, who will be expected to perform certain tasks. Now Mr. Shaw wants us to imagine a fantastic situation arising. He wants us to believe that, with the majority of workers understanding Socialism, one of their delegates would suddenly refuse to carry out instructions. Obviously, the position of the elected would be hopeless; a working class that had been capable of gaining political power would compel the resignation of such a delegate.

Towards the end of his first paragraph, Mr. Shaw is indeed highly imaginative, but not sound in his reasoning. He says that Nature does not make Socialism with a wave of a Marxian wand. Any Socialist is aware of this, of course. And he is aware of something else which Mr. Shaw has still to learn. It is this: Nature does not make Socialism at all—with any kind of wand. No, it is the working class who must establish Socialism.

Capitalism itself will help the workers reach Socialist understanding. The growing insecurity Capitalism brings to the working class, the failure of reform programs to change fundamentally its slave position and to end its poverty, the increasing gulf between the riches of the capitalist class and the poverty of the workers, all these things operate to the end that the workers become more receptive to Socialist propaganda. In time, the workers will see that there is no alternative to Socialism as a solution to their problems. Nor do Socialists proclaim this as a prophesy. The process is already taking place.

But to return to Mr. Shaw's passage about Nature. We believe that Mr. Shaw wishes to convey here the idea that Socialism comes as a steady growth; a bit of Socialism is established today, a bit tomorrow, and so on. In other words, Mr. Shaw is a believer in "the step at a time" theory, in Socialism arriving after a long series of reforms. He does not grasp the fact that Socialism is at rock bottom fundamentally different from Capitalism. No amount of reforms (which after all deal only with the problems thrown up by present society) can end private ownership in the means of production, can end capital and abolish the wages system. No amount of reforms can establish production solely for use and free access for the people to the means of life. Mr. Shaw's "socialism" consists of the Capitalist system with some modifications; in other words, Mr. Shaw is seeking, not Socialism, but an 'improved' Capitalist system. Indeed, he can see no further than Capitalism, for in his Utopia, the State, commodity production, capital, wage-labor, banking, etc., all essential features of Capitalism, will still exist. The State grew up with the evolution of private property as the power by which the owning class could govern (keep in subjection) the propertyless class. With the disappearance of private property, classes and class rule, i.e., with the end of Capitalism and the establishment of Socialism, the State will wither away. Similarly, commodity production, i.e., the production of goods for exchange, for buying and selling, cannot exist under Socialism, for commodity production, exchange of goods, buying and selling, presuppose private ownership. Wage-labor itself is evidence of commodity production and Capitalism, for with wage-labor, the worker driven on by economic necessity is compelled to exchange (sell) to the capitalist for money or wages the only commodity he possesses—his power to work.

No, Mr. Shaw, you have not yet learned what Socialism means, or you could not expect it to be arrived at by a long series of reforms of the present system; you could not write as you did in "The Intelligent Woman's Guide to Socialism and Capitalism": "for the political struggle between Capitalism and Socialism has been going on for a century past, during which Capitalism has been yielding bit by bit...and accepting instalments of Socialism to palliate them."

SOCIALISM IN ONE COUNTRY

Mr. Shaw still persists in the idea that "Socialism can exist in one country." I took pains in my previous article to prove that Socialism is impossible in a single country, that it involves international application. Should it happen that Socialist ideas spread more rapidly in one country than in others and the working class of that country gained political power before their comrades abroad, even then they could not have Socialism. They would be compelled to carry on a form of Capitalism until some other countries were ready to follow the same action. As we showed in our article, countries today are not self-supporting; each relies on imports from abroad. In such a world, Socialism could not exist in one country alone because that country would depend on Capitalist countries for goods and they would have to be paid for.

But as Socialists have often pointed out, this problem offers little difficulty, for in the advanced capitalist countries, Socialist ideas spread more of less with equal speed. And the reason for this is that Capitalism itself creates the desire for Socialism; wherever it appears, it nurtures its wage-slaves in more or less similar economic conditions.

Mr. Shaw, it appears, has fallen a victim to Bolshevik propaganda. He still contends that Socialism exists in Russia, though this time, one will observe, he does not attribute its existence to the application of Marxism. Russia is, of course, a Capitalist country. Here I will merely state that the great inequality of wealth distribution which is becoming more marked in Russia with the passing of the years should be sufficient to convince even Mr. Shaw that Socialism is not the social system there. Here I will be content to say that in Russia there is a hierarchy of social groups, some persons receiving incomes ten, twenty, thirty or more times larger than the ordinary worker; a division of wealth by classes exists in Russia.

Now the question I want to ask Mr. Shaw is this. In view of the fact that there is such inequality of income in Russia, how can he persist in calling the system there Socialist, when he himself, in his "Intelligent Woman's Guide to Socialism and Capitalism," stated there can be no Socialism where inequality of income exists? However, "equality of income" is a bourgeois concept that does not apply to Socialism which is a classless society where everyone receives according to his needs.

Let us now turn to Mr. Shaw's second paragraph. The first thing we notice is that it contradicts his first paragraph. In his first paragraph, Mr. Shaw says that to save Socialism in Russia, Stalin exiled Trotsky and liquidated his former comrades. Now, however, he informs us that the bulk of Stalin's work consists of bourgeois (i.e. capitalist) routine. Obviously, if Stalin's work now consists of capitalist routine, the social order in Russia is capialist. In other words, Stalin did not save Socialism in a single country, as Mr. Shaw claims in paragraph one. (But in actual fact, of course

Socialism was never in danger in Russia; it never needed to be saved, for it never existed.)

WHAT IS NECESSARY

Only in one instance does Mr. Shaw refer to Marx, although let it be remembered my original criticism of him arose because he distorted the teachings of Marx. Even now, when propounding on Marx, he ventures no further than stating something any beginner in Marxism knows: "Marx. . . dealt with epochs and classes." But even here, by his mode of expression, Mr. Shaw shows his failure to grasp one of the fundamental principles of Socialism. The fact is that when workers become Socialists they will not need the help of leaders—dead or alive. They will be capable of weighing the pros and cons of any proposition. Leadership, which Mr. Shaw believes necessary for the working class, is only possible where the masses are politically ignorant. With the spread of Socialist ideas among the workers, the workers will gain confidence, will cease to be awed by great names, spell-bound by leaders and misled by political careerists.

In his last paragraph, Mr. Shaw shows what he really thinks of Marxism. For him, it consists of day-dreams. Yet it is based on a scientific examination of past and present day societies. And as we have seen, Mr. Shaw is unable to disprove any of its fundamental teachings.

Mr. Shaw makes a grave error at the beginning of this section of his letter. He compares John Burns with a Socialist elected to serve on a Committee. The comparison is not valid, for John Burns, in spite of the Red Flag with which Mr. Shaw adorns him, never obtained his positions in the political arena on a Socialist program. Like all Labor leaders he contested his elections on a program of reform to be applied to the present system. Consequently he was backed by a reformist vote, that is, by people who were expecting Capitalism to continue even if with some modifications.

It is, of course, nonsense for Mr. Shaw to say, as he does at the end of his letter, that I discredit all the better-informed Socialists. It is true, however, that I always try to expose any individual or groups of individuals (e.g., political parties) who spread misconceptions about Socialism.

In view of his failure to show that he understands even the fundamentals of Socialism, Mr. Shaw is, I think, telling a tall story when he claims to be a better-informed Socialist than I am. He has yet to learn the first elementary principles of Socialism. When he has done that, he can build up his knowledge of the subject on a firm basis. Until he does this, Mr. Shaw will remain what he is: a bourgeois thinker with a Utopian scheme for reforming the present system.

In conclusion, I make the following points.

1. Shaw, so far in this controversy, has failed to show any knowledge of Marx or offer an adequate explanation as to why he undertook the review of Marxism when he doesn't understand it.

2. Shaw does not realise that before Socialism can be established the economic conditions must be ripe; that is to say, the means of production

must have been developed sufficiently so that enough could be produced for all.

3. Shaw's whole attitude shows that, for him at any rate, the establishment of Socialism does not involve the understanding of Socialism by the working class. This error is responsible for most of his fallacies as we have seen.

4. Lastly, Shaw does not know that Socialism means the common ownership of the means of life. This means that private property in the means of life will be abolished in all its forms. There will be no owning class and no working class; no capital and no wages system. Instead, every member of Society will have free access to the means of life.

C. ALLEN

Shaw Evades the Issue

[Arising from an article, "Shaw Versus Marx", in the May 1943, issue of The Western Socialist, a controversy with Mr. G. Bernard Shaw resulted. The reply to Shaw's letter is below.]

THE REPLY

Mr. Shaw is not only a master of dramatic art; he has also a genius for contradicting himself.

Readers of "The Western Socialist" will remember the glaring contradiction contained in his letter which was published in the December (1943) issue. In one paragraph, Mr. Shaw stated that Russia is socialist and, in the next, he spoke of the routine capitalist work with which Stalin is harrassed.

With this post-card, Mr. Shaw runs true to his usual form. He has now decided that "The Western Socialist" is not a journal he would care to receive. And yet previously he spoke of it with some enthusiasm. He said he was "indebted" to me for having brought the "W.S." to his notice.

Not being able to make up his mind seems to be one of Mr. Shaw's failings. But, of course, a few contradictions here and there are not very important from **his** point of view. He can publish a best-seller in which he warns against all imitations of Socialism. In that book, "The Intelligent Woman's Guide to Socialism and Capitalism," he claimed (wrongly, of course) that "Socialism means equality of income and nothing else." Later, without renouncing his former teachings, he can help propagate the myth that Socialism exists in Russia, where gross inequality of income is the order of the day.

And so does Mr. Shaw continuously reveal his muddled thinking and lack of logic. Unfortunately, he passes on this confusion to his reading public to the detriment of the working class and the socialist cause.

But Shaw thinks he knows. Perhaps success has gone to his head. I am not the first he has attempted to belittle when he has been criticized. Only recently he wrote the following as his concluding paragraph in reply to one of his critics in "The New Leader" (London, Feb. 26, 1944): "Stow it, Mr.

Brown. Put a sock in it.* And believe, if you can, that when I deal with Socialism and Capitalism I know what I am talking about."

Shaw's attitude to his critics is similar to that of many labor speakers' attitude toward the working class. Believing they tower above the working class, the labor leaders utter wise saws which they expect to be accepted without questioning. Should they be criticized, their first reaction is surprise, but their surprise soon gives place to indignation.

Thus Mr. Shaw, who believes (wrongly) he knows all there is to know about Socialism, now accuses me of "utter ignorance." And why? Simply because I dared to criticize him and BECAUSE HE CAN FIND NO ANSWER TO THOSE CRITICISMS. Against the science of Marxism, Shaw's witticisms are, to say the least, most inadequate.

Here I am reminded of a passage in Arthur M. Lewis's essay, "The Social Revolution." He is showing how the worker, ever in contact with the latest results of science during his working day, is better placed than the professional intellectual for getting a scientific view on life and social problems. "The. . .[socialist] worker of today," he says, "in all that relates to social philosophy, thinks more clearly than the professional intellectual. His environment brings him in daily contact with the latest results of science. . . The professional intellectual. . .is constantly engaged with ideas that have their roots in former modes of wealth production and his mind turns in vicious circles from which he finds no avenue of escape. Should he take up socialism and enter the movement, his first and greatest surprise is to find himself surrounded by hundreds of workmen who are fundamentally and undoubtedly his intellectual superiors. . ."

Mr. Shaw asserts that I misunderstand Marx, but he has not the time to waste in pointing out cases of misunderstanding. A strange assertion this, in view of the fact that already he has written some 700 words about me to "The Western Socialist." I challenge Mr. Shaw to give one single example where I betray a misunderstanding of Marxism. In contrast to this, I have given a number of examples of Shaw's inconsistencies and of his failures to understand Marx and the Socialist position.

Lastly, Shaw implies that Marxism is not based on facts and experience. Previously he said that Marxism consists of daydreams and that Marxists are impossibilists. What a waste of time to keep repeating these assertions, when if he is right and knows, he could demonstrate their truth in a simple, straightforward and logical answer.

But such an answer, I fear, is beyond Mr. George Bernard Shaw.

C. ALLEN

American equivalents for "stow it" and "put a sock in it" are shut up or fold up.

BIBLIOGRAPHY

Works by Bernard Shaw Cited in This Book

Androcles and the Lion; Nine Plays by Bernard Shaw. N.Y.: Dodd, Mead, 1948.

*Androcles and the Lion.*Baltimore: Penguin, 1969.

Autobiography (1898–1900). Selected from Shaw's writings by Stanley Weintraub. London, Sydney, Toronto: Max Reinhardt, 1970.

Back to Methuseleh. N.Y.: Brentano's, 1921.

"Commonsense About the War." *Current History of the European War,* Vol. 1, No. 1, N.Y. Times Co., 1914.

Economic Basis of Socialism; (Fabian Essay), Selected Prose; N.Y.: Dodd, Mead, 1952.

Everybody's Political What's What. London: Constable, 1944.

Geneva; (Bernard Shaw, Complete Plays with Prefaces). N.Y.: Dodd, Mead, 1963.

The Intelligent Woman's Guide to Socialism and Capitalism. N.Y.: Brentano's, 1928.

Last Will and Testament. Foreword by Wm. D. Chase (1st ed.). Flint, MI: Appletree, 1954.

Major Barbara; Six Plays by Bernard Shaw. N.Y.: Dodd, Mead, 1948.

Man and Superman; Nine Plays by Bernard Shaw. N.Y.: Dodd, Mead, 1948.

The Millionairess; Selected Plays of Bernard Shaw. N.Y.: Dodd, Mead, 1957.

Mrs. Warren's Profession: Bernard Shaw; Nine Plays by Bernard Shaw. N.Y.: Dodd, Mead, 1948.

On the Rocks. Max Reinhardt; London, Sydney, Toronto: The Bodley Head, 1973

Religious Speeches of Bernard Shaw; Penn State University Press, 1963.

Sixteen Self Sketches. London: Constable, 1949.

To Provident Landlords & Capitalists—A Suggestion and a Warning; Fabian Tract No. 3. London: Standring, 1885.

An Unsocial Socialist: N. Y.: Brentano's, 1903.

Other Authors and Works

Balabanoff, Angelica. *My Life as a Rebel.*N.Y.: Harper & Bros., 1938.

Berlin, Isaiah. *Karl Marx, His Life and Environment.*N.Y.: A Galaxy Book, Oxford University Press, 1959.

Blake, William J. *An American Looks at Marx.*N.Y.: The Cordon Co., 1939.

Boudin, L.B. *The Theoretical System of Karl Marx.* Chicago: Chas. H. Kerr, 1907

Chappelow, Alan. *Shaw the Villager.* A biographical exposition and critique, and a companion to and commentary on *Shaw the Villager.* Foreword by Vera Brittain. N.Y.: AMS, circa 1969.

Darwin, Charles. *The Descent of Man.* Modern Library ed., 1960.

________. *Origin of the Species by Means of Natural Selection.* Modern Library ed., 1962?

Engels: Frederick. *Anti Duhring.* Moscow: Foreign Language Publishing House, 1954.

________. *Condition of the Working Class in England in 1844.* Translated and edited by W.O. Henderson & W.H. Chaloner. Stanford, Calif.: Stanford Univ. Press, 1958, 1968.

Ferri, Enrico. *Socialism and Modern Science.* Translated by Rob't Rives Lamonte. N.Y.: International Library Publishing, 1900.

Hyndman, H.M. *The Economics of Socialism,* 4th edition. London: Twentieth Century, 1909.

James, Lewis G. *A Study of Primitive Christianity.* Chicago: Chas. H. Kerr, 1887.

Laidler, Harry W. *History of Socialism.* N.Y.: Thos. Y. Crowell.

MacKenzie, Norman, and Jeanne MacKenzie. *The Fabians.* N.Y.: Simon & Schuster, 1977.

Martin, James Stewart. *All Honorable Men.* Boston: Little, Brown & Co., 1950.

Marx, Karl. *Capital, Vol. I.* Translated from the third German edition by Samuel Moore and Edward Aveling. Edited by Friedrich Engels. Chicago: Chas. H. Kerr, 1906.

________. *Capital Vol. III.* Translated from the first German edition by Ernest Untermann. Edited by Frederick Engels. Chicago: Chas. H. Kerr, 1909.

________. *The Class Struggles in France.* With Preface by F. Engels. Translated by Henry Kuhn; N.Y.: New York Labor News Co., 1924.

________. *Introduction to a Contribution to the Critique of Hegel's Philosophy of Right.* First published in the *Deutsch-Franzosische Jahrbucher.* Issued by Arnold Ruge and Karl Marx. Paris, 1843.

________. *Theories of Surplus Value.* The posthumous manuscript on the "Critique of Political Economy" by Karl Marx. Edited by Karl Kautsky (in German). Volume I. Contains the results of Marx's studies of the history of the theory of value which were to have formed the fourth volume of *Capital.*

________, and Frederick Engels. *The Communist Manifesto.*Authorized English translation. Edited and annotated by Frederick Engels. Chicago: Chas. H. Kerr, 1945.

Morris, William. *News from Nowhere.* N.Y.: Vanguard, 1926.
Mussolini, Benito. *The Corporate State.* N.Y.: Howard Fertig, 1975.
Pease, E.R. *History of the Fabian Society.* London: Frank Cass, 1963.
Silone, Ignacio. *The School for Dictators.*Translated from the Italian by Gwenda David and Eric Mosbacher. N.Y. and London: Harper & Bros.
Webb, Sidney, and Webb, Beatrice. *English Prisons Under Local Government.* Preface by Bernard Shaw. N.Y., London, Bombay, Calcutta, and Madras: Longmans, Green & Co.
H.G. Wells. *The Science of Life.* (With J. Huxley & G.P. Wells). N.Y.: Literary Guild,, 1934.

Magazines, Newspapers, Manifestoes

The Clarion. (Short story by George Bernard Shaw). London: March, 1915.
Current History of the European War. Vol. 1; No. 1., N.Y. Times Co., 1914.
"Manifesto of the Socialist Party of Italy." In *Current History of the European War* Vol. 1, No. 1, Sept. 3, 1914. New York Times Co., 1914.
New York Times. (Column on George Bernard Shaw's defense of Mussolini.) Oct. 17, 1927.
New York Times. (Story on Wartime Operations of The Bank for International Settlements.) May 19, 1943.
Shaw, George Bernard. *A Manifesto.* (Fabian Tracts No. 2.) London: Geo Standring, 1884.
"The Socialist Movement in Great Britain." *The Times* (London), Jan. 9, 1904.
The Socialist Standard, London (SPGB) Review of *On the Rocks* by Bernard Shaw.

INDEX

DATE DUE
OCT 13 '97
CARD
DEMCO 38-297